MW00907113

Read My Lipstick

A Josephine Stuart Mystery

by
Joyce Oroz

Books by Joyce Oroz

Secure the Ranch
Read My Lipstick
Shaking In Her Flip Flops
Beetles in the Boxcar
Cuckoo Clock Caper
Roller Rubout

CHAPTER ONE

It was February first and I barely noticed the 85-degree weather, a quirky California coastal phenomenon sometimes lasting up to two weeks. Familiar lettuce fields and berry farms were just a blur as I drove toward my home in the foothills. I was in agony—consumed with the memory of Solow's pathetic howl as I walked away, leaving him in the care of Dr. Finley at the veterinary hospital in Watsonville. The cab of my pickup felt barren and lonely without my sweet basset.

I drove half a mile past the tiny town of Aromas and parked in front of my house. I plucked a cell phone from the cup holder and speed-dialed my best friend, Alicia Quintana. Aside from worries about Solow's dire condition, I had some good news for Alicia. Her pleasant sounding voice requested a message.

"Allie, good news (sniff), we got it—the mural job in Pajaro. Call me." I tried to sound chipper, but when I blinked, tears streamed down my cheeks. I should have been feeling happy about the new painting contract for my company, Wildbrush Murals, but my mind was on Solow. I couldn't rest until I knew he would be all right.

I thought about all the times Solow had made a fool of himself chasing Fluffy. The white cat typically ran circles around my short-legged canine. Fluffy's owner,

David Galaz, a "retired-at-fifty divorcé," had been my neighbor for over ten years. Unfortunately, he was in Minnesota missing all the Central California sunshine. Funerals are always a bummer; but David was a stand-up guy, and he made the trip to pay his last respects to his Uncle Theodore in spite of raging blizzards. It was no big deal that Sarah, David's ex-wife, would be at the funeral. I hardly gave it a thought.

I sat in the driver's seat with the windows down, letting the sun dry my tears and suddenly realized there might be important calls on the answering machine inside. I climbed down from my decade-old red Mazda truck, ignored Solow's empty bed on the front porch, opened the front door and stepped inside. Looking across the room, I saw no red lights blinking on the answering machine. No messages to cheer me up or break my heart.

"Forget that," I sniffed, deciding to take care of a few chores. I hauled Solow's two pillow-beds through the house and out the backdoor to the patio where my washer and dryer stood ready, taking advantage of a perfect opportunity to wash his bedding while he was away on a forced sleep-over at the vets. A little soap and water and what's that, the phone? I ran back to the kitchen and grabbed the receiver.

"Hello, Allie (hiccup)."

"What's the matter, Josephine? You sound awful."

"I'm so glad you called," I hiccupped. "I'm worried. Solow's in the hospital and Doctor Finley isn't sure if … oh, Allie, you should have seen him this morning, throwing up, shivering and his nose was hot. I should have known something was wrong when he didn't eat his dinner last night."

"Take it easy, Jo. You say he didn't eat? What's wrong with him?"

"He ate his baby blanket, you know, the silky blue one he's had forever"

"Ate what? I almost thought you said he ate his blanket."

"That's what I said. For weeks he's been ripping pieces off the blanket. I just thought it was a nervous habit." I pictured Solow's sweet jowly muzzle, sniffed and wiped my eyes.

"So how did that make him sick?"

"I never found the pieces but didn't give it a thought, really. This morning I realized the remaining piece of blanket was gone. I looked everywhere. I think he ate the rest of his blanket. I told the doctor it was made out of nylon, and he said it was probably caught in Solow's intestines." I put a tissue to my nose.

"Oh, dear, that's awful. But I'm sure Doctor Finley will pull him through." Alicia's voice faded. "What did Rosa think about it?"

"She wasn't there. I asked about her and one of the other nurses told me Rosa didn't show up for work yesterday or today. Didn't call or anything. The hospital was mobbed, reminded me of the supermarket at five o'clock if you added fifty cats and dogs to the crowd. I waited almost two hours to see Doctor Finley, but Solow slept through it all, bless his heart."

"I don't think Rosa has ever missed a day of work," Alicia sighed. "I'll call her later and see what's wrong."

"Right—and the good news is ... we got the job! We start work Monday at the Thornton Therapy Center in

Pajaro. How about that?" I said with as much gusto as I could muster.

"I'm glad they liked your proposal, Jo. I thought the sketches were terrific. A mural will be the finishing touch to their beautiful new building."

"Have you seen the building, Allie?"

"Well, just the outside every time I drive through Pajaro on my way to your house. I read in the Sentinel that it's 20,000 square feet and houses two large indoor therapy pools. How often do we get a painting job so close to both our homes? Looks like a fifteen minute drive for each of us, and if Kyle paints it will only be a half hour from his apartment in Santa Cruz, just another fun ride on his motorcycle."

I was sure Alicia was smiling. We had a soft spot in our hearts for the redheaded college student decorated from stem to stern with tattoos and piercings, including a nose ring that looked like it belonged on a fat bull instead of a lanky artist. I made a mental note to call Kyle.

"Isn't there a winter break at the University about now?" I asked.

"Ernie would know for sure, but I think the semester break was a few weeks ago. The Marine Lab didn't close, but the students were off." She knew the facts because her husband, Ernie Quintana, taught marine biology at the university in Santa Cruz.

"Holy moly! My washing machine sounds like it's ready to explode. Gotta run, Allie."

I dropped the phone, ran out the backdoor and flipped up the lid on the washing machine. The motor stopped along with the grinding noise, but something smelled like chicken roasted in machine oil. Everything seemed to be OK up top, so I dropped the lid down and the grinding continued. I threw the lid up again and silence reigned.

I circled the patio, hands on hips, brain working overtime. If I had a husband around I would have sent him outside to fix the stupid machine, but no, my poor Marty died seventeen years ago. That train of thought just made me feel sad, so I lowered my fifty-year-old reubenesque body down beside the maniacal machine. I scooted closer for a look at the underbelly, as my wavy auburn hair dusted the concrete patio.

There is nothing like putting your nose close to something dead. "Ugh!" I could call an expensive repairman or simply find a broom and sweep the crispy rodent out from under my washing machine. It took a lot of swishing to unhinge the little deep-fried critter. Mission accomplished. I wiped my forehead and dropped the lid down. The machine purred. I was doing mental pats on the back when I heard the phone ring. I dashed back to the kitchen.

"Hello? Hi, Allie, I fixed my washer. Can you believe it?"

"Wonderful. Next time I need an accomplished mechanic, I'll call you. I called Rosa's number. She's not home, or maybe she's too sick to answer the phone."

"I know you're worried, but maybe she had to go out of town for some reason."

"And not tell Doctor Finley? Rosa isn't like that."

"Are you hinting for me to stop by and see her?" I asked, as my own curiosity swelled. I had always enjoyed talking to Rosa, a pleasant thirtyish veterinary nurse who had worked for Dr. Finley for years. Even though we were basically neighbors, I had been to her house only once. I had picked her up to go to a soccer game a couple of years ago. Alicia's son, Trigger, had a soccer coach who was single and a nice guy. We figured he was just right for Rosa, but Rosa thought otherwise.

"Well, you both live in Aromas ... on the same street. I just thought ...."

"No problem, Allie. A little walk in the country might take my mind off Solow." I really doubted it, but the words sounded good. "Call you later. Bye."

I immediately set out on foot down my long gravel driveway, made a left onto the one lane, dead-end road named after Otis somebody, and stretched my legs for almost half a mile to Rosa's little house. Her home was a lot like mine, perched at the top of five acres, oak trees here and there and ocean breezes to keep the air cool and clean. Her house was an original adobe like mine, minus the window boxes full of gasping marigolds. She had a paved driveway and a row of very tall eucalyptus trees shading the back acres. Rosa's red Firebird, a hand-me-down from one of her brothers, was parked near the path to the front door.

I stood in front of Rosa's house watching a brilliantly red sun hover over a tiny piece of sparkling ocean barely visible between the coastal hills. David would have loved the view, I thought, and Solow would have enjoyed the walk to Rosa's. Why did I feel hesitant about going up to the door to ring the bell? After all, I had been to Rosa's once before.

Shimmering eucalyptus leaned eastward as a gust of wind sent a shiver up my spine. I became aware of crunching leaves and heavy purring. I looked down at a large orange cat with eyes the color of a bay in the Bahamas. He stood almost as tall as my dog. I remembered the big orange cat that never met a warm-blooded creature he didn't like and purred like an old motorboat. His purr was in overdrive as he circled my legs, leaning into me. I reached down and scratched Oliver behind his ears. He pushed his head into my hand and revved his motor.

I took a few more steps toward the solid oak front door. I felt eyes on my back and instinctively looked over my shoulder at the reddening sky. Half a dozen buzzard hawks circled high above the property, not an unusual sight, but somehow it gave me the creeps. I tapped with the brass knocker, waited, and then rang the doorbell. I pressed my ear against the smooth wood but heard nothing.

I skirted the house and peeked through a little window by the backdoor. There were no signs of life in the kitchen or the small dining area beyond. I pounded on the backdoor with my fist. Nothing. Too bad I couldn't just walk away, but that wouldn't be me.

Mom and Dad had mentioned many times over the years that I had inherited my curious nature from Aunt Clara. I hoped I wasn't turning into a nosy middle-aged woman, but I knew my aunt wouldn't have walked away from trouble and neither would I. I tried the doorknob. It turned, and I stepped inside.

"Hello? Rosa, are you here? Rosa, it's me, Josephine Stuart, your neighbor." I toured the house, kitchen first, broadcasting loudly the fact that I was looking for Rosa. I didn't want any surprises. The house was tidy, every-

thing in its place including Rosa's purse which sat on a
small oak table next to her bed. My heart did a zero-to-
ninety in one second with the realization that a woman
doesn't leave the house without her purse.

Two seconds later I was out the backdoor and stumbling over Oliver who was obviously on a campaign to
get food. I took a deep breath, turned around and
opened the backdoor again. Once inside, I flipped on
the light over the sink and hurriedly searched for cat
food. Two small stainless steel bowls sat on the floor,
side-by-side, in one corner of the room. One bowl held
water; the other bowl held a few dried-up clumps of
old cat food. I found more canned food in the fridge,
but it didn't look fresh enough for even the hungriest of
cats. I raced around the kitchen flinging open one cab-
inet door after another. Finally, I found a dozen or so
cans of cat food neatly lined up on a bottom shelf.

Oliver impatiently rubbed against my calves as I
worked the can opener. He spoke urgently in husky
meows. I scraped out the old globs and scooped in the
fresh. As soon as the fishy-smelling food hit the bowl,
Oliver was devouring it. When he finally lifted his head
to take a breath, I grabbed the bowl and set it outside,
along with a bowl of fresh water.

"Don't worry, Ollie, I'll feed you everyday until
Rosa comes back." I wondered how much food an im-
pressively large cat would need each day. Oliver me-
owed his appreciation.

I rounded Rosa's house and struck a swift pace
down Otis. It was getting dark as I walked past my
property and turned up David's driveway. I still had to
feed Fluffy. Fortunately, the kitty responsibilities had

temporarily taken my mind off Solow, allowing the pinched feeling in the back of my neck to subside.

When I finally reached my front porch, I panicked for a second because I didn't see Solow in his doggie bed. Then I remembered where he was and felt the pinch in my neck. By that time, all sunlight was gone and a sprinkling of stars had blossomed across the sky. I walked through the house, turning on every light and then the TV for company. That wasn't enough so I picked up the phone.

"Hi, Allie, I just got back from Rosa's."

"Was she home? Is she all right?"

"She wasn't home. It was weird, the car was there and so was her purse. The backdoor wasn't locked so I nosed around. Oliver acted like he hadn't eaten in days."

"Where could Rosa be? She would never leave Oliver without food."

"Don't worry about Oliver. I'm going to feed him until she gets back; that way I can tell you when she comes home." Home from where, I had no idea. Maybe I should have looked harder for clues, like, in her purse or her dresser drawers, but I had felt odd just being in her house.

"Thank you, Jo. I know Rosa will appreciate what you're doing. You know how she loves Oliver. Her brother, Pete Mendoza, lives in Castroville. Maybe he knows where she is. I hope his number's in the phone book."

"Don't worry, Allie, I'm sure there's a good explanation for all of this." Liar, liar, pants on fire, ran through my head. "See you Monday."

"Have a nice weekend, Jo." We hung up. I sat in my rocker with the receiver in my hand, feeling troubled on two fronts. I needed TV distraction. The local news flashed on ... something about a farmer loosing his crop of lettuce to a disease—a black fungus? I tried to concentrate, but it was useless. I needed food. Why would fungus-infested lettuce remind me that I hadn't eaten since breakfast?

I shuffled into the kitchen and warmed up some left-over leftovers. I didn't consciously taste the food, not even the chocolate ice cream that was supposed to make me feel better. My small but comfortable home had all the usual rooms plus a loft. With Solow gone, the place seemed cold, gray and tasteless—like my dinner. I stared at the TV, but I might as well have been watching an empty screen. The phone rang, snapping me out of my stupor.

"Hello." I tried to sound like my normal chipper self.

"Hi, Josie, it's David. I miss you and this weather is probably going to keep me here longer than I planned."

My cheeks felt warm at the sound of his voice, and I liked it when he used the nickname he had given me a few months earlier when we became "better acquainted."

"You mean your flight might be canceled?"

"That's right. The airport's closed as we speak. I'm hoping the weather will improve before Tuesday so I can come home. How's Fluffy?"

"Fluffy is fine. It's Solow who's having a problem. It seems my little porch potato ate his blanket and now he's spending time at the veterinary hospital." I tried my best not to sound overly worried.

"Hey, Josie, he's going to be fine. For a minute I thought you said Solow ate his blanket." We both laughed. "Just don't get into trouble until I get home."

"OK, David. Hope to see you Tuesday evening." I was smiling as I hung up. David always made me smile. All I needed was a cup of hot cocoa and a good rerun on the tube. I settled onto the sofa, mug in hand, and began watching a rerun of the very troubled Mr. Monk working his magic to solve a difficult case. I stared at the TV, trying to enjoy the mystery, but between Rosa's disappearance and Solow being so sick, it was impossible to concentrate.

I remembered the time Fluffy had mixed it up with a stray wire attached to a fence post. She ended up in Dr. Finley's office with an abscess on her little pink nose. Rosa Mendoza, the "Florence Nightingale" of animal nursing, made house calls to make sure Fluffy was healing.

Alicia had told me about the last boyfriend in Rosa's life, which went back to when she was in college, over ten years ago. After an abusive guy like that, no wonder she shied away from men. Since then, she and Oliver had lived together in her little house at the end of Otis Road. I should talk. All I had was Solow, and I didn't even know if he would be coming home.

My mug was empty, Monk was over and the late news came on. All of a sudden, I was wide awake. The camera zoomed in on Mr. Mendoza, Rosa's father. On camera, he explained that a mysterious fungus had blackened his entire fifty-acre lettuce crop in a matter of days. Samples of the diseased lettuce were being tested by government agriculture specialists. CAL-

OSHA had been called in to see if farm workers had been exposed to any toxic substances and the finding was that there had been no picking of lettuce in the last week, consequently, no sick workers. Sadly, Mr. Mendoza's two dogs were found dead in their kennel. They were being examined for cause of death.

The manager of a large farming conglomerate was also interviewed and said that his lettuce had not been affected. He expressed his fear that neighboring farmlands might become contaminated with the strange unnamed fungus.

The lettuce scene switched to a bloodbath story in the Far East just before I pushed the off button. My house was uncomfortably quiet without Solow's usual rhythmic snoring. I thought about Mr. Mendoza, a middle-aged widower. He lived in an old, but well kept, Victorian-style house on a front corner of his farm in Pajaro. His youngest son, Carlos, lived at home with his father and the two golden retrievers. How sad they must have been to lose their two beautiful dogs, not to mention fifty acres of lettuce.

I met the Mendoza family several years ago on Thanksgiving morning. Solow had a painful ear infection, the veterinary hospital was closed and I was desperate, so I called Rosa. She said that one of her dad's retrievers had just gotten over the same kind of infection and some of the medicine was left over. She told me to meet her at her dad's house before noon.

I arrived at the Mendoza farmhouse early. Rosa introduced me to her father, her brothers, Carlos and Pete, and Pete's wife and baby. Carlos was a moody eighteen-year-old. His older brother, Pete, was easygoing and smiled a lot, and their dad was very hospitable. If I hadn't had family of my own waiting for me, I would have accepted their invitation to stay for turkey dinner.

Rosa squeezed some medicine into Solow's ear and gave me the tube to keep. I thanked the family for inviting me to dinner and headed my truck in the direction of turkey dinner in Santa Cruz with my folks and their neighbor, Myrtle.

I remembered the Mendoza farm fondly, a labor of love for sure. They had produced organic lettuce and cabbage long before the big farms joined the organic way of growing crops. I hated to see a nice family like the Mendozas having bad luck ... or something.

Before going to bed, I checked my emails—something I do weekly if I remember. One email caught my attention:

Dear Ms. Stuart:

It has come to our attention that as owner of Wildbrush Murals Co., you have not signed an accident insurance form, which would protect your employees and all parties involved. Please report to my office, Monday, February 3rd, room 202. Thank you for your cooperation.

Cordially, Hans Coleberg, Coordinator of the Thornton Therapy Center Project

"First time I've been asked for that particular paperwork," I said to Solow, who I suddenly realized was not even in the house. I turned off the light, flopped into bed and stared at an open beam ceiling I couldn't see.

I remembered Solow as a puppy, clumsy and cute

with long ears dragging on the floor. At some point, my visualizing turned into dreams featuring a black fungus, which swept over my house, turning it and everyone in it black. Solow and I jumped into David's backyard pond and washed off the terrible fungus, only to have it leave a scummy black ring around the rocks. I scrubbed the rocks with my shirttail as buzzard hawks circled above, wearing sarcastic grins on their beaks.

CHAPTER TWO

I've always hated dark dreams that linger. But I love dark chocolate, David's dark brown eyes and black coffee … which reminded me that I needed a cup of coffee to get my body perking and eggs and sausage for strength. But when I thought about sausage, Solow's favorite, I remembered he was still in Dr. Finley's care, and again, I felt the ache in my heart.

As I went through the motions of cooking, I pushed Solow out of my mind by concentrating on Rosa's puzzling disappearance. The thing that bothered me most was her purse. I saw it in my mind, black suede with a wide shoulder strap and silver buckles. How could it be in her home when Rosa wasn't?

I didn't remember eating my breakfast, but the plate was greasy so I washed it. I showered, dressed and set out for a little walk to Rosa's. When I got there Oliver purred his heart out as he escorted me to the backdoor, an obvious ploy for food. We entered the house.

"Anybody home? This is your neighbor, Josephine … hello?"

I made a beeline for the bedroom and Rosa's purse. Nervously, I pulled it open and fished around for clues as to where she might be. I found a romance novel, cough drops, gum, Advil, lipstick, car keys and

Kleenex, but no wallet. I turned the bag upside down and shook it over her bed. When the purse was completely empty, I knew for sure there was no wallet with driver's license, money, credit cards and pictures. I scratched my head and looked around the room. Rosa's walk-in closet was neatly stocked with size ten blouses, skirts, slacks and nurse uniforms. I finally realized there was no way of knowing what might be missing since I didn't know what she had in the first place. One large suitcase sat on a shelf above the rack of hanging clothes. I reached up on tippy-toes and pulled it down. It was a typical lightweight, black fabric suitcase with wheels. I dropped it onto the bed and ran the zipper down. Empty. No smaller suitcase inside and no way to tell if there had ever been one. I finally abandoned the bedroom.

I checked the bathroom for a toothbrush, but what I found didn't help. A four-holed ceramic cup sat by the sink with three brushes of various types in it. Had there been a fourth?

I gave Oliver his daily ration of food and took off down the road. Next stop was Fluffy's house. Her urgent meows led me to an empty bowl on the kitchen floor. Once she had fresh water and food, I stepped out the backdoor. Fluffy enjoyed her own kitty door built into the bottom of the big door. I walked outside and once again admired David's backyard pond that served as a hot tub in winter. Leave it to David to invent something wonderful. When I reached home, the phone was ringing. I made a tired dash for it.

"Hello. Allie?"

"Hi, Jo, did you watch the news last night?"

"Yes. Isn't it awful? Those two beautiful dogs are dead and all the lettuce is gone. Poor Mr. Mendoza." I remembered the blackened field I had seen on my TV screen and shuddered.

"Seems very coincidental that Rosa is missing right when her father is having such bad luck. What do you think, Jo?"

"It's bad all right. But is it just bad luck? By the way, I checked out Rosa's house again. The only thing missing that I know of is her wallet. Either she has it, or it was stolen."

"Have you heard anything from Dr. Finley?" Alicia asked.

"No. Not today. He told me someone would call right away if Solow passed the blanket. If it doesn't pass through him by Monday, they'll have to operate." My neck tightened and the words stuck in my throat. I put a tissue to my nose and tried to think about other things.

"Jo, I'm thinking about having a visit with Rosa's father. Would you like to join me?"

"What time?"

"Well, I'm in the middle of preparing chili verde. I should be ready to go in an hour. See you at Mr. Mendoza's at two?"

"See you there," I said, and we hung up. I had enough time to check my painting supplies for the Thornton job, throw together a lunch and chug a mug of green tea. I crunched on celery smothered in peanut butter and listed colors of paint to buy.

The Thornton mural promised to be the largest

painting ever produced by Wildbrush Mural Company. We would paint an illusion of walls crumbling away to reveal an outdoor scene. Grassy hills would be the backdrop for a park full of children on bikes, skateboards and play structures. There would be a lake, trees, benches and paths for joggers. It would be an optimistic look at life, hopefully motivating all ages of temporarily disabled patients.

The state-of-the-art therapy center had two pools positioned side-by-side in a room forty-feet wide and sixty-feet long—enough room to park a blimp. We were set to paint fifty feet of out-door activity. I felt breathless just thinking about it. Hans told me that Mr. Thornton planned to work with mostly children. He wanted a mural that would encourage them to work hard and get well. I wanted to paint something that would make everyone smile.

I looked up from my paint list and noticed the time. Oops, I had just enough time to make it to Pajaro by two if I hurried. I grabbed my purse, rushed out to the truck and raced down Otis. San Juan Road was a different matter. I got stuck behind an extra wide tractor running at the speed of dirt—a common occurrence in our farming community. Near the end of my tedious drive, I spotted Alicia at the side of the road waving. She stood next to an older black BMW sedan parked about thirty feet from Mr. Mendoza's front yard. She waved and pointed to a wide spot in the road next to where she stood. I wondered why she wanted me to park so far away from the house, but I followed her directions. If I couldn't trust Alicia, I couldn't trust one soul on earth.

I slid down from my seat as Alicia rushed up to greet me. She took a couple of deep breaths and then gave me the scoop.

"Jo, I thought you'd never get here. Mr. Mendoza's barn was vandalized last night. I just thought I would warn you. He's really gone crazy. Said he wants to move back to Mexico and then he said some other things I can't repeat. I was worried he might have a heart attack."

"Is Carlos here to take care of him?" I asked, feeling uncomfortable about our visiting Mr. Mendoza at an awkward time.

"Of all times for Carlos to be partying," Alicia said. "He was gone all night and staggered home this afternoon in terrible condition. I drove up just as Carlos was crawling out of his friend's car. His father looked angry enough to kill him. Really, Jo, it was awful. Mr. Mendoza spoke in Spanish to Carlos. He threatened to disown his own son." Alicia's eyes were dark and wild as she gestured with her hands. Finally she wrapped her arms around her upper torso for comfort.

"Why don't we come back another time?" I asked, staring in amazement at the thousands of heads of black wilted lettuce surrounding the farmhouse and barn on three sides.

"I'm still concerned about Rosa. If her father knows where she is, I can relax. Please, Jo, I need your support."

"Don't worry, I'm right behind you," I said. Alicia turned and led the way down a dirt path sandwiched between an irrigation canal on our left and San Juan Road on our right. We turned into Mr. Mendoza's driveway and stopped short at the front steps of the Victorian. A disheveled young man sat on the top step, his head resting on his knees.

Carlos was a big guy. Maybe he was shy, or slow, or something, but that afternoon he was a slobbering drunk. If his father threw him out, Carlos had only gone as far as the front porch steps. He raised his head when he heard us coming and then dropped it as if it were made of lead.

One ring of the bell and a tired looking Mr. Mendoza opened the door. Under his thick mustache he wore a weak smile.

"Please excuse my son. He has never acted this way before. Won't you ladies come in?"

Alicia stepped inside and I tagged along. The spacious high-ceilinged front room was neatly arranged with ornately carved Spanish-style furniture. Each dark, heavy piece accented with pounded silver hinges, knobs and handles.

Light streamed into the house from a bank of four tall windows facing south. They were bare and provided perfectly framed views of the fields, railroad tracks and distant hills. The almost completed Thornton Therapy Center sat just a hundred yards away, looking like a humongous foreign object surrounded on three sides by jade green lettuce fields. Straight rows of green and brown stretched south to the hills and west about five miles to the Pacific Ocean. A dusty tractor road was all that separated the Mendoza's black lettuce farm from the neighboring one.

I jumped when the front door slammed, and Carlos staggered into the room. The liquor had put a smile on his face and gleam in his droopy eyes. His eyes were trained on the Hispanic beauty wearing jeans and a light blue t-shirt with a soccer logo on the back. He stared at her silky black hair and every inch of her slim body. Alicia ignored Carlos and turned to his father.

"Mr. Mendoza, has Rosa gone on vacation? I've been calling her, but she hasn't returned my calls." Before his father could answer, Carlos blurted.

"I know where ...."

"You don't know anything," his father snapped. "Go to the barn and help Andy put things in order. We had a visitor last night."

Carlos hesitated.

"Now!" Mr. Mendoza said, glaring at his youngest offspring and biggest embarrassment.

Carlos shuffled off to the kitchen and let the screen door slam as he walked outside.

Mr. Mendoza apologized again for his son's behavior but didn't have much else to say. I had an urge to run after Carlos and pump him for information, but instead I turned to Mr. Mendoza.

"Would you mind if we looked at your barn? I don't know anything about farming, but your house is lovely and I would like to see the grounds," I smiled sweetly.

Mr. Mendoza was obviously a proud man, and I figured he would want to show off his farm equipment—as if I cared about tractors. Oh well, I could look at his tractors all day if it helped us to get to the bottom of the Rosa issue. Alicia put on smile, but it didn't fool me. I knew it was covering her worry lines.

Mr. Mendoza agreed to show us the rest of the farm. We funneled out the backdoor into the glare of a not very warm sun. I sensed that the heat wave was just about over. Too bad David had missed it.

"This is my newest piece of equipment," Mr. Mendoza said, as he pointed to a large yellow and green tractor with two sets of double gigantic tires in the back. The driver's seat was surrounded by windows. No bugs in the teeth for Mendoza farmers. The tractor was parked on a concrete slab between the house and barn.

"What a nice tractor, Mr. Mendoza," Alicia said as we headed for the barn.

Carlos leaned against a wall just inside the open door of the barn, watching a man in his late twenties push a wheelbarrow full of debris. When Carlos saw us coming, he quickly grabbed a broom and began sweeping the concrete floor.

We entered the building and were shocked to see what looked like the aftermath of an 8.5 earthquake. Two small tractors parked at the far end of the structure were barely visible under all the fallen junk that had toppled off the storage racks. Metal pipes, plastic pipes and fittings were strewn across the floor and boxes of hardware had been dumped in a pile as high as my head, five-foot-six, to be exact.

Alicia and I just stood there, eyes wide, mouths open, unable to speak. Finally, I found my voice.

"This is outrageous! Why would someone do this to your barn?"

"Who could have made such a mess?" Alicia asked.

"Same SOB that killed my dogs and ruined my lettuce. Excuse my language ladies. If he comes around again, I'll ...." his face turned red as his voice trailed off. Mr. Mendoza leaned against the wall and shook his head slowly as if to shake away the terrible sight. He finally introduced us to Andy, the man behind the wheelbarrow. Andy was taller, thicker and a little older than Carlos. He worked fast and hard, his curly blond hair wet with sweat, while Carlos could barely aim his broom at the floor.

A red wool jacket stuffed into a fifty-gallon drum full of rags caught my eye. I picked it up and automatically shook the creases out, noticing that it was a "Liz Claiborne," size ten.

"Carlos, whose is this?" I asked, shaking the jacket like a toreador teasing a bull.

"Rosa's, I think."

Mr. Mendoza quickly walked over to his son but it was too late, the words were already out.

"It might belong to Pete's wife, Luisa; I'm not sure," Mr. Mendoza said, positioning himself between Carlos and me. "Would you ladies like to see the kennel?" It was an obvious ploy to get us away from Carlos.

"Lead the way," I said, wondering if he had forgotten that his dogs were dead. Then I thought of poor Solow. The short walking tour of the grounds included two large tin-roofed outbuildings and a painfully empty dog kennel. No one spoke as we hurried by the chain link fence surrounding a lengthy concrete slab. Two wooden doghouses stood side-by-side at the end of the run like tombs with pointy, shingled roofs.

I glanced at Mr. Mendoza. His eyes glistened, but the man kept his composure. Anger seemed to be the emotion of the day, not that I blamed him. I choked up just thinking about what Mr. Mendoza must have been going through.

"Thanks for the tour. We need to go now," I said.

"Yes, we should go, but please call me if you hear from Rosa," Alicia said, leaning toward her friend. They hugged. As a child, Alicia had been an orphan living on the streets of Tijuana until an American couple adopted her. Finally, she had lots of family. There was the family who adopted her and later, her husband's family and the Mendoza family. And, in a way, she had taken me in as a part of her extended family. She always invited me over for get-togethers, including dinner that night. How could I say no to chili verde, even if I had work to do that night in preparation for the "big job" at the Therapy Center?

"Allie, I'll see you at dinner time. Gotta run some errands first."

She waved goodbye and drove her green Volvo station wagon down the road toward Watsonville. I decided to take a little walk in the same direction, just one block, to the Thornton building. My cool-looking sunglasses didn't do much for watering, blinking eyes as I walked directly into the sun. I shuffled along the dirt strip between the ditch and San Juan Road. An eighteen-wheeler loaded with lettuce flew by, ruffling my hair, not to mention my nerves.

The extensive parking lot in front and to one side of the Thornton building was almost empty because the Center was not yet finished and opened for business. Three pickups with racks and built-in toolboxes were parked in the east side parking area just a few yards from the backdoor. In one of six spaces marked "RE-SERVED," a shiny new black Corvette cooled its wheels in the shadows of the two-story building. The only other vehicle on the property was a very old, barely-red Nissan pickup parked near a dumpster at the far end of the parking lot and only a few feet from a lettuce field. I tried to guess who was inside the building, probably one big shot, one janitor and three construction guys putting in overtime.

The backdoor was unlocked. I remembered going out that particular door after meeting with Hans a couple of months earlier. I remembered the long hallway, not yet carpeted, with doors on both sides opening into various unfurnished offices and meeting rooms. After passing six closed doors, I came upon an open area with two elevators and a staircase to the second floor. The stair rail was made of twisted copper tubing in tangled shapes, embellished with green glass globes here and there. Nice, but "Modern" was not my period. A three-foot by twelve-foot stained glass window featuring an abstract design added a bit of light and color to the alcove.

As I walked further, the hallway opened up on the right side to a gigantic room featuring two specially designed therapy pools trimmed with cobalt blue Italian tile. On my left stood over twenty yards of intimidating wall space. I ran my hand over the stucco surface to make sure it had been painted with the eggshell paint I recommended. The wall felt cold, smooth and ready.

I worried about the project being too big a challenge for my little mural company. I was a "Nervous Nelly" with a giant butterfly flapping around in my stomach. I fought to keep a positive, can-do attitude, telling myself that we would work hard, turn out a remarkable piece of artwork and keep everyone happy … I hoped and prayed.

For the first time since I arrived at the Center, I noticed the muffled hammering and sawing noises coming from somewhere on the first floor. I heard footsteps pounding up the hall, and looked to my right. A tall, thin dark-complexioned man rushed up the hallway toward me. His close cut hair looked like tiny white cotton balls and his long legs were slightly bowed. He seemed to be in a terrible hurry.

"Hey there," the old man gave me a friendly smile but kept on walking.

"Hey, yourself," I said, not knowing what else to say to the stranger. I finished my inspection of the pool room and began my return trip up the hall toward the backdoor. Suddenly I heard a thud, then a terrible crashing noise and groaning. I did a ten-yard dash to the foot of the staircase in time to see the old man roll down the last couple steps. The back of his head thumped on the concrete floor in front of me.

Everything seemed to be happening in slow motion. The man's nose and lip bled onto the floor. He couldn't lift his left arm to get himself up, and white sheets of paper were strewn all over the staircase, top to bottom. An empty metal wastebasket rested on the landing above us.

"Oh, my God! Here, let me help you up." My heart raced as I leaned over the old gentleman. He held out his right hand, I took it, leaned backward and after a couple of tries he finally pulled himself up to a shaky stance. He was heavier than he looked. I offered him a Kleenex from my pocket. He put it to his nose and tilted his head back to stop the bleeding. Big drips and little puddles created a morbid design on the floor.

"My name's Josephine. Can I call an ambulance for you?"

"I'll be fine," he said, as his right arm hung at his side, useless. I figured he had bitten his lip and bumped his nose on the way down. All in all, he was a rumpled bloody mess. I felt sick just looking at him.

"How can I help you?" I asked, wondering how he had slipped and tumbled down the stairs.

"Sorry, Ma'am. My name is Jim Keeper," his voice trembled. He touched his left hand to his right elbow and winced. "Josephine, I feel a little unsteady. Would you mind walkin' me to my truck?"

"Not at all," I said, wondering what I would do if Jim keeled over. The sound of our footsteps echoed off the walls as we trudged slowly to the backdoor. It seemed odd that no one else in the building heard the fall. No one came running. I opened the door for Jim and helped him across the parking lot to his old Nissan truck. He leaned against the tailgate, breathing hard. That was when I decided there was no way I would allow him to drive.

"Jim, I'll drive."

"I would appreciate that, Miss Josephine." He handed me the keys without a fuss. We walked to the passenger side, I opened the door and he gingerly lowered himself onto the seat.

"Which hospital?" I asked, afraid he might change his mind about letting me drive.

"Watsonville Hospital will be fine." He lifted the right arm with his left hand, letting it rest on his lap. The poor man squinted his eyes and tightened his jaw with every bump and turn as we wove our way through Watsonville. After what seemed like an eternity but really only minutes, I parked in the drive-up emergency parking area behind the three-story blue structure. A male nurse pushing a wheelchair across the parking area paused to look at the bloody-faced man and offered him a ride. Jim sat down carefully like a hen on her eggs.

The nurse pushed Jim straight to the admitting window, and I stood beside his chair in case he needed assistance. Mr. Keeper pulled all the right cards out of his wallet and the woman behind the window handed him papers to sign. Things were moving right along for Jim, probably because Sunday was pretty quiet in the emergency room. A perky young nurse with yellow hair hanging over one eye handed him some more paperwork and tried to make him smile.

"You don't look so good, Mr. Keeper. What does the other guy look like?" she joked, as she turned his chair and headed for a row of curtained cubicles.

Jim looked startled and started to explain. "I didn't touch the other ...." He squirmed in the wheelchair. The nurse and I locked eyes for a second. "I mean, I fell down the stairs and this nice lady here drove me to the hospital. Miss, can I have something for the pain in my arm?"

"Real soon. Try to relax," she said, as she helped the old man onto a narrow, but highly mechanized hospital bed. "Doctor Ikemoto will be with you shortly." She turned and bustled down the hall.

"Doc Ikemoto's one of the volunteers that's gonna work at the Therapy Center," Jim said.

"Have you already met the doctor?"

"Oh, no, but I know a lot of what goes on at the Center. Willy Thornton and I are like family." Jim smiled for a second, but the pain suddenly tightened his jaw and knotted his brow. "Miss Josephine, I'll be all right. You don't need to stay with me."

"I'm afraid I'm stranded here, unless I drive your truck." I smiled to let him know that I wasn't in a big hurry to leave.

"Miss Josephine, you can drive my truck back to the Center and I'll take a cab home."

"No, Jim, I have a better idea. I'll drive to the Center and exchange your truck for mine. When you're ready to go home, you call me." I wasn't about to take no for an answer.

"Did you say you drive a truck?" He cocked his head to one side. "A purdy lady like you drivin' a truck?" He looked like he wanted to laugh, but his ribs hurt too much.

"I'm a modern woman. I work as a muralist and I need a truck to haul my ladders and such. Besides, I like driving a truck." I winked at Jim and his cloudy eyes twinkled for a second. He looked at Alicia's phone number scribbled on the back of one of my business cards, holding it at arms length, and then dropped it into his shirt pocket.

"Is there anyone you want me to call?" He shook his head. "Don't forget to call me," I said.

"Yes, Ma'am."

I hated to leave Jim by himself, but after all—he was a grown man and the hospital staff would take good care of him. I hopped into the old Nissan pickup and drove straight to the Therapy Center. I parked Jim's truck and walked a hundred yards in the dark to Mr. Mendoza's house, climbed into my truck and headed to Alicia's, hoping I wasn't too late for dinner.

Alicia, Ernie and their ten-year-old son, Trigger, lived in a modest two-story house in the Watsonville Lake District. The house was ordinary, but their backyard lawn stretched all the way to the edge of Drew Lake, and looking east, across the water, were the grassy foothills. But what really mattered at Alicia's house were the people.

Ernie welcomed me with a hug, and then it was Trigger's turn. Even at ten, I knew Trigger would be a real looker when he grew up. As if that wasn't enough, he had his father's brains and his mother's heart. I smelled Alicia's wonderful Mexican cooking the minute I stepped into the house.

"Jo, you look frazzled. We were about to give up and eat without you," Alicia said as she put her hand on my back and steered me toward the dining room.

"I'm sorry, Allie. I had to take a sweet old man to the hospital."

Alicia and Ernie laughed.

"No, really, I did. I was checking out the therapy center before we start painting tomorrow. While I was there a man fell down the stairs and I had to take him to the hospital."

The smiles disappeared and everyone was quiet for a moment.

"How's the fellow doing?" Ernie asked.

"I think he'll be all right, although his left arm is probably broken. I'm not sure about his ribs."

"Auntie Jo, is that blood on the back of your sleeve?" Trigger said, making a face.

I twisted my arm to see my elbow. Sure enough, blood must have rubbed off Jim when I helped him up from the floor. Maybe it was on the truck seat too.

"Jim, the gentleman I was telling you about, was bleeding from his nose and lip. He was really shaken up. I told him to call here when he's ready to go home. I hope they let him go home tonight." I thought about poor old Jim, working hard on a Sunday at his age.

The chili verde was to die for and the rest of the meal was delicious, as usual. About an hour after we finished eating the call came. Not from Jim, but from a nurse. She told me Jim had tried to walk out of the building, but doctor's orders were clear. He could not leave without a caregiver.

"Miss, I just met Mr. Keeper. I'll be glad to drive him home, but ...."

"Ms. Stuart, the gentleman needs help just for one night."

"I'll be right down to pick him up." I put the phone down and scratched my head.

"Allie, would you mind if I take home a few left-overs?"

"Of course not. They're right here," she smiled knowingly and handed me two packages neatly wrapped in foil. "It seems you have another bird with a broken wing."

"Thanks for everything, Allie. I gotta go pick him up. See you tomorrow, nine o'clock." I hugged every-one. After all the warmth in the Quintana home, the starry night felt cold and bleak. A couple of miles later

I pulled into the hospital's loading zone. A plump, friendly nurse wheeled Jim out to my truck and helped him into the seat. She told him to be careful and wished him well. He waved goodbye. His right arm rested inside a shoulder-to-wrist purple cast, slightly bent and held up by a sling. I fired up the engine but kept the brake on.

"Mr. Keeper ...."

"Call me Jim."

"Jim, is there anyone at home who can take care of you? I understand you feel pretty good now that you're medicated, but you might need help if the pain returns."

"Miss Josephine, I'll be fine. Just drop me off at my truck."

"I'd rather take you home if there's someone there to help you." No way was I going to let him drive, all doped up.

"My grandson lives in a cottage behind my house. He'll be home later tonight."

"Show me the way," I said, thinking about all the work I had to do when I got home.

We drove a couple of miles and ended up back in the Lake District neighborhood. Jim's house was located on the north side of Drew Lake with a perfect view of the Quintana's house on the west side. I felt better just knowing that Alicia lived nearby in case of an emergency. I wondered about the grandson story, but decided I had done all I could.

"Let me help you out." I groped in the dark to open the passenger door and then held Jim's good arm while his feet made contact with the asphalt. A sensor light came on as we walked to the front door. His keys were still in my pocket so I unlocked the front door and then handed them over. The house smelled of pipe tobacco and leather. The brown leather sofa and matching chair were comfortably worn and the sage green carpet had a flattened path to the kitchen. The housekeeping wasn't the best, but for a bachelor, it was excellent. I helped Jim settle into his recliner.

"Just a minute, I'll be right back." I ducked out the door and came back with the leftovers wrapped in foil.

Jim smiled cheek to cheek.

"Don't know how to thank you. I'm gonna be fine now." Jim sat back in his chair, eyeing the food on the coffee table, probably wishing I would leave so he could sample it. I wrote down his phone number and walked to the door.

"Take care, Jim." I was headed home at last. I tried to convince myself the old man would be fine because I had no room for guilt with all my other worries such as Solow and Rosa, not to mention the first-day jitters of a new job. Besides, I planned to call Jim in the morning.

My house was dark and lonely when I got home until I played my messages.

"Josie, it's me, David. The weather's a little better. Maybe I'll make it home Tuesday after all." Short and sweet, it made me smile. I played the next message.

"Hi, Honey, this is your dad. Mother and I are leaving for the Mojave Desert with our hiking group. See you in a couple of weeks."—a typical message from my close to eighty-year-old parents.

Next message. "Josephine, this is Doctor Finley …." (Silence followed) My heart sank all the way to my toes.

I could barely breathe as my eyes stung and terrible fears bombarded my brain.

"Oops! Sorry, Solow was caught in his leash." Suddenly my spirits soared. Caught in his leash meant he was alive and standing up. Oh, God! The doctor continued. "He passed the blockage this evening. He's doing well, and you can pick him up in the morning." I did a jig all through the house, twirling round and round like a four year old. David would have laughed if he could have seen me. I sailed through all the work I needed to do, such as packing ladders, paint boxes and all essential tools into the bed of my truck by porch light. I felt truly blessed.

CHAPTER THREE

Seven a.m. arrived long before I was ready to open my eyes, until I remembered what Dr. Finley had said. I quickly rolled out of bed and let the hot shower wake me up. I had things to do before I could bring Solow home. I hurried through the natural beautifying process and dressed myself in clean but paint-spattered clothing, jeans and a long-sleeved pullover. Some of my old paint outfits had been around for seventeen years ever since my husband Marty died and left me to pay the bills.

After five trips to the Mazda, all essential gear had been loaded. The only thing missing was the confidence I needed to execute a mural of such proportion. I immediately buried that thought and grabbed Solow's leash, a thermos of hot tea, a toasted bagel and my purse. I tossed everything behind the passenger seat on top of a red folder full of mural sketches.

My first stop was Rosa's house. Oliver must have heard me coming up the road. He greeted me with soft meows and lots of body language, weaving in and out of my legs as I tried to hurry around the house to the backdoor. Once fed, he purred his appreciation.

Second stop, Fluffy's house. The prissy white fur ball lay curled up on a bench in the backyard waiting for food. She stretched and slowly made her way to my side. A little petting and some canned kitty gunk pacified her.

I thundered down Otis, then Aromas Road and onto San Juan for another ten miles of lettuce, cabbage and strawberry farms. I was in a hurry to see Solow, but an ungainly tractor kept me from breaking the speed limit, or even getting near it. There were just enough cars coming in the other direction to keep me from passing. I silently thanked the tractor driver as I passed a highway patrol car idling on the side of the road, ready to pounce.

Dr. Finley's office opened at eight-thirty, and I was there when Nancy unlocked the front door. Her job was to work the desk and comfort distraught people like me who called on the phone expecting advice and instant appointments. Nancy had worked with Dr. Finley at least five years, ever since Solow was a puppy.

"Hi, Nancy. How's my little hound dog?" I said, trying to contain myself.

"Solow's fine. Good as new," she smiled. I think Solow was one of her favorite patients; and I know he adored the tall, big-boned Swede with the touch of an angel. I followed her to the holding area where dogs and cats recovered from various ailments in wire cages only big enough for sleeping. Solow saw me first and howled.

"Solow," was all I could say before the lump in my throat choked off the volume.

Nancy opened the little wire door. Solow shot out of the cage and leaned his head against my knee. I squatted on the floor and wrapped my arms around him. All worries were forgotten in that special moment. I thanked Nancy, paid a fortune at the front desk and hiked Solow into the passenger seat of the truck for a short trip through Watsonville to my new job.

A few minutes later, we rolled into the Thornton Therapy Center parking lot. I parked three spaces from the backdoor, next to a familiar-looking black Corvette occupying the same reserve space as the day before. Next to it was Hans' white retro Lincoln. At least half a dozen pickups sporting racks and toolboxes were parked nearby, and Jim's barely-red Nissan pickup sat by the dumpster where I had left it. I hoped Jim was resting and healing and made a mental note to check on him later.

The roar of a motorcycle startled me out of my thoughts. Kyle, my youngest artist-employee, pulled in beside my truck, cut the engine and pulled off his flame-covered yellow helmet. I snagged Solow's leash from the back of the truck, clipped it to his collar and helped him down from his perch. His whole body wiggled with happiness as we exercised our legs around the perimeter of the parking lot. Kyle walked with us.

"Did Alicia, like, tell you I have all my classes on Tuesdays and Thursdays?"

"I haven't talked to her about it. Things got kinda hectic last night." I rolled my eyes with that under-statement. "I'm glad you're working with us again, Kyle. Don't worry, three days a week will be fine." We circled back to my truck.

"What kind of mural are we painting?" Kyle asked as he unbuckled black leather chaps from his long, skinny legs.

"It's going to be the biggest, most complicated mural we've ever done. Guess we better go in and see if they're ready for us, scaffolding-wise," I said as we grabbed tarps, a cooler and the folder of sketches. Before we had time to enter the building, Alicia drove up and parked alongside Kyle's bike. She joined us and gave Solow some loving pats. We entered the building and strolled down the hall past the alcove, home of one infamous staircase and two elevators. I noticed the floor had no bloodstains on it. We marched over to the giant "mural wall" opposite the therapy pools and gawked.

"Wow!" Kyle exhaled.

"Jo, it's huge!" Alicia gasped.

"I know," I groaned. I felt completely overwhelmed and my friends seemed to feel the same. The first ideas for the space had included a sixty-foot long, by twenty-foot high illusion of crumbling walls revealing a playground. My most recent meeting with Hans had the mural down to fifty feet by fifteen feet, which was still a formidable size and a threat to my composure. What if I failed? Over the last seventeen years of painting murals, I had never failed to complete a project. I told myself to get a grip.

"It's big, but I know we can do it, Jo," Alicia said with spirit and a sympathetic hand on my shoulder.

"Like, it's going to be OK, you know," Kyle chimed in as he scratched his head full of spiky red hair. "So, where's the scaffolding, man?"

"Sorry, guys. I need to talk to Hans about that. You guys can start measuring the fifty by fifteen-foot space and make some chalk marks. The mural will be centered on this wall, ending at the floor. Kyle, use the level and draw a horizon line at six feet. Ladders are in my truck. Solow can sleep on a tarp while I go upstairs and look for Hans." I turned to go.

"Hello, Josephine. Is this your fine crew?" Hans asked. His large, middle-aged body leaned against the wall as his clear blue eyes followed Solow. Looking like he might split a seam in his steel-gray Armani suit, Hans leaned down and let Solow sniff his hand, then scratched behind a long velvety ear.

"This is my team, Alicia, Kyle, and Solow."

Alicia stepped forward and shook Hans' plump hand. He was obviously delighted.

Kyle nodded from a distance.

"I'm glad you're here, Hans," I said. "I wanted to talk to you about scaffolding."

He cocked his head and looked around. "My dear, I'm afraid I forgot to inform our foreman of this project. I am so sorry. I'll go upstairs and give Chester a call right away. When you have time, I have a document that needs your signature." He turned and hustled his bulk to the elevator.

I looked at my friends in disbelief. "Did he say, Chester?" My mouth dropped open.

"Like, Chester Mathus?" Kyle asked.

"Wouldn't it be funny if it really was the Chester we worked with last summer?" Alicia said. "I wonder if he has recovered from that terrible accident."

We didn't have long to wonder because Chester, still young and handsome, hurriedly limped up the hall-way. He smiled when he saw us, and when he was close enough, shook our hands energetically.

"Hey, it's great to see you guys. How do you like the place?" he asked, brushing sawdust from his Levis. "It's very dramatic with those steel beams and stained glass windows," Alicia said.

"It's a bit cold looking without carpet. I suppose that happens last?" I said, trying not to give my actual opinion on the modernistic warehouse-looking structure.

"We're not doing carpet. The concrete floor will be sanded, dyed and coated to look like slate."

"Wow, that sounds like an interesting technique," I said, rubbing goose bumps on both arms.

"Got an SOS from the boss. Guess you guys need some scaffolding. Don't worry, I'll get the guys right on it." Chester was all smiles, happy to be working with old friends. The feeling was mutual. I had thought about Chester over the last few months, wondering if he had fully recovered from his truck taking a fifty-foot dive into the San Lorenzo River with him in it. Other than the slight limp, he looked good as new.

"A movable set-up eight feet high and about twelve feet long would be great," I said to Chester. He turned and did a hurried limp back to the west wing, as I tried to picture in my mind a realistic depiction of sky, fifty feet long and six feet high.

My workers were already heading in the opposite direction to collect all remaining equipment from the bed of my truck. I left Solow in the building and followed my friends outside.

"Jo, do you want all three ladders?" Kyle asked.

"We'll take all the ladders and every piece of equipment." I lifted a heavy plastic tackle box full of bottles of paint, and stuffed a folded tarp under my arm. I picked up a second tackle box with the other hand. My body complained but I didn't listen.

Kyle arrived at the mural wall with two ladders and Alicia set down two canvas bags full of equipment. We made two more trips, picking the truck clean. We stopped our organizing of equipment when we heard a rumble echoing up the hall.

Chester and another carpenter pushed two carts full of scaffolding pieces toward us. To me it looked like a nuts and bolts nightmare, but Chester and his helper had a couple of scaffolds assembled in record time.

I thanked the guys for the scaffolding just before another wave of self-doubt rolled over the tiny bit of confidence I had accumulated. Fifty feet was a daunting distance. I took a moment to pet Solow and regain my composure. He was good for lowering blood pressure, boosting morale and giving me unconditional love. I thanked God for Solow's good health and eventually felt calmer.

I had packed every tarp I owned, but twenty feet of floor space was still not covered. I scratched my head and decided to buy a couple of tarps on the lunch hour. I figured we would go through almost two gallons of sky blue, in three different shades, before we started the hills and foreground.

Alicia and Kyle measured off the mural lines. As Kyle drew the horizon line with chalk and a level, Alicia and I framed the mural area with masking tape, and then mixed up three buckets of blue paint in three different shades.

Solow lay on my jacket snoring and twitching his

paws as if he had Fluffy in sight.

By noon the preliminary work was finished, but I decided we should have lunch before embarking on the toughest sky we would ever be asked to create. Alicia had chores to do and I had tarps to purchase, so Kyle was elected to stay with Solow. I donated my home-made lunch to the starving student and headed for Watsonville. I passed through the little town of Pajaro, just two blocks from the Thornton Center. I drove past a couple of gas stations, a bar, two restaurants and a warehouse, crossed the Pajaro Bridge and entered Watsonville, a larger town by at least 40,000 people.

I cruised up Main Street where dozens of ornate and impressive turn-of-the-century buildings lined the street. I turned right on Green Valley Road and a mile later parked in front of ABC Paints. Five minutes later Steve carried my two newly purchased tarps to the truck, as if I couldn't do it myself. I didn't have a problem with a little chivalry now and then, especially when it came from a cute little gray-haired guy with the cocky attitude of a bantam rooster.

"You say you're working on the new Therapy Center," Steve said, looking unimpressed. "I heard that the councilmen rezoned that part of Pajaro just so big shot Thornton could build his Therapy Center. Pretty soon all the agriculture will be gone. You watch and see." Steve shook his head as he predicted doom.

"Thanks for the help, Steve," I said, firing up my Mazda. I pulled into traffic and headed down Freedom Boulevard to pick up a fast-food chicken salad. It was twelve-thirty and there were five cars ahead of me at the drive-up. I found my favorite music station and turned up the volume. In no time I had rock and rolled my way to the window where I paid for a salad and iced tea.

Five minutes later, I parked at the Therapy Center and entered the building carrying tarps and a boxed salad. I shivered as I walked past the staircase. Big concrete structures had never appealed to me. The cold feeling disappeared when Solow greeted me with a loving howl.

"Good sandwich, Jo. Like, what was in it?" Kyle asked as he sat on a paint box, chewing the last bite.

"Leftovers in a blender, spread on poppy seed buns with red onion slices and mustard." I watched Kyle's Adam's apple as he forced the last bite down his throat. He finished off the fruit and cookies while I ate my Mandarin Chicken salad and tossed a few bites of chicken to Solow. Alicia arrived sipping her soft drink from the Burger Box.

By one o'clock we were fully nourished and ready to paint. Tarps were down, tape was up, the scaffolds were in place, and the paint was mixed and ready.

"OK, you guys, you know the routine," I said. "Paint the darkest blue across the top and two feet down, end to end. I'll use the left scaffold, Alicia gets the one on the right and Kyle will use the eight-foot ladder in the middle area. We'll work fast and hope the air is cold and damp enough to keep the paint from drying too fast. Work the lighter blue into the bottom six inches of the darker blue and down another two feet. The lightest blue goes down to the horizon, of course. Let's do it!"

Solow looked inspired, but the rest of us knew how

much work it would be.

True to our fears, we used most of the blue paint and all of our energy. No one was allowed to stop until all the blue had been slathered on the wall using three-inch brushes and lots of muscle. Blending was always a fast and furious process; but at the end of the day, we had sky—a warm, sunny sky. I felt my forehead relax.

"Can you believe it's five already? See you tomor-row, Allie. Guess it'll be Wednesday for you, Kyle. I'll clean up. You guys get out of here." I didn't have to say it twice. Solow and I were alone in the cold silent pool-room until Hans appeared with papers flapping in one hand. He handed me a pen and I signed.

"Isn't that sky marvelous?" he said, hands on hips, head moving side to side taking it all in—all fifty feet. "You people really know how to paint. Do you think the sky should be a little darker?" He squinted at the wall as if he were an art critic.

"This is the sky portrayed in the proposal," I ar-gued. My cheeks were hot and the thought of repaint-ing the sky was worse than bamboo spikes under fingernails.

"Oh, sure, you're right. Can't wait to see what comes next," he smiled. "Lock the door on your way out." He turned and lumbered up the hall toward the elevators. I gulped some air and thanked the heavens for huge favors. I cleaned the brushes and stowed the gear against the wall, leaving the hallway clear of clut-ter.

When Solow and I reached the parking lot, all the carpenters' pickups were gone. The barely-red Nissan was still parked by the dumpster.

"Solow, maybe we should check on old Jim since I forgot to call him." I shivered as a gust of cold air whipped through the lot, pushing bits of litter and leaves across the asphalt. Yellow streetlights turned my truck an ugly orange, but I was glad for the light. Stars were out by the millions but no moon.

We settled into my cozy pickup, still shivering. I sat for a couple of minutes rubbing my fatigued right arm and wrist trying to gather some energy. Finally, we took off in the direction of the Lake District with the heater blasting. We passed Alicia's street and turned right on Cutter and then right on Lower Cutter, a one-lane road with no streetlights or sidewalks. Several older homes were nestled between the road and Drew Lake.

I spotted Jim's one story, sixties ranch-style house. The garage door was open. One side was empty; the other side housed a gray Chevy Tahoe SUV.

"Good," I said to Solow, "Jim's grandson must be here." I pulled off the road and parked in a wide spot. "Come on, big guy, let's go see Jim."

The front yard sensor light flashed on, exposing an uneven brick path to the front door. Cold air blew wisps of hair across my face and shivers up my spine. I pushed on the doorbell once—then again and again. Finally, I tried the door and found it was not locked. Solow growled softly as we entered the front room where one dim light illuminated Jim's favorite chair.

"Hello, Jim, it's Josephine." Jim sat in the chair with his head down and beside him, kneeling on the sage carpet, was a man in uniform. His head rested on Jim's left arm, the arm not in a purple cast. The young marine finally heard us and looked up, eyes swollen and red.

His thick lips trembled when he tried to speak. "My flight was delayed … if only I'd gotten here sooner," he said, in a husky voice. "Hi, I'm Josephine. Is something wrong with Jim?" I asked, already knowing in my soul that he was gone even though he looked like he was just napping. "Ma'am, I'm Corporal Justin Keeper, Jim's grandson." He rose up to his full 6' 3" and shook my hand. "I just got in from Afghanistan. I told Granddad in my letter I would be home yesterday. We ran into some bad weather and my flight was delayed. I walked in a few minutes ago and … I don't know what to do." Justin wiped his tears with a fist. "I should be accustomed to … death. But not my own Granddad, for God's sake." He folded back down to his original position on the floor with his head on Jim's arm.

My eyes welled up, and my throat felt like it had a boulder stuck in it.

I leaned closer to Jim and touched his hand. It was as cold as the night. Then I moved my hand to the suffering grandson, touching him on his shoulder. Solow sniffed Jim's boots, turned and trotted into the kitchen. I hadn't known the old man very long or well, but I felt sad that he was gone and sorry for the young man left behind.

"Did you know Jim had a terrible fall yesterday?" I whispered.

"I wondered about the cast. Last time I saw him, he was healthy enough to live to a hundred or more. How did he fall?"

"I don't know for sure how or why he fell down the stairs at the Therapy Center, but I think someone hit him," I said, thinking back to when the nurse had jokingly asked what the "other guy" looked like, and Jim started to tell us, but caught himself. It bothered me that the black Corvette had been parked outside the Center, yet no one heard the fall except me. I couldn't blame the carpenters. They were working in the west wing and couldn't have heard anything over all the pounding and sawing. I had a nagging feeling someone was upstairs with Jim when he fell.

"What makes you think someone punched him?" Justin asked, staring up at me with dark pools for eyes. "No one would punch my Granddad. Everyone loved him."

"It was something he said, but I could be wrong. Have you called anyone?"

"No. Not yet. I wanted to spend a few minutes alone with him."

"I'll take my dog for a walk. We'll talk about it later," I said on my way out the door. I walked Solow half a block and turned back. I boosted Solow into the truck and started the engine with the heater on high. I hadn't prepared myself mentally for a return to winter after the false little summer. I thought about the marine, tough as jerky on the outside, soft as cotton candy on the inside. I hated seeing him suffer; but after awhile, I knew I had to go back inside. One of us would have to call the authorities.

I opened the front door a sliver and peeked in. Justin had a drink in his hand. He raised it and said, "I love you, Pops," and emptied the glass in one long gulp.

"Justin, we're back. Maybe we should call now?" I

waited awhile for his answer, trying to be patient. Justin
finally nodded, giving me the OK to call 911. I dialed.
"911, do you have an emergency?" a female asked.
"Yes, sort of. A gentleman died in his sleep. We just
found him." I looked over at Justin. His eyes were brim-
ming with tears. I gave the woman on the phone the
address, and she said she would send the authorities
right away.
"Justin, can I get you something to eat or drink?"
He didn't answer. I looked around the kitchen, obviously a recent remodel judging by the new birch cabinets, black tile countertops and modern stainless-steel
appliances. I suddenly remembered Solow hadn't had
his supper.
"Justin, would you mind if I gave my dog something to eat?" No answer.
I opened the fridge and found a piece of leftover
roast beef in plastic wrap. Jim had never met Solow, but
I was sure he would have loved my dog and would not
want him to go hungry. Solow swallowed the slab of
meat whole and cleared his throat in time to howl at
sirens getting louder and then silent.
I heard the bell, opened the door and invited two
deputy sheriffs inside with a wave of my hand. Before
I could close the door, another siren dissolved into silence. An ambulance rolled to a stop in front of the
house, and two men in white made their way to the
front door. I held it open for them and stepped aside.
In order to give the men room to work, I made my
way through the crowd to the kitchen table and sat
down in a captain's chair featuring a soft cushion. It
was just right for a mature woman who had worked

hard all day. Maybe it was the painting or maybe it was mental stress, or both, but I was exhausted. It seemed like the day had been at least thirty-hours long, even though it was only seven p.m. Next thing I knew, someone was talking to me and shaking my shoulder.

"Josephine, ah … Ma'am. You can go home now." I thought it was Jim's voice breaking through a dream I was having. The misty staircase littered with papers disappeared and the dream ended. I opened one eye and lifted my head off the table to discover it was Justin. I blinked, yawned and looked around, finally realizing where I was.

Justin sank into a chair to my right. The house was eerily quiet. Jim's recliner was empty, and Justin seemed to be in shock. I reached out and put my hand on Justin's.

"Well, looks like your Granddad finally did it right," I said.

Justin frowned. "What do you mean by that?" he snapped, as his jaw tightened.

"Everyday we get up in the morning, live our day the best we can, try to ignore temptation, try to love our neighbor and all that good stuff. We go to bed at night, get up in the morning and try all over again the next day. I think that when we finally 'get it right,' we can go home to our maker. Your Granddad must have gotten it right."

Justin cooled his jets and even smiled for a second. "I see what you mean."

"I'm sorry for your loss. I only met Jim yesterday, but I know he was a good man." I figured Justin was a lot like him.

"Pop was eighty-two and still doing the books for Mr. Thornton. I told him to take it easy, travel or just relax. But no, he had to keep working." Justin dropped his head and wiped away another round of tears.

"Jim was an accountant?" I said in a small voice, thinking how I had mistakenly thought he was the janitor. What was he doing with a wastebasket full of papers?

"A damned good accountant. That's why Thornton would never let him leave. Jim worked on most of Willy's projects, always keeping things in the black. No pun intended," he smirked. Justin was as dark as Jim, but taller, heavier and his head was shaved—a formidable Marine. If I hadn't seen his tears, I would not have known the true Justin—the sensitive young gentleman sitting next to me.

"Did your Granddad get along with everyone? You know, Mr. Thornton and the employees?"

"Sure. He was practically family." Justin almost smiled.

"Do you know Jim's boss very well and Hans and …?"

"Josephine, may I ask why you're asking these questions? You said something earlier about Jim being punched. You meant it, didn't you?"

"We won't know what really happened yesterday until you get the coroner's report, but I hope you'll let me know what it says. I think the fall wasn't an accident." I handed Justin my business card. I couldn't shake the feeling that Jim had been struck before he fell, but apparently he hadn't wanted to talk about it.

"You look tired, Josephine, and your dog is dead to

the world." Justin bit his lip at his own choice of words.

"Will you be all right, Justin?"

"Sure. Don't worry about me. I have my cottage in the back … life goes on." He pushed back from the table and stood up. I started to stand. Justin took my elbow and helped me up. Solow woke up, stretched and followed us to the door.

"Thank you, Josephine … for everything."

"I wish things had turned out differently. You take care of yourself, Justin." I walked quickly to the truck before the young man could see me cry.

By the time we got home, it was after ten. I fell asleep in front of the TV without benefit of dinner or pajamas. In the middle of the night, I woke up sweating. Again, my dream was about a staircase littered with papers. I had been looking at the top stair but couldn't make out who was there. It was more like a feeling that someone was there.

Solow stretched out on the floor next to the sofa. He could have been in his warm doggie bed in my bedroom. Instead he kept watch over me, as I watched over him.

CHAPTER FOUR

Tuesday morning, I woke up on the couch with the feeling I had been swimming in a bucket of sadness. In reality, rain was pounding on the roof. It sounded even louder on the skylight in the dining room. My house usually felt warm and cozy in rainy weather, but this time it felt cold and sad because Justin lost his Granddad.

I finally pulled myself up off the sofa and stumbled into the kitchen where I foraged for food. Nothing looked appetizing. My neck felt stiff while my stomach growled like a mountain lion. I loaded Mr. Coffee and listened to the perk–perk as I thought about the Thornton Therapy Center.

After a good cup of coffee, I felt better and even looked forward to painting on the mural since the difficult sky had already been accomplished.

"Big guy, looks like Fluffy's waiting for you." I let Solow out the backdoor and the chase was on. He ran after Fluffy while she circled him effortlessly until she became bored with the game and headed for home. Watching Fluffy reminded me that it was Tuesday and David would be home around noon. I opened the door for my sopping-wet dog. He shook water on me, trundled down the hall and climbed into his bed.

After a quick shower and beauty routine, I washed down a bagel with a second cup of coffee, called Solow to the kitchen and gathered up my purse and jacket.

On our way to the front door, I noticed the answering machine was sending me red blinks. "All right, all right, might be something important," I explained to Solow. I pushed the button and recognized a favorite voice.

"Josie, you probably already know Denver is socked in since it's all over the news. It's a real blizzard. We were the last plane to land before they closed the airport. I couldn't get a straight flight to San Jose, hence the layover. Here I am, sitting in a plastic chair watching the news on TV in the Denver airport—about the Denver airport. Hope we can get out of here soon. Can't wait to see you."

Poor David. Like going to a funeral wasn't bad enough. I felt disappointed that I would have to wait even longer than expected. I pushed the button for my second message. The voice was vaguely familiar, but I couldn't place it right away.

"Josephine, I need to talk to you. Sorry, this is Justin … and thank you for …." Whether he was cut off or just stopped talking, I hadn't a clue. I figured he would call back later. In the meantime, I needed to feed two starving cats and get to work at the Therapy Center.

The rain slowed and then stopped as I trudged out to my rusty metal shed behind the house. I opened the door and looked around for spiders before stepping inside. I gathered up a couple of gallons of paint from the shed and loaded them into my truck. Next, I hefted sloppy-wet Solow onto his blanket positioned on the passenger seat. If Solow gained one more pound, he would break my back for sure.

Once Oliver and Fluffy were fed, we headed west on San Juan Road. As we passed the Mendoza house, I counted four people wearing white jumpsuits and headgear, bent over examining the lettuce field. I figured they were from the government, taking more samples of fungus.

We rolled into the Therapy Center parking lot where the usual pickups were parked. Alicia's Volvo and Hans' Lincoln were there too. Solow and I hustled down the hall to the giant poolroom and found Alicia already setting up for work.

"Good morning, Allie."

Solow sniffed the floor for the best possible place to take a morning nap.

"Jo, I'm glad you're here. I was just wondering if you wanted me to start on the clouds?"

"Sure. No one can paint them like you. I'll paint the hills." I studied the scaffolding to see if I could adjust the height myself. "Have you seen Chester?"

"No, I haven't seen him, but I hear a lot of pounding and sawing in the west wing."

"I'll be back," I said, and followed the noise to the other end of the building where three men were installing cabinets in one of many small examining rooms.

"Hi, I'm looking for Chester."

"Two doors down," a wiry old carpenter wearing white overalls said, pointing down the hall.

"Thanks." I turned on my heels, headed down the hall and practically ran into Chester as he exited one of the rooms.

"Don't tell me, you need help with the scaffolding," he said, in an exaggerated know-it-all tone, and then smiled showing off all his beautiful white teeth.

"Yes," I said, but I wanted to ask you another question." He shifted his weight, waiting for me to ask for another favor. "Were you here last Sunday afternoon?"

"Ah, yeah, I was here. Why?"

"Did you know Mr. Keeper, ah … Jim?"

"Sure, I know Jim. Good man, why?" Chester looked puzzled.

"Did you know that Jim fell down the stairs Sunday, right here in this building?"

"No. Nobody mentioned it to me. Is he OK?" Chester leaned into the next room to check on his workers. He straightened up in the hallway, looked deep into my eyes and asked, "What's this all about?"

"Wish I knew. Jim isn't all right. He's dead. He died in his sleep several hours after the fall." A lump was forming in my throat.

"Jeez! That's too bad," Chester said.

"Who drives the black Corvette around here?"

"Old Man Thornton's son, Garth," Chester said. "Poor little rich boy."

"What do you mean by that remark?"

"Garth spends his time getting kicked out of every college Willy gets him into. The kid takes stupid basket weaving classes and still fails—all the advantages and no ambition. You know the type."

Actually, I did know the type. Many years ago I had been an art major, and I remembered students who took art classes thinking they would be an easy grade.

Chester accompanied me up the hallway to the mural project.

"Good morning, Alicia," he said with the same sparkle in his eye that most men had when they looked at Alicia. She was used to it and couldn't care less because she loved her husband, Ernie. Chester finally turned his attention to my instructions and lowered one scaffold by three feet. Alicia's scaffold would stay at the full nine feet so that she would be able to paint a few wispy clouds.

"Chester, we'll need her scaffold down another three feet after the lunch break."

"No problem, Josephine." He turned and sashayed down the hall toward the west wing, boots tapping unevenly.

"Jo, do you want the same type of clouds I painted at the last job?"

"Exactly."

She painted clouds and I painted foothills until noon. As we worked, I told Alicia about everything that had happened in the last couple days. I thought it might explain the bags under my eyes; but most of all, I needed to vent. David wasn't coming home for awhile, Jim was dead and Rosa was missing. What I really needed was some chocolate, so naturally I asked Alicia to go to town with me and have a hot fudge sundae.

Alicia drove her station wagon so we could take Solow with us.

By the time we got back from lunch, pleasantly bloated, the scaffolding had been adjusted. I was ready for a nap, but how would that look to my co-worker? I sucked up some air and climbed to the top of my scaffold. Hills began to appear under Alicia's freshly painted clouds. Alicia followed me, highlighting the hills, giving them sunlight, shadows and depth.

"Jo, even though I never met Jim, I can see how his death has affected you."

"I'll be fine. It's just very sad."

"Speaking of sad, I've been thinking about Rosa," Alicia said. "I guess we should pester Mr. Mendoza some more. What do you think?"

"I think I'll be a lot happier when I know what's going on with the Mendoza family. Too much weird stuff going on." I dipped my brush into paint on my palette and worked subtle purple shadows into grassy green hills—only thirty more feet of hills to go.

"Jo, I just thought of something. You mentioned a black Corvette. You said it was parked in the lot Sunday." I nodded. "Well, I don't know if it means anything, but Carlos was getting out of a new black Corvette when I arrived at the Mendoza's house Sunday."

"Wow!" I blurted. "What are the chances there would be more than one new black Corvette in this little town?" I tried to make a connection between the Mendozas and the Thorntons. True, the house and the Center were only half a block from each other and each family had a son around twenty years old. So what? What would Mr. Thornton's son be doing at the Center on a Sunday afternoon?

"I was thinking the same thing. Shiny black Corvettes are not a common sight," Alicia said. "You didn't see anyone at the top of the stairs when Jim fell?"

"I didn't see anyone in the whole building except Jim. I remember feeling overwhelmed by the size of the mural wall and then Jim walked by and said, "Hey." A few minutes later I heard crashing and grunting from Jim falling down the stairs. I forgot my own worries real fast. He didn't make a big fuss, just asked for a little help to his truck. I barely knew him, but he seemed like a real sweet guy."

"Jo, would you like to drop in on Mr. Mendoza with me after work?"

"Sure, why not?" We painted in silence for a while until Hans walked up to the wall, commented on the lovely clouds and asked if Chester was taking good care of us. "Chester works hard to keep us happy," I said. "Always has."

"It sounds like you worked with the man before you came here." Hans reached up and ran his hand across the wall to see if the paint was still wet. Idiot! Fortunately, the fast-drying acrylic paint was already dry.

"Yes, as a matter of fact we worked with Chester several months ago. We're very happy to be working with him again. Have you talked to Justin Keeper?" I asked.

"Not in a long time. You know Justin?" I nodded and Hans continued. "Jim hasn't been to work since last week. I wonder ...."

"No one told you?" I scratched my head. "I'm afraid there was an accident right here in this building." I looked straight into Hans' round face.

"Here? What do you mean? Old Jim? I don't understand."

"I was here Sunday afternoon to take a few measurements when Jim fell down the stairs." I pointed in the direction of the staircase and then watched Hans' puffy eyes grow big. "I took him to the hospital where they set his arm, sewed his lip, braced his ribs and ran a few tests. I drove him to his house and left him alone. He told me his grandson was coming home, but Justin didn't get there until Monday afternoon and poor Jim had already passed away."

Hans took a deep breath and stared blankly at the wall. My own guilt for leaving Jim alone weighed heavily on my shoulders and made my heart ache as I relived that terrible night.

"I can't believe it," he said. "I thought he would outlive all of us."

"That's what Justin thought too. Do you know if anyone else was working Sunday?"

"Officially, no one works on Sunday. But the carpenters like to catch up on things so we let them. I'm surprised you were able to get into the building. The carpenters have been instructed to keep the doors locked." Hans looked down at his feet, but I doubt he could see past his belly. "Old Jim was a friend of mine, you know." He turned and slowly walked up the hall toward the infamous staircase.

"Someone didn't like Jim," I said to Alicia. My words hung in the air like a bad odor. We painted in silence as the sun made its way down to the Pacific Ocean. It was twilight when Alicia, Solow and I exited the building. The almost-red Nissan was noticeably missing. I figured Justin must have found someone to help him take it home. I wondered how Justin was managing.

"Jo, cheer up. Want to ride with me?"

"Sure." I sat down in the passenger seat of Alicia's green Volvo station wagon for the second time that day. Solow sat in the back, happy to be traveling. We would have walked, but there were no sidewalks or streetlights once we left the Center. Besides, the evening was already chilly. I pulled on my jacket and Alicia cranked up the heater.

Half a block later, we were parked behind an old Toyota pickup in front of the Mendoza house. In the dark, we cautiously made our way up the path to the front door. It was so dark I had to feel around for the doorbell. The porch light came on two seconds before Mr. Mendoza opened the door.

"Alicia, Josephine, nice to see you again." He stepped back and motioned with his hand for us to come inside. "Carlos, stand up. Ladies are present."

Carlos rolled his eyes and stood.

I was glad to see that both men were back to normal.

"Mr. Mendoza, I'm sorry to bother you," Alicia said as she sat down on the sofa beside me. "Have you heard from Rosa?"

"My dear, I want to apologize for not telling you sooner. We must be very cautious about her whereabouts. Rosa is staying with a relative. How long, I don't know. I wish I could explain everything, but these are ominous times."

"Oh, I'm so glad to know that Rosa is all right," Alicia said, her shoulders relaxing as if a great weight had been lifted. "How is the investigation going? The lettuce, that is."

"I think the agency has taken enough samples of black lettuce. The only thing the investigators have told me so far is that the well water is infected with a fungus. That happens to be the water we use for our crops. The house has city water." He smiled under his thick mustache. "Most of the farmers around here use public water, but I have a well."

"Is the well water stored in the tower near the kennel?" I asked.

"As a matter of fact, it is."

"Dad, tell them about the dogs," Carlos said, glancing at Alicia as if he shouldn't.

"It seems they were shot with tranquilizer darts powerful enough to put down big game, even elephants. The darts were obviously lethal for dogs. The poor things were probably shot from a distance and that's why we didn't hear any barking. Getting to the water supply was easy after that," Mr. Mendoza grimaced.

"What about the mess in the barn?" I asked. "Do you think the same person or persons did that too?" I asked.

"We don't know for sure, but I've installed an alarm system so we shouldn't have any more trouble," he said, glaring at Carlos who was sneaking another look at Alicia. "If trouble comes, we're ready." Carlos nodded his head and clenched a fist at his side. I noticed a shiny new shotgun hanging above the massive river rock fireplace. Carlos saw me look at the gun and grinned.

"Do you ladies like figs?" Mr. Mendoza asked. "It's the end of the season, but the tree is still loaded."

Alicia and I both agreed that we liked the fruit. The four of us paraded through the house to the backyard. Sensor lights flashed on. Mr. Mendoza handed us each a plastic bag, and we proceeded to fill the bags with ripe black figs. When my bag was full, I scanned the yard, looking for Andy. I didn't see him anywhere, but he could have been in the barn since all the lights were on. Finally, I spotted a hunched older Hispanic man pushing a wheelbarrow full of broken and ruined items. He went about his work, late as it was, oblivious to our presence.

"Thank you for the figs," Alicia said, as we walked through the house to the front door. "The family will love them and I'm so glad to know that Rosa is OK." We trotted back to Alicia's car with the porch light at our backs. Mr. Mendoza waved goodbye from the doorstep. Alicia fired up the engine, made a careful turn in the middle of the road and we pulled into the Therapy Center a minute later.

"Allie, did the Mendozas seem overly nice and friendly to you?"

"Well, they are nice people," she said, thoughtfully. "I think they don't want us to worry about them."

"I'm not worried. I think the Mendozas are ready for any unwanted trespassers."

"Good night, Jo."

"Night, Allie. See you tomorrow." I hoisted Solow into my truck, jumped in and headed into Watsonville to buy groceries. The parking lot was almost empty.

I entered the store and looked around for Robert, but didn't see him right away. I automatically grabbed the usual items and tossed them into my cart. As I rolled past the lettuce, I thought about Rosa and wondered what relative she was staying with and why. I found some nice artichokes and a bag of baby carrots, but my mind kept wandering away from vegetables. Finally, I gave up and headed for the check stand.

"Josephine, how's it goin'?" Robert asked, looking short and round in his new blue cashier's apron.

"Hi, Robert. What's new?" I said, hoping that nothing was new.

"I heard some bad news on KPIG this afternoon." He looked at me to see if I had already heard the news. My blank expression told him I hadn't. "Remember the dogs that were killed on that lettuce farm? The dart gun was stolen from Doctor Finley's office."

"How do they know that?"

"The doctor had reported a dart gun and darts missing a couple of weeks ago. The police finally put two and two together. The sedative darts were made for big animals like cows and horses, not dogs. Oh, and they think the fungus that killed the lettuce was a variety of stinking smut." Robert rolled his eyes and laughed at the name.

"That's very interesting. Anything else?"

"No, but if I hear anything I'll let you know." He expertly bagged my groceries, placed a closed sign on the counter and wheeled the bags out to my pickup.

"Thanks for the information, Robert. Have a nice evening."

"Yeah, you too, Jo." He reached into the cab and gave Solow a quick ear rub.

I drove away shaking my head and wondering what crazy scientist had named the stinking smut fungus. I pulled to a stop in front of my house, surprised and happy to see the porch light on. Golden light shone from the front windows. I wasn't in the habit of locking my doors. I thought of David. He was the one who always did nice things for me, like turning on lights and collecting mail and newspapers.

Solow leaped out of his seat and howled when he caught the scent of his friend. David had left a note on the kitchen table telling me how he had finagled a flight out of the Denver airport. He said he would tell me all about it Wednesday night if I would have dinner at seven, his place. I held the note to my cheek and closed my eyes.

Solow crunched kibble while my soup bubbled in the microwave. Soon we were both full and oh so tired. A little TV and off to bed where I dreamed about David eating a peanut butter sandwich with stinking smut growing on it. I grabbed the sandwich away from him and threw it. I turned my head and saw smut coming under the door and crawling up the walls. Solow barked at the fungus until it ran away on dozens of actual feet. The feet were all wearing shoes, but in the dream I couldn't quite see what type of shoes they were.

CHAPTER FIVE

I pulled the blankets over my head when the clock radio belted out an old Lisa Minnelli song. I reached for the off button without opening my eyes, and immediately fell back to sleep. Next thing I knew, Solow was howling to go out and the clock read eight-thirty. I was up in a flash, heart pounding, trying to get my bearings.

I let Solow out for a Fluffy chase, threw on some paint clothes and washed down a bowl of cereal with instant coffee. At five to nine I left the lovely hills of Aromas with the sun at my back and Solow at my side, wishing I had had time for a wake-up shower.

We whizzed past fields ranging from fallow to newly planted to ready to pick. The patchwork of vegetation gave the valley a richness of color and beauty until I passed by the Mendoza black lettuce farm. I watched two heavy-construction tractors scoop up dead lettuce mixed with black dirt and load it into four full-sized trailer trucks. They literally took the topsoil away to a hazardous waste dump.

The Therapy Center's parking lot hosted the usual pickups, including Chester's white Ford with its steel racks and built-in toolbox. I passed by the black Corvette and parked between Alicia's Volvo and Kyle's

Honda motorcycle. Across the lot was a red Jaguar with gold trims, an older white Lincoln and a familiar-looking black BMW sedan.

I entered the building with Solow on leash at my side. As we walked quickly down the hall toward the mural wall, I heard voices from an office above the stairs.

"My dad will hear about this!" Slam!

I looked up into the red face of a young man with shoulder-length brown hair and intense anger in his blue eyes. He practically flew down the stairs and rushed by me, heading to the backdoor. Not wishing to look like an eavesdropper, I did a fast walk to my friends down the hall.

"Hi, Jo," Alicia said, when she saw me coming.

Kyle was already painting more of the distant terrain. He stopped and looked over his shoulder. "Like, what's new, Jo?" he winked.

"What is that all about?" I asked. "What are you laughing at, Allie?"

"Oh, nothing, really," Alicia said, just before they both giggled. "We were just speculating why you're late this morning. Does it have anything to do with David getting back from his trip?"

"No. I haven't even seen him yet. I overslept." I saw the disappointment on their faces. I loaded my palette, picked up a two-inch brush and began shaping hills. Hours later, when the hills were finally finished, Kyle and Alicia pushed both scaffolds far down the hall and out of the way.

Chester noticed the contraptions on his way to lunch.

"Will you be needing these things again?" he asked, as he walked up to me.

"I sure hope not. You can have them."

"I'll have my guys break them down this afternoon." Chester took off for the backdoor.

My head clock must have been stuck on SLOW. I finally realized it was lunchtime and I hadn't packed a lunch. I was dying for some good hot comfort food. "How would you two Wildbrush employees like to have lunch with me, my treat?"

Kyle immediately dropped his brush in the water can and Alicia graciously accepted my invitation. We loaded Solow into her car; and just three blocks later, we were being seated by a pale pimply kid who worked in the Mexican restaurant called El Milagro. Solow rested in the Volvo.

El Milagro was an old metal packing shed on the eastern edge of Pajaro. It had been converted into a roomy and colorful place to eat. The no-frills eatery was packed with customers. We were served in a timely manner and the enchiladas were delicious, almost as good as Alicia's homemade Mexican food.

Kyle ordered a beer.

Alicia's mouth dropped open, and I stared at him as if he were my kid brother robbing a Quick-Stop.

"Like, I turned 21 over a month ago."

"Oh? I thought you were much older than that," I teased. Kyle seemed young and naive in some ways; but when it came to painting, he was like an old master. "So, did anything interesting happen at the Center before I got to work?" I was thinking about the ruckus I witnessed as I walked past the stairs on my way to the mural.

"Like, the cops were leaving when I rode up. Do you mean something like that?" Kyle asked, wiping beer foam from the end of his nose.

"Yes, I guess so," I said, wondering if the police were investigating Jim's death.

"I noticed two deputy sheriff's cars parked in the reserved spaces by the backdoor," Alicia said. "Four deputies were just leaving as I opened the backdoor. I didn't know the county could spare that many deputies at one time."

"Does seem excessive," I said. "Wonder what's up."

Our young waiter, who looked about fourteen, asked if we wanted anything else.

"Just the check please. Shouldn't you be in school?" I asked.

"Not me. I graduated high school last spring." He dropped the bill in front of me, turned and walked away in a bit of a huff.

Alicia threw a five-dollar bill on the plate. "For his college education," she said. Kyle added a handful of quarters, making me look bad if I didn't contribute to the college fund. The total tip ended up being more than the food bill.

Back at the Center, we climbed out of Alicia's Volvo and Solow sniffed his way to the backdoor. I noticed that all the cars were gone. I stopped off at the alcove, home of the infamous staircase, elevators and rest-rooms and handed Solow's leash to Alicia. "You two go ahead. I'll be there in a few minutes," I said. A couple of minutes later, I left the powder room and stared up to the top of the steps trying to remember whether I had

seen someone the day Jim fell. I couldn't remember seeing anyone, so I climbed the stairs and tried to remember from a higher vantage point. Nothing.

The door to Hans' office was two feet away and
open. I had seen the room a couple of times before
when I presented the mural ideas to him. It was a
dreamy office with south-facing windows, plush carpet and an over-sized mahogany desk. Mr. Thornton's
office was probably even better. I walked along the
landing to the next door, the one nearest the elevator
with William Thornton's name printed in gold letters.
My hand instinctively tried the doorknob. It turned. I
pushed the door open just a titch and leaned in for a
look. Just then I heard the elevator doors open.

"Ma'am, can I help you?" Startled, I looked over my
shoulder to see who was coming. I looked twice. I
couldn't believe my eyes. It was Andy from the Mendoza farm.

"Hi, Andy. I was ... ah, just looking for Hans. What
are you doing here?"

"I work here," Andy said as he walked past me.
Two doors down, he entered an office and closed the
door.

Rather rude, I thought. Out of curiosity, I walked
past the stairs and stopped in front of the door Andy
had just closed. Black letters on the door spelled, "An-
drew Anderson".

I was stunned. Andy had looked quite at home in
overalls out on the farm, but he looked just as comfortable carrying a briefcase and wearing slacks and a
sweater. I guessed he wasn't the first young man to
work two jobs for a living. Andy obviously wasn't

going to hang around to discuss it, so I marched down the stairs, turned left and headed down the hallway to our mural.

The scaffolding was gone. Alicia and Kyle were busy painting and Solow was having an afternoon siesta. I mixed up a few blues and began painting a thirty-foot lake that would eventually be filled with pedal boats and canoes run by strong, healthy children. Details around the lake, like paths, trees and bushes would be painted later.

"Jo, what if there was a slope to this part of the lawn? We could paint a skateboard trail."

"Good idea, Allie. By the way, did you know that Andy works here?"

"The only Andy I know is the blond fellow we met over at the Mendoza farm."

"That's the one." We looked at each other. "He has an office upstairs with his name on the door. Under his name it said, Computer Technologist. What does that mean?"

"Like, he programs all the computers for the company," Kyle said. "He's probably a trouble-shooter for any computer problems."

Alicia and I stared at Kyle and then at each other. This was more information than we had ever expected to hear from our co-worker. It still seemed odd to me that a trained computer expert would be working as a farmhand.

I painted automatically as thoughts of dinner with David made me smile. The room was quiet. I looked up to see Alicia and Kyle staring at me, probably wondering if I was thinking about David. I let them wonder.

My smile grew bigger. The afternoon dragged on, but finally five-thirty rolled around and we called it a day.

I noticed a black Beemer and a Gray Chevy Tahoe parked in the lot. The only person I knew with a gray SUV was Justin. Sure enough, he sat in the driver's seat reading a book.

"Good night, Jo. See you tomorrow," Alicia said and walked to her Volvo.

"Later, man," Kyle said as he slipped on his helmet and hopped aboard his Honda.

"Be careful, Kyle. It's starting to rain." I helped Solow into the front seat of my pickup and then walked across the lot to Justin's open window.

"Hi, Josephine. I hope you don't mind. I needed to talk to you."

"Justin. What a surprise. Are you OK?"

"I guess so. Hop in. Looks like it's starting to rain."

I climbed in. Justin took a deep breath, ran a hand over his shaved head and then spread both hands over the steering wheel. "The Coroner finished his report on Granddad." There was a long pause before he continued. "You were right. Granddad was hit on the head with a blunt object … and died from a blood clot in his brain." Justin's head involuntarily fell forward onto his hands.

I leaned toward him and put my hand on his massive shoulder.

"So what happens now? Is there going to be an investigation?"

Justin straightened up in his seat.

"The sheriff's deputies are investigating me, and they asked about you."

"Why me? Why us? We didn't do anything?"

"They questioned me early this morning, then talked to Hans at the Center and came back to me with more questions. Hans told them you were the one who helped Jim up and took him to the hospital. One of them, a little black guy with a temper, kept asking me if you had seen anyone at the top of the stairs."

"Wow, I must have just missed them. I was running a little late this morning, and my friends told me that four sheriff's deputies had just left the building. I had no idea they were looking for me. What should I do?" I asked as my heart raced and my face flushed.

"I would just wait for them to find you. Have you been able to remember anyone at the top of the stairs?"

"No, darn it. I try to remember. I even have dreams about it. In my dreams, I sense that someone is up there, but I can never see who it is." I shook my head slowly, as if to shake out the cobwebs. "Have you thought of anyone who would hurt your granddad?"

Justin stared at the raindrops on the windshield. "It has to be someone connected to the Therapy Center, an employee or family. Who works on Sunday, anyway?" he asked.

"I remember seeing a few pickup trucks, a black Corvette and Jim's truck."

"I'll bet anything the Vette belongs to the Thornton kid, but he wouldn't have a beef with Jim. He doesn't care enough about anything. He's pretty harmless. At least, that's what I've always thought of him."

"Does Garth have brown hair and blue eyes?" I asked.

"Yeah."

"Someone upstairs sure made him angry this morning, looked like he would pop a vein with that red face. He raced down the stairs all upset and angry about something." I looked over at Justin to see if he was listening. He just stared at the raindrops on the windshield, his mind on something he wasn't saying.

"Justin, call me if you find out anything new, OK?" I opened the door and climbed down to the wet pavement. "Thanks for the heads-up. See you later." He gave a little nod. I darted over to my mud-speckled truck, jumped into the driver's seat and gave Solow a pat on the head. I noticed the BMW was still there and guessed Andy worked long hours.

The clock on the dash read six o'clock. There was no way I would make it to David's by seven. After all, I had to feed Oliver, shower, and dress first. I pushed myself into high gear and drove straight to Rosa's house where Oliver impatiently waited for food. Solow raised his head and howled, letting Oliver know that a big cat-chasing dog was present. Ollie didn't care.

"Hi there, Ollie," I said as rain sprinkled my face. "Don't worry, food's coming." I wished I had had more time to spend with him. Poor cat was probably lonely, but fresh food would have to suffice.

I thundered down Otis Drive to my house, thinking about David all the way. We rolled up the driveway and hurried into the house. I filled Solow's bowl with kibble, turned up the furnace, ran the shower and laid out clothes to wear to David's. Once in the shower, I hated to get out. It felt good to be warm, but time was ticking; and I still had to fluff-dry my hair, add a little makeup and get dressed. The clock read five after seven. Yikes! I headed for the phone. I was just about to call David, when I saw that I had a message. Oh well, what was another minute? I pushed the button. "Hi, Josephine. This is Sarah. David asked me to tell you that he had to run down to Watsonville for ice cream and a jar of horseradish. Dinner will be delayed." Suddenly it was like my heart was in my slipper and Sarah was stepping on my foot. Why was Sarah, the ex, here and not in San Diego with her preacher husband? I knew she had gone to the funeral for Uncle Theodore in Minnesota, but I didn't think she would follow David home. What to do? Fake an illness? No, I wanted to see David. Sarah could just take a hike!

I took my time with the beauty ritual and changed my mind about what I would wear. I didn't own a red silk sari like Mom loved to wear, but I did have a baby-blue cashmere sweater that looked great with my navy blue wool slacks. A squirt of Essence of Plumaria and I was ready.

It was almost eight when I drove up to David's house. A dozen little golden lights led me up the drive-way to the sizable ranch-style house. Porch light flooded the wide brick entry. The garage door was closed, leaving me to wonder whether David was home or not. I had to ring the doorbell and hope for the best. I pushed the button and then wished I hadn't. I wanted to run back to my truck, go home to my comfort zone and be with Solow. But it was too late. The door opened. An older, plumper Sarah than I remembered opened her arms for a hug. I still wanted to go home, but I was an adult so I gave her a hug. She felt like a warm lumpy pillow, and I felt like a fool for not trusting her with David. After all, I had no claim on him.

"Josephine, it's been ten years or more and you look wonderful."

"Hi, Sarah. Yes, ah, ten years I think." I saw David walking toward us and smiled. "David, how was your trip?" We hugged. I made it a long one. Out of the corner of my eye, I watched Sarah's reaction; but her pale round face showed nothing but a simple smile. I remembered her when she was short and slim with long blond hair. The short was still there, but the hair was in a stylish boy-cut with spikes on top and her clothes were colorful and layered. "San Diego Casual" to cover the extra pounds.

"Are you ladies ready to eat?" David asked. He put an arm behind my waist and his other arm around Sarah and walked us to the dining room. Everything was already on the table as if they had been waiting for me to show up. David pulled a chair out for me and then one for Sarah. He sat between us at the head of the table and carved the roast.

"Too bad your husband isn't here, Sarah," I said. "We would have a foursome for cards after dinner."

"Oh, my goodness, I haven't seen him in years," she giggled.

I cringed. All traces of the high-tech, upwardly mobile Sarah I remembered were gone and so was her preacher husband. I didn't feel like giggling, but I did it out of nervousness. They just bubbled out of my mouth.

"More roast, anyone," David asked giving me a cheery wink.

"I'll take that little piece, thank you. So, how was

the funeral?"

"All we saw of the dear man was a lovely urn," Sarah said. "It was good to see the rest of the family though. I always liked that side of David's family, especially his Aunt Valena."

"So, you two got stuck in Denver?"

"We sure did." She tilted her head toward David's shoulder, laughing. "We had to sleep in our chairs. No showers and only airport food and drink. The whole city was shut down, you know. The first flight to California was to San Jose so we took it, and here I am," she smiled.

"It's nice to be home," David said, filling my wine glass.

"I'll have a little more please," Sarah said, holding her glass in the air. He poured as I choked on a piece of meat. A swig of water and I was OK for the moment.

"How are things going on the new job?" David asked. His dreamy brown eyes locked onto my green ones. I felt heat on my face and hoped I wasn't turning red. I was flattered but still not comfortable with Sarah sitting there working on her third beverage refill, not to mention living in David's house.

"The job is going well except for a murder at the Center," I said. The sheriff's deputies want to question me because I was there when it happened."

David's mouth dropped open and Sarah took a turn at choking on a piece of meat. After a short silence, David asked, "Who was murdered? Did you see who did it?"

"It was Jim, an accountant at the Therapy Center. And no, I didn't see the person who punched him at the top of the stairs. I just happened to hear Jim tumbling down the stairs and ran to where he was lying on the floor with a broken arm. I helped him up and took him to the hospital. Later that evening, I picked him up at the hospital and took him to his house in Watsonville. He seemed to be all right, and he said his grandson would be home soon." I squeezed my eyes shut, longer than a blink, remembering it all too clearly.

David covered my hand with his.

"So, how did the man die?" Sarah asked. "You said he was released from the hospital. I don't understand." She ran puffy fingers through her pointy hair.

"Everyone thought he was all right except for bruised ribs, broken arm and bloody nose. Oh, and a cut lip. I don't think he told anyone that he had been struck on the head before he fell, but the coroner caught it. The coroner's report said Jim died from a blood clot on the left side of his head." I pushed my plate aside. I couldn't eat the second half of my dinner. The meal was over for all of us as we sat in silence, reflecting on the demise of poor Jim.

"Josie, you look a little tired. Why don't I walk you to your truck? I know you're working tomorrow," David said. "Fluffy was the lucky one, seeing you every day. Thanks for feeding her." He helped me into my coat, put his arm around me and walked me to my pickup. He didn't linger because the night was cold and drizzly. Just a simple kiss before I drove home. A kiss I would tell Solow about, think about, wonder about and eventually dream about.

CHAPTER SIX

Thursday morning I stifled the alarm clock, stared at the ceiling and laughed to myself. I had certainly put the kibosh on David's dinner party the night before. Reflecting on all the sweet things he had said and done made me smile. But on the other hand, if possession was nine-tenths of the law, Sarah was in a better position than I.

Solow crawled out of bed ready for a good Fluffy chase. He usually preferred the backdoor, but that particular morning he ran to the front door. I opened it. To my surprise, two deputy sheriffs stood ready to knock. One male fist was already in the air as the door swung open. I backed up a few steps. A gust of frigid air crossed the doorjamb.

The young female sheriff spoke first. "Ma'am, we're from the sheriff's department." She flashed her badge. "This is Calvin Sayer and my name is Denise Lund. We need to ask you a few questions. May we come in?"

"Sure, come in, but do you mind if I go put on a robe?"

Solow kept them company while I scurried down the hall to my bedroom and slipped into a warm robe and perky penguin slippers. I ran fingers through bed-head hair to settle it down and trudged back to the living room feeling like Marie Antoinette walking to the guillotine. I was innocent, but who else would know that for sure since no one else saw the murder happen except the murderer. I sat down in my favorite rocking chair and began to rock slowly, wondering what would happen next.

"Ms. Stuart, our department is conducting an investigation into the death of a James Keeper. I believe you knew him," Deputy Sayer said, staring at his notes.

I tried to read his stony brown face. Sunlight from the window glinted off his bald spot, framed in tight black-going-grey curls. I forced a casual smile and nodded.

"How long had you known Mr. Keeper before he died?" He looked at me with piercing black eyes.

"Actually, I didn't meet Mr. Keeper until after the accident. He walked past me at the Therapy Center and said hello or something like that. A few minutes later, I heard him fall down the stairs. I got there in time to help him up. Jim wanted me to help him to his truck, but I insisted on driving him to the hospital." My rocker sped up a notch.

"You didn't call for help?" Officer Lund said, her light blue eyes cold as a glacier.

"Jim was trying to stand up. All he needed was a little help from me. His nose and lip were bleeding and one arm was obviously broken, but he was calm. He just wanted a little help." My rocker sped up another notch.

"Did you ask Mr. Keeper who hit him?" Deputy Sayer asked as he scribbled in his notebook.

"I didn't know he had been hit. I thought he just fell

down the stairs. He was pretty old, you know."

"We understand that Mr. Keeper's grandson ..." Deputy Lund paused and checked her notes, "Justin Keeper was with his grandfather when he died. Is that correct Ms. Stuart?" She sat straight as a broomstick with her shoulders back and her sharp chin jutting upward.

I told her Justin had not been present when his granddaddy died.

"Please continue, Ma'am," she said, in a way that grated on my nerves.

"Justin found his grandfather dead in his chair, just as I had left him the night before." I squirmed in the rocker and looked at the deputies. "Oh, sorry, I mean ... I left Mr. Keeper sitting in his favorite chair, but he was alive. He was fine. At least, that's what he told me." I felt my cheeks redden as the rocker kicked into high gear.

"Mr. Keeper didn't fall again, as far as you know?" Officer Lund asked, keeping an eye on my red face.

"Not while I was there."

The pair stood up. She handed me a business card and they filed out the front door.

"Thank God!" I said to Solow when they were gone. "I was beginning to think I was guilty of something."

I glanced at the clock and jumped in the shower. When I was clean and dressed, I ate my liverwurst and cheese-on-a-bagel breakfast while I drove to Oliver's house. I was running late, so I left Solow in the truck. I couldn't resist a quick visit to Rosa's room to see if her purse was still there. It was, but as I passed a little hall table with a telephone on it, I noticed something written in pencil on a piece of scratch paper. The paper was partially covered by a phone book. I picked up the note and held it up to the light from a window. It read, "PM at 5 call Jo for Ollie."

The writing was a fast scribble. Judging from the note, Rosa had intended to call me to ask for help with Oliver, but what was PM at 5? I stuffed the note into my pocket, fed Oliver and fired up the truck.

Solow and I sailed down the road singing to "Mack the Knife" on the radio. Solow's part was a long howl now and then. I skirted around a slow-moving tractor and minutes later pulled into the Therapy Center parking lot. I parked next to Alicia's Volvo, taking notice of every parked vehicle: a Lincoln, a Vette, a Beemer and several pickup trucks.

Solow and I proceeded down the hall to the mural wall where Alicia was hard at work making me feel guilty for being late.

"Good morning, Jo." She looked up from her work for only a second.

"Morning. Sorry I'm late again. I had visitors." I grabbed a brush and palette.

"Really? I thought you had a late night last night," she laughed and looked up to see if I looked embarrassed.

I stopped painting mid-stroke. "Last night's dinner didn't last long, but it seemed like an eternity. You'll never guess who David's houseguest is."

"Who?" Alicia turned to look at me.

"Sarah! Can you believe it? She followed him home after the funeral." I was having a hard time concentrating on my work. I stepped back and accidentally knocked over the water can with dirty brushes in it. "Here, Jo." Alicia handed me a roll of paper towels. "So she was there with you and David ... all evening? Where was her husband?"

"Sarah was not only there, she was drinking buckets of wine and hasn't seen the old preacher husband in years ... I'm telling you Allie, I felt sick. David asked me how work was going. Without thinking, I told him about Jim's murder. That put a real damper on the party. Nobody could eat after that, so I went home."

I sopped up the water with paper towels and then walked to the restroom for fresh water. As I passed the staircase, I heard voices coming from upstairs. The young fellow I figured was Garth Thornton thundered out of his father's office and slammed the door to Andy's office behind him.

Hans opened his door and walked out to the veranda. He looked down, saw me and motioned for me to come upstairs. I walked into his office still holding the empty water bucket. He pulled up a chair for me and we talked. He said he had been questioned by the sheriff's deputies and wanted to know if I knew why Justin requested an autopsy on Jim.

"I knew he wanted one to be performed," I said.

"Why would he want one?" Hans' double chin jiggled as he spoke.

"Because I told Justin I thought someone punched Jim, causing him to fall." I bunched my shoulders up and then let them fall, releasing tension in the back of my neck.

"You saw someone strike him?" Hans asked, wide-eyed.

"No, but something he said later, to a nurse, made me think that's what happened." I stared into the empty water can. "Turns out, I was right."

"The deputies were looking for you yesterday. Have you talked to them yet?" I nodded. Hans rubbed his chin and stared at me. "We hope there won't be news reports about this unfortunate event. Bad publicity for the Center, you know."

"It was a murder and that kind of thing usually gets out," I said, standing up to leave.

Hans stood and put a thick hand on my shoulder.

"We'll all do our best to get this matter over with quickly, won't we?" He sat down in his black leather chair and I left the room. I stood for a moment at the top of the stairs, listening. Not a sound was coming from any of the three occupied offices. I hustled down the stairs and fetched water from the ladies room.

Alicia looked up as I approached the mural wall. "Glad you finally found some water," she snickered.

"I know. It took a long time, but that's because Hans called me up to his office for a chat, or a threat, or maybe it was just advice. Anyway, he doesn't want the murder to get into the papers. I don't know what that has to do with me." I tried to put the whole thing out of my mind. It was time to concentrate on our gigantic paint project.

During the lunch hour, I took Solow for a short walk under a heat-challenged sun. As we passed by the Mendoza farm, I waved to Carlos who was sitting on the top step to the porch. He waved and then he bounded down the wooden steps and rushed past us to a black Corvette, which had just pulled to a stop at the side of the road. Carlos hopped in. The driver made a sharp U-turn and sped toward town.

Back at work, I told Alicia what I had seen at the Mendoza house. We speculated on Carlos and Garth getting together, while Solow took a recuperative nap.

"It sounds like Carlos and Garth are friends," Alicia said.

I finally noticed Chester standing a few feet away with a man-size measuring tape in his hand. "You're right, they are friends, but they're also tutor and pupil," he said, carefully stepping around our tarps and paint equipment as he measured the mural wall.

"OK, who's the student and who's the teacher?" I asked.

"Garth's the student and Carlos is the music teacher. Apparently Carlos is a real genius when it comes to the guitar and Garth wants to learn. Trouble is neither family wants their son to be a musician."

"So, Chester, what are you working on?"

"I'm measuring for the trim boards. Don't worry. They won't be installed until you people are finished with the mural. Nice clouds." Chester snapped his tape shut and strolled down the hall to his crew.

"Allie, something's been on my mind all morning. When I stopped to feed Oliver, I checked Rosa's house again to see if anyone had been around. Everything looked the same as always, but I found a note by the phone."

"Well, what did it say? Don't leave me hanging."

"All it said was, 'PM at 5 call Jo for Ollie.' That's it. The second part sounds like a reminder to call me to cat sit, but the first part has me stumped."

"PM, something at 5 PM? Maybe PM stands for a person. Pete Mendoza, her brother in Castroville?" Alicia offered.

"Wow! That could be it. Glad I brought it up. Good work, Allie." Out of the corner of my eye, I saw Justin walking down the hall from the direction of the backdoor. He turned left and walked into the alcove where we couldn't see him. I guessed he was going upstairs. A few minutes passed and he reappeared. He marched down the hall, sidled around the ladders and stood examining the artwork.

"Ladies," he said. "Nice clouds."

"Hi, Justin. Have you met my friend, Alicia?"

"Hello. Nice to meet you, Alicia. Josephine, I don't know if you want to go to Jim's funeral, but I thought I should tell you about it."

"I would like to go. Thank you for thinking of me."

"The service will be at Tiggy's Chapel tomorrow morning at ten." With his chin held at half-mast, he turned and started to walk away.

"Justin, do you have any family in Watsonville?" Alicia asked.

"No, Ma'am."

"Would you like to have dinner with me, Josephine and my family Friday night?" Alicia asked in her typical mothering way. "Home cooking," she smiled.

"That's awfully nice of you to invite me ... ah, I don't know what to say."

"Just say, yes," I said, realizing I would also be having the best food in town that night. "Alicia lives kitty-corner across the lake from you."

Justin finally smiled and agreed to come to dinner.

As he disappeared out the backdoor, Alicia said, "I asked him to dinner for a selfish reason. I've always wanted to hear what it's like to be in the service during a war."

"Allie, don't give me that. You know you want to help every stray you meet."

Alicia's cheeks flushed and she laughed. "Guess you're right, old friend." She dipped her brush into the dark green paint and continued creating yards and yards of grass. She added the lighter sunlit blades of grass later.

I was tired of painting lake water by the time five o'clock rolled around. I gave Alicia a few last-minute instructions for the next day, since I planned to go to Jim's funeral in the morning. We said goodbye. I washed brushes in the powder room and walked Solow to the backdoor. As we left the building, cold night air blew across our faces and Solow howled. I looked around. The parking lot was empty except for one black Corvette. Garth followed us out the backdoor and turned his key in the lock. I turned around and faced the young man.

"Hi, you must be Garth. I'm Josephine Stuart."

We shook hands and then he reached down to pet Solow. They were instant friends.

"My dad's out of town, so I help out around here. He'll be back tomorrow for Uncle Jim's funeral."

"It was nice to meet you, Garth. By the way, do you work here on Sundays?"

"No. Why?"

"Oh, nothing. See you tomorrow, Garth." I hoisted Solow into the passenger seat of my truck. Garth peeled out of the lot and I turned my attention to driving home. San Juan Road was dark except for an occasional pair of oncoming headlights and a few soft yellow lights emanating from farmhouse windows where families gathered for the evening meal. I loved to imagine perfect families living perfect lives in their picturesque houses surrounded by fields of thriving produce.

We crunched up my gravel driveway. I cut the engine and entered the cold, dark house. Solow took his sweet time waddling in behind me. I saw a tiny red light blinking in the front room, flipped on a light and pushed the message button.

"Hi, Josephine. This is Sarah. I was wondering if I could … maybe come over to see you for a minute." Oh, great. That was all I needed. Just then there was a knock on the door I had just closed. I turned on the porch light and opened the door.

"Sarah, come in. Did you walk over here in the dark?"

She nodded as Solow sniffed the flashlight she held at her side.

"It's a little spooky out there, but the stars are so beautiful here in the country." In her other hand she held a plastic bag containing something that smelled heavenly. "A little chocolate cake I baked for you." She smiled cautiously, setting the cake on the coffee table.

"Thank you, Sarah. Can you stay and have some tea and cake with me?" She had already shed her coat and asked where the bathroom was. While she took a powder, I turned up the furnace and put the kettle on for tea. The house immediately seemed warmer.

"Nice towels," Sarah said when she returned from the bathroom and sat down on the sofa.

"Thank you. They were a fiftieth birthday present from Mom and Dad. A few months ago, I painted the bathroom lavender, and Mom thought red towels would give the room zest. Go figure." I sat in my rocker for one rock. "Excuse me, I'll get the tea." My stomach was rumbling for real food, dinner actually. But I would make the best of it, even if it was Sarah.

When I came back with tea and cake, Sarah was bent at the waist rubbing Solow's tummy. He lay on his back in total bliss. I sliced the chocolate-on-chocolate cake and handed Sarah her piece on a plate. I took a bite of mine.

"This is my favorite cake, Sarah. How did you know?"

"David has told me all about you, even your taste in cake. I was all alone with nothing to do so I hit the cookbooks. David has some good ones."

"So, where's David?" I asked between bites.

"Modesto. Harley has jury duty. David's taking care of our granddaughter, Monica, for a few days." Sarah didn't look happy, but I was bursting with glee. "Harley thinks David is a more capable babysitter than I. Maybe he's right. It doesn't matter. I'm going home Sunday." She stabbed her cake with a fork.

I stuffed some cake into my mouth to hold back a smile.

"There's no jury duty on Saturday," I reminded her.

"David said he would stay in Modesto over the weekend so that he could spend time with his son. Well, he's my son too. I think David just wanted to get away from me. I do that to men." Sarah stuffed more cake in her mouth and swallowed. "I see how right you and

David are for each other, which tells me how wrong I was for him." She sipped her tea as if she were trying to extract a measure of comfort from it.

"Do you need a ride to the airport?" I asked, feeling generous.

"I was just about to ask if you could spare the time."

"My Sunday is free and I'd be happy to drive you to San Jose," I said with a smile.

"Actually, my reservation is for Monterey to San Diego."

"That's even better." Way better, I thought to myself. "Monterey is one of my favorite places. What time?"

"Three."

"We could have lunch on the wharf first." I really didn't mind Sarah as long as she wasn't running after David.

"Lunch is a great idea. I'm kind of looking forward to going home. I have four cats, you know." She smiled bravely, making me feel like a lout. We had second helpings of cake and tea and caught up on ten years of our lives. Hers had been a real rollercoaster, never really stable or happy. Mine was a dream compared to hers, and I figured it was only going to get better.

I drove Sarah back to David's house and then circled back to my comfy little home, where I curled up on the sofa and thought about how lucky I was. My contentment was reflected in dreams that night until they shifted into the recurring nightmare about a certain staircase littered with papers. I woke up with a start, but Solow's heavy snoring lulled me back to sleep.

CHAPTER SEVEN

It was Friday morning. Not a typical Friday, but a ten o'clock funeral Friday, which meant I could sleep in a bit longer and eat a real breakfast. I tried on my navy blue pantsuit and it still fit. I added fake pearl earrings and a light blue silk scarf.

After breakfast, Solow and I took a brisk walk over to Oliver's house. The grandiose orange cat was stationed at his bowl, confident I would show up and feed him. I couldn't help but love the big bubba. When he was fed, I left Rosa's house and jogged down Otis Road in my black mini boots, Solow trotting beside me.

Back at the house, I loaded up all the essentials—paint clothes for after the funeral, cooler, and purse. I helped Solow into the passenger seat, drove to David's house and tooted the horn.

Sarah came out with Fluffy in her arms.

"Would you like a lazy dog for the day?" I shouted.

"You know I would." Sarah put Fluffy down, giving her a running head start, and then helped Solow down from his seat. He ignored Fluffy. My porch potato had completed his walk and was apparently too tired for a Fluffy chase.

"Bye, big guy," I said, and set off for Tiggy's Chapel in downtown Watsonville. The little chapel was extra fancy and so was Mr. Tiggy. He greeted me at the door smelling like roses, wearing a suit made for a smaller man, his mouth fixed in a plastic smile.

Justin sat in the left front row pew. I approached him, anxious to know how he was holding up. He stood and we hugged.

"Hi, Josephine. Have a seat." He patted the bench beside him.

"Should I? I mean, shouldn't Jim's family be here in the front?" I whispered.

"The only family he had was me." Justin scooted over a bit and I sat down. I could see Jim's casket, lid open, to the right of the podium. There were enough flower arrangements to keep half the town sneezing, and a framed eight-by-ten photo of Jim tucked amongst the flora. A few people wandered up to the casket and looked down at the old man's remains. I preferred to remember Jim the way I had left him Sunday night— smiling and relaxed in his easy chair.

"Thank you for coming, Josephine."

"I liked your granddad." I handed him my card with Alicia's address written on the back. "Don't forget, dinner tonight at Alicia's." I didn't know what else to say, so we sat quietly. I have no idea how long the ceremony lasted. All I know is we stood up to sing about ten times, I cried through "Amazing Grace," we stood up to read scripture about five times and finally we stood up to leave.

When we turned around to exit, I noticed the chapel was about half full and not a black person in sight, except for Justin and one sheriff's deputy sitting in the back row. Everyone filed out the door to the street, beginning with the back row. As Justin and I passed Deputy Sayer, who had moved into the foyer, he said, "Ma'am, Sir," and nodded his head. I figured he was there to keep an eye on we the suspects.

"Is Deputy Sayer the guy who questioned you?" I asked when we were out on the sidewalk.

"Yeah, and a woman, Officer Lund. I have to go now." He turned and walked to the black limousine parked in the alley. Justin would go to the gravesite, but I needed to get to work at the Therapy Center. As I walked down the sidewalk toward my truck, I couldn't help noticing Garth Thornton standing beside a red Jag parked at the curb. A group of people joined him at the car. The only person I recognized, besides Garth, was Hans. He saw me coming and extended his hand for a handshake.

"Josephine, I thought you barely knew Jim. Nice of you to come down here today." He put a hand behind my waist and introduced his friends. A skinny, busty woman wearing a red dress and heels stepped up and cranked my hand like a water pump.

"My, my. So you're the muralist we hired. I'm Tavia Thornton, Garth's stepmother." She pointed a long jeweled finger at Garth who had just made himself comfortable in the Jag's backseat. She shook back a mass of blond hair that threatened to tangle with her heavily mascaraed lashes, and said proudly, "and this is my son, Mark." She smiled and pointed to a blond, pointy-nosed teenager with blue eyes and pouty lips. He sat in the front passenger seat, oblivious to everyone, playing a hand-held electronic game.

"It's lovely to meet you, Joan. The clouds you

painted really are an inspiration." Tavia smelled like gardenia blossoms and a dirty ashtray. I took a step back, but she stepped forward into "my space."

"It's Josephine, and you can thank Alicia for the clouds," I said, stepping back again, and feeling socially inept around such well-developed theatrics. Tavia stretched her red lips into a smile, turned and wiggled her way around the Jaguar to the driver's seat.

"And this is William Thornton," Hans said. Willy and I shook hands. The man was an average-looking, clean-shaven guy wearing a very expensive suit.

"I would have met you sooner, Josephine, but I've been out of town," he smiled.

"Darlin', get in the car," Tavia crabbed as if Willy was a wayward four-year-old. Willy dutifully climbed into the backseat next to Garth. She laid some rubber as Hans and I walked down the block to my truck and his car.

Back at the Therapy Center, the usual carpenters' trucks were present, along with the BMW but no Jag. The building was lunchtime quiet. I found Alicia and Kyle sitting on five-gallon paint buckets, eating home-made burritos. We always packed extra food for Kyle.

After lunch and a change into work clothes, I settled into the paint routine which simply meant painting more boring lake water. Hours later when the water was finally finished, I began adding rocks and walking paths. Kyle painted a cluster of redwood trees and Alicia added shadows. With fifty feet of mural space, it was weird how often we found ourselves all working in the same area dodging each other's elbows. I finally re-assigned the work, and tried to keep everyone in his/her own space.

"Jo, did you see Justin at the funeral?" Alicia asked.

"Yes, I talked to him. He seems to be managing fairly well. I feel sorry for him, losing the only family he had. By the way, I met the Thorntons."

"That's nice."

"Like, what do they drive?" Kyle asked.

"A red Jaguar with gold rims." Just then Chester walked up to me. I turned and he grabbed my arm as I started to trip over the bucket of paint behind my left foot. "Thanks," I sputtered.

"Did I hear something about ol' Jim's funeral?" Chester asked. "Guess you're wondering why I didn't go. They're pushing me to get this project done before the first. Besides, I hate funerals."

"I went, but I guess Andy didn't," I said, hoping to learn more about Andy.

"Andy didn't go to his own mother's funeral. You know the type." Chester shrugged.

All of a sudden, a loud annoying fire alarm shrieked through the building. We looked up and down the hall while Chester took off running toward the alcove and staircase. The three of us followed at a slower pace but in time to see the contractor taking the steps three at a time. He yanked open Andy's office door where smoke was curling up from the floor. As the door swung open, a plume of smoke forced Chester back against the copper railing.

"Call 911," Chester shouted.

Alicia already had her phone out, dialing.

I cautiously proceeded up the stairs, trying not to breathe deeply as the smoke had a nasty smell like burnt rubber or plastic. I peered into the room. Chester was beating Andy's printer with a throw rug. He walloped the smoking machine over and over while Andy stood silently watching, unable or unwilling to move. Beside the desk, papers were burning in a metal trash can and flaming ashes found their way to a stack of papers atop the desk. Chester zapped the pile with the rug, killing the flames with one blow. The printer smoked a little, but the flames were finally out.

I retreated down the stairs, anxious to get away from the toxic smoke. Chester and Andy sat down on the bottom staircase, breathing deeply between coughing fits.

"The fire trucks are on their way," Alicia said.

Kyle leaned against the railing, four stairs up, until he was pushed aside by three firemen lugging a sizable hose. One helmeted firefighter ran up the stairs to check out the situation. A few seconds later, he was back, explaining that everything was under control.

"You guys OK?" the young fireman asked. Chester and Andy nodded. "I'll look around and make a report—won't take long." The other two helmets took their hose back to the truck while the young fireman did his investigation.

Andy sat, silent and stone-faced.

When Chester was finally breathing normally, he excused himself to go home.

I followed him out the backdoor. "Chester."

He turned around.

"What do you think started the fire?"

"Looks to me like it started in the trash can," he coughed. "Maybe the idiot dropped a cigarette in there.

Who knows?"

"Andy smokes?"

"Not that I know of, but he might have started." Chester coughed again, jumped in his truck and took off. I wondered why a big guy like Andy would just stand there and not take action to put out the fire. He didn't even step outside his office to call for help. I was standing in the parking lot, shaking my head, when I realized the sun was very low in the sky. I turned to go inside and bumped into Andy who seemed to be in a hurry to leave the building. His cough was much worse than Chester's, but that didn't stop him from rushing past me to his BMW and peeling out of the parking lot.

I went back inside and found Alicia and Kyle down the hall cleaning brushes. They must have realized what time it was about the same time I did. I missed Solow and couldn't wait to go home.

"Kyle, see you Monday?"

"Sure. Like, I'll be here," he said with a bit of excitement in his voice. After all, where else would he find as much excitement?

Alicia slipped into her jacket and followed me to my truck.

"See you at my house, Jo."

"Oh ... yeah. See you there." Wow, I had forgotten all about dinner.

"Are you busy tomorrow?" she asked. I shook my head. "I'm planning to go to Castroville. Would you like to join me?" I immediately knew why she wanted to go to Castroville. The small town was famous for growing artichokes, but she wasn't looking for artichokes. Pete

Mendoza lived there, and I was sure Alicia wanted to find Rosa.

"I'd love to go, Allie. I'm as curious as you are about Rosa, and I'm wondering how much longer I'll be feeding Oliver. Don't get me wrong; I love that big old bubba. But I would like to know what's going on."

"See you at the house," she said and turned her Volvo toward Watsonville.

I backed up and left the parking lot. As much as I wanted to see Solow, I remembered the grocery list in my purse. Five minutes later, I pulled into the grocery store parking lot with its bright lights and full parking lot. Oh yeah, it was the eve of Super Bowl weekend and everyone was stocking up on the essentials: charcoal, chips and beer. My essentials included kibble, fruit, cereal and laundry detergent.

"Hey, Jo," Robert said, as I entered the building. "Did you hear about the murder?"

"Hear about it? I was there." I pushed my cart down the produce aisle, letting Mr. Know-It-All suffer for a few more minutes.

"Are you kidding me?" he asked, breathlessly.

"No kidding." I let him wonder for a couple more minutes as I sampled the grapes. "I was there when Mr. Keeper fell down the stairs. In fact, I went to his funeral today. Did you just find out? I thought you got around better than that, Robert."

"I heard it on KPIG this morning," he mumbled, his chubby shoulders in a slump. "Did you see who pushed him?" Robert was in my way, keeping me from reaching the sack of potatoes I was after.

"Excuse me, Robert," I said as he backed up two

steps. "The answer is, no."

"No. What?"

"No, I didn't see who hit him." I dropped the potatoes into my cart and rolled it over to the pet food aisle. I waited for a couple of forty-niner fans to push their baskets forward so I could reach the last bag of Solow's favorite kibble. A very tall blond woman with an amazing reach grabbed the sack despite the crowds of people. I opened my mouth to protest but just in time realized who the lady was.

"Josephine, how's Solow doing?" Nancy smiled and handed me the sack.

"Nice to see you, Nancy. Solow's just fine. Fat and lazy, actually."

"I hear you're working with my brother, Andy." Nancy dropped a box of doggie treats into her shopping cart.

"Oh ... yes, Andy. He works upstairs. I didn't realize he was your brother." But when I thought about it, they certainly looked like family. "How long has your brother worked for the Thorntons?"

"Well, let's see," Nancy looked up at the ceiling for a minute, "must be almost six years now. He started working for Willy at the Santa Cruz office the same year I was hired at the veterinary hospital."

An old man wearing a forty-niner red and gold jersey banged his cart into mine and apologized profusely. Nancy and I realized we were causing a lane blockage so we separated. She waved, "Nice to see you, Josephine."

"Take care, Nancy," I shouted over the crowd of football worshipers. I pushed my cart to the next aisle, noticing that Robert was nowhere in sight. I threw a few more items into my cart and forged a trail through the mass of shoppers to a checkout stand. Robert was ringing up a million items from two carts piled high with chips and beer. I pulled in behind the potato chip connoisseur who needed two carts and a bagger to haul his Super Bowl supplies out the door. After a long wait, it was finally my turn.

"So, Josephine, did you hear about the Research Center?" Robert asked, smiling smugly. "It's going to be built next to the Therapy Center. I hear it's going to be a big one."

"You got me. I hadn't heard about that." I wondered exactly where it would be built. "More KPIG news?"

"Actually, I was reading today's Pajaronian in the lunchroom. They said the property has already been re-zoned. All they need now is a vote from the city council to make it final. Who's going to say no to a Solar Research Center?"

"There goes another farm," came a familiar voice. I looked to my left and smiled at Steve from the paint store.

"Steve, do you know about the research thingy Robert's talking about?"

"Sure, it was in the Pajaronian. This whole place is going to ruin. Just wait and see." Steve was busy separating his milk, bread and cereal-type groceries from his Super Bowl chips, dips and beer.

"Which side of the Therapy Center gets the Re-search Center?" I asked Steve.

"I don't know and I don't give a rat's rear-end. It's a crime, I tell you, taking people's farmland. I'm not a farmer, but I know when rights are being violated."

"OK, guys. Gotta go." I carried my grocery bag in one arm and bag of kibble in the other, and dropped everything into the back of the truck. Ten minutes later I parked in front of Alicia's house, walked up the lighted path and rang the doorbell. Trigger and his little dog, Tansey, met me at the door.

I hugged Trigger, maybe for the last time. He was ten and I worried that he might become self-conscious about hugs, but I figured he would always call me Auntie Jo. Just then a gray SUV pulled up next to my truck. Justin strolled up to the open front door.

"Hi, Josephine … and this must be …."

"This is Trigger. Trigger, meet Mr. Keeper."

"Call me Justin," he said, and ruffled Trigger's hair as if they had been longtime friends. Trigger's mouth dropped open as he examined the medals on Justin's uniform. He led us into the house, as Tansey bounced along behind us.

Ernie stood up from his bar stool, hugged me and held his hand out to Justin. They shook hands as Alicia called out from the stove across the room.

"Hi, you guys. Hope you're hungry. Trigger washup, honey." She turned back to the pot of mole she was stirring.

"Anything I can do?" Justin asked.

"Sit down here with me," Ernie said as he pulled out another bar stool. "I'm sorry to hear about your grandfather."

"Thank you, Sir." The men chatted while Alicia and I carried food to the table. Trigger showed up with clean hands and face and offered Justin a seat beside him at the table. The table-chatter faded away as our mouths filled with chicken mole and homemade rice and beans.

Justin was as comfortable as an old sofa with the Quintana family, and everyone looked happy to be entertaining a real Marine. They did their best to help him forget his troubles.

I enjoyed dinner, but it had been a long day. I was tired and I missed Solow so I skipped dessert and made my excuses for leaving a little early.

"Tomorrow at noon," Alicia said, as I turned to leave.

"Wouldn't miss it. Goodnight, everyone."

I climbed slowly into my truck and headed home. It was nine o'clock when I drove up David's driveway. I heard a howl from inside the house and smiled. The door opened and Solow greeted me with his tail wagging his whole body.

Sarah stood beside the door with a cell phone to her ear.

"Jo, hang on a minute." She said a few words into the phone and handed it to me.

"Hello? David, how are you? Sarah told me about Harley's jury duty."

"I just wanted to let you know that I'll be home soon. Harley thinks the trial will end Tuesday or Wednesday."

"I guess Sarah told you she's leaving Sunday."

"Sure did, and you're driving her. Glad you two are getting along so well. I miss you, Josie. Monica wants to know when you'll read to her again."

"As soon as I can. Tell her I miss her … and you too, David."

"I'll let you go, Josie. See you soon."

"Bye, David." I stared at the front door until Sarah spoke.

"Josephine, are you all right? Come sit down." She led me to the dining room where she had set the table for two. You must be hungry."

"You prepared a dinner for both of us?" I said, still feeling warm from the sound of David's voice and not wanting to take my attention away from the memory of it.

"Sure did. Do you like baked salmon, scalloped potatoes and artichoke salad?"

"Sarah, you're spoiling me with all my favorite foods."

She disappeared into the kitchen and came back with individual salads. On a scale of one to ten, the food was over the moon. Unfortunately, I was already stuffed. Oh well, I thought, I had experienced worse problems than having to eat all my favorite foods on a full stomach.

I wondered if the dinner was just a plot to fatten me up so that Sarah would look slim compared to me. I gave up that idea quickly. Sarah was being friendly and open about everything and didn't even notice that I dropped some of my dinner into Solow's strategically positioned and ever-ready mouth.

"So, how's the mural coming along?"

"It's fine, but I haven't had much time to think about mural work. It seems like there are so many pressing issues to think about these days, like murder, a missing friend named Rosa and I just heard that more farmland is going to be lost."

"What do you mean? Lost?" Sarah cocked her head. "Even though I'm working for the Thorntons, I was never happy about them building the Center on farmland. Now, it seems, another chunk of land is going to be developed. Another family will lose their farm to industry. Actually, it will be to an Electronic Research Center. At least it won't be a shopping mall."

"You've got to fight back, girl. Don't let the filthy rich hypocrites take the land away from the people. You have to fight, organize and save the farmers from ruin."

"You sound like you've had experience with this sort of thing."

"You better believe it. Remember the 'Whitehill verses Gable' case? They wanted to fence off blocks of oceanfront property. I was there with hundreds of warriors—people who fought for justice. We won, and the fences came down after we spent a whole week camped out in the middle of the street and one night in jail. Then there was the case of the shopping carts for the homeless … you just have to fight for what's right. You can do it." Sarah wiped sweat from her forehead with her napkin.

"But I don't know where to start. I don't even know who's behind it."

"Get the information you need and then call the 'Rent-a-mob' and picket or whatever you have to do to bring these guys down." Sarah wiped her lips with her napkin. "How about a cup of decaf and some raspberry pie?"

"Coffee would be great, but no pie, thank you." I petted Solow's head and hoped I had enough room for a few sips of coffee. Sarah came back with steaming mugs and a smile a mile wide.

"I could help you ... you know ... to stop the slimy land grabbers," Sarah said sweetly, not losing the smile for a second. "I know I'm supposed to leave Sunday, but I would be willing to stay with you a few days and organize things. What do you think?"

"What about your cats?"

"My sister takes care of them. A few more days won't hurt." The smile started to fade as I took my time answering.

"I think that might work." I felt like such a coward. "Are you sure it won't inconvenience you?" I asked, looking into my mug for help. I never liked having houseguests, but at least she wouldn't be staying at David's house.

"I'm so excited!" Sarah jumped up from her chair, put both hands over her red cheeks like a dramatic teenager and rolled her eyes to the ceiling. "I just remembered someone who can help us. He's the cutest little man, but wild when it comes to a cause. He owns ABC Paints in ...."

"Watsonville, on Freedom Boulevard," I said, propping my chin up with two palms.

"Oh, you know Steve?"

"Sure. I buy some of my paint supplies there, and you're right, Steve's a pistol. Sarah, I hate to break this up. It's almost eleven and I'm exhausted. It's been a long day."

She circled the table and put a hand on my shoulder. "I should have realized how tired you are. We'll talk about everything later, and in the meantime I'll get busy organizing." Sarah walked me to the door.

"So I guess I'm not taking you to the airport Sunday?"

"Of course not, I'll be helping you from now on. Goodnight, Josephine."

"Night, Sarah. Dinner was lovely." I wondered how I could have been so easily manipulated into having a houseguest. Maybe that was how she trapped David into marriage twenty-eight years ago. Solow followed me to my truck and I hefted him into his seat. I climbed in and drove half a block to my home sweet home.

CHAPTER EIGHT

Dawn caught me by surprise. I had planned to sleep late, but Solow whimpered to be let outside. Unfortunately he didn't know a Saturday from a weekday. Once he was outside, I tried to go back to sleep. I was almost there when the phone rang.

"Hello. Steve? What ...?"

"Like I said, Sarah called me and we wondered if you wanted to meet us at Denny's for breakfast. We could discuss our strategy. Jo, are you there?"

"Sorry, Steve. I'm a bit under the weather this morning, and I have a meeting to go to in a couple of hours—maybe next time. Bye." Steve's call reminded me of dinner with Sarah and our conversation. Good grief, I had enough problems without Sarah and her sidekick, Steve, ruining my life.

Solow howled. I gave up any thoughts of sleeping late and let him in. A strong cup of coffee would fix everything. Mid-morning, when most of my housekeeping chores were finished, Solow and I took a windy walk over to Rosa's. Ollie met us outside the front door, daring Solow to come closer. Solow hid behind my legs.

The three of us trotted around the house to the backdoor and into the kitchen. It felt good to be out of the wind. I set about filling the food and water bowls for the big bubba kitty that kept wrapping himself around my legs, purring like a broken muffler. Because Rosa's house was always neat and clean, dried mud on the kitchen floor in the shape of footprints caught my eye. I shuddered.

My first thought was to run, and then I remembered that Solow would growl if anyone was around. I quietly peeked into every room including Rosa's bedroom. I could have sworn I left her purse near the bed. What was it doing on her little desk?

I walked back to the kitchen and stood next to one of the muddy prints obviously made by a man with big feet. Solow sniffed around. Someone had been in the house. I was more than ready to go home, but Solow had taken up sniffing everything in every room. If only he could tell me who and what it was all about.

We left Oliver happily scarfing up kitty food, purring between bites. We walked home with a pale sun overhead and the wind at our backs. Solow collapsed into his doggie bed on the porch, and I went inside and flopped down in my rocker. A blinking red light caught my attention. I pushed "play."

"Hi, Josephine. This is Steve. Ah … maybe I missed your call. Sarah and the gang are meeting in front of the Salinas Civic Center at noon. See you there."

I listened to the next message. "Jo, it's Sarah. I hope you don't mind. I painted an extra sign for you. You looked so tired last night and I was full of energy. Steve and I worked until four in the morning. It's going to be great. See you at noon."

"What? Don't tell me they're already organized."

Solow heard me ranting from outside and howled to come in. I was stunned. There was no way I was going to give up Castroville for the Salinas Civic Center. Rosa was higher on my to-do list. I checked out the sign on the front porch, which I hadn't even noticed earlier. It read .... SAVE OUR SPINACH. I rolled my eyes, let Solow in and then called Alicia.

"Hi, Allie, are we still on for Castroville?"

"Of course. I heard there's going to be a big protest march today in Salinas. If we leave a little early, we could see what it's all about."

"Good grief!" I groaned. "I mean, yeah, I guess we could do that. I'll be over about 11:30." I had never picketed before and I really didn't want to start; but on the other hand, I was aware that agriculture was being gobbled up by new construction and that bothered me. My comfort zone said, "Stay out of it," while my higher self said, "Get involved."

I left Solow at home, drove to Alicia's and from there, we motored down Highway One in Alicia's Volvo station wagon. We drove past the little town of Castroville and made a right into downtown Salinas. I talked as Alicia drove. Finally she spoke.

"Are you sure you saw footprints? Maybe it was mud from Ollie's feet."

"No, Allie. These were not little pawmarks. Someone with good-sized feet was in that house. Solow went crazy sniffing all over and I'm not sure, but I think Rosa's purse had been moved."

"Shall I park here?" Alicia asked.

"Looks fine. A little walk won't hurt us." I dropped two quarters in the meter and we headed down the sidewalk. I saw state and federal flags flapping in the wind above the Salinas Civic Center, our county seat, two blocks away. I turned my coat collar up and hoped the sun wouldn't disappear behind dark clouds moving in fast from the west.

We passed a KPUT minivan with saucers and antennas sprouting from its roof. Just a few parking meters down was another van with "KPIG Radio" written in bold letters across the back. At least a hundred people marched in an elongated circle in front of the Civic Center. Some pushed strollers; others carried hand-painted signs stapled to long wooden sticks. One very old man beat on a little drum. As we came closer to the noisy crowd, we were able to make out the words of the chant.

"Hey-hey, ho-ho, taking our farmland is a no-no." The chant was repeated over and over and led by high-stepping Sarah. She saw us, waved and stepped off the curb into the slow-moving traffic. She threaded her way across all four lanes, signage and all. She didn't look back. If she had, she would have seen Steve and the whole group of marchers following her like rabid bunny-hoppers doing the conga.

"Hi, Jo. Are you and your friend going to join us? Where's your sign? I left one on your front porch last night. Maybe you didn't see it."

"No, I guess I didn't," I shouted over the noise. The racket became too loud for conversation and the honking from frustrated drivers was even louder.

Sarah looked over her shoulder. "Steve, what are all you folks doing over here?"

Steve opened his mouth but nothing came out. At

that same moment, a microphone was shoved in front of my face and a very tall Hispanic man wearing a three-piece suit leaned down and asked my name. "Josephine Stuart, why?" I turned my head and saw a geeky guy with a TV camera pointed at me. "Good grief!" Unfortunately everything was captured for posterity. Alicia put a hand over her mouth stifling a giggle. Sarah stepped closer to the mike and shouted. "We want justice! We need agriculture! Don't take our land! We all agree that big government better back off. The people have spoken." She smiled for the camera, turned and led the whole battalion back across the street, bringing on the honking horns once again. I had the feeling most of her speech had been used before for other causes.

"I'm cold. What about you?" I asked, hugging myself to keep body heat from escaping out of my jacket.

"Me, too. Let's go," Alicia said. We turned and walked toward the Volvo. I looked back over my shoulder in time to see half a dozen police cars pulling up in front of the Civic Center with red lights flashing. I was glad to be going in the other direction. Fifteen minutes later, Alicia turned off the highway and headed into Castroville. The town was famous for its 1947 artichoke queen, Norma Jean (Marilyn Monroe).

Alicia followed her handwritten directions to the Mendoza house, which turned out to be an average-looking, white-stucco, ranch style with a red-brick chimney and blue shutters. The only thing that stood out was the fact that the house and yard were immaculate and the rest of the neighborhood wasn't.

As we parked at the curb, I noticed drapes in the front picture window part for a second. A concrete walkway led straight to the front door. I rang the doorbell. Three locks clicked. Before my finger left the button, the door swung open. We entered and the door immediately closed with a thud behind us.

Pete smiled at Alicia but looked at me as if I were trespassing. "Nice of you to stop by Alicia." They hugged.

"Pete, this is my friend, Josephine Stuart."

"Yes, now I remember. We met a few years ago on Thanksgiving at my father's house. How are you ... and your dog ... what was his name?"

"Solow. We're fine. It's nice to see you again, Pete." I felt a bit awkward as we stood in the living room with lights on and all the drapes closed. Pete offered us seats on the sofa and then disappeared down the hall. The house was quiet for a Saturday afternoon—no radio, TV, dishwasher, or even child noises. I looked at Alicia's face in the dim lamplight. Her lips were tight and a couple of worry lines marched across her forehead.

Pete's wife, Luisa, entered from the hallway with Pete behind her. Her shoulders were even with his, but thicker. She looked much bigger than the last time I saw her.

Alicia stood and they hugged.

"What a surprise, Alicia." Luisa looked at me. "We've met. You're Josephine?"

I nodded. She smiled and took a seat opposite the sofa.

"How are you, Luisa?" Alicia asked. Luisa patted her belly and laughed.

"I'm going to have a baby," she cooed, "in May."
Her smile was radiant.

"I'm so happy for you. I guess you're wondering
what Josephine and I are doing out here in Castroville.
Rosa and I have been friends for a long time, and I've
been worried about her."

I watched Pete's face as he looked at Luisa.
The uncomfortable silence finally ended when Alicia spoke.

"We know Rosa hasn't been home for over a week.
She hasn't gone to work and Josephine has been feed-
ing Oliver. I thought she might be staying with you."
The ultra silent house put me on edge. "Alicia and
I are concerned about Rosa. She would never leave
Oliver ...." I stopped talking as Rosa walked into the
room.

Alicia's mouth dropped open. She jumped up from
her seat and rushed to her friend. After the hugs, Rosa
stood next to her brother with her arm around his back.
Alicia walked back to the sofa and sat down.

"Pete and Luisa have been kind enough to let me
stay here. I know you two won't tell anyone where I
am. Papa and Carlos are the only ones who knew, until
now. You see, I received a death threat two weeks ago,
but it sounded crazy and I thought it was just a prank.
Part of the threat concerned Papa's farm and his dogs.
If he didn't sell the farm, terrible things would happen.
As soon as I found out the dogs were dead, I showed
Papa the note and he insisted I stay with Pete until we
find out who wrote it."

"Why didn't someone call the police?" I asked.

"Papa thinks the police aren't to be trusted. Like the

government when it takes your land," Rosa said.

"Has anyone offered to buy the farm?" I asked.

"A couple of the big conglomerates have been try-ing to buy it for years because we have a very good well. Even the small farmer next door has tried, but I think there is someone else. Papa doesn't want to sell, period." Rosa stared at the floor. "But I think he's weak-ening. Says he might sell now because he's worried about me, but I told him not to give in."

"Did you have time to pack before you came here?" I asked.

"I only had time to grab my wallet and some clothes before Pete picked me up and drove me here." Rosa shuddered. "We didn't know how soon they would come looking for me. I was so scared. Did you get my message about feeding Ollie?"

"No. Maybe my message machine swallowed it. It's been known to happen," I said and Alicia agreed. "But don't worry, I feed Ollie every day. I love that old cat." I couldn't help grinning at the thought of the big purr machine. "By the way, Rosa, has anyone been to your house lately?"

Pete cleared his throat. "I was there yesterday around noon. Rosa gave me a list of things to pick up. You know, books, more clothes and stuff like that."

"I'm so relieved it was you. I saw muddy footprints in the kitchen and didn't know what to think."

"Actually, I don't remember going into the kitchen." Pete rubbed his chin for a moment. "I remember un-locking the front door, going straight to the bedroom closet, back through the living room and I locked the front door on my way out. I don't remember going into the kitchen at all."

"Who could it have been?" Rosa stammered. The room was uncomfortably silent as Pete pulled up a piano bench and sat down. Something moved in the hall. On second look, it was a little girl pushing a doll buggy. Her dark eyes looked half awake as she parked the buggy and stood quietly beside her daddy.

"Honey, you remember Alicia," Pete said.

"Martina, it's so nice to see you," Alicia said. "Were you napping?"

The little girl nodded, let go of her buggy and crawled onto Alicia's lap. "I go to school now. Did you know that?" She squirmed around and then smiled at Alicia, totally ignoring me. But she was only a baby the last time I saw her and she didn't know me from any other older woman.

"Can I get you something to drink?" Luisa asked.

"No, thank you, dear. We just wanted to stop by for a minute to see about Rosa." Alicia helped Martina down from her lap, and we stood up to go. "Rosa, call me if you need anything. And please be careful."

"Thank you, Alicia. You're so sweet. Thank you, Josephine for feeding Oliver." She hugged us both. "I hope you won't have to feed him much longer," Rosa said with a weak smile.

Alicia and I sidled out the door into the bright sunshine and gusty wind. No one followed us outside and the front door closed the second we cleared the threshold. I heard two locks click and then the deadbolt. Instinctively, I looked up and down the street to see if anyone was watching us. I didn't see anything strange, just cars parked here and there at the curb and a couple of lawns being mowed.

Alicia drove without speaking.

"Are you feeling better now that you know where Rosa is?" I asked.

"I suppose. I have mixed feelings about the whole thing." Alicia stared at the road ahead as if she were hypnotized. "Maybe Mr. Mendoza should sell the farm and retire from all that hard work. Maybe Carlos would go out on his own and make something of himself."

"I just wish we could find out who's making the threats and stop this whole thing. That way the Mendozas would be free to live where they want, farming or not farming. Do you think Mr. Mendoza is keeping the farm so he can pass it on to Carlos?"

"Probably," Alicia said. "But if that's the case, then Mr. Mendoza doesn't know his son very well. Carlos isn't interested in farming. Hungry?"

"What? I mean, yes. I'm hungry." My stomach did a happy dance as we pulled into a fast-food joint. Alicia ordered Mandarin Chicken salads at the microphone in front of the big drive-through menu. She paid for them at the window, and then parked the Volvo around the corner where we had a fine view of Watsonville traffic. We were only half a mile from her house, but it seemed like Alicia wanted to talk rather than go home.

"What's on your mind, Allie?"

"When I hugged Pete ... I felt something tucked into the back of his jeans, you know, at the waist. It felt like a gun. I'm sure it was a gun." Alicia turned her head to look at me with dark, penetrating eyes.

"Is that a bad thing?" I asked.

"Jo! A gun! The reality of this whole thing is really upsetting."

"I know what you mean, but think about how safe Rosa is with her brother. That's got to be a comfort, isn't it?"

"I suppose," she muttered. Her salad had barely been touched. Mine was gone.

"How about a movie matinee to take your mind off of Rosa?" I offered.

She shook her head. "Jo, thanks for going with me today, but now I need to catch up on housework and spend time with Trigger and Ernie." Alicia parked the car in her garage. I followed her into the house. After a ten-minute visit with the boys, I said my goodbyes and took off in the truck. Since I was so close to Justin's house, I thought I would drop in and see how he was doing.

Four blocks later, I parked in Jim's driveway. The garage door was closed and no one answered the front door, so I walked around the house to the cottage in the back. Being in the back was not a bad thing. Being closer to the lake was a beautiful thing. From where I stood, I could see Alicia's house and Trigger's pedal boat tied to the dock.

The cottage was straight out of a Disney fairytale. Steep red tile roof, river rock chimney, green shutters and a red Dutch door. It seemed like a witch with a poison apple might arrive at any moment. I stepped up to the door and knocked.

Justin opened the top half of the door, holding a book in his other hand.

"Josephine! What a surprise. Come in." He opened

the bottom half of the door. We walked past the kitchen and into a small living room. He offered me a chair in front of a large window facing the lake. I sat staring out the window watching two gray Toulouse geese with orange feet and bills, waddled across Justin's lawn as if they owned it.

"You were right, I can see your friend's house from here," he said. "The Quintanas are nice people."

"Yes, they are. I just left their house and thought I would see how you're doing. This place of yours is so picturesque. You must love it here."

"I lived here with my granddad all through high school. Lots of good memories. When I went off to college, my holidays were spent here; but now it's not the same ... without him." Justin's mouth tried to smile, but his eyes looked sad.

"Are you any closer to figuring out who punched him?" I asked. Justin shook his head. "Did you know that Andy Anderson works for Mr. Mendoza and for Mr. Thornton?"

"I knew he worked for Willy. Where are you going with this?"

"Don't you think it's odd that Andy is a computer geek who works as a farmhand on the side?" I scratched my head for effect.

"I don't pretend to understand it," Justin said. "Andy knows that Willy's been trying to buy the Mendoza farm for years. I don't know why he would cross the line and work for Mendoza, unless Old Man Thornton put him up to it. We sat in silence pondering the ramifications. Justin stared at the geese while I mentally added Mr. Thornton to the list of people wanting to buy the Mendoza farm.

"Would you like something to drink, Josephine?"

"Thank you, Justin, but no, I just had lunch."

"I have something I think I should show you. It may or may not be connected to Granddad's death." He walked to the other side of the room where a built-in bookshelf covered the entire wall. A zillion books were packed into the shelves, mostly paperbacks. Two taller shelves at the bottom were built to hold larger books. I watched Justin stoop down and come up with a dark leather briefcase, well used and overstuffed.

"This was Granddad's. I found it when I cleaned out his office at the Center." He placed the briefcase on the coffee table, unzipped it and let the thing flop open, exposing a two-inch stack of paperwork. I noticed an email printout on the top of the stack.

"I've been busy going through insurance contracts, bills and that sort of thing. Finally, this morning, I got around to his briefcase." Justin handed the email over to me.

From … Megamalls.com to Thorntonenterprises.com
January 25 at 6:32 pm
JCP is out. Pajaro location does not suit them. Bath and Beds, Lazy Lunch and Harper's Buffet are in. Still haven't heard from Kiddie Kapers and Animals R Us. Meeting with HC Friday.

"Why do you think Jim saved this email?" I asked.

"It sounds like a mall is going to be built in Pajaro, but that's crazy. We would have heard about it. Besides, the only land available is zoned for agriculture." I watched

Justin raise one eyebrow, and then Steve's prediction of agricultural ruination flashed across my mind.

"What if the Electronic Research Center dropped out and a mall took its place?" Justin suggested with a serious frown on his face.

"That would be criminal. Two years ago the people of Monterey County voted against a proposed mall in Pajaro," I stammered. "What if Mega Malls got away with it? And who, exactly, is building the Electronic Research Center anyway?" My jaw muscles tightened and my throat went dry. "Justin, this is insane. It must be a mistake."

"I skimmed through the stack," Justin said as he laid a hand on the pile of paper in the open briefcase. "The email you read is the only email I found. It was folded up real small and stuffed down inside a pouch on the inside-back of the briefcase. Everything else is Granddad's work ... figures and that sort of thing."

My mouth dropped open as I considered a scenario that came to mind.

"Justin, the night Jim fell ... what if he was gathering or downloading a bunch of emails and put them in the trash can? What if he was going to take the trash to his truck instead of the dumpster? Maybe that's why he parked his truck way out by the dumpster." I was scaring myself as the wild scenario started to make sense.

Justin's eyes had changed from relaxed to alert. He stood up and began pacing the length of the room. "It kinda makes sense, I guess. Maybe Granddad suspected foul-play."

"The real question is: how did he discover that

email? It was obviously sent to Mr. Thornton. By the way, where is Jim's office located?"

"When you go up the stairs, turn right at the top. It's one door past Andy's office." Justin stopped pacing and scratched his head. He mumbled to himself. "Couldn't be Andy."

"What did you say?" I was all ears. "What about Andy?"

"Nothing, just thinking," Justin said. I had so many questions, but Justin looked like he needed a rest from sad thoughts and wild plots. "Did I tell you that my leave has been extended? Another three weeks."

"That's great. I'll call if I learn anything new." I stood up to leave.

"Glad you came by. You might want to keep your theory quiet for a while. You know, until we know more."

"You're right. I'll keep it quiet, but I intend to keep my ears open. Thanks for sharing, Justin. Take care." I walked out into the cool sunshine with a lot on my mind. I didn't even remember driving home. I only remembered parking next to David's Miata, which was parked in front of my house. Sarah was unloading a suitcase from the passenger seat.

"Josephine, how was your meeting?" Obviously Steve had passed the meeting information along.

"Extremely productive," I smiled. Solow crawled out of his porch bed and rubbed his long body against my calves, probably thinking about dinner. "Ok, Solow, let's go inside and pour some kibble." He trotted into the house, sniffed the two large suitcases in the dining room and galloped over to his bowl on the kitchen floor.

"How was your day?" Sarah asked, setting down a third suitcase.

"My day was great. Oh, Sarah, I'm afraid your bed is in the loft." I pointed to the narrow, rickety staircase opposite the living room sofa. I watched her carry one suitcase atop her head, like a native carrying water in a crock from the communal waterhole. Her hips had no wiggle room between the wall and the railing. She sucked air like a vacuum cleaner and swore like a politician when she tripped on the top step.

I finally took pity on Sarah and carried one of her bags upstairs. I was sure she could manage the last one. After all, she had invited herself to stay at my house. Years ago I discovered a surefire way to keep guests from staying too long. I simply kept the old, lumpy, coil-spring bed I inherited from my grandmother. It was the only extra bed in the house.

"Thank you, Josephine. Don't bother with the last suitcase. I'll get it." I knew she would get it because I certainly wasn't going to. I hustled down the stairs and began planning a dinner for two. It was only five-thirty, but I wanted to get dinner out of the way. Peanut butter on toasted rye with coleslaw—simple, but wholesome.

Sarah was still breathing hard when she entered the kitchen.

"What can I do to help?" she asked. I handed her a couple of plates, forks and napkins. She set the table, I flipped on the TV and we settled down for the evening meal. I had just taken a bite of melted peanut butter when I saw myself being interviewed on the five o'clock news. The peanut butter refused to go down as I stared in stunned silence at the news reporter who talked about my plan to stop urban sprawl.

"Look, Josephine. It's Steve and me and Jasmine and look ... it's Mr. Snow with his wife and four boys." She was so tickled to see herself and her friends marching round and round she almost fell off her chair.

"Oh, my God! Did you see that?" I shouted.

Sarah laughed again when the camera captured Steve cracking his cardboard sign over the kisser of one of the three bronze dolphins featured in a fountain statue in the center of the Civic Center plaza. He had missed the pesky councilman and whacked the bronze dolphin by mistake.

"Sarah, why isn't anyone else mentioned? Just me?"

"We all knew it was your idea, and we didn't want to take any of the credit away from you." She smiled wide as if she had done me a great favor.

"Actually, I'm not entirely into ...."

"That's OK, Josephine. We don't mind giving you the credit. Have any wine to go with dinner?"

"Sure. There's one open in the fridge." I didn't mention it had been opened on New Years Eve so David and I could make a toast, and it might have turned to vinegar.

Sarah brought the wine and two glasses, and we clinked to a successful first march.

"First march?" I gulped.

"Yes, we're just getting started. Don't worry. Everyone's going to do their part."

I finished my glass of wine, excused myself and went to bed. I was not a good hostess or a good protester, but I promised myself I would try harder in the future.

CHAPTER NINE

By the time the sun came up, I was more than ready to forget the reoccurring nightmares and roll my tortured body out of bed. I pulled on a robe, tippy-toed past my snoring basset and headed to the kitchen to brew some coffee.

"Good Morning," Sarah said, waltzing into the kitchen wearing pink pajamas and a cheery smile.

"Morning," I croaked in my un-caffeinated voice. I filled Mr. Coffee and pushed his button. "You can use the bathroom first, Sarah. I'm going to check my emails." Actually, I just needed time to wake up and be alone with my thoughts.

Solow waddled his way down the hall and into the kitchen, warming up his short legs for a run with Fluffy. I let him out and she made a fool of him shortly before he begged to come back inside, tail between his legs.

"You poor beast. Fluffy did it again, didn't she?" I poured him some kibble, freshened his water and rubbed his ears. He crunched kibble as I checked for emails. There were two from Steve and one from Hans Coleberg. I read the emails from Steve.

"Josephine, hope you can join the gang Sunday at 2:00 on the Pajaro Bridge. Bring your sign and any instructions you may have for us." Steve's second email,

"Josephine, bring all your friends."

Oh boy! I needed an excuse and fast. Luckily, Sarah was still in the shower when I called Alicia.

"Hi, Allie, it's me. I need a favor."

"What kind of favor?" She sounded like I had woken her up. Oops, I checked the clock and it was only six-thirty, Sunday morning.

"I'll explain later. I just want to know if I can come over to your house at two this afternoon?"

"Sure, I guess so …."

"Thanks, Allie." I hung up just in time to hear Sarah turn off the shower. I sat in front of my computer looking busy as Sarah made her way to the loft wrapped in a beach towel. The bathroom was clear so I took a turn. Her shower had seemed short enough, but my shower started out lukewarm and went frigid from there. Unfortunately, my old hot water heater was only good for one hot shower every sixty minutes.

When I was finally dressed and ready for the day, I ambled back to the kitchen where breakfast smells filled the air. Sarah flipped pancakes and fried sausages. I heated syrup in the microwave and stirred up a batch of orange juice from frozen concentrate.

"Sarah, did you sleep well?" Silly question, I thought, considering the bed.

"Yes, eventually. I stayed on the phone several hours after you went to bed. Steve wanted to come over, but I told him you had already gone to bed. I had a lot to do, people to call. You know how it goes." She shrugged, as if it were all in a days work. I knew about the rally at the Pajaro Bridge, but I wondered what else they had cooked up.

"By the way, I have a meeting at 2:00 in Watsonville today. Papers to sign, sketches to go over, you know how it goes." I shrugged as if the meeting couldn't be helped.

"Oh, Josephine, I was hoping you could make it to the protest today. It starts at two o'clock, and we plan to stop traffic this time."

"Darn. If only this meeting weren't so important. I'll try my best to meet up with you later," I lied. I didn't want to lie, but I didn't want to be arrested at some fool protest march. After breakfast I read Hans' email.

"Ms. Stuart, I would like to see you in my office Monday morning. Hans Coleberg."

The note sounded cold. I wondered what he wanted and then a picture of me in front of a TV camera flashed across my mind. Good grief, did he think I was the organizer of the protesters? Why would he care anyway?

"What's wrong? Get a crank email?" Sarah asked, studying my face.

"It's my boss. I'm not sure what his problem is." I shut down my Mac, picked up the broom and began sweeping the kitchen floor while Sarah loaded the dishwasher. An old John Denver favorite emanated from the radio and Sarah sang along, her hips swaying side to side as she worked.

My mood was not a singing or dancing mood, so I excused myself from the room and took Solow for a walk. I was glad to be in the fresh air and sunshine. We walked at a leisurely pace up Otis Road to Rosa and Oliver's house. It was only eight-thirty, but Ollie acted like he had missed several meals already. He rubbed the side of his face up and down my pant leg, vibrating and drooling as he purred. Solow lagged behind, keeping his distance from the big bubba.

"Here you go, Ollie." I set his bowl down on the concrete just outside the backdoor and then went back inside with Solow. I scanned the kitchen to see if anything looked suspicious. The footprints I saw the day before had almost disappeared because of heavy traffic from a cat, a dog and me. The floor just looked dusty.

"Solow, let's go old boy." We slowly walked home, giving me some time to think. Sarah wasn't a bad person. I just had a low tolerance for self-invited houseguests who didn't give me a clue as to when they planned to leave.

The slow pace was just right for Solow. By the time we approached my mail box, I had already shed my jacket. As we walked up the gravel driveway, I saw a classic red Volkswagen bus parked between my truck and David's Miata. It was plastered with half a dozen sticker messages all over the rear. The special California license plate was a definite clue as to ownership, "ABC PNT."

Solow settled into his porch pillow bed and I went inside. Steve and Sarah stood kitty-corner to each other, leaning over the kitchen table. Brushes, bottles of poster paint and big squares of white cardboard littered the table. Sarah looked up first.

"Would you like to join us, Josephine?" she asked, flushed and smiling.

"Yeah, join us," Steve said. "You're probably good at thinking up new slogans. We need all the help we can get."

"Sure. Why not?" I rolled up my sleeves, picked out

a brush and copied what they were doing. The slogans were, LEAVE OUR CABBAGE ALONE, FARMERS ARE NOT FOOLS and HONK IF YOU LOVE PRODUCE. To ease my conscience, I figured I could help with production and skip the marching. Steve had done his best to get me to march; but in the end, he would have to do it without me.

Steve's arm bumped Sarah's and she let out a couple of school girl giggles. By noon the room was wall-to-wall signs. Steve took the dry ones outside and stapled them onto long flat sticks, using an industrial-size stapler. His bus was stuffed end-to-end with signage.

I made peanut butter sandwiches for everyone. We ate them sitting at the patio table in the backyard while Steve filled me in on city politics.

"I have a friend on the board of supervisors in Salinas," Steve bragged. "He told me that a final vote on the Pajaro rezoning is coming up Thursday night. Wait till they see us at the Civic Center Thursday night …. "

"Land-grab? Are you talking about property for an Electronic Research Center?"

"Of course." Steve smiled at me as if I were ten years old and clueless.

"Steve's friend is voting against it," Sarah smiled proudly.

"Who's voting for it?" I asked.

"You've probably heard of Hector Castro and his two lame councilmen friends. Unfortunately, there are only five council members so we have to convert at least one of Castro's followers to our side. I think public opinion will help; and we know how to create public opinion, don't we?" he winked at Sarah. She blushed. I looked into Steve's animated face. "Have you heard anything about a mall to be built in Pajaro?" I tried to look nonchalant as Steve narrowed his dark eyes. "I just thought you might have heard a rumor or something." I glanced over at Sarah to see if she reacted to my question. Her mouth had dropped open, as if a great sin had happened right under her nose. Steve washed down the last of his second sandwich with iced tea.

"Some people think Hector is up to something like that, but we have no proof." Steve took another gulp of tea. "The guy has a lot of money, you know. People have accused him of having conflicting interests. His pals are doing pretty well, too. One of them has a Lazy Lunch franchise over in Salinas." Steve squinted his eyes at me again, probably noticing the startled look on my face.

"That's interesting," I said, looking away.

"Do you remember where you heard the rumor, you know, about the mall?"

"Not really," I lied. Sarah and I began clearing the table. No offer of help came from Steve, who probably preferred fix-it jobs in the garage to kitchen work. I thought about David and how comfortable he was with male or female-type chores.

Sarah and Steve took off in the VW, heading for the Pajaro Bridge. I followed in my truck with Solow riding shotgun, ears blowing in the wind. Steve was a slow driver for someone fired up over an important issue. Maybe the old VW couldn't do better than thirty miles an hour. I hung back several car lengths and watched him talk and Sarah giggle all the way to town.

San Juan Road usually had very little traffic unless you counted slow tractors and eighteen wheelers loaded with fresh produce. But there were no tractors or big rigs in sight. The closer we got to town, the slower traffic became as tons of bumper-to-bumper cars squeezed into the tiny town of Pajaro.

It was only one-forty-five, but hundreds of people were already lining the main street. They congregated on the sidewalks, waving their signs and yelling at traffic. A couple of blocks before the bridge, I made a quick decision. I turned left on Allison and made a right onto a rutty little back road beside the railroad tracks. I finally connected up with Salinas Road. Getting onto Salinas Road was difficult since traffic was barely moving. Finally I was able to make a left turn and bully my way into the slow flow.

Solow hung his head out the window, probably hoping for a little speed. Avoiding the Pajaro Bridge meant circling around to Highway One and then back into Watsonville. It was costing me an extra seven miles in time and gas. There was no easy way around the protesters. Sarah and Steve would be very happy.

"How about that, Solow, we made it," I said, pulling to a stop in front of the Quintana house. Solow howled, letting the neighborhood know he had arrived for a visit with Tansey and her family. I helped him down from his seat, followed him to the front door and pushed the doorbell. Trigger yanked the door open, bent over to pet Solow and then remembered me.

"Hi, Auntie Jo, Mom's upstairs."

"Thanks Trigger." I walked inside and looked up

the stairs.

Alicia dragged a vacuum down the stairs and into the entry hall closet.

"Hi Jo, don't mind me. I'll meet you in the backyard." She motioned for Trigger to take me out to the back lawn.

Ernie stood up from his lounge chair when he saw us emerge from the sliding glass door.

"What a nice surprise. Have a seat, Jo." He extended his hand toward a wicker chair with a soft pillow seat. I sat facing the lake with Solow flopped at my feet.

"Ernie, how can you stand to live under these conditions?"

"Very well, thank you," he laughed. I thought about Justin living at the lake in his adorable cottage and looked in his direction. The "Disney" cottage was only five or six properties away, about three hundred yards as the duck flies. I watched the two gray geese resting on the shore, surrounded by black coots and several varieties of wild and domestic ducks.

"Why are all the ducks and geese on that one beach?" I asked.

Trigger's hand shot up as if he were in a classroom.

"They go where people feed them," Trigger explained. "At five o'clock they will be over there at the Carters." He pointed to the opposite side of the lake. I heard the glass door open and close. Alicia walked over to me and dropped Tansey in my lap.

"You sure know my weakness, Allie." I stroked the little sheltie as she settled in. Solow didn't even notice the canine on my lap because he was already snoring.

"So, what's up, Jo?" Alicia pulled a chair close to

mine and sat down.

"I guess I told you, Sarah is staying at my house for an undisclosed amount of time. Steve came over this morning, and we painted signs for another protest march. I wasn't about to get involved in stopping traffic and maybe getting arrested. Call me 'chicken,' but count me out. Anyway, I needed an excuse and you were it ... again."

"I'm not sure I understand what the protesters hope to accomplish," Ernie said.

"The way I understand it, there will be a vote by the Board of Supervisors Thursday to determine whether or not an Electronic Research Center can be built in Pajaro," I said.

"That would be the property east of the Physical Therapy Center," Ernie said.

Alicia's mouth dropped open. "You don't mean the Mendoza farm!"

Ernie nodded.

"Where did you hear that?" I stuttered.

"Read it in the Pajaronian. I thought you knew."

"Honey, you didn't tell me," Alicia wailed. "I had no idea the Mendoza property was at risk." She laid both hands across her chest.

"I ... I'm sorry ... darling," Ernie winced. A long silence followed.

Finally, Alicia stood up. "Iced tea, anyone?"

"Sure, I'll help you." I jumped up, handed Tansey over to Trigger and followed Alicia to the kitchen. I poured tea while Alicia placed homemade oatmeal cookies on a plate. "What are we going to do, Allie?"

"I think we need to talk to Mr. Mendoza right away.

Do you want to go with me, Jo?"

"OK. Now I almost wish I was protesting at the bridge today." All of a sudden, the cause seemed more important to me and no less than desperate for the Mendozas. I felt ashamed that I had shirked my civic duty to make trouble and defy the law.

Alicia and I spent a few minutes eating cookies and sipping tea before we excused ourselves and took off for Pajaro in her Volvo. After twenty-five minutes of driving the long way, part of it through crowds of people, we finally arrived at the Mendoza farm. Several young-adults carrying signs trotted by the house on their way to the gala. Mr. Mendoza peered out the front window at the swarms of spike-haired and tattooed protesters. He opened the front door when he saw us.

"Come in." He hugged Alicia, laid an arm on my shoulder and motioned for us to sit on the sofa. "So what's on your mind, ladies?"

"We're worried about you and your farm," Alicia's said.

"So I guess everyone knows that the county wants my property. It's not up to me any more. It's up to the supervisors." His shoulders caved and his mustache drooped.

"That's what the protest march is all about," I said, brightly. Please don't give up, I thought to myself. "Where there's a will there's a way."

"Wasn't that you, Josephine, on the TV?" He worked up a little smile. "You organized all this for me?"

"Ah, something like that," I gulped. "By the way, is Andy still working for you?"

Mr. Mendoza opened his mouth to speak, closed it and shook his head. After an uncomfortable silence, he said, "No, not any more. You see, he and my son, Carlos, used to hang around together in high school. Even though Rosa was a couple of years older than Andy, she was always nice to him ... you know, like she had another kid-brother.

Alicia and I hung on every word.

"I'm so sorry. Can I get you ladies something to drink?"

"No, thank you," we said in one rapid voice.

"Well, it seems Andy was repairing one of Mr. Thornton's computers when he found an interesting email. I don't know spit, excuse me, about computers, but anyway, this email mentioned my farm so he hurried over with it."

"What did it say?" Alicia asked.

"I haven't told anyone about this email except my boys, but I guess I can tell you. Someone with the initials HC sent it to Thornton. It said something like, "We want you to go ahead with Mendoza's lettuce and take out the dogs for good measure." Mr. Mendoza took a deep breath and looked at the ceiling for a moment.

"A few days later, Andy was back here with another email." Mr. Mendoza squirmed in his black leather recliner. "It said something like," "If the dogs aren't enough, get the daughter." Signed HC

"That was when I asked Andy to help out around here, just a few hours a day and earn some extra money. I liked having an extra hand around ... just in case."

"No wonder you whisked Rosa away," I said.

"Once the dogs were dead, I knew they meant busi-

ness. Rosa finally told me she had been threatened. I
called Pete and he picked her up in a hurry, about five
o'clock in the morning. Rosa's been with him ever
since. She was safe; the dogs were gone. I figured I
didn't need Andy anymore and he understood."

"Mr. Thornton has sent me several offers on the
property over the years, but I refused to sell. I guess he
decided to try a different approach. He wasn't such a
bad guy years ago, but with a naggy wife like Tavia any
man would go sour."

"So you're pretty sure it was Willy who destroyed
your lettuce and killed the dogs?"

"Maybe, I don't know who actually did the dirty
work." Mr. Mendoza stared straight ahead at the
river rock fireplace where the new shotgun hung
over the mantle. "My property has already been re-
zoned without my approval, and it won't matter
whether I want to sell or not if the board of supervisors votes to take my farm. You say there's a protest
march at the brid …."

Sirens screamed by the house. Then another set, but
higher pitched. Like lemmings, we hurried to the front
door. From the porch we saw several sets of blinking
red lights atop police cars plus two black police vans
just a block away. We heard shouting, sirens, and fireworks four blocks away.

Dozens of young protesters fled the Pajaro Bridge
fiasco and made their way southeast, past the three of
us. They tossed their signs along the way, many of them
landing on Mr. Mendoza's front lawn.

I ran down the steps and across the front yard to
pick up a few signs before they could be trampled. I

held two signs in one hand while I bent down for another. Just as I raised up, a white van with TV dishes and aerials on the roof pulled up behind Alicia's Volvo. A young, overly made-up woman wearing a low cut black pantsuit bounced out of the vehicle and shoved a microphone in front of my face. Out of the corner of my eye, I saw a cameraman crouch down for a low-angle shot.

"Good grief!" I said, before I had time to think.

"Hello, Ma'am. KPUT would like to know how you feel about the arrests made here today. How does this affect free speech?"

"Ah … I'm just, I mean, I think its fine to protest something you think is illegal or unreasonable. The public should have its say. It's our first amendment right to speak out. We need to preserve our agricultural land and …" I was cookin', but the woman jerked the mic away and jumped back in the van with the camera guy. The driver whipped a U-turn and headed back to Pajaro.

I grabbed two more signs and dropped all of them in a pile near the stairs. By that time, Alicia had collected signs from half a block away. We recovered at least twenty printed slogans and eventually stuffed them all into her station wagon. She hugged Mr. Mendoza, said goodbye and told him not to worry. I waved a "thumbs-up" to the unhappy farmer as we headed southeast on San Juan Road. Alicia made a five-mile loop heading toward the foothills and then north to the Lake District, skillfully avoiding the havoc in Pajaro.

"I hated to leave Mr. Mendoza alone, so I asked him over for dinner tonight," Alicia said, staring straight ahead at a slow-moving RV. "I hope you can be there too. I'm sure we can find something for Solow to eat." In other words, don't use him as an excuse to go home.

"I'd love to," I said, after a second to consider the invitation. I dreaded going home to Sarah and Steve and who knows what else. I missed my quiet life with Solow.

"Jo, do you get the feeling that Mr. Thornton and City Hall are working together?"

"I can't see it any other way. The problem is how to stop them." My cell phone began playing Beethoven's Fifth. I fumbled through my purse and fished it out. "Hello."

"Josephine, this is Sarah. Steve and I are going to have a sleep-over at the Salinas jail tonight. Giggle. Do you think you could pick us up tomorrow morning?"

"Ah … sure. I can hardly hear you with all that noise. Who's with you?"

"Two sheriff's vans full so far. Lots of nice people." She sounded like she was having a good turnout for a Tupperware party instead of being thrown in the clink.

"Gotta go. Everyone's waiting to use the phone." Click.

Alicia stared at me.

"That was Sarah. She wants me to break her out of jail tomorrow." We laughed till our sides hurt, and I thanked God I hadn't marched. If I had, I would probably be looking through bars instead of going to a fine dinner at Alicia's.

"It's almost five and I need to stop at the store for a couple of things," she apologized. "Do you mind?"

"I'm not going anywhere, just dinner at your house.

I'll go to the store with you."

The Watsonville Market was packed with sweaty, discourteous and disheveled young adults fresh from the demonstration. They were loud as they talked and laughed, still high on the thrill of defying the law for a worthy cause, which they probably knew very little about. I was pushed and elbowed most of the way to the produce aisle.

"Ouch!" Alicia screamed as someone's hiking boot stepped on her sandaled foot. She snatched up a clump of fresh cilantro and a head of lettuce. I dropped three tomatoes into a plastic bag, grabbed a sweet onion and we headed to the checkout at the front of the store. The line at Robert's check stand looked shorter than the rest, but only by a few baskets.

"Hi, Josephine. Did you march today?" Robert asked when we finally made it to his register.

"No, I didn't, but it looks like attendance was good." Alicia paid for the groceries and I picked up the sack and turned to go. "See you around, Robert."

"Right. I heard that some of your friends made it to the pokey in Salinas." I smiled back at him as if it were an everyday thing to have your friends locked up in the slammer, and then I remembered that I would have to drive twenty miles to Salinas in the morning.

Alicia drove home and parked in her garage along-side Ernie's compact Toyota. She touched her left foot and whimpered. I had forgotten all about it.

"How's the foot, Allie?"

"I won't know until I walk on it." I walked and Alicia limped into the kitchen where Trigger was pouring kibble for the two dogs.

"What's the matter, Mom?" Trigger asked, as he took the sack of groceries from me.

"Honey, you had a call from Mr. Mendoza," Ernie said. "He can't make it for dinner. Something came up. I take it you invited him over?"

"Yes. We talked to him today and he seemed so alone. Carlos wasn't there and his whole street was in chaos because of the protest march in Pajaro." She plopped down into a leather chair on wheels parked at her kitchen desk. I noticed her foot looked gray in spots and slightly swollen.

Alicia explained to Ernie what happened to her foot and he quickly found a little foot stool and a sack of frozen peas. "Nothing's too good for my baby," he joked, trying to make her smile.

"Allie, tell me what to do and I'll make dinner," I offered.

"The tamales are already steamed. You just need to warm them up and make the salad. I see Ernie has already made the beans and rice. Trigger, you can set the table. Wash your hands first."

By the time dinner was over and Solow and I were ready to go home, Alicia's foot looked black and blue and quite swollen. But, since she was still limping around, I figured it would be OK by the next day.

"Allie, if your foot hurts tomorrow, stay home, OK? Kyle and I will be fine without you." She nodded, everyone hugged and Solow and I headed home. I thought about the protest march all the way home. I switched on the lights and the furnace and then called Kyle.

"Hi, Kyle?"

"Like, yeah."

"This is Josephine. You sound awful. What happened?"

"My feet are killing me. I've been, like, marching all afternoon and then a cop whacked me with his baton just because I wouldn't get out of the street."

"Don't tell me you were in Pajaro."

"How did you know that?"

"Kyle, I'll be late to work tomorrow and Alicia might not be there at all, so you just continue painting the playground area ... sketches are in the red folder. If Hans asks for me, tell him I'll be there quick as I can."

"Playground, red folder and what?"

"Never mind. I won't be too late, I hope. Thanks, Kyle." I hung up and pressed the message button.

"Hi, Josie. Remember me? Sure seems like a long time away from you." David sighed. "You must be keeping busy. Every time I call, you're out. I'm still in Modesto so call me. Bye."

I put on the 10:00 o'clock news, turned the sound down and called David.

"Hello, Josie? Can't believe it's you."

"You're right, David, I've been so busy I meet myself coming and going. Guess who didn't go back to San Diego and moved in with me instead?"

"No, she didn't. That woman needs a job, or a man or something," David laughed. "I think I know what's been keeping you so busy. I watched the five o'clock news and now you're on again. You look like Rita Hayworth in her prime," he chuckled.

I looked up at the screen just in time to see myself being interviewed by a woman in a black pantsuit showing plenty of cleavage.

"Good grief! You mean I'm in the news in Modesto, too?"

"Yes, same thing I saw at five." The camera picked up on an army of police hustling protesters into two black vans. I saw a short cocky guy yelling at the police as they tossed him into one of the vehicles, and then they skipped back to a scene from earlier in the afternoon where hundreds of protesters held hands across the Pajaro Bridge, blocking it for hours.

"Look, they're using tear gas, David. Oh, did you see that woman take her top off ... oh, now they're all doing it. I wonder if Sarah participated in that event?"

"If I know Sarah, and I do know Sarah, she's in it all the way," he laughed. "How did you get involved in this stuff, Josie?"

"I'm not too involved, it just looks like I am. It's a long story and I hope to tell it to you in person one of these days."

"Like I said, Harley thinks the trial will be over first part of the week. I hope so. I miss you. How's Fluffy doing?"

"Oh, ah ... she's fine. I miss you too, David. Sweet dreams." We hung up. "Holy cat chow. I forgot about Fluffy." Solow looked up as I said the "Fluffy" word. "Let's go next door." Solow was up in a flash, ready to see his old nemesis. I grabbed a jacket and flashlight, and we pushed through knee-high grass all the way to David's house.

High clouds hid all traces of moon and starlight. If I hadn't known it was February, I would have sworn it was Halloween night. Eucalyptus trees rustled and an owl hooted in the distance. Solow stayed close to my side until I entered David's house and turned on the lights. We checked Fluffy's bowl on the kitchen floor. A few bites remained. They looked somewhat fresh. Even though Sarah had probably fed the cat in the morning, I refilled the bowl figuring I would have little time in the morning.

CHAPTER TEN

Monday morning I awoke to Johnny Mathis singing "That Certain Smile" on my clock radio. I let Johnny finish his song before I hit the off button and rolled out of bed. I sat on the edge of the mattress listening to the pitter patter of rain on the roof, feeling embarrassed all over again. Why did KPUT have to interview me? There were plenty of colorful characters to talk to. David must have thought I'd lost my mind.

Solow looked up from his doggie bed with love in his eyes, expecting food and a walk. "Want to go out?" He padded to the backdoor, did a U-turn and ducked back to his bed. I didn't blame him. It was wet and ugly out there. The pitter patter turned into a deluge as a roll of thunder rattled the windows. Solow's instincts had been right. Unfortunately, being a responsible human, I could not stay in my warm bed and sleep the day away. I had to spring the law breakers and then paint for a living.

I hurried through my morning shower, packed a lunch, fed Solow and myself and then we fed Ollie who was soaking wet, which made him look like he had lost ten pounds. He rubbed against my legs until my jeans were soaked. I took care of Ollie and headed home for a dry pair of dry pants. As I raced through the front door, I noticed I had a message. I pushed the button.

"Hi, Josephine. Hope you can pick up Steve and me around eleven this morning? Don't forget, it's the Salinas jail on Natividad Road. Thanks. You're a dear."

I plopped down on the sofa, hung my head and tried to gather my wits. It was only eight o'clock. Everything I needed for work was already in the truck and Solow waited patiently for me to start the engine. That settled it. I zipped up my dry Levis, ran through the rain to the truck and left Aromas.

San Juan Road started out looking normal, but the closer we came to Pajaro, the more rubbish I saw along the sides of the road. The people who dropped their water bottles, candy wrappers and picket signs were probably the same people who would march for a cleaner environment. Garbage floated on two feet of rain water that had collected overnight in the ditches lining the road.

The torrential rain slowed to a sprinkle as I lowered Solow out of the front seat. We scurried across the Therapy Center parking lot to the backdoor, entered and didn't stop until we were standing in front of the mural. I shivered, reminding myself that I had signed a contract to finish the painting, and that was what I intended to do.

An hour later I looked up from the pedal boat I was painting, to see Kyle shuffling down the hall. As he came closer I noticed something under his nose.

"Morning, Kyle. What's on your lip?" He let his fingers slide across his upper lip as if remembering something.

"I'm growing a mustache. Don't you remember? I had it last week."

"Sorry, guess I was too busy to notice."

Kyle looked disappointed. The mustache looked like a red, short-haired caterpillar crawling above his lip. It didn't go well with the ring in his nose.

Hans joined us wearing a lemon-sucking face. Judging by his thinning grey hair and expanding waistline, retirement wasn't far off.

"Good morning, Hans," I said, brightly.

"Yes … and I need to speak with you in my office." He twirled around and lumbered back to his upstairs retreat.

I dropped my brush into the water can. "Kyle, I'll just be a minute. Don't finish the whole painting while I'm gone."

"How could I … yeah, I'll save some for you, Jo."

I heard Hans close the door to his office, as I climbed the steps and knocked on his door.

"Come in, Josephine." Hans swiveled his chair around and waved me into a black lacquer chair with a rattan seat. "I don't know if you are aware of Mr. Thornton's interest in the Mendoza farm. Most people don't realize what goes into a project like the Solar Research Center." He looked at me to see if his words had registered.

"I didn't know Mr. Thornton was planning to build the Center. Where did you say he would like to build it?"

Hans brushed invisible lint off his immaculate trousers. "So this is the first you've heard about the new Center?" He raised an eyebrow as his double chin fell to one side.

"Oh, no, I saw the Solar Research Center proposal on TV, but they didn't say anything about whose farmland would be taken. How many acres will the Center need?"

"Ms. Stuart, I know, and you know, that you are trying to keep the Center from ever happening. Your picketing won't make a bit of difference to the supervisors, but it's very disturbing to Mr. Thornton since you are his employee." Hans pulled open a file drawer and rummaged around until he found the contract I had signed the week before.

"Do you happen to remember signing this?" He waved the stapled, two-piece contract in the air. "Remember the part about conflicting interests?"

"Mr. Coleberg, I'm not behind the picketing and I haven't done any of it myself. The camera man just found me." I knew how bad it looked. I tried to get comfortable in the hard chair and hoped my hot cheeks and beads of sweat across my forehead wouldn't give away my nervousness.

"It was my friend, Sarah, and her friend, Steve, who organized everything."

"And you just went along for the ride?" His upper lip curled in disbelief.

"I didn't even join the march or the protest. I happened to be in the neighborhood and the stupid reporter made it sound like I was in charge of everything." I flicked away a drop of sweat that ran down my forehead and pooled above my eyebrow. I heard voices and footsteps.

The door opened and Han stood up. "Good morning, Mr. Thornton … and Tavia. What a nice surprise," he cooed.

I stood up. Tavia grabbed my hand and patted it as if I were her long lost friend. "Joan, darling, so nice to see you again," she gushed.

"It's Josephine," I said as Willy shook my other hand.

"Fine job you're doing downstairs. Keep up the good work." He didn't mention marches or pickets or anything. In fact, I was very quickly ignored so I excused myself and left the room. I walked past the stairs and Andy's office, stood for a moment in front of Jim's office door, tried the knob and entered. The room looked as though it had gone through three spring cleanings and a car wash for good measure. The shelves were bare, along with the desk. Pale wintery light from a window enhanced the sad look of the room. I turned to go, but stopped when my eyes caught sight of the hapless metal wastebasket, scarred with dings.

"So, we meet again, darlin'," Tavia said, leaning against the door frame, one high-heeled foot holding her weight while the other foot rested against the door. She wore a black leather miniskirt, black heels and a sweater that looked like it came from a white rabbit. Her hair was a black-rooted blond ponytail and her face and body looked as natural as something manufactured by Mattel.

"Hi, Tavia … ah, I just wanted to see where poor old Jim used to work."

"Yes, well, this was his little ol' office. How did y'all know?"

"His name's printed on the door." I moved across

the room as Tavia backed out into the hallway. "I need to get back to work. See you later."

"Yes, y'all have a nice day." Heavy perfume had me holding my breath as I passed by her starved body.

All the way back to Kyle, I tried to put my finger on what made me feel so creepy when Tavia had appeared. She was polite to me. I had no quarrel with her, so why did I get the shivers every time I smelled her perfume?

I loaded my brush with paint and began working on another pedal boat, but it was difficult to concentrate on my work. Kyle was doing his part, probably lost in thought like me. A half hour later, I realized it was time to go get the jailbirds.

"Kyle, I'm afraid I have to run down to Salinas on an errand. See you in an hour."

"Before lunch?" he asked, sounding like the starving college student he was.

"Don't worry. I won't let you starve. And by the way, you're in charge of Solow." I hurried down the hall, out the backdoor and into a downpour. I was soaked just getting to my truck. All the way to Salinas, I ran the wipers on high. I poked along at 35 mph, barely keeping up with the rest of the traffic heading south on Highway One.

Finally, I left the highway, cut through Salinas on Natividad Road and parked in the public parking lot near the jail, better known as the Salinas Sheriff's Correction Bureau. Three figures moving toward the back of the building caught my eye. I let the engine idle so my wipers would keep working. I finally decided it was probably some other tall black young man with a shaved head being escorted to the backdoor by two uniformed deputies. I cut the engine, ran to the front entrance and pushed the door open.

"Josephine, hi. We're over here," Sarah shouted from down the hall. I saw her waving as she and Steve stood up from their seats on a bench beside six other protesters. They were smiling as if they had just come from a relaxing stay at a luxury spa retreat. My colorful paint clothes blended nicely with their wrinkled and worn looking tie-dyed T-shirts. I stopped in front of two long benches loaded with people sitting shoulder-to-shoulder.

"Anyone going to Watsonville?" I asked. No one spoke. "My little truck only seats two people ... I just thought-never mind."

"It will be fine, Josephine. I'll sit on Steve's lap." Sarah smiled down at the unshaven macho man. Steve's eyes became big and round at the thought of someone twice his weight sitting on top of him all the way home.

"I have a little errand to run. Could you two wait here a few more minutes?"

Sarah giggled and nodded. Steve took a deep breath, and they both went back to their conversation with a couple of young protesters.

I wanted to check out the man I saw in the parking lot who looked way too much like Justin. I didn't know where I was going as I hurried down the hall, made a right and headed toward the back of the building. Ahead of me three people walked abreast of each other. I bumped up my pace and as I came closer, I decided the one in the middle was definitely Justin. He towered over the deputies.

"Justin!" I yelled. He tried to turn his head as they all stopped on a dime. I recognized Deputy Sayer with his balding head and khaki uniform. Deputy Lund, wearing the same mannish type khaki uniform, recognized me.

"Something we can do for you, Ms. Stuart?" she asked.

Seeing a pair of silver handcuffs around Justin's wrists left me speechless. I just stood with my mouth open.

Justin asked the woman if he could speak to me. She nodded slightly. "But make it quick," she barked.

"Josephine, I need you to take care of … Megan, ah, my cat." He looked into my eyes as if he wanted me to understand something. Something important.

"Sure. I didn't even know you had a cat," I said. Oh dear, did I say the wrong thing? Justin's jaw tightened and his stare was intense. Maybe he didn't really have a cat. I hoped I didn't mess anything up for him.

"Can you get my keys?" he asked Deputy Sayer, as he pointed a finger at his right Levi pocket. The man awkwardly reached into Justin's pocket and threw me a set of keys. The threesome turned and continued down the hall.

"Wait a minute," I shouted, as I ran up behind them. They all stopped and turned to look. "Justin, where are they taking you? Are you under …?"

"I think so. Just take care of Megan. I'll get a lawyer."

"No problem. I love cats."

I watched deputies Sayer and Lund steer Justin over to a desk in an alcove where another uniformed deputy sat ready to create a pile of paperwork. They pushed their prisoner down into a chair and stood close by, ready to take on the Marine if they had to. There was no doubt in my mind that Justin could take on all comers with muscle to spare, cuffed or not, if he had wanted to.

I finally decided there was nothing I could do for my friend except take care of Megan, whatever that meant. I walked back to the benches full of ex-protesters, feeling a huge weight on my shoulders and a pain in my heart. Justin had suffered the loss of his grandfather and now he was locked up ... but why?

Sarah saw me coming up the hall. "Josephine, what's wrong?"

"Nothing, just thinking."

"We have a plan for Thursday, you know, for the council meeting," she whispered, looking around to see if anyone heard.

"That's great, but I think we should go now." Steve jumped up and led the way to the front entrance. Outside, buckets of rain fell on us as we ran for the truck. Steve held the door for Sarah, which meant she would be on the bottom. He climbed up onto her lap while she giggled. I felt like a chaperone at a sock hop for twelve-year olds.

"Steve's plan is so exciting," Sarah said, her voice muffled by the manly body leaning against her. We definitely had too many hot bodies steaming up the windows.

"So, what's the plan, Steve?" I couldn't see to drive

an inch until the fog cleared, so I started the engine and flipped on the defrost.

"I have a few ideas," he said, his shoulders bent forward and his head pressed against the ceiling. "We'll pass out leaflets to the public a couple of hours before the meeting, you know, explaining our position. That's not all. We'll set up a TV interview for you with KPUT. Should I make it for Thursday afternoon?" Steve asked.

"Ah, I think ... oh yeah, I have a dentist appointment that day." Lying had gotten easier with practice.

"That's OK, Josephine. Steve looks great on TV and he speaks so well." Sarah giggled. "You don't mind, do you, Steve?"

"I don't mind if it's OK with you, Josephine."

"I don't mind," I said, feeling greatly relieved.

Steve held onto the window visor with both hands as I made a sharp turn onto Natividad.

"By the way, you can let Sarah and me out at my paint store. My friend, Alberto, parked my VW up there." After Steve's instructions, we rode in blessed silence all the way to Watsonville. I pulled up in front of ABC Paint. The middle-aged teenyboppers jumped out.

I whipped the truck around, headed over to Pajaro and parked beside Alicia's Volvo at the Center. Solow met me halfway down the hall, his tail in a non-stop wagging mode. As we walked up to Kyle and Alicia sitting on paint cans eating their lunch, I noticed my friend wore an unusual sort of boot on her left foot. It was big and black with Velcro straps.

"Alicia, what's with the boot? Are you OK?"

"It seems one little bone was broken so I have to wear this thing for at least four weeks," she smiled.

"The good news is, I can get around pretty well and even paint. I picked up some fast food for lunch. Care for some nachos?"

"Sounds good. I need to drown myself in comfort food. You won't believe my day so far." I told my two friends all about the jail experience. When I was finished, Alicia asked me why I thought Justin didn't own a cat named Megan.

"In the first place, the cat would have to be Jim's because Justin was usually away being a Marine. In the second place, I don't remember seeing any sign of a cat on the property, in the main house or in Justin's cottage. No food bowls, rubber mice, nothing."

"Maybe he was trying to, like, tell you something," Kyle offered, his mouth full of bean burrito.

"Yes, what sounds like Megan?" Alicia asked, as she stared at the ceiling.

I kept searching my mind for an answer, feeling like it was right under my nose. Justin had given me the keys to his house, so I planned to start there right after work. I ran the Megan thing through my head over and over as I painted children in canoes and pedal boats. Normally, I would have projected myself right into the painting. In my mind, I would have been the child in the boat, but I couldn't concentrate on my work until I figured out what Mega … oh, my God! My heart skipped a beat. I knew.

Five o'clock came slowly, but finally it was time to go home. I followed Alicia as she kah-thunked down the hall in her black boot. Kyle and Solow were the first ones out the door. The night was cool, dry, and moonlit. Stars appeared in the east even before all the streaks of crimson had faded from the west.

"Good night, Jo," Alicia said, and Kyle repeated the sentiment.

"Good night you guys." I hurried to my truck and hiked Solow into his seat. I was so excited about my revelation I could barely think about driving. We made it safely to Jim's house on Lower Cutter, only to discover a deputy sheriff's patrol car sitting in the driveway. The patrol car lights were off. Two uniforms sat in the front seats with steamy drinks. We kept on going down the narrow road until I found a place to turn around. As we passed the patrol car a second time, I thought I recognized Officer Lund. I hoped she hadn't seen me. I mentally canceled plan A and went directly to plan B.

CHAPTER ELEVEN

I left Lower Cutter and drove four blocks to Alicia's house. Ernie answered the door, hugged me and patted Solow's head.

"Josephine, how are you? Come in." He scratched his head. "Allie just got home from work. She didn't say you were ...." I heard Alicia's boot kah-thunking to the front door.

"Hi, Jo. What's up? Come in ... it's cold out there."

"Allie ... I have an unusual request. Ah, actually, I was wondering if I could borrow the pedal boat ... just for one little trip?"

Alicia cocked her head to one side. At her request, we moved into the living room and sat down. Trigger ran into the room from the kitchen and plunked himself down next to me.

"What do you think about Jo using your boat, Trigger?" Ernie asked his son.

"You mean now, in the dark? Can I go too? Mom never lets me go in the dark."

"I just need your boat for a short little ride. I think you should stay here, honey. It's cold tonight."

Trigger folded his arms and puckered his lips.

"Now, honey, I'm sure Jo has a very important reason for wanting to use your boat. It would be nice if you would let her use it, don't you think?" Alicia said, looking at me as if I had gone completely bonkers.

"Sure, you can use it," Trigger grumbled and ran up the stairs to his room. Solow followed Tansey, who followed her master. I felt like following them but decided to hurry up with plan B. Justin was depending on me.

"Let me help you with the boat," Ernie said. He flipped on the backyard floodlights and we made our way across the wet lawn, dodging puddles all the way to the dock. The lake water was as black as Garth's Corvette except on the eastern side where a quarter-moon reflected on the water. The pedal boat bobbed up and down, rubbing noisily against one of the dock pilings. A large bird beat its wings across the lake.

"Just show me what to do," I whispered.

"Sure. Why are we whispering?"

I automatically looked to my left, at Justin's cottage. "I just don't want to attract attention."

"I see." Ernie smiled but didn't laugh at me even though he probably wanted to. He must have thought I'd lost my mind, but he untied the rope and told me how to pedal. "Just like a bicycle. Push hard. You can do it." He held my arm as I climbed down three wooden steps at the end of the dock and leaped onto the hard plastic bench seat of Trigger's boat.

"Thank you Ernie," I whispered. My feet found the pedals. I pushed hard and then harder. The boat moved a bit. Another round of pushing and another couple yards forward. At that rate, I worried the sun would come up before I reached Justin's beach. Pretty soon I figured out how to use my weight to get things moving and finally had a rhythm going. I imagined a fellow behind me, pressing me onward with the beat of a drum. My legs began to ache, but there was no time for self-pity.

The aerobic workout finally paid off. I tied the boat to Justin's dock, gingerly stood up on spongy legs and climbed onto the wooden structure.

My heart was racing as I stole across the dock and jumped a couple of feet down to the little beach. Off to my right, a duck quacked a single quack and I jumped. I took a deep breath and kept going, maneuvering my feet around various groupings of ducks sleeping on the sand and lawn. I thought about the duck poop I couldn't see and was probably stepping on.

Moonlight glanced off the long front window of Justin's cottage. It was the only light on the half-acre property. I skulked across the lawn, aiming a little left of the moon's reflection, not able to see the ground under my feet. As I approached the cottage, I took a step, slammed my foot into a brick curb, fell to my knees and bit my lip quietly. I sat for a moment listening.

Air swished by my left ear as something swooped and flapped its wings—maybe a bat. I cringed. All my irrational childhood fears rose to the surface. I jerked my head around, right and left, to make sure there were no more winged critters near me.

I stood and slowly crept up the path beside the cottage, keeping in the shadows. At the front corner of the house, I turned right and faced the front door. Fortunately, the cottage could not be seen from the road because Jim's house obstructed the view.

I pulled out the keychain Justin had given me and

tried one key after another. The fourth key turned and I was in, but what to do about light? What if someone wandered into the backyard and found lights on in the cottage? I heard a dog bark next door and was paralyzed for a moment, unable to think.

Finally my mind began to work, not really well, but enough to notice green digital numbers on an appliance about ten feet away. I felt my way into the kitchen area and opened the microwave oven door which sent a weak trail of light into the room. I looked around to see if the blinds were closed. When all the curtains and blinds were tightly shut, I headed toward the bookcase in the living room. The microwave light didn't reach that far so I used my hands to feel as I shuffled along. I remembered how Justin had picked up the briefcase by reaching down and to his right.

I smelled musty books in front of me. My senses were heightened to a point where I could have given Solow's expert nose some competition. I bent down and ran my hand along the bottom shelf until I came to a large object. Not a book. I hoisted the heavy leather case up to my chest and smiled.

The smile quickly disappeared when I heard footsteps outside and saw the bobbing lights from flashlights. I froze for a second, gathered my wits and ran for an open door to my right. I heard men talking outside, and then a woman laughed.

"The door isn't even locked," the female said.

I entered a dark room and managed to knock my sore foot into a bedpost. Clumsily, I felt my way along the walls, located a closet and ducked inside. I pushed hanging jackets and slacks in front of me and tried not to breathe as I cowered in the corner of the closet, sitting on the briefcase, wondering if I could plead insanity if I were discovered.

A female laughed sarcastically.

"Look at this. He left his microwave open. Men!" I recognized Deputy Lund's voice.

Someone turned on lights in the living room, sending light under the closet door. I panicked, pulled some shirts off their hangers and draped the clothing over my head and body. I curled myself onto a tight ball, hoping to look like a pile of laundry.

Heavy steps tromped over the wood floor in the living room.

"It's a big old briefcase. You can't miss it," a man said, clearing his throat.

I heard the search, the moving of furniture, books hitting the floor and lots of mumbling and swearing from two males. But the worst was when I heard footsteps near the closet door. Someone was in the bedroom. There was more shuffling of stuff, a big sigh, silence and then, "ah-hah".

Oh no! Not the clos ... I thought to myself.

The closet door opened and light streamed in. I held my breath as I sat paralyzed, unable to think or even blink. The toe of one shoe stuck out. I pulled it back under a shirt sleeve as my heart thundered in my ears. It seemed loud enough to wake the whole neighborhood, but the searcher didn't hear it and left the room. Streams of perspiration ran down my forehead. My mouth felt dry and time stood still as I waited an eternity for the lights to go out.

"Officer Lund, did you check in there?"

"Sure did—the closet, too."

"I told you we should search the SUV."

"Yeah, yeah, we'll do it now."

"Cal, we're already on overtime. Let's not take too long, OK?" she implored.

"It's important that we recover these files, ma'am," the second man said, after he cleared his throat and blew his nose with a loud honk. I heard the front door close. The voices faded and the neighbor dog barked as they walked the path up to Jim's front door.

I sat still, collecting my thoughts. Finally, I tucked the briefcase under my arm and stood up on wobbly legs. I slowly felt my way to the living room and then the door by the kitchen.

Once I was outside I sucked in a deep breath of cold air and listened to water slapping the dock a hundred feet away. I crept down the path, sliding my left hand along the side of the house. As I approached the end of the building, a stream of light caught me from behind. I fell forward onto the wet grass. Still holding onto the briefcase, I crawled like a snake around the corner of the house, stood up and ran past the front window. I slid behind a giant rhododendron bush, heart pounding and sweat running down my face.

Deputy Lund yelled to her partner. "Over here, hurry. Someone's behind the house," she shouted, as she waved the flashlight back and forth across the lawn trying to find me again.

Heavy footsteps raced down the path. Another flashlight bobbed around, spotlighting piles of indignant ducks.

I knew it was only a matter of time before they

looked behind the bush. I had to keep moving so I ducked behind a prickly holly tree (ouch) and then crept over to a clump of young redwood trees. From there I scrambled over the neighbor's rickety five-foot-high fence. Ms. Occupant flipped on the porch light just as I landed on top of her backyard decorations. Within my reach was a gazing ball, a miniature white-plastic picket fence and several concrete gnomes. I sat nose-to-nose with a pink plastic flamingo until the woman went back inside.

I finally caught my breath, stood up and angled myself around most of the yard stuff. A child's plastic chair caught me by surprise and sent me chin first into a large pile of leaves. The briefcase flew ahead, knocking down a bearded gnome.

"What's all that racket? Who's out there?" Ms. Occupant shouted, as she stepped onto her little porch, giving me the pulse of a race horse. I huddled in the shadows, barely breathing. She finally slammed her door and turned out the light.

I heard Officers Sayer and Lund discussing who or what might be in Justin's yard and then what was going on next door. I had to think fast and hide the briefcase. The deputies would be hopping the fence any minute. I felt around in the dark for the case, found it and tucked it under the pile of musty leaves.

The two sheriff's deputies climbed over the fence just as I bellied down to the sandy beach and slipped into the water like a thirsty trout. A snorkel would have been nice, but it wasn't an option. I held my breath, closed my eyes and swam underwater in the direction of Trigger's boat. I didn't bother to open my eyes because the water was darker than Tavia's black pumps and smelled like duck droppings. On one breath and tons of adrenalin, I was able to swim almost fifty feet. I stopped suddenly, gasping for air when my head hit the side of Trigger's pedal boat. My head throbbed and stars floated in front of my eyes.

"Did you hear something? Look over there and I'll go this way," Deputy Sayer ordered. I watched them train their flashlights on one piece of junk after another all over the neighbor's property. I saw the lights change direction and bob down the beach to Justin's dock and then full circle back to the cottage and beyond. By that time, my body was numb and my lips were in a non-stop tremble. I held onto the side of the boat, trying not to imagine what kind of slimy creatures might be swimming in Drew Lake at night.

The neighbor dog barked again as the sheriff's deputies retreated up the path to Lower Cutter. I listened until I could hear nothing except the lapping of water against pilings. Carefully I climbed into the boat, which was no easy task in wet clothes, untied the rope and pedaled my shivering body over to Alicia's dock.

"Ahoy! How was the trip, Josephine? You're drenched!" Ernie said as he helped me onto the dock and secured the boat.

My mouth trembled too much to answer. My whole body trembled and shook until I thought I would shake all my teeth loose.

Ernie put his arm around my waist and helped me to the backdoor where Alicia waited.

"What did you do, fall out of the boat?" Alicia asked with big round eyes and a hand held out to help me.

As soon as she steadied my other side, Ernie let go. A minute later, he was back with a big white blanket. He wrapped it around me and they both helped me into a chair. The shivers wouldn't stop.

"Jo, what happened?" Trigger yelled as he charged down the stairs, two at a time. "Did my boat sink?"

"No, Trigger, your boat didn't sink. Let's give Josephine a little time to warm up."

"OK, Dad." Trigger automatically reached out to pat my hand. "Don't worry, Auntie Jo. I don't care about that old boat anymore."

"Jo, come with me. A warm shower will do wonders," Alicia said, helping me up from the chair. She wobbled and tipped toward Ernie. He steadied her and held my elbow with his other hand.

"Honey, I'll help Jo upstairs. You sit down and put your foot up. Doctor's orders!"

Ernie helped me upstairs, gave me a clean towel and a soft terrycloth robe and then headed downstairs. My skin stung under the warm water, but I stayed until the stinging subsided and I was squeaky clean.

I thought about the third person in Justin's cottage. Who was he? Why did he want the briefcase, and how would I retrieve it? Nothing could be done about Megan that night so I shoved it out of my mind. I wrapped myself in the terry robe, dried my hair with Alicia's hair dryer and joined the Quintanas downstairs.

"Thanks, you guys. I feel great now." I sat in front of a crackling fire in the big brick fireplace. Trigger ran upstairs and came back with a pair of Alicia's slippers.

"Thanks Trigger, for everything. What's that

heavenly smell?"

"Ernie made a pot of albondigas soup. The meat-balls are guaranteed to warm up your insides," Alicia said, smiling. "But first let's go upstairs and find some-thing for you to wear."

I followed Alicia to her bedroom, wondering how in the world I would be able to fit my size twelve bones into her size six clothes. Luckily, I was able to stuff my mature body into a pair of sweat pants and shirt. In the meantime, my wet clothes were being run through the washer and dryer.

"Jo, did you go to Justin's house tonight?"

"Sure did. I figured out what Megan sounds like ... Megamall. What do you think?"

"But what about Megamall? What's the signifi-cance?"

"It's a long story. Justin showed me an email from Megamall that Andy gave to Jim. It was about building a mall in Pajaro."

"How can that be? The mall was voted down, re-member?"

"I remember, but someone is lining up the various shops and anchor stores." I took a deep breath and sighed. "Someone wants Jim's briefcase real bad. I al-most got caught taking the thing. It's in the neighbor's yard under a pile of leaves for now. Hope it doesn't rain again."

Alicia's mouth dropped open. "What are you going to do?"

"Do you happen to know anything about Justin's neighbor in the old blue house with white trim and a palm tree in the backyard?" I watched her look at the ceiling, trying to remember the blue house across the lake.

She shook her head. "I don't know anyone on that side of the lake except Justin. Sorry."

Just then we heard Trigger bounding up the steps. "Soup's on!" he yelled, turned and ran back down to the kitchen. Because of Alicia's foot, we took our time going down the stairs. The albondigas soup was served with individual corn and cheese quesadillas.

"This is a wonderful meal, Ernie. When did you have time to do all this?" I asked.

"All in a day's work," he smiled. "Actually, Trigger helped."

"Daddy stayed home today. He took Mama to the doctor this morning."

"All in a day's work?" I laughed. Pretty soon we were all chatting about one thing and another. I felt so relaxed I could have stayed all night, but I had things to do at home. After dinner, Trigger gathered my clothes from the dryer and brought them to me.

"Thank you, big guy." I excused myself to change. When I came back, Solow and Tansey were lapping up leftovers from a couple of bowls on the kitchen floor. As soon as the bowls were empty, we took our leave.

I thought about the boat trip to Justin's as I drove home. Who was the man looking for the briefcase? I suddenly became aware of my surroundings when my headlights glommed onto an old Volkswagen bus parked in front of my house.

"Good grief!" I checked my watch. It was almost nine. "I wish I could be home alone, except for you, Solow. I love having you around." He licked my hand as I helped him down from his seat. The porch light went on and the front door opened.

"Hi, Josephine," Steve said. "I was just leaving."

"We've had the most glorious day," Sarah swooned. To Steve she giggled, "See you."

He raised a hand, thumb pointed up and climbed into his bus.

Sarah and I entered the house and I immediately collapsed on the sofa, but Sarah was still full of pep. "Steve talked to his councilman friend. He said the Solar Research Center, parking lot included, will take up less than four acres of the fifty-acre parcel. He thinks someone has plans for something much bigger."

"I think he's right," I said.

Sarah squinted one eye as if to say, "How do you know that?" But I didn't go any further with the subject because my eyes were heavy, my house was warm and the sofa was soft under my aching calves.

Sarah rambled on about whatever until I couldn't hear her any more.

I dreamt I was belted into a speedboat heading for downtown Salinas. Suddenly angry picketers stopped the boat and crowded around trying to grab shoes off a giant pile of high heels in the back seat. I noticed Tavia was driving. She cranked the wheel and the boat spun around, skimming right over the protesters. They were all flattened out like paper dolls. A gust of wind blew them away.

CHAPTER TWELVE

I finally convinced my tired achy body it was time to get out of bed. It was Tuesday, a work day, so I rolled out of bed, pulled on a robe and found Solow in the kitchen with Sarah. She was reading the newspaper aloud to my adoring dog.

"I hope he gets more out of the paper than I do," I said.

Sarah giggled. "I'd trade all my cats for just one Solow." She took a sip of coffee and offered me a cup. "Is there anything I can do for you today? I don't have much going on."

"Yeah, shop around for a new body. I need to replace mine. I think the odometer hit two hundred thousand last night." I took a sip of hot coffee.

Sarah scrunched her eyebrows together. "You don't look too bad ... except for the scratches on your face and hands." She paused for an explanation, but didn't get one. "Oh, by the way, an attorney named Mr. Wellborn called. He wanted you to call him right away. He gave me his home phone and cell phone numbers." One eyebrow rose upward. "Like more coffee?"

"Sure, I need all I can get." I let Solow out for a run and came back to the kitchen table. Sarah and I drank coffee and talked about the weather until I felt like I was energized enough to call Mr. Wellborn. It was early, only seven forty-five, but the man answered on the second ring.

He cleared his throat.

"Ms. Stuart, on behalf of my client, Justin Keeper, I called to find out if you had any success finding the poor cat named Megan?" The man's voice reminded me of someone, but I couldn't put a face to it.

"I had her, but she got away," I said. Sarah must have been listening from across the room. She stared at the newspaper, trying to be polite and not eavesdrop, but I knew she was curious.

"Do you expect to find her again … soon?" He emphasized the soon.

"I'll capture the little rascal today for sure. Tell Justin not to worry."

"Thank you, Ms. Stuart. My client will be happy to see his cat safely tucked away." He cleared his throat again and continued. "I would like very much to see this cat once it is in your possession. Are you available this evening for dinner … Green Valley Grill, shall we say … seven?"

"Uh, sure. But what if I can't find Megan?"

"Call me."

"OK, Green Valley Grill at seven." I heard a click and hung up.

"Everything all right, Josephine?" Sarah asked, studying my face.

"Oh, sure. But I won't be home for dinner tonight. I'm going to take a shower now." I drifted down the hall and into the bathroom—alone at last. Warm water comforted me as my mind traveled ahead of real time.

I wondered how I would face Mr. Wellborn and Justin if I failed to retrieve the briefcase. I reluctantly turned off the shower and prepared myself for work.

Sarah had prepared Eggs Benedict with berries and cream on the side, the perfect send-off from an under-appreciated houseguest. After breakfast my first stop was Oliver's house and the first thing I noticed was a fresh little puddle of motor oil on the asphalt driveway. I stood beside my truck for a moment, thinking. Whoever left the oil was obviously gone.

Oliver appeared from behind the house looking for love or food or both, his motor on overdrive. Too bad he couldn't tell me who had leaked the oil.

"Hi there, ol' buddy." My voice caused his motor to rev up another notch as he made figure eights around my legs. "Let's get you some food."

As soon as Ollie was fed, watered and loved, I motored down Otis, trying to formulate a plan to rescue Megan. I parked next to Alicia's Volvo, noticing that the parking lot had all the usual vehicles, Tavia's red Jag, Garth's black Vette, a white Lincoln, a black BMW and scads of pickups.

I hustled inside and down the hall to where Alicia stood contemplating the mural. I parked my purse and little cooler out of the way of hall traffic, stepped back, and saw that the mural was beginning to take shape.

"Good morning, Jo. Where's Solow?"

"Morning, Allie. I left him home with Sarah. She's crazy about him. She even read the newspaper to him this morning."

"How are you feeling today?" She inspected me carefully. "The scratches look a little better this morning.

Too bad about that cat fight with Megan." We laughed.
"I talked to Justin's lawyer this morning. He wants
Megan, and I promised to get it for him. Today! How
am I going to do that, Allie?"

"Maybe I can help. I'll talk to the people in the blue
house if they're home. Meanwhile, you run to the backyard and grab the briefcase."

"You have a real flair for undercover work, don't
you? It might work. After all, who wouldn't talk to a
gal with a gimpy foot? Can you come with me on our
lunch break?"

"You're the boss," she laughed.

Once that was settled I put my mind on the mural.
We painted until the lunch break, dropped our brushes
in water and headed for the backdoor. Just as I passed
the stairs, I remembered I needed to visit the restroom.

"I'll meet you at the truck. Here are the keys." I
handed them to Alicia, turned and entered the powder
room. Inside the state-of-the-art granite everywhere
lavatory, the air smelled like cigarette smoke and gardenia blossoms. Tavia stood in front of the ten-foot mirror watching herself blow smoke through her nose like
a self-absorbed dragon.

"Tavia, how are you today?" I asked, obviously
catching her in a personal moment.

"Oh, … I'm peachy fine, Ms. Stuart. How sweet of
you to ask. Remember, honey, just because we're
friends doesn't excuse you from a certain little contract
you signed. I hope your work as a painter keeps you
busy and out of trouble for the next few days. Politics
doesn't become you."

"What do you mean …?" Slam. Tavia was out the

door and I wondered if she meant I shouldn't march or protest or what? I seriously considered marching after that scolding, but then I thought about the Salinas Correction Facility and dropped the idea like a hot picket sign.

Luckily, I made it to my truck without running into any more big shots with threats to throw at me. Alicia sang along with a twangy country tune on the radio as I climbed into the driver's seat.

"Everything OK, Jo? You look angry."

"Sure, I'm OK. I don't have time to worry about Ms. Thornton."

"You ran into Tavia?" she asked.

I nodded. "She seems very interested in my extra curricular activities. She thinks I'm a protest marcher working in the opposite interests of the Thorntons. Actually, I'm just a quiet farm sympathizer."

"Maybe she watches the local news," Alicia smiled.

"I know how it looks. Hans thinks the same as Tavia." I made a right onto the Pajaro Bridge and minutes later we were driving down Lower Cutter to Jim's house. "Allie, do you know what you're going to say to the neighbor if he or she happens to be home?"

"I'm going to take a survey for Golden Days Magazine," Alicia said.

"I've never heard of that magazine. Is it new?"

"It's about ten minutes old," she laughed as she pulled a notebook out of her purse. "The first questions will be: Are there any retired folks living in the neighborhood and how do they feel about retirement activities in Watsonville?"

I parked the truck in a grassy wide spot just one lot

short of Jim's house. Alicia and I separated. She walked
two doors up to the blue house and I walked a shorter
distance to Jim's. The place looked quiet, no cars
around and I didn't hear any voices. I cautiously
walked down the driveway to the narrow path at the
side of the house, and found it so much easier to navigate in daylight.

The path ended. I turned left, crossed the vacant
lawn and headed down to the mini-beach. Dozens of
mallards swam by, followed by two large Toulouse
geese who probably thought they were ducks. I had a
clear path to the next door neighbor's beach. Once I
passed the fence, I hung a left into Ms. Occupant's cluttered yard. The pile of leaves was still there. I bent
down to swipe the leaves away.

"Whatcha' doin'?" a little voice asked. I jumped,
which was silly because in my mind I knew immediately it was a young child speaking. My heart restarted.
I looked up to the porch where a preschooler stood
alone holding his ratty little blanket to his ear. He wore
half his lunch on his face and shirt.

I waved and smiled, acting casual and trying to
blend in with the backyard décor. I grabbed the briefcase and stepped back, feeling foolish in front of the little boy. I backed into the fence, rounded it, turned and
ran. I made it across the beach and lawn before the
barking began. The dog was big, brown and separated
from me by a wimpy chicken wire fence. I didn't try to
make friends.

As I approached the front corner of Jim's house, I
looked to my right and saw Alicia standing at the
neighbor's front door. If I had taken another step forward,

the occupant would have been able to see me. I waved at my friend until she saw me in the corner of her eye. She talked a moment longer and then I heard the door close. We both headed for my truck. "Piece a cake!" I said to myself.

"What are you smiling about?" Alicia asked.

"A little munchkin scared me. I was so nervous I almost wet my pants, but I got the briefcase. I sure hope Megan will help to Justin." I turned the key and we motored across town to the Therapy Center. "Thanks for helping me, Allie. Did your magazine survey work?"

"Actually, I had to cut Greta off when I saw you waving. She loved having an audience for her volumes of information. Everything you would ever want to know about the neighbors," Alicia chuckled. We were still laughing as we walked into the Center, but the mood was cut short by angry words from upstairs.

"You can't tell me what to do. He's my friend," Garth shouted.

"You're just like your father. Always think you're right, don't you? You think you're so smart. Well, I say you can't go. Thorntons do not associate with little ol' farmers and sons of farmers," Tavia screamed.

"He's my friend. Take it up with my dad if you want." A door slammed upstairs. Garth tore down the stairs and out the backdoor, barely missing us as we did our best not to look like eavesdroppers. Alicia and I hurried down to the mural, ate our lunches quickly, and did some serious painting until 4:30.

"Let's call it a day, Allie. You've been on that foot way too long. Besides, I have to go home and change for my dinner appointment."

"Wonder what Mr. Wellborn looks like," she winked.

"I just hope he's a good lawyer for Justin's sake," I said, remembering the misery I had seen in the young Marine's eyes. "See you tomorrow." I walked to my Mazda pickup and Alicia kah-thunked her way to the Volvo station wagon.

"Have a nice time, Jo." Alicia laughed and waved.

On my way home I noticed Garth's black Vette parked in front of Mr. Mendoza's house. I wondered how the old farmer felt about Garth. Was he judgmental like Tavia?

What about Tavia's son, Mark? Did he have any farmer friends? I doubted it.

I drove past lettuce, cabbage and berry farms until the road headed up into the foothills to my snug little home. I was happy to see that a certain VW bus wasn't there.

"Josephine, how was work?" Sarah asked, as she and Solow met me at the front door. "You're home a little early. I'm washing sheets and towels today. Shall I wash yours?"

"Sure. Thanks, Sarah. How was your day?"

"You'll never guess who came home today." Before I could make a guess, she continued. "David is finally home."

My heart did a little dance. "Is he home right now?"

"Actually, he drove to the grocery store. Said he would be back in time to see you before you leave for your dinner date," Sarah said.

"Great. I mean, I can't wait to see him." I wished I hadn't agreed to meet Mr. Wellborn for dinner. Why did

Sarah have to tell David I had a date?

"What's the matter? You look pale," she said.

"Just tired, I guess." I turned and walked to my room where I planned to flop down on my bed and rest. One problem, the blankets were in a pile and the sheets were missing so I wandered over to the kitchen and sat at the table.

Sarah joined me. "Actually, I threw your sheets into the washing machine before you got home," she confessed. "I just want to help out as much as I can until Sunday."

"What happens Sunday?" I tried to sound interested.

"Did I forget to tell you? I'm sorry. I fly home Sunday. But don't worry, Steve's taking me to the airport."

"How long have you known Steve?"

"Oh, Steve and I go way back to high school. He had so many girlfriends he never even noticed me; that is, until I filled out in the twelfth grade." She blushed. "We dated a few times before I went away to college."

It was easy to imagine the rest. Tall, dark and handsome David came along and Steve was forgotten.

"Is Steve still the romantic guy you used to know?" Solow squeezed under the table between the chairs and rested half his body on my feet.

"We've changed." She looked down at Solow.

"Guess I'll get myself cleaned up for dinner." What I really meant was, I'll fix myself up before David gets back from the store. I hadn't seen him for a long time and I missed him like crazy. My heather-green pantsuit with black scarf and heels would suffice.

At six sharp the doorbell rang. Sarah jumped up

from the sofa and opened the door. "David, what beautiful roses ... they must be for Josephine."

I jerked my rocking chair to a halt and stood up. "David, it's nice to have you home again." He set the roses down on the coffee table.

"Hi, Josie." He gave me a tender hug. "Hope you have a vase for these." He smiled, picked up the long-stemmed red roses and handed them to me.

"David, they're lovely."

"Guess I won't see you tonight." He straightened his shoulders.

"I have a business meeting tonight at seven," I explained, as if he didn't know already. One of his eyebrows stretched upward.

"It is business," I said. "I'll explain it all later. Would anyone like a cup of coffee?" Sarah nodded and rushed to the kitchen to take advantage of another opportunity to be helpful around the house. After arranging the roses in a large vase, I sat down at the kitchen table and listened to Mr. Coffee perk his little heart out. David sat across the table from Sarah and me, but his eyes were trained on mine and I wished Sarah was already back in San Diego. In no time at all, it was six forty-five.

"I'm afraid I have to go now," I said, feeling like I was turning my back on a prince to have dinner with a possible ogre. I hoped Mr. Wellborn would be tolerable company.

I sped down San Juan Road to Watsonville, turned onto Penny Lane and made a sharp left into the parking lot reserved for Green Valley Grill patrons. I couldn't help noticing a very distinguished-looking gentleman in a three-piece suit standing near the entrance, patting his nose with a handkerchief.

I watched him through the windshield as I opened the briefcase, pulled out the infamous email, folded it three times and stuffed it into my purse. As I approached the four-story building, the gentleman locked eyes with me and cleared his throat.

"Ms. Stuart, I presume."

"Mr. Wellborn, call me Josephine." His chiseled features looked even better close up. His light brown hair, streaked with gray, was combed back and still damp from a shower with lavender soap. He smelled better than Mom's apple pie. However, his most outstanding feature was the color of his eyes. Cobalt blue.

"And I'm Charlie." A deep dimple appeared in each cheek when he smiled.

"Nice to meet you, Charlie. I hope you didn't have to wait long." I noticed he was an inch or two shorter than David, but still on the tall side as men go. He cleared his throat.

"Shall we go in? It's a little nippy out here."

We entered the building, rode a slow elevator to the third floor without a word and stepped out onto the teal carpet of the Green Valley Grill. The greeter immediately showed us to a table in the far corner against a wall of windows. I had the feeling Charlie had used this table before. The tips of redwood branches brushed against the glass, back-lit by headlights from Green Valley Road traffic. A candle flickered as Charlie and I chatted.

After we ordered our dinners, I handed him the email. He unfolded it, read quickly, refolded it and put it in his breast pocket.

"Thanks for capturing that rascally old cat," he said,

with a movie star grin.

"I just had the craziest thought." I looked into his very blue eyes and forgot what I was about to say.

"Oh? What's your crazy idea?" he asked.

"Um, oh yeah ... I was just wondering if you have ever been to Justin's house. The lake is beautiful, you know."

"As a matter of fact, I was there last night. I had a couple of officers take me through his house to see if we could find Megan. Unfortunately, Megan was gone and it was too dark to see the lake." He brought out a handkerchief and blew his nose discretely. Poor man must have had allergies.

"Yes, you really missed something if you didn't see the lake," I said, ending my fishing expedition. Charlie gave no indication he knew I had been in the cottage that night so I changed the subject.

"Do you think Justin will get out on bail?"

"I think so, but you never can tell for sure. Depends on the judge. Unfortunately, some of Justin's story doesn't hold together, and then, of course, there's motive."

"What do you mean, motive? Justin loved his grandfather more than anyone in the world. He worshiped the man," I said loud enough to turn a few heads at tables near us.

'I'm sure he did. On the other hand, he had everything to gain as the only living relative and beneficiary. Maybe he couldn't wait for the old man to ... you know ... die."

"That's nonsense and you know it." My cheeks burned.

"Now take it easy. I'm just telling you what the

prosecutor will try to use against Justin. After all, someone has already come forward and said he saw Justin's SUV at the Therapy Center the day of the murder."

"I was there. Justin and his SUV were not. Period!" My jaw tightened.

"I didn't say I believed the sighting," he smiled. "Care for dessert?"

"No, thank you. I have to get home to feed my dog." I tried to believe Charlie could help Justin, but it wasn't easy. We drank our decaf in silence. Charlie handed me his business card: H.C. Wellborn, Attorney at Law. "Big wow," I thought.

"Josephine, if you learn anything new concerning the case, please give call me. I want to help Justin all I can, believe me." His pleading made me feel like a fool.

"Sorry. I'm sure you have his best interests at heart. Please say 'hi' to Justin for me when you see him." I gathered up my coat and purse, and we walked through the restaurant to the stairs. Minutes later, I was driving down the road in my cozy little Mazda truck while Charlie cruised out of the parking lot in his classic late-fifties white Jaguar convertible. He seemed to have it all.

I had a strong urge to see David, so I drove up his driveway instead of mine. A light was on in the garage. The big double door was closed so I peeked through the little window in the side door. I saw David sitting on a stool, tapping one foot to music coming from an old radio on the shelf behind his head. His hands were busy cleaning a small metal gizmo with a grimy rag.

"Hello," I said, as I pushed the door open. The extra-wide garage housed two cars, one lawn tractor

and two work benches but didn't have room for much
else. I made my way across the room toward David. He
hadn't heard me, but he finally saw me coming.

"Josie, thought you were out on a ...," he smiled. I
put my hands on my hips.

"I told everyone it was business. Is that so hard to
believe?"

"I don't care what it was about. I'm just glad to see
you. Let me clean up a little and I'll meet you in the
house." He walked over to the utility sink and scooped
up a glob of grainy soap out of a short, round tin. Minutes later he joined Fluffy and me in the kitchen where
I had turned on the lights and the coffee pot.

"Now my home feels homey." He gathered me up
in his arms and we stayed that way for many wonderful minutes. "Let's go sit down," he said. I led the way
to the living room where we settled into his soft sofa.
Fluffy positioned herself between us and proceeded to
fall asleep.

"The meeting tonight had to do with proving
Justin's innocence." I began.

"Justin is the grandson of the man who was murdered?"

"Yes, Jim was murdered and Justin didn't do it, but
I think someone is trying to frame him by saying they
saw his SUV that night at the Center. Justin wasn't there
and I'm certain of it. Justin is as innocent as I am." I had
disturbed Fluffy with my ranting. She jumped down
from the couch. I sucked in a few big breaths.

David reached over and massaged the back of my
neck.

"Did I ever tell you that you're beautiful when

you're defending a friend?"

I couldn't help smiling. I was putty.

"Anyway, Justin's in jail, but we're hoping Megan, I mean a certain email, will prove to be someone's motive for murder." I probably sounded like a babbling idiot.

"So you went to dinner with ...?"

"Justin's attorney, Mr. Wellborn. I had to deliver Meg ... I mean, the email. I had retrieved it from Jim's briefcase which was in Justin's house."

David squinted, giving me the feeling I needed to do more explaining.

"You see, when I saw Justin at the jail, he asked me to take care of his cat named, Megan. Actually, that was code for an email he wanted me to find for him at his house."

"Where did you find this email?" David asked.

"It was right where Justin left it, in Jim's briefcase on the bookshelf. Crossing the lake in Trigger's boat was the hard part, but the swim was the worst." I rattled on and on about everything that had happened while David was gone. He still had a puzzled look on his face as he pulled me closer.

Around two in the morning, I woke up on David's couch in a sweat. The nightmare was worse than ever. I had watched Jim fall down the stairs all over again, and watched papers flying in slow motion from the trashcan as Jimmy Buffett sang Margaretville.

David was asleep in the La-Z-Boy; so I spread a lap blanket over him, kissed his forehead and went home.

CHAPTER THIRTEEN

Wednesday morning, I awoke feeling like I had just come back from a vacation in the Bahamas, only better. David had a way of making me feel good. I stretched, sighed and finally rolled out of bed. I found Solow in the kitchen listening to Sarah reading the newspaper.

"Josephine, how was your date … I mean, meeting?" She tried to contain her smile.

"Fine."

"Is he married?"

"I don't know. It never came up," I chirped.

Sarah's smile turned into a look of concern. "I was just reading an article in the newspaper about Justin being held for the murder of his grandfather. They say a witness saw him coming out of the Therapy Center the afternoon of the murder. According to this article, Justin stands to inherit two million dollars worth of property and stocks," Sarah said. "But you still don't think he did it?"

"That's right. Guess I'll take my turn in the shower. Looks like Solow will be staying with you today." Sarah smiled and patted his adorable head.

"Steve called last night. He's coming over to paint more signs today. Tomorrow's the big day."

"Yes, that's right. Let me know if I can help." I took off down the hall before she could think up something for me to do. After my shower and breakfast, I drove up to Rosa's and fed Oliver.

"You sweet ol' cat." Big Bubba purred while he ate. I made a mental note to buy more cat food next time I shopped. His supply was running low. I hopped into my truck and by nine o'clock I was standing in front of the mural trying to calculate how many more days of painting would be needed to finish.

"Morning, Jo," Alicia said. "How was the meeting?"

"Hi, Allie. I thought that was you kah-thunking down the hall. The meeting was fine, I guess. Mr. Wellborn seemed happy to have Megan."

"I read the paper this morning. It's not looking good for Justin."

"I know. We have to help him somehow," I said, as Kyle joined us.

"Like, why are you two so serious?"

"We were just talking about our friend, Justin, who's in jail."

"I heard he murdered his own grandfather."

"Don't believe everything you hear," I snapped. There was nothing else for me to say on the subject. An uncomfortable silence ensued as we turned our attention to painting. I brushed in a red canoe with three youthful passengers. Alicia worked on a giant oak tree and Kyle painted a couple of skateboarders.

"Painting's lookin' good," Chester said, as he walked past us on his way to the upstairs business offices. On his way back he mumbled. "I shoulda' told Hans where to go."

"What's wrong, Chester?" I asked.

He stopped and turned to face the mural. "Hans wants me to be an informant. It's not my job to rat on my friends."

"What does he want to know?" Alicia asked.

"Guess I might as well tell you since I don't plan to cooperate with the jerk. I'm supposed to keep tabs on you guys. If I hear anything about protest marches and stuff like that, I'm supposed to tell him." Chester stepped back two steps. "Where's the dock for those pedal boats and the canoe?"

"Good idea," I said. "I'll put a dock over here. Thanks."

Chester made a two-finger salute and sauntered down the hall. When he was out of sight, Kyle said, "Does that mean I'm not supposed to march with my friends anymore?"

"It means we don't discuss it at work, but what we do on our own time is nobody else's business." I was starting to think of marching as good exercise. "Anyone want to go to lunch at El Milagro ... on me?"

"You mean it?" Kyle asked.

"Of course she means it. She didn't pack a lunch." Alicia winked at me and we all dropped our brushes into the water bucket. As we walked outside, Alicia said, "Ernie packed my lunch with enough calories to choke a whale, bless his heart. He thinks I'm helpless with this broken foot."

"He should see you paint. You're as good as ever."

"It's kind of nice when he fusses over me. I don't mind at all." She smiled as she drove the three short blocks to El Milagro. The parking lot was full and cars were parked up and down the street. Alicia pulled into a space that had just been vacated by a delivery truck. I noticed an old red VW bus parked two spaces away from us with a license plate I recognized. College students and colorful characters of all ages were standing around in groups in the parking lot talking.

As we entered the establishment, the noise level tripled. It looked like every table was taken and people milled around talking to each other excitedly. I was seriously thinking about leaving, when over the voices of a bazillion customers, I heard my name. I turned and saw a familiar fellow, short, gray-haired and feisty like a rooster. He waved his arms to get my attention. Next to Steve, Sarah was tearing into a giant burrito.

We joined our friends sitting at one end of four tables pushed together to make one banquet-size table. Many of the people sitting around it were college students, but a few really raggedy ones looked like they might have been recruited from the soup kitchen in Watsonville.

"Hi, Steve, Sarah. What's going on?" I asked.

Steve motioned for the waiter to bring three more chairs. He shouted over the other excited patrons who were engrossed in conversation as they ate Mexican food.

"This is our headquarters, you know, to stop the land grab and save agriculture."

"Yes, so it is." I smiled, as the three of us took our seats. The same pimply kid who had waited on us last time rushed over to take our orders, probably remembering the historically fat tip we had given him the week before. We shouted our orders and the scrawny young man took off for the kitchen. Kyle talked to the people sitting to his right. Fellow students, I suspected. A number of his friends had enough tattoos and piercings to keep their parents on Prozac for years. "Josephine, we printed some wonderful fliers today. Would you like to see one?" Sarah asked, just before she made a sizable bite into her burrito. I nodded. She unfolded a green piece of printed paper the color of pea soup. One line caught my eye. "Eminent domain means farmers unfairly lose their land. The county wins again unless we stop the taking of private property in order to glean more taxes."

I looked up at Sarah, ready to compliment her on the hundred-word masterpiece full of grease stains. But a familiar black microphone caught my eye and grazed my nose.

"What the ...?" I grumbled. Across the table, wedged between Sarah and Steve, was the woman from KPUT, wearing a low-cut ruffled blouse. She leaned across the table, showing off her assets as she held the microphone.

"What can you tell us about this secret flier, Ms. Stuart?"

"I, ah ... think it is well written. Hopefully it will, ah ...." I stammered, as the fuzzy black instrument was pulled away and the KPUT reporter stuck the mic under Steve's nose. Steve wasn't shy. He chattered on and on until the woman grew weary and followed her cameraman out the door.

"Nice job," I assured Sarah, as I handed the piece of green paper to Alicia for her inspection.

"It's really very informative. I just hope it will help, for Mr. Mendoza's sake," Alicia said, handing the flier back to Sarah. "By the way, Sarah, I have a couple of dozen signs in my garage."

"What signs?" Sarah blinked.

"Josephine and I recovered some of the signs from the Pajaro march."

"That's wonderful, Alicia. Thanks so much. I'll tell Steve to go get them. Do you still live at the lake?"

"Yes, I do. If I'm not home, just go through the back-door of the garage."

"Did I tell you, Steve's friend has volunteered to take us up in his helicopter tomorrow so we can drop the fliers all over Salinas—like green rain. He usually sprays the crops, but city hall will be much more fun," she giggled. "And we plan to put green food coloring in the fountain."

I tried not to roll my eyes. "Anyone know the weather report for Thursday?" I asked.

Sarah jerked her head up with a mouth full of beans. She swallowed.

"If it rains we might have to change our plans," she said, looking at Steve for advice. Steve didn't look up because he was in a huddle with three student-types standing behind his chair. Near the huddle, a young woman with jet-black hair and a snow-white face an-nounced she needed to leave. She had to hitchhike back to her job in Santa Cruz. She said goodbye to Kyle and took off with a backpack slung over her shoulder.

Finally our food arrived via a ten-year-old girl. Probably a family member hired two minutes after the crowd arrived. Kyle ate all of his combination special plus a donated chicken taco from my plate. Alicia ate her enchiladas slowly as she conversed with a young couple sitting across the table.

"I think it's wonderful that you would take the time to picket against something you feel is wrong," Alicia said.

"Yeah, well, we know Steve. If he says go, we like, go," the young man said.

"I, like, go where Dillon goes," his friend smiled and took another bite from her end of the burrito they were sharing. All of a sudden I felt a hundred years old. Alicia was hip. Sarah and Steve were close to my age, but they were still able to relate to the modern youth. I was lost. If I had been a mom and raised teenagers, maybe I would have been able to understand the younger generation.

"Josephine," Sarah shouted, trying to get my attention. "I talked to David today. I tried to get him on the team, you know, marching. He doesn't want anything to do with it. I wondered if you could try."

"If David said he won't march, there's nothing I can do about it," I said, smiling a secret smile. Sarah would never understand David, but that was fine with me.

My painters had finished eating, so I paid the bill and suggested we go back to work.

"See you tonight, Sarah." We pushed our way through the crowd, out the front entrance and over to Alicia's car.

Back at the Therapy Center one could hear a pin drop in the mammoth interior. No sawing, no scraping, no hammering. I scratched my head. Being of sound mind and a curious nature, I strolled down the hall, well beyond the mural, to the unfinished construction area. I heard Hans' voice coming from one of the unfinished examining rooms, so naturally, I stopped and listened from the hallway.

"I have been in contact with Mr. Thornton, and he wanted me to remind you that he expects your work to be finished by next Friday. May I remind you of the contract you signed. Mr. Thornton will pay the estimated cost and no more. If all your work is satisfactory, we will consider including you in a very lucrative building project coming soon in this very neighborhood. Any questions?"

"Sounds good. We'll be out of here next Friday, right after we get paid," Chester said.

I spun around and dashed back up the hall to the mural. I grabbed a brush just before Hans arrived, huffing and puffing. He stood, red faced, several feet back, studying the painting and then marched up and down the hall taking in every detail.

"Will there be a slide?" he asked. "I always loved the slide when I was … anyway, the painting is certainly coming along. How much more time until you finish?"

"It will be finished next Thursday or Friday," I said. "And yes, there will be a slide and swings."

"Very well. Mr. Thornton will be pleased."

I wondered if Mr. Thornton even cared. It seemed to me that Hans and Tavia were the ones who had their undergarments in a twist over every little thing. The carpenter racket had resumed. Hans walked up to his office and the tension in my neck disappeared.

"Kyle, I love your guys on skateboards. How about

a skateboarder being pulled by his pet dog on a leash?"
I said.

"Cool, man. Like, I can do that," he laughed. "I'll
paint Solow."

I painted two rowboats and their occupants plus a
diving board at the edge of the lake with a junior diver
in mid-air doing a swan dive. Alicia painted a swing
hanging from the limb of the giant oak tree. A little girl
sat on the seat with her legs stretched forward and her
hair flying out behind her.

The ideas were endless, but the time left for painting
was running out. If Hans hadn't been such a dolt, I
would have painted a few extra days for free just to get
all my ideas into the painting. When four-thirty finally
rolled around, we cleaned our brushes and stowed our
gear. Kyle pulled on his leather jacket and tucked his
yellow flamed helmet under one arm.

"See ya." He turned to go.

"Hey, Kyle, if you march Thursday, save a little energy for Friday's painting, OK?"

He nodded without turning around.

"Oh, speaking of Friday," Alicia said, "Trigger
wants you to come to the school play. It's Peter Pan and
he plays the part of Captain Hook ... which reminds
me, I have to work on his costume tonight."

"I'd love to go. Would it be all right if I invited
David?"

"Absolutely! They're trying to earn money for sci-
ence camp." The price is twenty dollars a person. Can
you believe it?"

"Good grief. Inflation has hit the schools." I shook
my head in disbelief. We walked to our vehicles and

said goodbye. I noticed the lot was empty except for Andy's old BMW. I walked back into the building, climbed the stairs and knocked on Andy's door. Not waiting for an answer, I pushed the door open. The room was dark except for a green glow from one computer screen.

"Who's there?" Andy said as he jerked his head up from the desk. He looked up at me. "What's the matter? What time is it?" He looked around the room as if it were all new to him.

"You must have fallen asleep. Do you have a minute?" I asked, as I flipped on the overhead lights.

Andy blinked and shielded his eyes with both hands. "Sure ... but ...."

"I just wanted you to know that I know about the Mendoza emails."

Andy pressed both hands to his forehead and moaned.

"I was wondering if you gave an email to Jim? Justin has been accused of murdering his grandfather, and I'm just trying to prove he didn't do it."

"Is Justin in jail?" Andy asked, clearing his throat.

"Yep, and I don't know if his lawyer is a real believer in Justin's innocence. If I could just find more evidence to prove someone else had a motive, maybe they would release him. How did you happen onto the Mendoza emails?"

"I worked on Willy's computer a couple of Fridays ago and needed to see if the emails were coming through all right. Well, this one caught my eye so I downloaded it. Actually, I downloaded a few others, too. Jim walked in just as I was reading the last one. He saw the one from Megamalls on the screen and asked for a copy. I gave him the one I was holding." Andy shook his head back and forth slowly. "I should have refused to give it to him."

"Why was Jim taking a wastebasket down the stairs?" I pressed.

"He must have been snooping around Sunday and found the other emails in my trash basket. Maybe he was trying to take the emails out of the building."

"What if someone saw Jim? Saw what was in the basket and tried to stop him with a punch or a push?" I said. But that didn't make sense. I figured Garth was on the property that Sunday afternoon because I saw his Corvette. But why would he care? The young man had anger issues, but I couldn't imagine him hitting a nice old man like Jim. The only other people around were the carpenters.

"All I know is that the basket was empty when I came back to work Monday." Andy shut down his computer and grabbed his jacket from the back of a chair near the window. We walked out of the building together.

"If you happen onto another interesting email, I hope you'll donate it to the cause."

Andy pulled a ring of keys out of his pocket and locked the backdoor. "I'll think about it. If they catch me, I'll be looking for a job." He climbed into his car, but I held the door open.

"By the way, I know your sister, Nancy. She's Solow's favorite nurse, and she works with Rosa." Andy slammed the door.

I gave up trying to get a few more words out of the

sullen young man, and headed towards home. I imagined a quiet evening, a long bath, a cup of tea and a bowl of soup. Simple nourishment to counter the major calories I had consumed for lunch. All my wishes were whisked away the moment I saw a certain VW bus in my driveway. I climbed out of the truck and walked slowly through the cold night air to the front door.

"Hi, Josie," David said, as he held the door open for me.

My evening plans suddenly took a turn for the better.

"David. What a nice surprise."

"Sarah thought it would be fun to invite two bachelors over for a home-cooked meal. Who could turn that down?" he laughed, looking sharp in his light-blue polo shirt and Levis. As we walked through the dining room, I noticed how beautiful my dishes looked in candlelight. I made a mental note to create the same scene with just David sometime.

We walked into my brightly lit kitchen where Sarah stirred spaghetti sauce with a long wooden spoon. Steve sat at the little kitchen table formulating plans aloud and on paper for the following day. He had drawn a map of downtown Salinas and scribbled little notes all over the page with a time schedule at the bottom. He handed it to me.

"What do you think, Josephine? Do you want to add anything?"

"Looks like you thought of everything. The fellow dressed as an artichoke is a nice touch. Are you still going to turn the fountain green?"

"Thanks, I knew I forgot to write something down."

Steve retrieved the paper, made a notation, leaned back in his chair and sighed. "We picked up the signs at Alicia's house today. Thanks for recovering them."

"Glad to be of help," I said, as we moved into the dining room. David pulled a chair out for me. I sank into it with a sigh.

"Coffee or wine?" Sarah asked.

"I'll have coffee, thank you. I'd like to be awake for dinner."

"You had a late one last night, didn't you," she said. David winked at me and I suppressed a giggle.

"I'm sorry, Sarah, did I wake you when I came in?"

"I'm a light sleeper. Always was," she said, dumping the cooked pasta into my colander to drain.

David pulled a large salad bowl out of the fridge and began tossing the greens with two forks. Sarah grabbed the garlic bread out of the oven just as I was about to ask what was burning. The loaf was barely singed.

We carried food into the dining room and settled down to the business of cleaning our plates. I must have looked like I needed sleep, because the men left shortly after dessert. Sarah turned on the TV and flipped over to the ten o'clock news.

Suddenly I was wide awake and flushed like a school girl. On the TV screen, the familiar reporter-gal with the microphone at El Milagro asked me what I thought about the secret flier. Again, I had been caught off guard and could barely spit out my words.

"We watched the interview earlier on the five o'clock news," Sarah said.

"Was David here?"

"Sure. He got a big kick out of it."

"That's funny. He didn't say a word about it to me. I feel like such a fool."

"Don't worry. You can do no wrong in his eyes." Sarah shook her head as if to make sense of David's affection for me.

I smiled and tucked her words into my memory for safekeeping.

Solow was already in his bed snoring when I crawled under my blankets.

I dreamt about a fuzzy black KPUT microphone lying on a silver cookie sheet in a very hot oven. The microphone was slathered in butter and sprinkled with garlic. I ignored billows of black smoke pouring out the side of the oven door as long as I could. When I finally pulled the tray out, there was only a pile of black ashes on the tray. I felt relieved.

CHAPTER FOURTEEN

I realized it was Thursday, D-day. "Deliver the vote for Mr. Mendoza." I sat up in bed, stretched and finally put my feet to the floor. I hadn't made up my mind whether I would march or not as shades of "picket-phobia" danced in my head.

I pulled on my robe and wandered down the hall to the kitchen where Sarah stood in an ankle-length multi-colored skirt, hot-pink sweater, long purple scarf and large dangly earrings. It was the perfect outfit for a tall hippie or young college student, but not flattering on a squat middle-aged protester. Her eyes were still puffy from sleep as she sipped on a mug of coffee.

"Good morning, Josephine."

"Morning. You look like you're going somewhere."

"Actually, I have an interview to go to. Steve and I will be questioned by KPUT at their Salinas studio. Wish me luck," she giggled, nervously. "Steve will probably do most of the talking. He's so good with words." She smiled, took a last sip from her mug and wrapped a thick, hand-knit shawl around her shoulders. Poor woman was stuck in the eighties.

"So, is anything going on with you and Steve, other than marching, that is?"

"I don't know." Sarah's eyes studied the floor.

I wished I hadn't asked. She went out the front door and I prepared myself for work. Solow followed me everywhere, even into the bathroom. I think he wondered what his day would be like without Sarah. I decided to leave Solow at home and ask David to feed him, in case I decided to join the march in Salinas. I dialed his number.

"Josie, I didn't expect a call from you so early in the morning. What's up?"

"I called to ask if you would feed Solow his dinner tonight. I know Sarah will be getting in late, and I'm not sure about my schedule yet."

"Don't know if you'll march or not?" he chuckled. "Don't worry about Solow. I'll take good care of him."

"It's just that Mr. Mendoza will lose his farm if the vote goes the wrong way. I'm tempted to march, but I have a real problem with the possibility of going to jail. Hopefully, by the end of the day, I'll know what to do."

"Whatever you decide, it will be the right thing. Quit worrying."

"Thanks, David. I needed that. I'll see you later." Click.

What a pal, I thought. He's always on my side no matter which side I take. Just as I set the receiver down, the phone rang.

"Hello, dear. We came home a couple of days early."

"Hi, Mom. Everything OK?"

"Of course, we just decided to help you with your campaign to save the farmland."

"You watched TV out on the Mojave desert?" I stammered.

"It was so cold at night that we had to abandon our

tent and move into Myrtle's RV."

"And, of course, she had her television on and you saw me?"

"Yes, that's how it was. Your father insisted we help out."

"How do you feel about it?"

"The cause is good … and I just love a good demonstration," she laughed.

"I thought so. When will I see you?" I pictured my parents taking over the march, leading everyone down the main street and ending up behind bars.

"We haven't exactly planned our day yet, but I'm sure we'll find you at the main event." She sounded like we were all going to the circus. Actually, there were a few similarities like clowns and the artichoke man. We hung up.

Outside it wasn't officially raining, but the fog was wet enough to keep the wipers wiping. I drove up to Rosa's and fed Oliver. Everything looked the same as usual so I took off for the Therapy Center. I pulled into a parking space beside Alicia's Volvo. Parked in the drizzle were a white Lincoln, a red Jaguar, a black BMW and several pickups.

I hurried to the back door, trying to escape the cold mist. I wondered if my fake fur-lined jacket would be warm enough for an evening of marching in Salinas, if I decided to do it.

Inside, I found Alicia leaning toward the mural. She was adding a few chickadees to an intricate, two-story birdhouse hanging from an oak tree.

"Morning, Gimpy. How's the foot today?" I shouted over the hum of construction.

"Good morning, Jo. The foot is better. I only wish it were healed so I could march."

"I didn't know you wanted to."

"It would take something terribly important for me to march, but I think Mr. Mendoza's farm is just that," she said, staring at the fancy birdhouse.

"I'm thinking about marching. I just want to help anyway I ..." My mouth suddenly snapped shut like a Venus flytrap with a bug on its petal. Heat pushed filled my cheeks.

"You were saying, Ms. Stuart?"

I whipped my head around.

Hans stood two feet behind me, arms crossed, upper lip curled slightly and I swear his eyes where shooting flames.

"Hans ... didn't see you there," I stuttered.

"Obviously." He began pacing up and down the length of the mural, inspecting every detail. "No slide? Huh."

"It's coming, don't worry," I said, but I knew that wasn't the bur in his britches. I wondered how much of our conversation had been overheard.

"Is there something I can do for you, Hans?" Just then a couple walking down the hall caught my eye. It was Ms. Hippie and her favorite rooster.

Hans followed my gaze. "Friends of yours?" he asked, as the couple drew near.

"Hans, I'd like you to meet Sarah and Steve.

"Nice to meet you, sir," Sarah said, and turned to me. "Josephine, you should have seen our interview. It was smashing! I couldn't wait to tell you all about it." Her eyes were wide, like she had just had an Elvis sighting. "We debated one of the supervisors, Mr. Castro, for the longest time. Steve was terrific."

I blanched and Hans scowled.

"I need to talk to you in my office at your first opportunity," Hans said, just before he turned and huffed his way up the hall.

"What was all that about?" Sarah asked. "His face is so red."

"He's worried that I might be involved in a demonstration which goes against the Thornton's interests, and I think he should worry." I smiled because I finally knew what I had to do. No Hans or Tavia on the face of the planet could stop me after Hans' pathetic little speech.

Alicia and Sarah discussed the interview while I explained to Steve some of the things we would be adding to the painting—that is, if we were still employed. I promised myself I would march even if we were all fired and I had to pay Alicia and Kyle out of my own pocket. It would be worth it just to see Hans' face when the council's "no" vote came in.

"Would you gals like to join us for lunch at headquarters?" Steve asked.

I looked at Alicia. She nodded and I said we would see them at noon. Sarah and Steve left us to our work. I stalled as long as I could, but finally I made the trip up to Hans' office. The door was open. I walked in and saw movement under the far window. It was Tavia, Hans' backup, or maybe she was his backbone. Sitting at the other end of the black leather couch was her son, Mark, ears plugged into music and thumbs working an electronic game. Tavia glanced at me and turned back to her book. She looked dressed to kill in a gray silk suit, red scarf and red high heels.

"Hello, Tavia, Mark." No answer.

"Josephine, we have gone to great lengths to overlook your behavior …."

"Wait a minute. What I do on my own time is my business," I said, and the painting is progressing according to schedule."

"That's not the point. You have blatantly acted against the interests of this company," Hans' voice quivered. "Our friends are becoming concerned."

"And those friends are …?" Hans tightened his jaw until it looked like steam might suddenly shoot out both ears.

"I'll wait to hear from Mr. Thornton," I said over my shoulder as I marched out of the office. Alicia looked surprised to see me back at the mural so soon.

"I set ol' Hansy straight. I just hope we still have a job. But until Mr. Thornton tells me to leave, I'll keep painting." I was still steamed as I picked up a brush and went to work painting the framework for a play structure. I had never painted anything so fast.

"You have real spunk, Jo. I'm proud of you. I only wish I could march too."

As soon as twelve o'clock rolled around, we vacated the building. I drove the two of us down to El Milagro with the windshield wipers on slow. The place looked like it had been invaded by a small nation. People were lined up just to enter the building.

"Hey, everyone, let the injured lady through please," I shouted above the chatter.

People stepped aside for Alicia, and I followed close

behind to the entrance. Several informed citizens in the crowd recognized me from TV and raised their voices as they waved a two-finger, "V" salute.

Once we were inside, the robust smells of Mexican food overpowered any doubts about staying for lunch. Sarah motioned us over to a table where she and Steve were distributing piles of pea-green fliers to enthusiastic re-distributors.

"Hi Josephine, Alicia, have a seat," Sarah said, pointing to a couple of white plastic chairs piled high with green papers. She bent over, lifted the piles one at a time and dropped them into boxes on the table.

Alicia and I settled into our chairs just as the pimply high school graduate arrived to take our order. I saw a familiar face at the other end of our long table and waved.

Kyle turned red and waved weakly.

Sarah and Steve stood up and greeted a friend who had just arrived. The fellow was thirtyish and handsomely Latino. He wore a baseball cap and matching green jacket with a black whirlybird logo embroidered on the left front pocket.

"Josephine, I'd like you to meet my friend, Alberto."

Alberto smiled wide, his dark eyes twinkled.

"Nice to meet you, Alberto," Alicia said.

His smile grew even bigger.

"Alberto is our helicopter pilot for today. We take off in less than an hour," Steve bragged, just before he gulped down the rest of his beer and ordered another.

"Will it be just the two of you dropping fliers?" I asked.

"That's right," Steve grinned. "This is my chance to

ride in a chopper."

Sarah nudged me, opened her purse and pointed to the contents. Inside were three little bottles full of green food color. She giggled like a school girl who had just put one over on the teacher.

"It's for the fountain," she explained.

I turned away and rolled my eyes to the ceiling.

Our food arrived, we ate, we talked and then it was time to go back to work. Alberto and Steve headed outside, each carrying a big box of green fliers. The mingling crowd stepped aside as we followed the men through the parking lot.

I scanned the area for my truck, but the first thing that caught my eye was an orange and green helicopter parked in the middle of a vacant lot next door to El Milagro. We watched the guys open the chain-link gate, walk over to the cute little single-rotor copter, heft the boxes inside, and climb into their seats. The bulbous bug-like machine took off straight up, made a circle around the restaurant, tilted and headed west.

Alicia and I climbed into my truck and zipped over to the Therapy Center. Just as I turned off the engine, there was a loud whap-whap-whap sound and the orange and green helicopter appeared in my rear view mirror. It landed in the Therapy Center's almost empty parking lot directly behind my Mazda.

"Good grief!" I was shocked. Alicia just stared out the back window with her mouth open. We jumped out of the truck and stood frozen, waiting for the chopper blades to stop rotating. Steve climbed out of the copter, staggered toward me and put his hand on my shoulder. It felt like I was the only thing holding him up. He tried to speak, but turned his head just in time to keep his lunch from landing on my chest. I stepped back as it splashed on the blacktop.

Alicia gagged slightly, paled and excused herself back to work.

"Sor...ry, Josephine." Steve pointed to the helicopter. "Can't do it ... I might be coming down with something. You can do it."

"I can do what?"

"You can take my place. You have to. Hurry, before your boss comes out and sees you." He let go of my shoulder, bent down at the waist, took a deep breath and then straightened up. "Please, Josephine, you have to."

"But ... I've never ...."

"Neither had I, but you can do it. I know you can. Please. If I weren't so sick I would do it ...."

Alberto motioned for me to get in.

I forced myself to take the first ten steps, then ten more. My heart was racing as I climbed into the bulbous windows-everywhere cab and strapped myself in. I donned the headset Alberto handed me, tightened my safety belt until my tummy cried "uncle" and a second later we were in the air. Part of me loved it and the other part was scared silly. After a few miles, the scared part calmed down and the joy of flying took over. I began to enjoy the patchwork of agriculture below us, the stormy gray ocean to my right and our destination in the distance, the city of Salinas.

"You're not turning green like Steve, so I guess you're OK?"

"I'm doing well, all things considered," I shouted

into my head gear. I finally noticed two boxes of green fliers at my feet. "What's the plan?"

"I thought you knew," Alberto said. "Aren't you the organizer of all this?"

"I know. You saw me on TV. Actually, Steve is the man with a plan. I have no idea where he wanted to drop this stuff. Downtown might be good, I guess."

"Downtown it is," he shouted back as the flying machine tilted to the right.

The landscape appeared slightly unreal, looking through windows covered with tiny droplets that were more like fog than rain. As we approached Salinas, a stiff wind tossed us side to side causing my fish taco to feel like it was learning how to swim. Quickly I focused on the landscape and wished David could see what I saw. I went so far as to wish he was flying through the air instead of me.

"Is that the Civic Center?" I pointed down and to my right.

"Looks like it," Alberto answered.

Suddenly my stomach was in my neck as we lost altitude. Beads of perspiration appeared across my forehead and ran down my nose. "Are you OK? You look a little pale."

"I'm fine. I just want to know how we get the fliers out of this helicopter."

"No problem. I just open your door from over here and you push them out." The helicopter hovered over city hall. I watched Alberto push a button on the dash. Air rushed in under my door. I screamed and slapped a hand over the mic positioned over my mouth. I told myself to be strong even though we were only a few hundred feet above the streets, Civic Center and traffic. The bulbous glass-door raised up a few more inches, giving me just enough room to shove the first box out.

Just as the second open box sailed down to earth, trailing green papers, I heard something even louder than Alberto's chopper. I looked up and to my right. A bigger helicopter hovered beside us. KPUT was painted in big black letters on the side and a big black camera stole our privacy.

"Oh my G...!" I screamed.

Alberto laughed as he closed my window and made a tight left turn that lasted until we were headed east, back to Pajaro. I looked over my shoulder. The KPUT copter was following the paper trail. If one of the empty cardboard boxes hit the mayor on the head, KPUT would be there to show it to the world.

I was so much happier with the door closed. I took a deep breath and thanked God for getting me through a really tough moment. I even took an interest in the landscape again. Finally, we landed next door to El Milagro. Steve ducked down, not that he needed to, and ran to the copter. He opened my door and caught me as my legs wobbled like Jello.

"You look a little unsteady, Josephine," he said, as if he could do better.

"Too bad you missed the sights, Steve. It was fantastic."

"Thanks, Al. We owe you," Steve yelled.

Alberto waved and took off.

I was happy to see him go, but I would never let Steve know that.

Sarah sat in the VW bus keeping warm. Steve offered me a lift and I accepted.

"How did you like the ride?" Sarah asked, as I crawled into the backseat.

"Nothing like it in the world. By the way, was I supposed to let the papers out over Civic Center?"

"Sure, I just hope no one saw you," Steve said. Sarah laughed and I groaned as he stopped the bus near the backdoor of the Therapy Center.

"Thanks for the ride. Hope you feel better, Steve." I hopped out, waved goodbye and took a few steps to the backdoor of the Center. Just as I opened the door, Andy rushed past me, not saying a word. I guessed he was headed for a late lunch. I found Alicia sitting on a paint box leaning down to paint a path near the bottom of the mural. She heard me and straightened up.

"Jo, where have you been?"

"You won't believe it even if I tell you."

"I'd believe it," Hans said, walking up behind me. "Why don't you people pack up and go home before I lose my good manners."

"What?" Alicia asked. "What's going on?"

"I'll tell you later. Let's go," I said, as Hans turned and stomped back up the hall. Alicia washed her brushes, grabbed her purse and we left the building. It was only two o'clock so we caravanned over to Alicia's house. I asked her to turn on the TV.

"That's why Hans is so angry," I pointed at the screen.

"Jo, that looks like … can't be. Is it you?"

"Every time I turned around that blasted KPUT was there, snapping pictures or taking live video."

Alicia slapped her knees and howled with laughter.

"Allie, do you think I broke any laws when I dropped the boxes over city hall?"

"They could get you on the litter law for sure, five-hundred dollars ... or is it a thousand?"

CHAPTER FIFTEEN

Five minutes after I left Alicia's house the weather changed from ugly to actual thunder, lightning and rain, but I was fired up and ready to march, thanks to Hans. It was four-thirty by the time I parked my truck on West Alisal in downtown Salinas, just three blocks away from the main event. I pulled my red umbrella out from under the seat, dropped the truck keys in my pocket and left my purse in the cab.

Looking down West Alisal, I saw multitudes of people already congregating in front of the Civic Center. As I plodded down the street, leaning into the wind, two Greyhound buses stopped in the middle of congested traffic and let a hundred or so senior citizens disembark. As soon as the old folks hit the sidewalk, they unrolled bright green banners and began chanting as they marched. The women wore clear plastic rain hoods, the men donned baseball caps and everyone wore raincoats and galoshes. Someone familiar caught my eye.

"Mom, what are you doing here?" I shouted over a clap of thunder.

"Hello, dear. I brought some concerned friends with me." She smiled and waved her hand to show that these were her people. Mom wore a green visor over her clear plastic hood, lime green overalls, and matching rain boots. She had always been a trendsetter.

"Here comes your father," Mom shouted, pointing to a minivan with a Bowl & Bowl logo on the side. My Dad and seven bowling buddies jumped out, all wearing their maroon team jackets. They made their way across the street through throngs of people. Each man carried an identical sign on a stick, which read, "Council Vote NO!"

Dad saw me. "Hi, honey. Where's your mother?"

"She's marching ... over there by the fountain. Oh my, that fountain water is really green." I looked around. Pea green fliers were everywhere, soggy and draped over benches, trashcans, treetops and even a few umbrellas. The rainwater had soaked them even before they washed into the storm drains. The drains already hosted gobs of soggy fliers and, as I watched, the water deepened at the curb.

"I'll see you around, sweetheart," Dad yelled over his shoulder, as he slogged across the street to join his fellow marchers. A motley group of several dozen young people walked toward me.

"Jo, like, what do you want us to do?" Kyle asked, shrugging his bony shoulders. I recognized his old girlfriend, Kellie, at the back of the mob. She wore a very wet t-shirt, a long clingy skirt, sandals and no umbrella. The guys were just as unprepared for rain.

"Since you and your friends don't have rain gear, maybe you should march in a smaller circle under the eaves over there." I pointed to the entrance to the Civic Center. They scurried through ankle-deep water across the plaza to the three-story building.

The next group to arrive was packed inside a red VW bus. Sarah stepped out first, then Alberto and half a dozen other people each carrying a sign. Steve drove away to look for parking.

Sarah hurried across the street to where I stood. "How do you like the fountain?"

"It's ... um, really green. Who did it?"

"David."

"No way! He wouldn't ... oh, hi David. I didn't see you over there," I stammered.

"Hi, Josie." He ducked under my umbrella and kissed my cheek lightly. "So what now, boss?"

"I'm not the boss, but I guess we just join the circle." I looked across the street as Trigger's soccer team filed out of a minibus. Trigger saw me and waved. The bus driver climbed down from his seat and stopped traffic so the kids could cross safely. A full-size school bus pulled up behind the little bus and the entire Watsonville band clamored out. Within a couple of minutes, they were marching to their own music up and down the sidewalk across the street from Civic Center.

"Look up the street, Josie. Isn't that the Castroville Jazz Band?" David pointed at some thirty senior citizens playing instruments as they sashayed down the street. At this point, the police had stopped traffic, except for participants, and put up blockades. It seemed to me the police were going out of their way to help the protesters.

"David, look, aren't those tractors?" I pointed up the street. A large yellow and green tractor led the entourage of mobile farm equipment. Several tractors pulled flat trailers full of farm workers singing, "Hey,

hey, don't take our land away." Carlos and Garth sat with the first group of people, strumming their guitars. It was probably the first time ever that farmers, farm workers and illegals, were on the same side of an issue.

Streetlights flickered as a bolt of lightning came close to hitting the roof of the Civic Center, followed by a roll of earth-shaking thunder. I jumped and pushed against David. He wrapped his arms around me as if I were a child afraid of thunder, which wasn't far from the truth. The rain pelted us as we marched around and around endlessly. My stomach told me it was past dinnertime, but duty called. I needed to march, needed to do my part, so I pressed on.

People just kept arriving until we were talking thousands, not hundreds, of bodies. KPUT set up camp across the street. I watched them carefully, not wanting to be caught off guard. I saw the cameraman point his camera at a swollen storm drain. I could imagine what he was saying into the mic and who would be blamed for the coming flood.

A stiff wind and a huge crowd pushed us along in a giant oval pattern around the dolphin statue and stone benches. A few seniors had already hit the benches, but they still chanted with everyone else. "Ho, ho, hey, hey, don't take our land away."

A man in an artichoke costume danced around the KPUT van, probably hoping to be videoed for TV. His leaves were soggy and pointed down instead of up like a real artichoke. After all his antics, he finally gave up, sloshed across the street and sat on a bench looking like a dejected green man.

"David, I'll meet you at the fountain after I go find

a restroom." I hiked up the front steps to the Civic Center and glanced at my watch. It was almost seven and the meeting would be starting soon. Once inside, I closed my umbrella, tucked it under an arm and looked down the crowded hallway to my left and then my right. To my right a long line of women had queued up for the restroom. I planted myself at the end of the "line to nowhere" that seemed not to move at all. After ten minutes of not moving forward, I decided to find a powder room out of the mainstream, one that would be harder for the average woman to find.

I marched up the stairs to the second floor where I heard loud angry voices coming from behind partly open double doors. I lingered in front of the extra large doors just long enough to see one gentleman shout at another.

"What have you done with Anderson?" the man asked.

"I don't know where he is and if I did know, I wouldn't tell you … you old crook!"

I wondered if this was business as usual for the board of supervisors.

Two doors down, I discovered a restroom with no one in it. As soon as I closed the door to my stall, I heard two women enter the restroom. They slammed their individual toilet-stall doors and one spoke to the other.

"Can you believe it? The most important vote in years and Curt is missing."

"Something's wrong. I know Curt and he would never miss a meeting, let alone an important vote," the other woman said. "I'm out of paper over here. Hand me some, would you?"

I left without seeing either woman. On my way to the stairs, I paused again at the entrance to the supervisor's chambers.

"I move we discuss items fourteen A and B while we wait for our fifth supervisor," a gentleman at the podium suggested. I noted the room was packed with spectators, many of them standing. There was a general hum of discontent in the large room. I moved on, but not expeditiously. I wasn't looking forward to going outside to fight the elements on an empty stomach. I stood in the foyer for a minute, watching the protesters through a long row of tall windows. I saw David at the fountain talking to my dad. Mom was easy to locate. She was the lady in green with the bullhorn, waving her sign with gusto as an army of seniors followed like green sheep.

Finally I stepped outside under the eves where Kyle and his friends were camped. They sat on the ice-cold concrete, sharing body heat and singing to the rhythm of Kellie's tambourine. Mr. Artichoke had joined their clique, probably to get out of the rain. Kyle, wearing a forced smile, flashed me the peace sign. His usually red spiky hair hugged his cold, wet head.

I popped opened my umbrella and carefully maneuvered my body down the slippery stairs. I wedged myself through the flow of marching humanity, ending up at the fountain where David and Dad stood soaked to the skin.

"Dad, you're drenched. Get under," I said, lifting my umbrella up over his head.

"Thank you, honey." But it was really too little too late. Poor David was obviously cold and wet too, but uncomplaining.

"This whole effort might turn out to be useless," I said.

"What makes you think so, Josie?" David asked.

"When I went inside, I got the impression that one of the supervisors didn't show up for the meeting. Do you know who Curt Anderson is?"

"Sure." David said. "He's in the paper all the time. I think he teaches biology at Hartnell College, but he's also a supervisor ... and coach for a kid's soccer team in Watsonville." David shook his wet head like a puppy after a bath. "Let's march down the street to the coffee shop," he said, just before Dad sneezed.

"Yes, let's go. Your mother will be fine," Dad said as he watched Mom leading her entourage with vigor.

I noticed that the Watsonville band had disappeared and the tractors were heading north at about seven miles per hour. At that rate, they would be back in Pajaro just before sunrise. The Jazz Band stood in a tight circle on the plaza, too tired to march but still blowing their horns. As we left the crowd behind, I noticed the water in the street was level with the sidewalks. My truck sat directly across the street from the coffee shop in water up to its hubcaps.

Picketers, thick as flies in a pig barn, swarmed in front of the little café. Picket signs were stacked against the brick façade, ours included. We squeezed inside, ordered coffee and stood near the front door warming our hands on the sides of the hot mugs. I held my cup out from my body each time someone tried to pass by, trying to avoid a burning splash.

"Well, this is relaxing," David joked. I rolled my

eyes and Dad sneezed. Just as the coffee cooled enough for us to drink, four people filed out the door and we were able to sit at last. Bread crumbs and puddles of mustard and catsup where still on the table, but I didn't care. My bones needed a rest and the cast iron ice cream chairs served us well.

"So, what's this about a missing supervisor?" David asked.

"While I was in a restroom upstairs, I happened to hear someone say that Curt Anderson is missing." I took a sip of coffee. "With only four supervisors, we might have a tie, don't you think?"

"It's possible," Dad said. I don't know the rules here in Salinas, but in some cities the Mayor can break the tie."

"I think the Mayor is a supervisor, so I don't think he can break a tie in this case," David said. Dad nodded thoughtfully.

"Look out there. Where's everyone going?" I asked, just before a lightning bolt lit up the street and thunder rattled the windows. We gave up our seats and made our way to the front windows where we stood in a puddle of water that oozed in under the door. People were leaving the main event in droves, wading across the street through knee-deep water. Cars passed by sending up rooster tails, knocking over pedestrians and blocking the road when their motors stalled. Another finger of lightning, followed by bone-jarring thunder, sent even the most resolute picketer running for cover.

"Time for me to find your mother," Dad groaned. We followed him out the door and down the street through ankle deep water, weaving through the flow of humanity.

"Dad, she's getting on the bus ... over there." I pointed to one of the two Greyhound buses parked across the street. Mom climbed the stairs and disappeared into the bus as dozens of seasoned citizens fought the current, trying to reach their ride home. Picket signs were used like canes or crutches until they inevitably washed away. A minibus with a Bowl & Bowl logo on the side pulled in behind the second Greyhound.

"There's my ride, honey. Will you be all right?"

"Sure, Dad, my truck is just up the street." We hugged. He turned and began the trek across class-two whitewater.

David and I watched until Dad was safely inside the minibus.

Several white pickups stamped with the city emblem arrived. City employees placed sandwich signs all around warning people of the obvious flooded roads. One city truck parked at the curb where we stood. I approached the driver. He rolled down his window.

"You might check the storm drains." I smiled, and pointed to a drain a few yards away. He looked at me as if he had seen my picture in the Post Office recently.

"Let's go back to the coffee shop," I suggested to David. "The water isn't as deep there and then we can cut across the street to my truck."

David took my arm and walked me to the café.

A minivan drove by, splashing cold water over our heads.

"That wasn't funny," I shouted at the minivan. David laughed and pretty soon, we were both doubled over. We hurried across the street. I found my keys and prepared to drive home. "Where's your car, David?"

"I had Sarah drop me here this afternoon. I had business at the Civic Center and figured I could ride home with you."

"Weren't you taking a chance? How did you know I would even be here?"

"Wherever there's trouble, I know you'll be there. And here you are." He smiled and I pretended to take offense.

"I'll take you home if you feed me when we get there," I said.

"I like the subtle way you do things." He climbed into the passenger seat. Our bodies shivered and our teeth chattered for miles. Finally the heater put out enough heat to warm us. He asked about my new job.

"Hans called me up to his office today."

"Oh, what's up?"

"He kinda' hinted that if I marched I would be fired."

"What does Mr. Thornton have to say?"

"Guess I'll find out tomorrow when he returns from a trip to the east coast."

"I admire what you did, Josie."

"I got carried away with the moment. Now I'm worried about my job." I reached up and wiped the windshield with a wet sleeve. "What happened to you, David? Sarah thought you would never do something like this."

"Sarah doesn't know me like you do." I took that as a compliment, even though I had guessed wrong about what David would do. My cheeks warmed as I drove up David's driveway, parked and we ran through the rain to the front porch.

Solow met us at the door with a happy bark and lots of tail wagging. I made a fuss over him until he had had enough and finally curled up on the living room carpet for an evening nap.

"Bless his heart," I said. "You'd think he marched half the night."

"I fed him before I left," David said. "Why don't you take a warm shower while I stir up some food?"

"How did you know that's what I wanted to do?"

"Psychic," he laughed, handing me a fresh towel and bathrobe.

As soon as I warmed up from the short shower, all I could think about was food. I towel dried my hair and wrapped myself in David's big terrycloth robe. The aroma of grilled cheese sandwiches and hot tomato soup pulled me into the kitchen. It was almost 10:30 and food never tasted so good.

"I watched the 10:00 news," David said, "and I didn't see any interviews with you, just one quick shot of you dumping fliers out of a helicopter." He stifled a smile.

"So, did KPUT blame me for the flood?"

"Not exactly, but anyone could put two and two together."

"In other words, it was plainly my fault."

"Don't get upset. What you did was brave and wonderful. It wasn't your fault it rained."

"What about the vote?"

"You called it. It was a tie and Curt Anderson didn't show up." He shook his head. "There will be another vote next Thursday."

"Oh, brother! I hope there won't be another protest march."

"I wonder if your houseguest will go home before all this is settled," David said, as he spooned out the last drop of soup in his bowl and then shivered.

"David, your lips are still blue. I think it's your turn to warm up in the shower. I'll get a fire going in the fireplace. Go! And don't worry about the dishes.

When David finally reappeared, he looked irresistible wearing his navy blue sweats. The fire blazed and a bowl of warm popcorn sat on the coffee table along with mugs of hot chocolate. We sipped our frothy drinks and forgot all about the flooded town of Salinas, the missing supervisor and the murder I hoped to solve someday.

CHAPTER SIXTEEN

I remembered Thursday night as if it were a dream, a dream to end all dreams. It was just the four of us—me, David, Solow and Fluffy. I remembered driving Solow home and crawling into my bed well after midnight. And then I thought further back to the Salinas experience, back to the nightmare of a crazy helicopter ride and an inconvenient storm.

It was 8:30, Friday morning. The phone rang. I reached over and grabbed the receiver.

"Hellooo," I swooned.

"Expecting David to call?" Alicia asked, with a chuckle.

"As a matter of fact … maybe. What's up, Allie"

"I forgot to ask you if we work today. Kyle will be there at nine."

"Oh, no! I'm not even out of bed yet. My plan was to go to the Center around noon to see if Mr. Thornton is back. I don't think we should paint anything else until we know if we're fired or not."

"Better call Kyle right away." Alicia said. "Maybe he hasn't left home yet. You can get back to me."

"Thanks, Allie. Bye." We disconnected and I called Kyle. After about ten rings he finally picked up. He sounded like he'd been run over by at least two trucks.

"Guess your engine's a little rusty after last night," I said.

"Like, I didn't get to sleep until an hour ago," he groaned. I thought I heard Kellie's voice in the background. "Is this still a workday?"

"Not for you, brave marcher. I'll see you Monday unless something comes up, like, we get fired or something." I thought about an upcoming and possibly ugly encounter at the Therapy Center.

"Jo, what did you say?"

"Nothing, Kyle. See you Monday. Bye." I hung up and called Alicia to tell her I would meet her for lunch. She suggested her place. That was fine with me. I shuffled down the hall toward the sound of Sarah reading the paper to Solow in the kitchen.

"Good morning, Josephine. Here's a picture for your scrapbook, if you want it." She held up the front page of the Sentinel. I recognized myself in a certain helicopter and hoped no one else would. Just then the phone rang.

"Good morning, dear. Have you seen the paper yet?" Mom asked, sweetly.

"How do you always sound so awake in the morning?"

"I guess it's because I see so much potential in a new day. How are you feeling, honey?"

"Not as bouncy as you, but I'm fine." I smiled when I thought about Leola and her bullhorn.

"Your dad took the paper to the coffee shop this morning. He wants to make sure his friends see it. We're so proud of you, dear."

"I haven't read the article yet. Do they blame me for

the flood?"

"Of course not. Some people might draw that conclusion, but don't worry about it."

I knew Mom was being as kind as she could be. We said goodbye.

"By the way, there's a message for you." Sarah pointed to the answering machine in the living room.

"Thanks, Sarah. I'll check it out after breakfast. All that marching gave me an appetite." I made breakfast pancakes and fried eggs.

"These pancakes are delicious. I'm going to miss this place," Sarah sighed.

"You're here until Sunday, aren't you?"

"Yes, but I wish I could stay until this farmland thing is settled. Steve says we shouldn't march again. We don't want to overdue it and have popular opinion go sour."

"I think Steve is right, but I'll miss having you around. To be honest, I wasn't real happy to have a houseguest in the beginning, but I think we have co-habitated very well." I felt angelic for telling the truth, finally.

"To tell you the truth, I wasn't crazy about your loft and the cold showers and ... oh, never mind. It's the hospitality that counts," she giggled, as I felt a pinch of guilt in the back of my neck. "I was hoping Steve would ask me to stay longer." Her eyes stared at her empty plate and all of a sudden, I felt a knot in my throat.

"I'm only working half the day today. Maybe we can get together ...."

"Josephine, what if I made dinner for everyone? You know, David, Steve, Alicia and Ernie?" What do you think?" It was amazing how fast her mood changed.

"That sounds wonderful, Sarah. Should I shop for anything on my way home?"

"Don't worry about a thing. David said I can drive his Miata as long as I want. I'm going to look through your recipe books and make a shopping list." The minute Sarah became "Martha Stewart," I lost the pinch in my neck along with my feelings of guilt. I ate the last pancake, excused myself and went to the answering machine.

I listened to Mr. Wellborn telling me that Justin was out on bail, but that we needed to get together to talk about Justin's defense. He said I should meet him at the Green Valley Grill Saturday night at eight. Same weird working hours, I thought.

I decided to call Mr. Wellborn later and turned my attention to getting ready for possible work. I drove to Oliver's house, fed him and headed into town. The sun shone on the green fields as if there had never been an untimely storm messing up our protest march.

I arrived at Alicia's house early, 11:00 a.m. to be exact. I heard her kah-thunk, kah-thunk, kah-thunk her way to the front door.

"Josephine, you're early." She motioned for me to enter.

"Nobody needs me at home. Sarah takes perfect care of Solow, the laundry, not to mention the house, so I thought I'd come over here and bug you.

"Don't forget Peter Pan, you know, Trigger's play tonight at the school."

"I totally forgot. Guess I'll call David." He didn't answer so I left a message inviting him to take me to the play.

"Alicia, what would you say to a visit with Justin?"

"Is he out of jail?" she asked.

"Yep, his attorney, Mr. Wellborn, called this morning."

"Let's go now," she said, as she pulled a windbreaker out of the coat closet. I nodded and we climbed into my truck. "Have you talked to Justin yet?"

"No, I just got the call this morning. Mr. Wellborn wants to meet with me to discuss Justin's defense … Saturday night. Can you believe that?" I felt my cheeks redden.

"Sounds like a date to me," Alicia laughed.

"The man thinks he's God's gift. Here we are. You'll love the cottage in the back." I parked the truck, and peg-lady and I walked slowly to the little house behind the big house. I knocked and Justin opened the door.

"Good morning, ladies. What a nice surprise," he said, smiling. "Come in."

We passed by the little kitchen/dining room and moved on to the living room and a comfy sofa with a view. Outside, the lawn and beach were littered with ducks, some preening, some sleeping. Two large gray geese comingled with the ducks as if they were family.

"Lovely view you have, Justin," Alicia said. "I can see my house from here. How are you feeling now that you're finally home?"

"Much better, thank you. Hope I never have to go through that again. Mr. Wellborn says I might have a defense, but we need more evidence." Justin flopped into a chair across from us and stared at the floor.

"You're innocent—what more does your attorney

need to understand?" I asked.

"By the way, thanks for taking care of Megan. Hope she wasn't too much trouble."

"No trouble at all. I love cats," I said.

Alicia smiled but kept her mouth shut.

"So, Justin, who said they saw you at the Center the day that ... well, you know. Mr. Wellborn wouldn't tell me when I asked him."

"Apparently, Mrs. Thornton saw me enter the parking lot as she was leaving," Justin said, scowling. "I should have told you before. My flight really was delayed, but for only a couple of hours. I got into town around six Sunday evening. Granddad wasn't home so I drove down to the Therapy Center. I looked around for his pickup but didn't think to look way back to the dumpster. I gave up and headed down to my old hangout, the Long Foot Bar."

"Wow, that puts a monkey wrench in your alibi," I said.

"Anyway, I got home from the bar around two a.m. I didn't wake up Monday until noon. Granddad's front door was locked, he didn't answer his phone and the truck was gone, so I figured he had gone to work. He usually works until five. I waited until a little after five and let myself in with my key. A few minutes later, you came in." Justin held his head in his hands as if it were too heavy to stay upright on his thick neck.

"It wasn't your fault. You didn't know he was in the house, or hurt for that matter," Alicia said, leaning forward as she wiped a tear from her cheek.

"But if I had gone into the house earlier, I might have been able to save him." Justin's voice cracked.

"That means that Tavia was at the Therapy Center Sunday evening, but I don't remember seeing her Jaguar in the lot." I stared at the ceiling, trying to remember everything, from Jim, to the clutter of papers on the stairs and then up to the two feet at the top of the stairs. Black high heels came into focus. Suddenly, I knew who killed Jim. I was finally able to remember the shoes as they turned and disappeared from view. I listened to Justin confirm what I already knew.

"She was driving a black Corvette," he offered.

"That's it. Tavia did it!" I shrieked.

Justin's eyes looked dark and angry.

"Dios mio!" Alicia gasped, placing a hand over her mouth.

"Tavia was trying to keep Jim from taking the emails Andy had accidentally found in Mr. Thornton's computer. Why would she care about the emails?" I asked. "Justin, is Mr. Thornton a bad guy? You know what I mean. Is he … honest … or not?"

"All I know is that my Granddad worked for Willy long after he should have retired. He wouldn't have done that for just anybody. Willy was Pop's friend." Justin took a deep breath and sighed. "Granddad thought Willy was an honest man."

"How about the Thorntons as a couple? Are they close?"

"I only know what Granddad told me and he wasn't much of a gossip. He mentioned a separation a few years ago. Tavia was fooling around, but that was before I joined the Marines."

"Who was the unlucky guy?" I couldn't help asking.

"I'm not sure … but he was a big shot, well known around town. I think his name was Dirk or Curt or something," Justin said.

"The real question is whether Tavia is capable of murder, and other crimes?" I said. "We need to find out what she's up to and gather evidence."

Alicia and Justin nodded their heads. Easier said than done, I thought, especially when it came to amateurs like the three of us. How in the world could we prove what we knew to be true?

"Josephine, watch out for Wellborn. He thinks you're hot." Justin smiled.

"And I was going to warn you. Your attorney doesn't sound convinced of your innocence. I'm afraid Alicia and I have to get back to the Therapy Center now to find out if we're fired. Hans is very upset with me for getting involved in the land-grab protest."

"That reminds me," Justin said, I watched the ten o'clock news last night." He tried to look serious, but he couldn't hold back the grin. "How did you like the helicopter ride?"

"It was my first and definitely my last ride in one of those things." We all stood up. Alicia hugged Justin and he hugged me.

"I can't tell you how much your support means to me," he said to us as we walked out the door into the sunshine.

Motoring down Lower Cutter, I asked Alicia if she would like to stop in Pajaro for tacos or something.

"That would be lovely," she said.

I parked in the almost empty El Milagro parking lot. "Good, no crowd today," I said. We found a table by the window and the pimply kid waited on us. We ordered tortilla soup and chicken tacos. The boy's eyes looked bloodshot and his shoulders slumped.

"Are you OK?" Alicia asked.

"Not really. Yesterday I worked. Then I marched in Salinas and had to come back here to clean up the restaurant after the party last night. I didn't get home until after midnight and here I am again." He turned and dragged himself back to the kitchen.

"Where are the violins?" I rolled my eyes.

"Look, Garth and Carlos are sitting over there in the corner," Alicia said.

I turned my head to see. They saw us and waved. Garth looked pale and his eyes were red and puffy with dark circles under them. But I figured half the population of Pajaro was in the same condition after the big march.

"Come on, Allie. Let's sit with the guys."

"But, I don't think they … all right. I'm right behind you," she said, as she kah-thunk, kah-thunked her booted foot across the terra cotta pavers.

"Hi, guys. Any news on whether Wildbrush is still under contract with the Thorntons?" I asked.

"My dad's back. You should ask him," Garth said. Carlos smiled at Alicia and offered her a seat at the table. I didn't wait to be invited. I just pulled up a chair.

"I'm sorry the vote was a tie last night," she said to Carlos.

"It would kill my dad to lose the farm. I wouldn't be happy either. I hear the government only pays half what the property's really worth," Carlos stared into his half-empty mug of beer. "So how was the helicopter ride?" A slow smile crossed his face and Garth chuckled.

"I don't recommend it, especially in the rain. Garth, do you remember a couple of Sundays ago when you dropped Carlos off at his house ... in a rather sorry state?"

Carlos laughed, keeping his eyes on the beer foam.

"Sure, and I remember seeing you there." Garth nodded in Alicia's direction.

"What did you do after you left the Mendoza farm?" I asked. Garth cocked his head to one side. "I have a good reason for asking," I persisted.

A long moment passed before he answered.

"I parked the Vette at the Center and took my step-mother's Jag down to the gas station to put air in the tires. Actually, they didn't need air so I stopped at the Long Foot for a cold one." He looked at me to see if I needed more explanation. "She had called and asked me to hurry down to the Center. Said her tire was going flat. I'm her little puppet, you know." He gulped some beer and wiped his mouth with the back of his hand.

I felt sorry for Garth, and so did Garth.

"So, Carlos, how's your dad holding up?" I asked.

"He got a big charge out of watching you on TV, dropping those fliers." Carlos laughed.

Garth interrupted his friend. "Sorry, ladies, but we have to go. This should cover the bill." He dropped a couple of twenties on the table and they walked out the door.

"It all fits, Allie. Tavia switched cars with Garth. That's why Justin saw her in the Vette.

"Maybe she didn't want anyone to know she was at the Center so she asked Garth to take her car ... giving a lame excuse like 'the tires need air,'" Alicia added. We finished our soup and then tackled the tacos.

"These tacos are wonderful," I said. "Oh, that reminds me, Sarah wants you, Ernie and Trigger to come over for dinner tonight."

"That sounds great. We will either be celebrating our work or our dismissal. Which do you think it will be, Jo?"

"Let's go find out." I laid the two twenties on top of the bill. "The kid can finish graduate school on a tip like that." We hurried into the truck and two minutes later we climbed out, kah-thunked across the Therapy Center parking lot past a red Jag, a white Lincoln and a black Porche.

We entered the building cautiously, looking down the hall at Willy and Hans studying our mural. They heard Alicia's kah-thunks and turned their heads. Tavia was noticeably missing, which helped to keep my blood pressure within normal limits. As we came closer to the two men, Willy Thornton smiled.

"The painting is coming along beautifully, ladies. Hans tells me you expect to finish by next Friday." He reached out and shook our hands. Hans didn't make eye contact.

"I'm glad you like it," I said, trying to keep my smile at a modest size. Inside my head fireworks were going off. I was too happy to think straight. I noticed that Alicia looked mighty cheerful as well. Hans looked devastated, which only added to my euphoria.

Willy and Hans excused themselves and walked on down the hall, probably to tour the heart of the construction zone. Alicia and I happily grabbed our brushes and went to work. It was a great relief not to be fired, but it was absolutely wonderful to know that our client loved the mural.

About twenty minutes later, the suits walked back up the hall and past our painting. Willy held up his thumb and smiled as they passed.

"How does it feel to have job security?" Alicia asked when they were gone.

"I can't wait to tell David all about it."

"You'll probably get a chance at dinner tonight, or maybe at the play."

"Just because I invited him doesn't mean he's going. Maybe he has plans."

"He has plans for you and you know it, Jo."

I tried unsuccessfully not to blush. "What time is the play?"

"Seven. Maybe you should ask Sarah to plan an early dinner, and I'll see if Ernie can leave work a little early." We put our brushes in water and rummaged through our purses for the cell phones. Sarah didn't answer so I left a message. Ernie answered Alicia's call and said he would leave the lab early. As we began painting again, Chester strolled up behind us and watched.

"You girls make it look easy. Nice job." Chester continued up the hall and out the backdoor. A couple of hours later, we called it a day, cleaned up the work area and kah-thunked out to the parking lot. Alicia said she would see me around five and climbed into her Volvo.

I waved to Alicia, turned and started to climb into my truck. Suddenly I saw red lipstick letters on my driver's side window. A chill went up my spine: WATCH

YOUR BACK WOMAN. The red looked red enough for Tavia to wear. I kicked the front tire, and looked down when my toes complained. The tire was flat.

"Oh, my ...!" I murmured and stormed around the pickup, kicking one tire after another. They were all flat. The parking lot was empty except for a white Lincoln and I wasn't about to go to Hans with my problems. I pulled out my phone and called my towing service. I waited impatiently for at least half an hour. I had tried to call David, but my once trusty phone chose that moment to suffer low-battery syndrome.

Finally, a tow truck pulled up and a burly woman climbed down. She was thirtyish, blond and built solid like her truck. She took care of the paperwork first.

"Somebody doesn't like you," she grinned as she wrote down the pertinent information and handed me a yellow carbon copy. "Did you call the police?"

"No. I think the perp is my boss." I shrugged my shoulders, shedding a little tension as I laughed at my predicament.

"At least the caps are still here." She filled the tires and wished me luck.

CHAPTER SEVENTEEN

The sun set, stars twinkled and a silver moon bal-looned up over the hills as I drove home. I barely noticed the headlights behind me. My driveway was cluttered with cars: David's Miata, Steve's bus and the Quintana's Volvo. I drove up onto a low bank of weeds bordering the parking area and cut the engine. It took a minute to gather my wits. I felt completely dis-combobulated by the lipstick prank. I finally climbed out of my truck and walked toward the porch light. David met me at the door wearing a worried face.

"Josie, are you all right? Here, sit down." He hov-ered near me as I flopped down on the sofa. Everyone stared from the dining room table where they were fin-ishing up their plates of lasagna.

Alicia stood up. "Jo, you look like you've seen a ghost. What's wrong?"

"I had four flat tires! Someone wrote with lipstick on my window … 'WATCH YOUR BACK WOMAN.' What's going on?" I asked, shaking my head slowly, trying to make sense of it all. Solow sidled up to me and rested his head on my knee.

"Did you see anyone around?" David asked, as his warm hand found my cold one and held it tight. "Do you know anyone who would do something like this?

Didn't you say your employer was upset with your getting involved in the protesting?"

"Mr. Thornton isn't upset with me, but his wife hates my guts." The lasagna aroma wafted my way and my stomach growled. "Guess I should try to eat something before we go to the play."

David smiled and helped me up from the sofa.

"Jo, you don't have to go to the play if you're not feeling up to it," Alicia said.

"But I want Auntie Jo to see me. I'm playing Captain Hook," Trigger pleaded.

"I wouldn't think of missing the play. I'm feeling much better now," I lied.

David pulled out a chair for me. A satin heart-shaped box of chocolate candy sat on the table next to my plate.

"For me?"

David sat down beside me. "Happy Valentine's Day, sweetheart."

"Oh … I, ah … love chocolate. Is it February fourteenth already?" Tears welled up, but I managed to keep them at bay. I felt off balance, shaken and pitiful. The little girl inside me wished she could hide under the table long enough to get her head together. I laughed out loud at myself and felt a teeny bit better.

"We were worried about you, Josephine," Sarah said. "It was getting late and I thought something awful had happened … oh, I guess it did. You poor thing." She squeezed Steve's arm. "Sweetie, pass the salad down to Josephine."

I wondered if Steve had remembered to do something for Sarah for Valentine's Day.

Sarah disappeared into the kitchen and came back with seven little bowls of spumoni ice cream balanced on a tray. "Please excuse us, Josephine, but everyone's in a hurry to get to the play on time," she said, placing a dessert in front of each guest.

"Don't mind me. I'll catch up," I mumbled over a bite of lasagna.

After a few more bites of heavenly pasta, I rushed down the hall to change my clothes and run a brush through my hair. David and I were the last to leave the house. We climbed into the Miata and followed Steve's slow VW bus all the way to Pajaro. We caravanned across the bridge into Watsonville, then turned right onto Merritt Street to the school.

We followed Steve's bus into the parking lot and immediately realized it was completely full. David circled the neighborhood and finally pulled into an empty parking lot behind a dentist's office. The bus had disappeared down the street. From there we high-tailed it down the sidewalk.

Two blocks later, we entered the school's multi-purpose room. David bought our tickets just before Sarah and Steve rushed in the door. The four of us positioned ourselves against the back wall behind the back row of a full house. The lights dimmed and a rotund red-faced teacher, wearing a colorful muumuu and black cardigan, walked up to a podium to the left of the stage area. After several announcements, she waved her thick arm for the curtain to open.

Overhead lights dimmed as the stage lights clicked on, revealing a hand-painted set created by ten-year-olds. Positioned in front of the painted background stood an old-fashioned canopy bed and a chest of drawers. Wendy sat on the bed reading to John and Michael. I hadn't seen a school play since my own school days, and this one was a kick.

The second act had just begun when all of a sudden the lights flickered twice and went out. I heard children stumbling around the stage and a murmur throughout the audience while the teacher told everyone to stay put in a shrill voice, without benefit of a microphone.

"Ladies and Gentleman, as you can see, our power is out. Flashlights are coming … ah, here come the flashlights, folks. Thank you, Mr. Quintana," she said as Ernie walked up the aisle carrying several lights. He distributed them to five key parents who used them to lead people to the restrooms or to the main entrance if needed. Most of the audience waited patiently in their seats for the lights to come on.

After a good twenty minutes in the dark, the lady in the muumuu stepped up to the podium again and made an announcement.

"I'm very sorry we are not able to continue with Peter Pan tonight. However, I want to thank our volunteers, Mr. Anderson, Mr. Quintana and Mrs. Burns for their many hours of help with this project. The play will be presented again tomorrow night. Mrs. Burns will stamp your hand at the door so that you may attend tomorrow night's production free of charge."

Since we were already standing near the exit, we left in front of the crowd. Luckily, we had moonlight to help us navigate the sidewalk as we headed for the Miata. The night air was cold but refreshing. It looked like the whole town was blacked out. The only lights we saw were flashing red lights from two police cars as we rounded the second block. About fifty yards down the street I saw more police cars, flares, and a tow truck. A light pole stretched across the street.

"Drunk driver?"

"Probably," David said. I climbed into the Miata, praying there were no more drunks on the road.

"Would you mind stopping at the grocery store on the way home? Oliver is almost out of food."

"No problem. How much longer are you going to have to feed that cat?"

"I wish I knew. I'm thinking until we get a yes vote from the supervisors. At that point Rosa can come home, but Mr. Mendoza loses his farm."

"What if it's a no vote?" David asked, as he angled into a parking space at the well-lit market on the other side of town.

"If it's a no vote, she might still be in danger. But Mr. Mendoza can keep the farm."

I watched Robert push a long row of carts toward the front entrance of the store. David and I stepped out of the Miata and walked up to the store entrance where my friend was picking litter out of each shopping cart.

"Evening, Robert."

"Oh, hi, Jo. Hear about the hit-and-run across town?"

"We just came from there. Didn't know it was hit-and-run. Anybody we know?"

"For awhile I thought it might be you. This friend of mine told me he saw a woman driving a red pickup down the street like a maniac." Robert laughed at his own words. "She rams an old parked VW bus. It jumps the curb and slams a power pole. My friend was right there when it happened. Even got the license. He looked pretty shook up." Robert walked with us into the store and down the pet food aisle.

"That's a lot of coincidences, don't you think?" I said to David.

He frowned. "Not many older VW buses on the road these days," David said. "Robert, did your friend happen to tell you the color of the bus?"

Robert shook his head. "He didn't say. I'll see you guys up at the checkout."

"Are you thinking what I'm thinking, David?"

"Yeah," he laughed, "I'm reading your mind. We'll call Sarah as soon as we get out of here. Cat food's over there." He pointed to the next aisle.

We loaded about twenty cans of cat food into a hand basket. It was a good thing we didn't need anything else because the Miata only held two people and one grocery bag. We hurried to the checkout counter.

"So, Josephine, how was your helicopter ride?" Robert's grin was all over his chubby freckled face.

"How do you know it wasn't someone who looks like me?"

"Cause KPUT said it was you."

"They didn't! Did they?" My cheeks were hot. People in the line stared at us. David paid for the cat food, Robert bagged it and we raced out the door. I borrowed David's phone as soon as he dug it out of the glove compartment.

"Guess I'll call home," I said, punching in the numbers. All I got was my own annoying voice telling me to leave a message.

"Don't look so worried. Maybe they didn't go straight home. After all, it's Valentine's day," David reminded me with a wink.

"You're right, but maybe I should call the hospital."

"It happened while we were at the play, remember?"

"Oh yeah, you're right. I'll call Alicia and let her know what happened." I punched the numbers and Ernie answered. I started to tell him about the hit-and-run, but he cut me off and explained that Sarah and Steve had caught a ride from the Quintanas over to Steve's house in Watsonville.

"That's great," I said, "that is, the part about getting a ride."

"Steve was pretty upset. He's had that bus since dinosaurs roamed. I don't know why he doesn't drive the Chevy pickup parked in his garage. Guess he'll have to now. His bus looked like an accordion. The front and back were pushed to the middle. Good thing no one was in it."

"What happened to the pickup truck that got away?"

"I didn't know it was a truck," he said. "It must be drivable because it left the scene. Hope someone caught the driver's license."

"Thanks for the info, Ernie. Bye." We disconnected. David drove us up San Juan Road to Aromas. Just as we were making the turn onto Otis, a fast moving car rounded the corner from the opposite direction, braked, fish-tailed and almost side-swiped us. Because there were no streetlights on the little country road, it was impossible to see the driver.

"Wow! That was close!" I said, as my heart froze for a second.

"Yeah. What are your plans for this evening? It's only 8:30. Any dates with attorneys?"

I ignored his snooping. "Care to stop at Rosa's on our way home?" I asked, finally feeling calm again. I figured David didn't need to know about the upcoming meeting with Mr. Wellborn, at least not until there was an absolute need-to-know.

"Next stop, Rosa's," he laughed. Finally, we were both feeling relaxed after a stressful day. The automatic security light over Rosa's front door blinked on.

"We have to use the backdoor. I keep it unlocked since I don't have a key."

David lifted a corner of the welcome mat, revealing a nice shiny key.

"Your way or mine? Front door or back?" he teased.

"All right, David. You win. I don't know why it never occurred to me to look there."

David turned the key, opened the door, and flipped on a light. I entered and he followed carrying the bag of cat food. Instantly I smelled stale cigarette smoke, tinged with an ultra-sweet perfume. My skin prickled.

"Someone was here recently," I announced, holding my breath as I looked around. Something caught my eye on a little table across the room. I hurried over to the end table for a closer inspection.

"The nerve! David, someone burned a black spot into the table top and left this filthy cigarette butt smeared with red lipstick. Who would do such a thing?" But I knew who—I just couldn't believe she would do this to Rosa. And then there was the trespassing aspect, and what about the deadly threats ... from ... Tavia? The possibility stuck in my mind like flies in summer.

"There must be an explanation ... don't you think?" David said as he pawed his chin.

"Let's put the cat food away and get out of here." I felt like my privacy had been violated along with Rosa's. We quickly stacked the cans in the cupboard while Oliver scratched on the backdoor, letting us know he wanted to join the party. I let him in and screamed.

"Oh, my God! Now she's picking on a poor helpless cat!" I pointed at Ollie's face. His nose had been smeared with red lipstick. He sent his little pink tongue up to clean it off, but it would take a million tries. I grabbed a tissue, wiped the red gunk off as gently as I could, picked him up and cuddled him.

David put an arm around my shoulders. "I think you know more than you're telling me, Josie."

"I'm more than 99% sure that Tavia Thornton did this—the same person who flattened my tires and wrote on my window with lipstick. She wants me to know it's her."

"What's her problem?"

"She's angry because I walked in the protest march after she warned me not to."

"That's all?" David scratched his head. "How does her husband feel about it?"

"He's fine. Thinks our painting is wonderful. No problem. I think his attitude might be part of her problem."

"OK, Ollie, out you go." I set him down on the concrete patio, closed the backdoor and followed David out the front door. I turned the key in the lock and slipped it into my pocket. David turned the car around and we headed back down Otis to my house. While he drove, I threaded Rosa's key onto my key ring for safekeeping.

"Home at last," I said, but my smile faded quickly as David's car came to a halt beside my truck. Even in the wimpy light from the front porch, I could see that the front end of my Mazda was seriously smashed. I leaped out of the Miata and practically fainted. My head was spinning. I felt like I would explode.

"How in the world?" David said, almost to himself. We looked at each other and at precisely the same second, we both came to the same conclusion. His mouth dropped open and I screamed.

"David, my truck hit Steve's bus!" I almost felt guilty of the crime in an unrealistic way. Maybe I drove Tavia to do it. I shook my head and let anger take over. "How dare she hurt my truck. How dare she ... but ... how did she do it?"

I opened the passenger door and stuck my head inside. I saw a lone key still in the ignition. I ran my hand over the seat and found the little black magnetized key case that used to be attached to the underside of the left front wheel well. I had placed it there myself in case I was accidentally locked out of my truck. I tried to hide the tears burning my eyes and blurring my vision.

"Come on, let's go inside. It's cold out here," David said, as he guided me into the house.

I sniffed the air. Good, no unusual smells, just Lasagna.

He walked me to the sofa. "Sit. I want to know more

about Tavia," he said, as he circled the room turning on lights. "But first, I'll call the sheriff."

Solow entered the room looking like we had woken him from a deep sleep. Just looking at him brought my blood pressure down by double digits.

David called the sheriff. "Someone will be out here within the hour," he announced. "Now, what about Tavia?" He sat down and stretched an arm around my shoulders. I needed to release some more pressure before I blew a gasket, so I told David about all the latest developments concerning Jim's death and Justin's predicament. When I finished, I felt better, but David looked worried. We sat quietly, thinking.

"And that's why I have to meet with Mr. Wellborn tomorrow night." There, I said it.

David didn't say a word.

"What if you came with me? You know all about the case now, and maybe three heads would be better than two." And that would keep me from being alone with Charlie. I almost smiled at the thought of dining with two very handsome and distinguished men at the same time.

"If you think I would be able to help somehow ...."

"Then it's settled. Pick me up at six-thirty tomorrow night." I snuggled closer, listened to David's heart beat and eventually things didn't seem quite as bad.

Fifty minutes later, an official sheriff's car parked in front of my house. We listened for a knock. After waiting several minutes, David got up and opened the door. I followed him outside. We found Deputy Sayer crouched in front of my truck, examining it with a flashlight while Deputy Lund took fingerprints from the cab.

Sayer looked up. "Ms. Stuart, good evening."

Before I could say anything, David stepped forward. "Hello officers, I'm David Galaz. I called to report the stolen truck."

"What makes you think it was stolen, ma'am?" Deputy Lund asked, looking into my face, ignoring David as she pulled out a pen and notebook. "Isn't this the pickup we're talking about?" She pointed a thumb at the truck behind her.

I nodded and shivered at the same time.

"Would you like to come in and sit down?" David asked.

The deputies followed us inside and sat stiffly on the sofa. David took the rocker. I sat in my recovered wing chair I inherited from my grandmother.

"I'm going to tell you right now, Ms. Stuart, we have a witness to a hit-and-run and your license number was mentioned," Deputy Sayer said, as Solow laid his head across the man's boots and fell asleep.

"How fast do you think you were traveling when you hit the vehicle?" Officer Lund asked in a flat tone.

I ground my teeth together, squinted and growled my answer. "I wasn't driving. Tavia Thornton stole my truck, ran it into my friend's bus and then dropped it off here. Before she did that, she broke into Rosa's house and smeared lipstick on Oliver's nose and before that she flattened all four of my tires. I'll show you the paperwork from the towing company." I reached down and pulled my purse from the floor.

"There!" I flashed the yellow carbon copy in front of Deputy Lund. She cocked her head to one side, trying to read the small printed document.

Deputy Sayer wrote something in his notebook.

"I could hardly believe it myself, but it's true," I said. The room was silent except for Solow's snores.

"Mr. Galaz, did you witness … ah, Ms. Stuart's story?"

"Yes, sir, most of it," David said. "Josephine and I went in my car to see a play. When we came home, well, you saw the truck." He rocked back and forth.

I proceeded to fill in the details while the officers listened, and scribbled on their pads, looking skeptical as if they were being duped by a shyster. I had a hard time convincing them on certain points, but I persisted until Officer Lund called it quits. Her eyelids were drooping.

"I read the lipstick on your truck," Lund said. "May I see a sample of your lipstick?"

I quickly rummaged through my purse and handed her a tube of "Merry Cherry."

"Don't leave town. We'll be in touch," Officer Lund warned, as she dropped my lipstick into her pocket. She stood, stifled a yawn and walked to the door.

Officer Sayer slowly pulled his feet out from under Solow, trying not to wake him. By the time he joined Deputy Lund at the door, Solow was there to see them off.

CHAPTER EIGHTEEN

Saturdays were usually housework days for me. After my coffee, half a bagel and a walk to Rosa's to feed Ollie, I inspected my humble abode for dirt, dust and clutter. Nothing. Sarah had kept the house spotlessly clean all week. It seemed there was nothing to do and no one to talk to, not even Solow. He was exhausted from our walk in the neighborhood and crashed on the floor. In no time, he was chasing Fluffy in his dreams.

I dipped into my box of chocolates and called Alicia.

"Hi, Allie. The worst thing happened last night. I still can't believe it myself. You'll never guess who smashed Steve's bus."

"I don't know, but I think you're about to tell me."

"It was my truck." I waited for her reaction as I imagined how Steve's bus must look as a twisted accordion.

"I thought you were going to tell me what happened," she said.

"It's the truth. It was my truck, but we think Tavia was driving."

"How could she possibly … I mean … how do you know …?" Her voice trailed off.

"I'm still steamed, but last night when I saw Oliver

wearing lipstick and there was a cigarette butt on the end table ... and then to find my poor truck ready for the junkyard ... well, I came unglued. Poor David had to help put me back together. I'm not really together, but I can fake it. He called this morning to see if I was OK. Allie, I gotta go. Someone's at the door." We disconnected and the front door opened.

"Sarah, what's the matter?"

She scratched her head and turned back to look at my truck again. I caught a glimpse of the back end of what I figured was Steve's green Chevy pickup as it headed down the driveway toward Otis.

"What a coincidence. You crashed your truck last night. Are you OK?"

"No, I didn't wreck my truck, but someone else did. That's how my Mazda looked when we came home last night from the play. Actually, we think Tavia was driving it and she hit Steve's bus."

Sarah's jaw dropped. "Steve is so angry. It took me all night to calm him down." A tiny smile flickered across her lips. I guessed it hadn't been all bad.

"I'll run the whole situation by Mr. Wellborn tonight. Legal stuff, you know."

"Another date?"

"Not a date, a meeting," I corrected her. "Have you had breakfast?"

"I had scrambled eggs at three this morning, but yes, I'm ready for a little something. What did you have in mind?" she asked as she floated into the kitchen wearing rumpled clothes and her hair in a rat's nest. "By the way, I'm not leaving Sunday, that is if it's OK with you. Steve needs me."

"You're welcome to stay," I said, thinking about my clean house and how much Solow enjoyed her company, not to mention how guilty I felt about Steve's bus. I hoped Steve had deeper feelings for Sarah than just being needy. I prepared waffles with blueberries and whipped cream. We talked, ate, sipped hot coffee and let the calories fall where they could do the most harm.

Suddenly, Solow howled.

"Solow, come with me," I said, feeling a little spooked and wondering who had knocked at the front door.

"Alicia. What a surprise." Solow howled his approval as the tail wagged the dog.

"I came right over because you, ah ... sounded strange over the phone. Everything all right? I see your truck really was in an accident."

"Sure was. Would you like a cup of coffee or waffles?" She nodded and we walked to the kitchen. The three of us sat for over an hour hashing out the "Tavia problem." We didn't come to any great solutions, but the sisterly support was comforting.

"I didn't know Ernie was involved in Trigger's drama class," I said.

"He and Curt Anderson are the only dad's that help with everything ... soccer, plays, fundraisers, you name it. Curt's been at it for years," she said. "I help out once in awhile but not like those two."

"Allie, are you talking about the supervisor—Curt Anderson?"

"Yes. Why?"

"He's the guy who's missing ... the one who didn't vote Thursday."

Alicia put a hand to her mouth as a little squeal leaked out.

"Everyone is looking for Curt."

"I didn't realize he was missing. I didn't see him at the play last night, but I just thought he was helping the children backstage."

"Is Mr. Anderson a yes or a no vote?" Sarah asked.

"He might be a no vote," Alicia shrugged. "Maybe Andy knows where his dad is."

"Are you saying that Andy at the Therapy Center is Curt's son?" Bingo! I should have put the two together sooner.

"That's right. I thought you knew, Jo—after all, you know Nancy from Dr. Finley's office."

"Well, girls, all we have to do is find Mr. Anderson and talk him into voting no at Thursdays meeting," I said. Alicia and Sarah nodded their agreement.

"I'll ask Steve to track him down. He's pretty good at that sort of thing," Sarah's cheeks flushed. For about the tenth time I silently hoped Steve felt about Sarah the way she obviously felt about him.

I grabbed my reading glasses and flipped through the phone book. I found A, for Anderson. My finger stopped a quarter of the way down the numerous listings for Anderson.

"Anderson, C., 1215 Long Dr., # 303," I recited. "I'll give Mr. Anderson a call." I dialed. After twenty rings, I gave up. We were silent for a minute, thinking.

"Hold on. I'll get a map." I dug through my kitchen junk drawer like Solow after a gopher. "Got it." I spread the map of Monterey County on the table and we leaned in for a closer look.

Sarah put her reading glasses on. "I see it." She put her finger next to the street name. "I know where this is. It's one of those pricey gated-condo places on the beach near Moss Landing. I think it's called 'Fore at the Water.' Has a fabulous golf course and everything. I saw it being built about fifteen years ago when David and I were looking for a place to buy."

I tried to picture David living in a condo. Impossible. David loved his apricot orchard, his little tractor-mower, country living and the sweet little town of Aromas way too much to downsize into a condo with a balcony, even if it had a view of the ocean.

"Are you thinking what I'm thinking, Jo?" Alicia asked.

"Parts of it. If we leave now we could be back in time for lunch."

"I'll call Ernie and meet you in my car." She picked up the phone and dialed while I filled my pockets with doggie treats, clipped a leash to Solow's collar and helped him into the back seat of the Volvo next to Sarah. I had a plan, but it involved Solow's cooperation.

Alicia kah-thunked across the gravel driveway to her car and climbed in. Sarah studied the map while Alicia drove us through Watsonville. We entered Coast Highway One going south and five miles later turned right on Pelican Lane. The two-lane road curved right and left and back again, but basically headed west toward the ocean. It wound through at least a mile of cypress and pine. Between the trees, we glimpsed the cobalt blue Pacific Ocean.

"That's the gate up ahead, just around that bend," Sarah warned. Alicia slowed the Volvo, cranked the wheel to the right, and cut the engine. I admired the five-foot high rock walls on both sides of the road curving to the left and leading up to a small rustic building adjacent to an electronic gate.

"We can't go in there. We don't know anyone," Sarah said.

"What if my dog wandered in? I'd have to go get him, wouldn't I?"

"Um, I guess that could work," Sarah said.

Alicia was already out her door and helping Solow to the ground. He sniffed the air and wagged his tail as she clipped a leash to his collar. He had miraculously landed at the edge of a virgin forest full of exotic animal smells. He strained at the leash, pulling Alicia off balance.

I grabbed her arm to keep her from falling. "Alicia, you wait here and be our getaway driver."

She looked at her boot, nodded and climbed back into the driver's seat.

Sarah stood next to me with wide eyes.

"Ok, let's go," I said, as Solow howled. We crossed the street and followed the rock wall about fifty yards, all the way up to a small weathered cottage beside an ornately designed iron gate. The exit road next to it had a twin gate, which opened automatically for vehicles leaving the compound.

"Look, there's a bike path between the gate and the building," Sarah whispered.

"Perfect." I walked up to the front corner of the cottage and let Solow sniff a doggie treat. I dropped my hold on his leash and threw the biscuit as far as I could. The treat landed well past the cottage and half way to the edge of the slough that meandered through the eastern side of the property.

"Fetch!" I whispered to Solow, but he didn't see the biscuit. I tried again. This time I aimed for a rhododendron just five feet from the far side of the building. Solow saw it and took off running, right under the gate controller's window. I watched Solow find the treat and then pulled on Sarah's jacket sleeve.

"Let's go," I whispered. We crept along single file. I peered in the window as we passed, but didn't see anyone. Darn. All that whispering for nothing, I thought to myself. We caught up to Solow, but I let him drag his leash and run ahead of us until we rounded a sandy hill shaded by a grouping of cypress trees. I wanted him to look like a runaway, at least until we were a comfortable distance from the gate.

"Sarah, I forgot to ask you how big this place is."

"You can see the buildings from here," she said brightly as she pointed down the coast about half a mile. We passed a dozen empty tennis courts surrounded on three sides by lawn, a lawn bowling setup surrounded by benches and several offshoots of the main golf course. As we passed over a tributary of the slough, Solow made a mad dash under the bridge hoping to rouse out a flock of coots resting in the sand. The birds filed into the water before he was even close.

We crossed over several rustic river rock bridges that crossed and re-crossed a winding stream carving its way through the property. As if the reed-rimmed waters on our left weren't beautiful enough, to our right, beyond the sand dunes, lay the sparkling Pacific Ocean. I cranked my head this way and that, soaking up the beauty as waves pounded and crisp salty air tickled my face like butterfly kisses.

"I could live here," I heard myself saying.

"I don't remember why David and I didn't buy a condo," Sarah said. "This place is lovely." Solow's energy seemed to be fading. I took control of his leash and encouraged him to keep going. His stubby legs galloped as his body moved forward slowly.

Finally, the first four-story building was close enough to make out details such as parking lots, outdoor staircases, balconies and ramps—not a good place to live for the old or physically challenged.

"Most of the apartments are empty at this time of the year," Sarah said. No wonder we hadn't seen a soul except for one party of golfers. In the distance, I saw a string of mostly empty parking lots. The first building contained forty apartments, each with a spectacular view of the ocean on one side and slough and golf course on the other. It was dubbed The One Hundred Building. We needed the Three Hundred Building, so we kept marching south along the bike trail.

Eventually we passed a second building and finally stood before the third. It looked exactly like the first two, which resembled heaps of misplaced timbers stacked high along a windy beach. All four structures, including decks, ramps and stairs, had been created from unfinished redwood that had aged to a pale silver gray, adding to the overall understatement. The outer architecture belied the richness of the interiors, I realized, as I cupped my hands and peeked into a few windows on the first floor.

"Now, what?" Sarah sounded out of breath as she

gazed up at the third floor.

"I guess we should knock on Mr. Anderson's door. Come on Solow." We were all huffing and puffing by the time we zigzagged up several outdoor ramps and a set of stairs to the third floor apartment, number 303. Solow flopped down in front of the door, panting and completely tuckered out. I pushed the doorbell, waited and pushed again.

"I heard something," Sarah whispered between gulps of air.

I wanted to peek inside, but the blinds were closed. I pushed the button one more time and then knocked with my knuckles in case the bell was broken. "It's time for plan B," I whispered as I hooked the end loop of Solow's leash over the doorknob and motioned for Sarah to follow me down the stairs. We stopped at apartment 203 on the second floor, directly below 303, and seated ourselves on cold splintery steps.

"Now, what?" Sarah asked, trying to catch her breath.

I opened my mouth, but Solow cut me off with a double-barreled bark. A minute later, he let out a mournful howl and then another. It broke my heart to leave him in a strange place, three stories up, but it had to be done. Half a dozen howls later, I heard the door at 303 open and close and all was quiet.

"Ok, now we go looking for my dog," I said. "If you don't want to go upstairs again, I'm fine alone. But if I don't come out after fifteen minutes, call 911."

Sarah shivered, and said she would use her phone if necessary.

I climbed the stairs and rang the bell. The door opened.

"Hi, my name is …."

"I know who you are. You're Josephine, the gal in the helicopter, right?" His blue eyes twinkled. "Is this your dog?"

I stepped inside. "Yes, he is. His name is Solow." I scratched behind Solow's ears as he leaned against my knee. "I didn't catch your name," I said, looking up at the very tall, blond, middle-aged gentleman wearing gray sweats and Mickey Mouse slippers.

"Curt Anderson," he said, holding his hand out to shake my hand. The way he did it struck me as a pre-programmed act from years of campaigning. Robotic or not, it was a warm handshake. "Would you care for a cup of coffee?"

"Oh, thank you, but I just came to pick up my dog … actually, that's not true." I struggled to find the right words. "I wanted to discuss something with you."

"Could it have something to do with my not voting last Thursday?" He cocked his head to one side. "I've been following the story, and I know how important it is to you."

I glanced around the large room flooded with light from giant windows facing the ocean. I couldn't help myself. I moved past a couple of easy chairs and an iron and glass coffee table toward the windows for a closer look at the ocean.

"It's fabulous. The water is so close."

"Yeah, I never get bored with the view. The water is different everyday—today it's blue, but yesterday it was silver and choppy." He sat on a tweed hassock stroking Solow's back.

"Mr. Anderson, I came here to plead with you to

vote no ...."

"Believe me, I'd love to. But there's a problem with that."

"Can you tell me the problem?"

"No ... that is ... I don't want to involve anyone else." He stared at Solow's backside. The smile was gone.

"Just tell me if the problem involves any of these people: Mr. Thornton, Mrs. Thornton, Garth, Hans, Andy, Nancy, Rosa, Mr. Mendoza, Hec...?"

"Hold it. Obviously, you know some of it already, and I guess you know about me and Tavia?"

I nodded, even though I didn't know much.

"All I can tell you is that my son, Andy, is in love with Rosa. Always has been. Tavia knows it and she's using it to her advantage."

"What about Hector Castro?" I asked, feeling like I was on the brink of finding out what was really going on.

Curt sighed. "Tavia says ... someone ... is pressuring her to pressure me to vote yes."

"What if you show up at the council chambers Thursday and vote no?"

"All I know is that I don't want to endanger anyone else. That's why I don't answer the door or the phone. I know your intentions are good, Josephine, but people's lives are in the balance. If you keep up the good work, maybe the public will get what they want." Curt stood up, walked to the wall of windows and stared blankly at the horizon.

"Did you know that Rosa is safely hidden?" I asked. He nodded his head.

"Just one more question. Since you teach biology, do you know how a person might obtain samples of a certain smut variety of fungus?"

Curt's chin dropped a titch, but he didn't answer. I walked to the front door. He didn't move. I said goodbye. He said nothing. Solow and I traipsed down the stairs to number 203.

Sarah giggled, holding her thumb and index finger half an inch from each other. "I was this close to calling 911, and then I remembered I didn't have my phone with me," "What took so long anyway?"

"Mr. Anderson is a very nice man, maybe too nice. I noticed he had a recent visitor who leaves cigarette butts around."

"Maybe he smokes."

"Do you think he wears red lipstick when he smokes?"

"Tavia?" Sarah raised a hand to her lips.

"I think so. Seems she has Curt under her thumb." I helped Solow to his feet, gave him a doggie biscuit and we started the long trek back to Alicia's car. I glanced over the rail and recognized a green station wagon in the parking lot.

"Josephine, isn't that Alicia's car?" Sarah waved her arm above her head a few times and, sure enough, we saw a little hand in the driver's seat wave back. Sarah forgot her weariness and thundered down the stairs with amazing speed. Solow and I could barely keep up. Once we were all seated in the car, Alicia had a flood of questions.

"I'll answer your questions after you tell me how you got past the gate," I said.

"Easy. I walked up to the window and asked the nice woman to let me drive in. I told her that my silly friends were looking for a lost dog." Alicia laughed as she drove us across the compound, out the automatic exit gate, right on Pelican Lane and eventually eased her car into Highway One traffic heading north.

By the time we reached Watsonville, I had told my friends everything Curt and I discussed, to the best of my imperfect fifty-year-old memory.

"Do you think you convinced Curt to vote no?" Alicia asked.

"I think he would like to vote no. Trouble is, I couldn't convince Curt to show up next Thursday. I think he's afraid Andy or Rosa will get hurt if he votes no. I told him Rosa is in a safe place, but I think he's worried about Andy."

Alicia dropped us off at my house and hurried away to run errands. I circled around my truck. The sight of it made me sick with anger. I followed Sarah and Solow inside the house and slammed the front door. I called Barry, my insurance guy. He didn't sound like he understood what happened to my truck. I repeated the story several times. He finally told me to get an estimate at the Watsonville Body Shop and hung up.

"Sarah, I have to take my truck down to the Body Shop on Airport Boulevard. I'll see you later this afternoon."

"I'm glad, because Steve's coming over and I think he would flip if he saw your truck the way it is, not that it was your fault."

"OK, good, the place is open until two. Gotta run." My sick little truck coughed and sputtered all the way to town, but made it without incident. It was almost two o'clock when I opened the front door to the Body Shop. The girl behind the counter looked like she had just swallowed an ugly bug. Even her hot pink lipstick seemed to fade.

"Hi. My name is …."

"I know. Ms. Stuart, please fill out this form," she said, shoving a couple of papers across the counter as she snapped her gum. She was the only one in the four-desk office. A young man in white overalls paced the parking area outside the front windows. I handed the finished papers to the gum-snapping girl. Seconds later the young man appeared with keys to a rental. He hurried me out the door to a gray, bottom-of-the-line four-door Chevy.

"Thanks for the car. You might want to wipe the pink lipstick off your neck," I said, still smiling a mile down Airport Boulevard. I decided to stop at the drugstore for a few non-food personal items. Sarah kept the kitchen well stocked with food, thank goodness. I didn't know if I could handle another one of Robert's stories at the market.

I drove to the shopping center and angled my rental car into a parking space between two pickup trucks. As I walked by the white truck on my left, a familiar voice called out my name. I did a tight little pirouette and circled back to the driver's side of the truck. The driver grinned.

"Hey, Chester. How's it going?"

He eyed my rental. "I hear you've been working on your rap sheet." The grin grew wider.

"Which part are you talking about?"

"Well, KPIG had you in the news today. Apparently you're a hit-and-run artist."

"Cute. So they still think I smashed Steve's van. Actually, I think the deputies have a bias against me."

"Did you hear about Garth?" Chester's voice was suddenly husky.

"No. What about Garth?"

"Poor kid collapsed at the Monterey airport last night. He was walking his dad to the check-in counter and just dropped to the floor. Willy canceled his trip and rode to the hospital in the ambulance with Garth. Turned out to be a chemical problem."

"I never thought of Garth as the type," I said.

"He's not. The drug was arsenic. A dash in his food day after day did the trick. They think it was Tavia. Seems she and Mark disappeared last night. I think Willy finally sees what that woman's all about."

"Should I go to the hospital … or call … or something?"

"There's nothing we can do. They think he'll pull through. Willy's keeping a cap on it. Only reason I know what happened is because he needed me and my friend to pick up his car at the airport. I was with Willy this morning when the tests came back."

"What about the witch … I mean, Tavia?"

"There's already an APB out for the wicked witch of the west."

"Just for the record, I didn't hit anyone with my truck. I'd tell you the rest of the story, but it's very long. See ya Monday," I waved goodbye. A cold sad feeling settled in my chest as I watched Chester fire up his truck. I said a prayer for Garth as I drove home, wondering what kind of son Mark was, and was he safe.

CHAPTER NINETEEN

I drove the rental car up my driveway and parked next to a green pickup truck I assumed was Steve's. I had been thinking about poor Garth all the way home, remembering how pale and tired he looked the day before at El Milagro.

Solow jumped up from his porch-lookout bed and greeted me with a throaty howl and lots of tail wagging. I patted his head and thought about my big date with two handsome gentlemen in less than three hours.

"Hi, Josephine," Sarah shouted across the room over country western music streaming from Steve's old boom box. Steve didn't look up, just stared at the Chinese checkers game laid out on the kitchen table.

"Hi, guys. Think I'll go take a bath." I took my phone into the bathroom with me, called Alicia and filled her in on the latest Tavia crime. She promised not to tell a soul. While I soaked in bubbles, the phone rang. I grabbed it off the counter.

"Mom, glad you called."

"Hello, dear. I, ah, called to invite you to a little soiree I'm throwing Sunday afternoon for our dear friend, Myrtle. It's her eightieth birthday, but don't let on that you know how old she is. She's sticking with sixty-nine ... year after year after year."

"I think I can make it tomorrow. Why did you wait till the last minute to let me know?"

"I tried calling a couple of hours ago ... honey. I don't want to seem critical, but your name has been mentioned on KPIG," she blurted. Ah hah, that was the real reason for her call.

"Oh, that. Don't worry, Mom, they got it all wrong. I didn't hit a Volkswagen bus or anything else. The police are out to get me these days, but I explained everything to them last night and I picked up a nice little rental car today."

"But I thought you said you didn't hit ...."

"That's right, Mom. Someone else used my truck to hit the bus."

"Dear, I'm afraid we have a bad connection. Talk to you later, honey."

I was a couple of slow blinks short of falling asleep in my bubbly vanilla-scented paradise, when the phone rang again.

"Hi, Jo."

"Hi, Kyle, ready to go back to work Monday?"

"Like, we aren't fired or anything?"

"Nope, Mr. Thornton loves our work."

"Ah, I guess I'll see you Monday. You don't have to go to jail or anything?"

"No, of course not. It wasn't my fault ... which incident are we talking about?"

"KPIG said ...."

"Don't believe everything you hear from a stupid radio newscast. See ya Monday."

The bathwater had turned cold and the bubbles were long gone so I toweled off, dressed and joined the outside world. The house was strangely quiet. I found a note from Sarah on the kitchen table explaining that Steve wasn't feeling well, so they were going to his house to watch a movie. The meaning between the lines seemed to be that Steve had heard about my truck getting together with his VW. Maybe he listened to KPIG or some other misinformed conveyor of news.

"Well, Solow, it's too bad Steve hates me, but when he learns the truth he'll get over it. Wonder how long that will take?" I curled up on the sofa, picked up a mystery novel and began to read, dozing off in the quiet privacy of my own little sanctuary.

I awoke to someone knocking. Solow stood with his nose close to the front door, wagging his tail like a basset ready for a Fluffy chase. It was already dark outside when I opened the door and received a warm David-hug.

"What time is it?"

"Six-thirty, just like you ordered," he said, clicking his heels together.

"Good grief. I'm not ready," I shouted over my shoulder as I hurried to the bathroom and the make-up drawer. I ran a brush through my hair and poked earrings in my ears. Ten minutes later, I was set to go, except for puffy, sleepy eyes.

"Ready, beautiful?" David asked. "Nice little rental." He pointed his thumb outside.

"It'll do."

"Did they say your truck was totaled?" he asked.

"Totaled? No, they haven't told me anything yet. I certainly hope it's not totaled."

"My Jeep awaits." He bowed and then escorted me

to his four-wheeler. Solow followed us and let David
lift him into the backseat. "He can sleep in the Jeep just
as well as the house," he said. I smiled at his thought-
fulness.

As David drove, I filled him in on the latest news
about Tavia and Garth. He didn't say a word. His jaw
tightened. He stared straight ahead, aiming his vehicle
at the far side of Watsonville.

David parked the Jeep at the Green Valley Grill at
seven-fifteen. I immediately spotted Charlie standing
near the entrance to the building, talking to a pretty
young woman wearing a black dress and smoking a
cigarette. We walked over to the attorney.

"Charlie Wellborn, I'd like you to meet my friend,
David Galaz." The men shook hands as the girl disappeared into the building. Charlie looked suave and self-
assured in his three-piece suit, but David was a
stud-muffin in Dockers, turtleneck and a cardigan. He
stood two inches taller than Charlie and had scruples
Charlie never even heard of.

"Are we a threesome tonight?" Charlie asked, clearing his throat and looking like he was late for a date in
another county.

"Hope you don't mind, but we have things to discuss," David said, as we walked inside the building and
rode the elevator to the third floor. David maneuvered
me out of the elevator with a possessive arm around
my shoulders. Charlie followed.

The three of us stepped over the threshold into the
restaurant entry where the young woman in black was
already back from her smoke break and ready to show
us to Charlie's favorite table. But we had become a

threesome and needed a bigger table. The greeter suggested we sit at the bar and she would call us as soon as a table became available. We took the three stools near the end of the bar next to a heavy set man slumped over his martini. I immediately recognized Hans and wished I had a date in another county. He turned his head.

"Ms. Stuart, … lovely to see you." Hans said in a slurred version of the English language.

"Hans, I'd like you to meet David Galaz and Charles Wellborn." Was Hans actually being nice to me? If he was, it was probably due to his inebriated condition.

"Charlie?" Hans said. "What are you, ah, never mind. Did you know that Garth … oh, sorry, can't talk about that." Hans propped his head up on one hand as he stirred his drink with the olive stick. He gulped his martini, slapped money on the bar, stood up on wobbly legs and turned to leave.

"Do you have a ride home?" I asked. He didn't answer, just headed for the elevator. I ran after him. "Have you had dinner, Hans?"

"Not exactly."

"Join us for dinner … please." I grabbed his coat sleeve and with a little help, he clumsily pivoted around so that he faced the bar again.

"Well, maybe one more for the road."

"No. I mean it's time to eat." I glared at the bartender, silently daring him to serve Hans another drink. The greeter walked up to Charlie with news of an available table. David steered Hans by his elbow as the four of us filed through the dining room to a table in the center of all the tables. Charlie quickly dropped into the seat next to me. David helped Hans into his chair and then sat down beside him.

Before the hostess left, I asked her to have someone bring a cup of coffee to our table. She nodded knowingly, while Charlie cleared his throat and fidgeted with his tie.

"I'm not sure that this is an appropriate situation for the discussion of Justin's defense," Charlie said to me in a raspy voice, followed by more nervous throat clearing.

"David knows everything I know about the case and I'm thinking Hans might be of help to us." I looked over at Hans with his head hanging low and wondered if he would be conscious, let alone helpful. My gut feeling was that he had fled the Tavia camp once he found out about Garth's poisoning. I had insisted Hans stay with us; so whatever happened, it was my fault he would hear our conversation.

Charlie settled down, sipped his white wine and stared at the flickering candle in the middle of the table. I couldn't help but notice how much his profile looked like Tom Selleck's. Our waiter appeared and we ordered. David had to take over for Hans who stared at his menu like an incoherent dolt.

"So, David, tell me about your line of work," Charlie said, handing my friend one of his business cards featuring gold lettering and a head shot of Mr. H.C. Wellborn.

"Retired." David answered with no mention of his apricot orchard, his volunteer work or his V.P. position before retirement.

"How is Justin's case looking?" David asked.

"There's always a possibility the jury could find him not guilty, but there were no witnesses for the defendant," he said.

I turned toward Charlie, red faced and ready to attack. "No witnesses my foot!" I hissed. "What am I, mashed potatoes? I was there. I pulled Jim up from the floor. I saw the feet at the top of the stairs. Tavia's feet, actually."

"Tavia, who?" Charlie asked, his eyes squinted, his voice smooth.

I suddenly felt like everyone in the restaurant was staring at me.

"How many Tavias do you know? Tavia Thornton, of course, and I saw her feet. She was the one at the top of the stairs. She's done lots of terrible things lately, like poisoning her stepson and crashing my truck and lipstick on Oliver ...."

Hans nodded his head up and down and then began shaking it side to side, looking like he was deeply disturbed by the line of conversation. He was definitely more alert, thanks to the tone of my voice. People at other tables seemed interested too.

"I trusted ... Tavia," Hans whimpered.

"Exactly what did Mrs. Thornton say to you, Mr. Coleberg?" Charlie asked.

"She told me she saw Justin ... the day Jim fell. She told me Garth was ill and she wanted to help him ..." Hans' chin rested on his chest as a tear made its way down his fleshy cheek. "She lied to me. She used me ... and she used my friend, Willy ... poor Willy."

"What do you mean when you say she used you?" Charlie squirmed in his seat next to me. "How do you know she lied?"

"I thought she wanted to build the Re ... search Center ... but no, she wanted a mall instead. I found an email ... she threw away ...." Hans' voice faded as a grimace twisted his flushed face. "She lied to Willy."

Charlie practically gulped his wine as he listened to the pitiful man.

"So, Charlie, how did it happen that Justin hired you to be his lawyer?" I asked.

"I work for Mr. Thornton, his family and associates. Naturally, I offered my services to poor Justin as soon as I was informed of his arrest."

"It wasn't so you could find out how much Justin knew about the murder?" I asked in my most angelic voice.

"That doesn't even deserve an answer," he snapped.

Our food arrived. No one looked hungry, but we put fork to mouth and tried to enjoy the food, except for Hans. His shaky hands could barely handle the cup of coffee that was periodically refilled by an ambitious tip-seeking busboy. Charles clammed up, I was steamed, David simmered and Hans was pickled. Fortunately no one asked for dessert, just a bill so we could leave the uncomfortable dining experience. Charlie split the bill with David.

David steadied Hans in the elevator, keeping him vertical and then helped him into the passenger side of the Lincoln. I drove Han's car while David and Solow followed in the Jeep. We traveled about ten miles north of Watsonville up Highway One to the small town of Aptos. Thankfully, Hans knew his way home and in no time we arrived at the smallest house in his up-scale neighborhood. His house was located just behind the tenth hole of a very prestigious golf course and surrounded on both sides by lovely homes. I parked the Lincoln in his driveway.

David opened the car door and helped the large lump of a man climb out. We each took an arm and guided Hans into the house.

"I want to go to bed," he said, barely able to mouth the words. After a few wrong turns, we finally discovered his bedroom upstairs. Hans melted into the bedspread. David pulled his shoes off, and I wrapped him up in the bedspread like a giant enchilada. Poor man had no one to keep him warm. A framed photo of his deceased wife sat on the bureau. David and I trotted downstairs and out the front door.

"David, what did you think of Charlie? Is he the snake I think he is?"

"Well, I just met the man. You have to give him a little slack because he's a lawyer."

"The man just sets me off," I said, more to Solow than David. Solow was sitting up, enjoying his ride home in the manly jeep. David pulled into my driveway and parked behind the rental car. The house was dark. I figured Sarah was still at Steve's house.

"How about a cup of decaf and a slice of banana bread?"

"Sure. Sounds like something Sarah used to bake."

"She still does, and … she cleans my house and she loves Solow. As a houseguest, she's worked out pretty well." I opened the front door and immediately smelled the perfume I hated along with stale cigarette smoke. I told myself that as long as I hated the perfume and not the woman, I was not being hateful. David turned on a light and we looked around.

"That does it! She burned a hole in my coffee table. I'll kill that good-for-nothing woman." So much for trying not to hate thy neighbor. I stormed through the house, followed by Solow, looking for any other evidence the witch might have left behind.

"She just wanted me to know that she could break into my house any time she pleased. How did she know I wasn't home? David, how did she get in?"

"I think we left the backdoor unlocked."

"Yeah, I guess so. We were in a hurry and I forgot to lock it. I never worry about locking up when Solow's home, but we took him with us at the last minute." I pounded my fist on the kitchen countertop. "From now on every door will be locked." I rubbed my sore hand. "Guess we should report the break in."

"Do you want me to make the call?" David asked.

"Would you, please? They would probably hang up on me, or else I'd lose my temper or something." I popped another comforting Valentine chocolate in my mouth. There were only three left in the heart-shaped box and when David came back to tell me about his phone call, there were none.

"Same old thing. They'll be here sometime within the hour." He ushered me to the living room sofa, built a fire in the fireplace and turned the TV to an oldies music station. Five minutes later, there was a knock at the front door. David opened it.

"Evening, folks." Deputy Sayer flashed his badge as if we were meeting for the first time. Deputy Lund, looking bored, marched inside ahead of her partner.

"You had a break-in this evening?" she asked. Her eyes searched the room. "Can you describe the damage?"

"Right there, on the coffee table," I said as I removed a National Geographic from the burn spot. I had kept the damage covered, hoping to quell my anger.

"That's it?" She looked at me like I was a cockroach walking across her lunch.

"Actually," David said, "we aren't as concerned about the burn mark as we are about the fact that an intruder felt compelled to make herself at home on private property."

"Do you know who the intruder was?" Deputy Sayer asked.

"It was Tavia Thornton," I said, matter-of-factly. "The same woman who killed Jim, flattened my tires, poisoned Garth ...."

"Wait a minute, ma'am. What makes you think that Ms. Thornton was involved?" Deputy Lund asked, trying to drown out my voice which was getting louder by the second. "Take a deep breath, ma'am."

"We know it was Tavia because when we left the house at seven, there were no burn marks on my tables. When we came home at ten, there was a burn mark on my table like the one she made on Rosa's table. And her smelly perfume was all over my house."

Deputy Lund rolled her eyes and let Deputy Sayer take the floor.

"Ms. Stuart, we just want to know why you think someone broke into your house while you were away. Do you have a relative or friend who might have ...?"

"No! I know very few people who smoke and none

who would break into my house, except my boss, Tavia Thornton."

"And just how did this boss person break in?"

"Actually, I left the backdoor unlocked. But she had no right to ...."

"Ma'am," Deputy Lund interrupted, "unless your damages exceed $500.00 dollars, we can't continue with the investigation. Obviously the table ... well, I'm sure it has sentimental value, but that's not enough." She was already inching her way toward the door, but Sayer got there first.

"We'll be in touch." He opened the door and they disappeared into the night.

"Now, what?"

"Josie, honey, we know what happened. Now we just have to be more careful until she's caught. I want you to try to relax and let the police do their job."

"I know she'll be caught eventually, but right now I'm just so angry." I felt like a keg of dynamite with a short fuse. Scratch a match on my nose and I'd blow up everything in sight. David tried his best to snap me out of my horrible mood, but all the kindness in the world couldn't get my mind off that woman. Finally, he said he was going home so that I could get some sleep.

I locked the doors and Solow and I shuffled off to bed. I fell into a dark dream state where I watched Tavia circling my head riding a wet mop, cackling and letting the grubby thing slap me in the face as she made her turns. I saw a fuse dangling from the mop handle and struggled to reach high enough to connect the flame from my match with the string. Before I could make contact, she flew away leaving me holding the match.

CHAPTER TWENTY

Sunday morning I woke up feeling rested. I let Solow out the backdoor for a Fluffy chase and started my shower. Over the sound of rushing water, I heard Solow barking and figured he was having a good run with David's cat. I laughed to myself as I imagined Fluffy running the usual circles around my poor, short-legged basset. Solow's barking stopped before my shower ended. I began thinking about other things, like what a downer I was the night before. I didn't blame David for leaving early.

As I toweled off I heard the front door slam and quick, pounding footsteps coming closer.

"Josephine, are you in there?" Sarah shouted.

I quickly slipped my robe on, opened the bathroom door and looked into a pale round face with quivering lips and teary blue eyes. Sarah stood gasping for air, looking white as the proverbial ghost. I put my arms around her as her body shook like an unbalanced washing machine.

"What's wrong, Sarah?"

"She took Solow!" she half screamed, half cried. We have to catch her …."

"Who did what?" I didn't want to believe I heard what I thought I heard.

"Tavia! She took him in her car … I thought I saw her driving down Otis a minute ago, just before Steve dropped me here. The car went by so fast … it wasn't until Steve dropped me off that I made sense of what I saw … a red Jaguar, a dog in the back seat … a woman driver with black hair and a young man sitting next to her." Sarah shivered.

"A woman with black hair? Are you sure?" I took a step back as all the blood drained from my head. "Dang blasted …!! She must be wearing a wig. She's flipped out!"

"I know it sounds crazy, but I recognized Solow. My first thought was, where is Solow going? My second thought was … I remember you saying that Tavia drives a red Jaguar with gold trim."

By that time I was jamming myself into Levis and a pullover sweater, and thinking wild thoughts of what I would do to Tavia if I caught her. Burning at the stake would be too quick. My jaw clenched as I shoved my feet into Nikes and grabbed a windbreaker.

"Are you sure her hair was black?"

"Oh yes, it was black all right, and the boy was blond."

"Sounds like her son, Mark." What kind of woman would introduce her fourteen-year-old to a life of crime. I grabbed my purse, slammed the door and we scrambled into the Chevy loaner. Gravel sprayed behind us as we fishtailed down the driveway to Otis, and swerved onto San Juan. I pushed the gas pedal to the floor.

"Tighten your seatbelt, Sarah." I glanced to my right. She was whiter than the dotted line down the middle of San Juan Road. From the top of the hill we saw a line of cars waiting for an unusually long freight train. The guards were down and red lights flashed.

"Look, Josephine. That's the car I saw." She pointed to a red Jag at the head of the line of waiting cars. I slowed down as we approached a silver SUV, last in the line of at least fifteen cars. I watched the slow-moving train and noticed that the caboose was only a couple of lettuce fields away. It would pass by us in less than a minute, the arms would go up and we would be bringing up the rear.

I pulled off the pavement onto dirt and slowly passed one car on the right, then another and so on until we were only two cars from the Jaguar. The train was gone, the arms went up and I fought to cut in between a dump truck and a blue station wagon.

"Look out!" Sarah screamed, crouching down in her seat, expecting the wagon to scrape us or worse. Finally, I was able to wedge my little car between the two vehicles, but the truck took forever to gain any speed. Billows of black smoke clouded our windshield and polluting the air. Sarah gagged and coughed as I yelled a few angry words at the truck driver.

"Sure hope he turns off at Murphy Road, otherwise we're stuck at thirty miles an hour all the way," I said, as if Sarah were listening or cared. She hung onto her door with white knuckles, crouched and quiet. "Hang on, Solow. We're coming," I whispered.

We followed the dump truck all the way to the Pajaro Bridge with no passing opportunities, even though it was Sunday morning and traffic should have been light. As we approached the bridge, I spotted the infamous Jaguar idling at a stoplight with about a dozen cars behind it. Time was moving so slow for me. I wanted to push the gas pedal down hard instead of waiting for the light to turn green. Finally it turned and the cars began to move forward, but I needed to pass a few and shorten the gap.

"Oh no! Construction signs. The left lane is closed." I banged the steering wheel with my fist. "I don't see any workmen. Who works on Sunday anyway?" I pulled into the left lane where cars were merging to the right. Instead of merging, I squeezed between a few orange cones until I had passed half the cars.

"Stop!" Sarah screamed. "There's an open pit in front of us."

"I know. I just saw it." Blast it anyway. I began inching my way back into traffic, but no one wanted to let me in except for a blue station wagon which put us behind the smelly old dump truck again.

As we motored up and over the Pajaro Bridge, I looked down at the next red light where a red Jaguar idled at the head of the pack. The light turned green and the Jag turned left across the intersection.

"At least we know she's headed toward the freeway," Sarah said.

"Keep watching." By the time we reached the intersection the light turned red. I thought about running it, but something inside wouldn't let me. Not even for Solow's sake. So we sat for another eternity. Finally the light turned green, we made a left onto Riverside and headed toward the freeway.

"Oh, Josephine," was all Sarah could say as she covered her mouth with both hands. The same train we had waited for ten miles ago was now crossing Riverside Drive. We were first in line but it was a very long train, probably ninety or a hundred cars. Silently I cursed all the industries that used the railroad, like the quarry, the lumber camps, even the farmers.

The train disappeared down the tracks at about eight miles per hour, the arms went up and we sped down Riverside toward the freeway. No sign of a red Jag. I had two choices. For no reason at all I chose to head north on Highway One. We passed up the Green Valley exit and took Airport Boulevard. The airport was kind of a "Mom and Pop" airport, small but popular and located near the freeway exit. I figured we could circle back through Watsonville, maybe stop at Steve's and call for help. But as we passed the airport, Sarah did a double take.

"Turn! Turn! Look!" she screamed, with her head against the windshield as she pointed madly at the parking lot beside the runway. I pulled a U-ee at the signal light and turned right, straight into the parking lot. We screeched to a stop beside a red Jaguar with gold trim. The car was empty, but running across the tarmac was a black-haired woman in high heels.

Running like crazy behind his mother was Mark, carrying a heavy bundle wrapped in a blanket with a basset tail hanging out one end. They clambered into a small, white, six-windowed private jet. By the time we jumped out of the car, the plane was halfway down the runway.

I reached into my purse, pulled my cell phone out and watched the jet take off. It made a wide half-circle and headed east. I dialed 911.

"Hello, I have a terrible emergency."

"Your name, please."

"Never mind that. There's an APB out for Tavia Thornton and she just stole my dog."

"Ma'am, this sounds like a matter you can settle at the police station ...."

"You don't understand. She murdered someone and then she tried to poison her stepson and then she took my ...."

"Ma'am, slow down. You say her name is Tavia, what?"

"Just get the police out to the Watsonville airport fast ... please." I hung up, dialed David's number and left a message. Next I called the Quintanas and left a message.

Sarah held her hand out for the phone. "I'll call Steve. He'll know what to do." She dialed. "Steve, are you busy?"

"Yeah, I told you I had a big order of paint to mix. Why? You sound out of breath."

"Oh, Steve, it's awful. Poor Josephine. I know you're upset with ... ah," Sarah put one hand over the speaker, looked at me and blushed. "But Tavia dognapped Solow and they took off in a jet plane. Jo is beside herself with worry."

"Where are you?"

"We're at the Watsonville airport."

"I'll just put the tops on these buckets of paint and get right down there. Don't worry." He hung up.

Sarah looked relieved, but not me. After all, what could Steve do?"

"I think I'll walk over to that building." I pointed to a modest one-story office building at the southern edge of the runway. "Why don't you sit in the car where it's warm and wait for Steve?"

Sarah agreed to stay with the car so that Steve could locate us. She looked like she was going to cry. That was a luxury I could not afford for myself, at least not yet.

I walked half a block barely feeling the cold, even though I had rushed out of the house wearing only a thin wind breaker over my clothes. My heart was aching. I finally reached the building bearing the sign that had caught my attention. It read, "Helicopter Flight School." I burst through the door, happy to see Alberto's smiling face behind the desk.

"Josephine, nice to see you again," Alberto said, as I dashed across the room. "Don't tell me you liked the helicopter ride so much you want to learn to fly one." His smile was a mile wide until he realized I wasn't smiling.

"Alberto, I'm afraid I'm in the middle of a crisis. I wonder if you could answer a couple of questions?"

"Here," he pulled out a chair for me, "please sit down. My student won't be here until nine o'clock." He hovered like a mother hen. "What seems to be the problem?"

"It's a very long and terrible story. Right now I just need to know if every plane that takes off from this airport needs to file a flight plan."

"Well, no. Why do you worry about that? You're trembling. Can I get you some water, a cup of coffee …?"

"No, thank you. Did you happen to see the jet that took off about five minutes ago?"

"No, I didn't. Planes take off about every five or ten minutes around here. So many … I don't even notice them any more." He shook his head back and forth slowly.

"I really need to know where a certain jet is going. My dog has been stolen and he's on that plane." I pointed to the ceiling.

"Maybe Hal saw it take off." Alberto led me outside and over to the office next door where he held the door and followed me inside.

"Hal, got a minute?" Alberto leaned over Hal's desk while I found a seat near the front windows. They talked for a minute, Hal shrugged his shoulders and then Albert motioned for me to join the huddle.

"Josephine, I'd like you to meet Hal." We shook hands.

"So you're looking for your friends?" Hal asked. I rolled my eyes to the ceiling and Hal got the message. "Do you know the type of plane ….?"

"In the first place, I'm assuming it was a jet. I don't claim to know one plane from another, but it had six round windows on the side." I looked at Alberto, hoping he would remember seeing something.

"Sounds like a private jet." Hal said. Alberto nodded. "Only a hand full of them around here."

I glanced out the window toward the runway hoping to see a small white jet land and a darling old dog disembark, but all I saw was a police car pulling into a parking space. The car was black and white, not green like the sheriff's cars that were so prevalent in my life around that time. Sarah and an officer climbed out of the car. She was leading him to Alberto's little office, but I stepped outside and waved them over to Hal's office.

"Josephine, are you OK?" Sarah asked in a quivery little voice.

"Fine, but Tavia won't be so good when I ...."

"Ma'am, I'm Sergeant Williams. Can you describe the victim, rather, the dog that was stolen?" Williams was young, tall, handsome and already moving his pen across the top page of his notebook. I automatically compared him to Deputies Lund and Sayer, and quickly decided there was no comparison.

"Solow is a typical basset hound, about the size of my coffee table. He eats a lot and sleeps every chance he gets. He's brown and black and white, depending on which end you're looking at." I brushed a tear away and continued. "He has the cutest long ears and his feet are extra big." I couldn't go on because it felt like a tennis ball was lodged in my throat.

"His collar is brown leather," Sarah offered.

"Ma'am, where was your dog when it disappeared?"

"In my own front yard! I let him outside for a Fluffy chase. I heard him bark a few times when I was in the shower, but it wasn't until Sarah told me she saw Solow riding in a Jag that I thought anything was wrong."

Sarah burst into tears. Holding mine back became that much harder.

"What time was it when you realized your dog was missing?" he asked.

"Ah, let me think. I finished my shower just in time for the KPIG eight o'clock news. That's when Sarah told me she saw Solow in the back seat of Tavia's car. I threw on some clothes and here we are." I ran my fingers through damp, tangled hair.

"I see," he said, looking at hair that must have looked like it came straight out of a blender. "You mentioned someone named 'Tavia.'"

"Yes, she's my employer's wife. She killed Jim, poisoned Garth, crashed my truck and stole my dog, all because of a farm that the county wants to take away from poor Mr. Mendoza." I took a breath.

The sergeant pulled up a chair and sat down. "Let's take it from the top," he said, looking slightly fatigued. Sarah and I told the whole story, helping each other remember details as we talked. Alberto and Hal sat with mouths open, hanging on every word, especially the part about dropping fliers from a certain helicopter. About ten pages and one hour later, we all stood up and stretched.

"Ladies, you can go now, I have your statements," Officer Williams said, turning around to talk to Hal.

I walked behind the desk and thanked Alberto and Hal for trying to help. Alberto gave me a bear hug and wished me luck. Hal gave me an encouraging smile, while Sarah held the door open looking a little lost.

"I don't understand why Steve isn't here yet."

"Isn't that him in the green truck?" I pointed to a Chevy pickup idling in the parking lot near my loaner and the red Jag. Sarah saw it and picked up the pace. A cold wind slapped our cheeks and stabbed my broken heart. But at that point in time, I was impervious to any aggravation except the existence of Tavia.

"Hi, Steve. I thought you'd never get here," Sarah said, leaning against his door.

"Yeah, well I tried to get here sooner, but one customer after another came into the store and my help was overwhelmed." He shrugged his shoulders and pushed his lips into a pout. She fell for it, reached through the open window and ran her hand down the side of his face. He managed a pathetic smile.

"Hi, Steve. Thanks for coming down here to help us," I said.

He forced a polite smile. "Sarah says your dog's been stolen. I really like that old hound. What can I do to help?"

"We thought you might know what we should do," Sarah whined.

"First, call the police."

"We've already talked to Sergeant Williams. He's going to try to help us," she said. "I just thought you might know something else we could do."

"No, I don't know what you can do except wait for the police to do their work. I'm sorry, but I have to get back to the store." He leaned toward Sarah and she kissed him. We watched the pickup dart onto Airport Boulevard and disappear into the blur of traffic.

"Let's go," I said.

"But where?"

"Who knows Tavia really well? I think we need to talk to Hans." I pulled my loaner into traffic and motored west to the freeway.

"I thought you hated him after all the things he said, upsetting you and ...."

"I think Hans will be more cooperative now that Tavia almost killed his Godchild. We ran into him last night and he was completely distraught over Garth being poisoned. He was drunk at the time, but hopefully he still hates Tavia." Ten minutes later, we were cruising through an exclusive, woodsy Aptos neighborhood. I parked in Hans' driveway beside the Lincoln.

"So, how do you know Garth is his Godchild?" Sarah asked as she climbed out of the car. "And how do you know so much about Hans, like, where he lives?"

"I was in his bedroom last night and saw his family photos on the bureau."

"Oh."

CHAPTER TWENTY ONE

Sarah and I scrambled out of the car and up the path to Hans' front door. It took quite a few rings of the doorbell and some heavy knocking before Hans appeared, puffy and red-faced, obviously enduring a headache the size of a beach ball.

"Oh, it's you," he growled out of habit.

"Sorry to disturb you, Hans, but I need to know where Tavia might go if she flew out from the Watsonville airport."

"Huh?"

"She stole my dog. We followed her to the airport, and we saw Tavia, Mark and Solow get into a jet and head east."

"Come in, ladies." It seemed his memory of the night before finally came into focus. "Sit here." He pointed to a pristine white couch with mauve accent pillows at each end. The whole place looked like it had been decorated expensively thirty years ago and not disturbed since—probably not since his wife died. Hans flinched as he lowered himself gently into a matching white chair.

"If you're still upset with Tavia, maybe you can help us find her," I implored.

"Mr. Thornton called from the hospital this morning.

He said Garth is having a tough time." Hans sniffed and went on. "You say she took your dog? Why on earth would she do that?"

"I don't know why she does half the stuff she does, but I have to find Solow."

"You say she flew out of Watsonville? That would be the private jet and their pilot, Jamie Walsh. I've known her for years … sorry, ah, you want to know where Mrs. Thornton might be going."

"With her son, Mark," Sarah added.

"Yes, yes I see. Well, I don't think it would be to their estate in Connecticut or the beach house in Miami, but maybe … it might be the cabin at Tahoe." He looked at the ceiling, trying to remember if there were any more possibilities.

"Can you give us an address for the Tahoe cabin?" I asked, impatiently.

"Oh, I can do better than that. I'll drive you up there; you see, I have a score to settle. Did you ladies bring any warm clothing, jackets and the like?"

"You really would drive us up there? Right now?" I couldn't believe my ears.

"Absolutely. What about jackets?" he asked in earnest.

"Actually, we've been on the run since eight o'clock. No time to pack."

"Very well, I'll fish around for some cold-weather gear." He galloped up the stairs like a man half his age. A man on a mission. Five minutes later he stood in front of us with an armload of jackets, scarves, leggings, gloves and knitted hats. "As you can see, I hate to get rid of things … my wife's things, that is." He dropped the whole pile onto the couch between us.

Sarah's eyes lit up as she pulled a pink scarf with matching cap and mittens from the stack. A wool jacket fit Sarah nicely once the sleeves were rolled up twice. My black all-weather jacket was loose, but satisfactory. I gathered up a whole set of teal green accessories. Once I had everything I needed, I looked up to see Hans pulling his warm clothing out of the coat closet by the stairs, along with a tin box that was smaller than a breadbox and had a lock on it. The three of us dashed out the front door. We threw our newly acquired winter gear into the trunk and jumped into the old, but impeccably clean, white Lincoln. Sarah sat in the front seat and I took the back.

"I can't believe I'm being spontaneous," Hans muttered. "If only my wife could see me now." He backed down the driveway. "I was a bit of a dud years ago."

It wasn't hard to imagine Hans as a dud, but I kept my mouth shut.

About a hundred miles of scenery zoomed by and Hans hadn't said a word. We sped through Sacramento on Highway 80 and then tackled the Sierra Mountain Range. The Lincoln rode like a dream as it powered up the mountains with spirit. The man knew his way and wasn't stopping for anything.

My stomach growled, reminding me that breakfast and lunch had never happened. A couple more hours and it would be time for dinner. I wondered if Tavia had given Solow enough food and water. I decided to call David and let him know what we were doing. Just as I pulled the phone from my purse, it rang. "Hello?"

"Josie, I got your message. Are you OK?" David

sounded like he was breathing hard. "I just got home. How can I help?"

"You won't believe where we are—that is, Sarah, Hans and I. We're halfway to the Thornton's cabin in Tahoe."

"Honey, don't do anything crazy. Have you called the police?" He sounded frantic at that point. He knew my bent for getting into tight situations which were not my fault.

"I wish you were here, David, but you could help by calling the Tahoe police for us. We'll be going to … Hans, what's the address we're going to?"

"Four-forty Northwind Boulevard at Incline Village," Hans answered.

I repeated the address to David and asked him to call Steve right after he called the Tahoe Sheriff. He said he would see me soon. I doubted that. We hung up and the miles droned on.

"Looks like we'll have to stop for gas pretty soon," I said, popping my last "tic tac" into my mouth. "Hope they have food."

"I hadn't thought about food or gas. But you're right, we will have to stop. I remember a service station about ten miles from here with some sort of food establishment next door." He leaned forward in his seat, white-knuckled hands held the steering wheel as he stared straight ahead with unblinking eyes.

Sarah busied herself trying to find radio music to please all of us. When a station faded out of range, she found another. She wasn't complaining about hunger, but she fidgeted like she was ready for a restroom break. I knew how she felt, but we had to hold on for ten more curvy miles.

"You really know your way around up here in the mountains," I said to Hans.

"I spent many happy vacations up here with the Thorntons and Jim and Jenny—she was Jim's wife before she left him." Hans' voice softened a tad as he reminisced about the old days. "Anyway, we went on holiday with them several times. Old Jim was quite the athletic skier in his day. Someone told me he almost made it to the Olympics. He was that good. Of course, that was long before I knew him."

A Shell station appeared on our right and next to it was the Dinky Diner.

Hans angled the Lincoln into an empty space next to a gas pump.

"We'll see you at the Dinky Diner," I shouted to Hans. Sarah ran to the restroom in back of the gas station. I walked about thirty feet over to the Dinky Diner. Their accommodations were exceptionally dinky. Getting out of the little restroom was harder than getting in. I had to straddle the toilet in order to get the door open and make my exit. I didn't even try for the water faucet a la carte, that came without soap or towels. I trotted outside, into the frigid air and back to the Shell station restroom. I darted in as Sarah stepped out.

A few minutes later, the three of us were settled into hardback chairs arranged around a small oak table with a centerpiece consisting of bottled catsup, mustard and Tabasco sauce. My stomach did summersaults as I thought about salty, greasy food.

"I saw a little patch of snow along the side of the road," Sarah said.

"We'll see a lot more snow from now on. You might want to wear jackets the next time we leave the car," Hans said.

Our waitress, wrinkled and worn like my favorite leather purse, stood between Hans and Sarah. Her eyes were the color of Solow's favorite blanket, pale blue, and her voice sounded dry like she had been cheering for hours at a football game, but her attitude was friendly. She handed out three well-worn menus.

"Coffee, honey?" she asked, leaning toward Hans.

We all said, "Yes," and she headed for the kitchen.

"Look, blueberry crepes … oh my, and spinach soufflé … and a crab melt. I don't know what I want," Sarah sighed, her eyes raking over the grease stained menu. "It all sounds so good."

I looked around to see what other people were ordering, but the only other customer in the place had just finished his meal. A few French fries remained on his plate. Oh well, I was hungry enough to eat dirt at that point.

Hans ordered a hamburger, Sarah asked for a chicken pesto personal-size pizza and I ordered the crab mango bisque with jumbo shrimps on the side. We sipped our coffee and discussed the weather while we waited for the food to arrive, but no one wanted to bring up the subject that dominated our thoughts. Silently, I wondered if Solow was scared, if he was hungry, if he was alive.

"My, my," Hans said as he was served a giant burger with dozens of fries, a pickle that could choke a horse and a big smile from the old woman. My expectations grew until I laid eyes on my jumbo shrimps which were quite small, all three of them. They were dry, freezer-burned and barely heated. The crab mango bisque arrived in a small chipped bowl and smelled like yesterday's fish. Sarah's pizza had obviously come from a dinky frozen package.

Hans offered us some of his fries and we accepted, but even with that, Sarah and I were still hungry. Our waitress didn't miss a beat. She had a dessert menu in front of us before we could mutter "apple pie." The pictures were inviting and I was sorely tempted, but we had urgent business down the road. Sarah opened her mouth to speak, but I quickly told the waitress we wanted the bill and no dessert. Sarah looked disappointed until her memory brought up the reason for the whole ridiculous chase in the middle of February in snow country. She gave me a brave smile.

Hans sipped his coffee, looking comfortably stuffed.

"It's only three o'clock and it's already getting dark outside," Sarah said.

"Storm's coming," Hans replied, as he paid the check. He was the kind of old-fashioned guy who would always insist on paying a lady's way. Besides, he owed me for all the nasty things he had said to me over the past week.

We rushed outside to the car, shivering as we climbed in.

"That wind is sure cold," Sarah complained, her teeth chattering like castanets as she slammed the door. The car heated up quickly. We drove past heaps of dirty snow from previous storms lining both sides of the four-lane highway and made good time all the way up to Donner Summit. As we headed down the mountain, fresh flakes of snow covered the windshield. Hans turned on the wipers and slowed the car down. Minutes later, everything was white: the sky, the ground and everything in between.

It was hard to know where the road was so Hans aimed the car down the middle, between three-foot walls of old dirty snow. But the old snow was quickly turning pure white like everything else. The car began to slide, right to left, and then left to right as Hans over-corrected.

"Have any chains?" I asked as sweat trickled down my back.

"I keep them in the trunk." He pulled the car over to the right, sliding to a stop against a mountain of old snow. It was hard to tell if we were off the road since every surface was covered with several inches of white fluff. Hans opened the trunk and we quickly pulled out our foul-weather gear. He dragged out a box of chains, dropped it beside the back right tire and reentered the car. Sarah and I scrambled back inside.

"Now, what?" I asked, impatiently.

"We wait for a tow truck and we pay the man to put the chains on. That's how it's done. Don't worry. They patrol up and down the highway all day and night helping people like us."

"Couldn't the three of us put them on?" I asked. Hans shook his head. We zipped up our jackets and let the Lincoln take on a mantle of snow. About every ten minutes Hans would start the engine long enough to warm the car. Half an hour ticked by. I could have spent that time saving Solow from whatever Tavia had in mind.

"Won't be long now, ladies." Hans opened his window and a bearded face appeared. He told the tow truck driver, wearing orange rubber overalls, where the chains were and the guy went to work. Hans did his part. The bearded gentleman told him when to roll forward and when to stop. Finally, the chains were on, the man was paid and we were motoring down the highway at a full thirty miles per hour. Clank. Clank. Clank. Traffic was extremely light and there were none of the usual interstate big rigs.

Sarah flipped through the radio stations until she found one that came in loud and clear. The announcer was in the middle of warning everyone of an impending storm in the Sierras. According to the weatherman, the worst of it would hit around midnight. Chains were required on the roads that were still open. I thanked God that Highway 80 was one of those roads.

I sat back and imagined my reunion with Solow, how I would crouch down and hug him and scratch behind his velvety ears. He would whine and cry, telling me all about what had happened to him.

Sarah cranked her head around to look at me in the backseat.

"I was just thinking about ... ah, what's wrong, Josephine?"

"Nothing, just thinking about Solow."

"I know. I was too. Funny, I don't spend much time thinking about my cats, but that old sad-eyed dog had me on the first wag of his tail," Sarah sighed. "But he'll be fine, you'll see."

"Hans, how much farther?"

"We've already passed Boreal, Soda Springs and

Donner Lake. "We'll take Highway 267 down to Lakeshore Boulevard to Incline Village. Half an hour or less." The snow hadn't let up. It was almost dark at four o'clock.

Suddenly my phone played a little tune causing me to jump out of my skin. I was wound way too tight. "Hello?"

"Josie, I'm at the four-forty Northwind address ...."

"David? Is that you? What do you mean you're at four-forty?"

"That's right, Steve and I got a ride with Alberto."

"You rode in a helicopter ...?"

"No, Al flies airplanes, too. In fact, he owns one. We were lucky to get here before the storm. We checked out the address, but no one's around except half the Nevada police force." He sounded like he was shivering. I couldn't believe we had gone that far just to have Tavia slip through our fingers. I started to speak, but my phone made some static noises and went dead.

I relayed David's message to Hans who shook his angry crimson head.

"Now what?" I asked.

"I know another place we can try. Tell me if you see a phone booth."

"Hans, those things went out with the dinosaurs. But I'll try." We had already made the turn onto Highway 267 and twenty minutes later, we were cruising near Kings Beach on Lakeshore Boulevard. Quaint, North Pole-looking stores, gas stations and office buildings lined both sides of the street. Their pointy snow-capped roofs and colorful shutters were storybook cute. Snow-laden pine trees grew between and behind the buildings, giving the place even more country character.

"Stop!" Sarah shouted. "On the left, look … isn't that a phone booth?" Falling snow made it hard to make out details, but yes, we all agreed it was a phone booth. Hans parked in the lot close to the booth and disappeared inside. His body fit wall-to-wall. I saw him write something on his hand and then return to the car.

"Got it! Curt's address. I knew it was on Northwind," he mumbled to himself.

"Now, what?" I asked as the car made a U-ee in the empty parking lot and then clunk-clunked down Lakeshore. The village looked like a town preparing for a storm, few cars and no pedestrians. Yellow lights glowed in a couple of windows but most were shuttered and dark.

As we crossed into Nevada, people didn't seem to know that a storm was coming. Maybe Nevada was impervious to snow, wind and major chill. The Crystal Bay stores and casinos had their lights blazing and people walked along the sidewalks as if it were an evening in June.

As we rolled through Incline Village, Sarah said, "Oh, I know this area. David and I used to play golf right up there." She pointed to the left, up Northwind Boulevard. Hans signaled and turned left. The Lincoln moved up the hill and then slowed. The average house on that wide street was at least a dozen rooms, two stories with four-car garages situated on two acres of land and surrounded on three sides by pine trees.

Hans drove us past three sheriff's SUVs clustered in front of one large home. Official red lights swirled as people milled around pointing flashlights. I guessed it was the Thornton's cabin and David was probably there. I wanted to see him, tell him all my fears and cry on his shoulder. But Hans showed no signs of stopping.

"Hans, aren't we going to …?"

"No!"

He drove a block past the Thornton house, followed the road as it made a sharp left, continued another three blocks and parked at the curb. He pointed to a large house about sixty yards up the street with a black SUV parked at the curb. My pulse quickened.

CHAPTER TWENTY-TWO

Sarah and I sat in the Lincoln pulling on hats, gloves and scarves as Hans fiddled around with something in the trunk. Only two houses in the last three blocks had lights in their windows. The home Hans had pointed to was dark. At least, no lights showed in the front. As soon as we were properly bundled, we climbed out of the car and entered the big chill. Snow fell diagonally in wind driven flurries.

"Hans, slow down. We can't keep up with you," I shouted, as we scurried to catch up to the bobbing light from his flashlight.

Hans twirled around and faced me. "Quiet! Just do what I do," he hissed. I noticed a bulge in his jacket pocket. Sarah and I didn't say a word. We just followed in Hans' big footprints past the black SUV. Snow stung my cheeks. I pulled my knitted cap down over frozen ear lobes. Sarah trudged along behind me, wrapping and rewrapping her scarf until it covered her nose.

If there was a sidewalk under the snow, we couldn't see it in the dark. We turned left, followed Hans' light up a long circular driveway and stopped in front of wide steps leading to extra tall, double-doors. The fifty-year-old house was built out of knotty pine. Facing the street were two giant angled windows that peaked in the middle giving the appearance of a ghost ship land-locked in a sea of pine trees and snow.

"I don't see Hans," Sarah whispered as the sound of her chattering teeth cut through the night.

"I can't see his footprints anymore," I whispered, bending down for a closer look. I finally discovered more footprints heading to the right side of the house. We skirted halfway around the building, feeling our way in the silent darkness.

"Eek!" I squeaked, stepping back from Hans' bulk. It was like hitting a giant "Sponge Bob," and then Sarah ran into me. Hans raised a finger and pointed to a sec-ond-story window where a slim line of yellow light es-caped from under the blinds. My heart skipped a beat. Sarah gasped as we stood still, huddled together, wait-ing for Hans to tell us what to do.

"I've never been in this house," he whispered. "I'm not a friend of Curt Anderson's."

"What now?" I whispered, impatiently.

"Stay here. I'll check the doors." Hans walked away, pointing the flashlight toward a set of wooden stairs an-gling up to a deck. A minute later his light was gone.

"I'm so cold," Sarah moaned. "How long do we have to stand here?"

"Beats me. I don't have any idea what he's up to." All of a sudden I heard a dog barking inside the house. Lights went on inside and out. Tears stung my eyes and my heart leaped for joy. Then came a long, mournful howl. My baby was calling me. But there were other sounds coming from inside the house; feet pounding down stairs, angry shouts, more barking and then more pounding on the stairs, some unintelligible shouting, two shots from a gun and thump, thump, crash. Solow howled long and hard.

Sarah and I clung to each other fearing the worst.

Finally, all was quiet. The porch light helped a lot as I crept up the back stairs onto the snow-covered deck. I turned to my left and found the backdoor, protected from the weather by a little pitched roof. I tried the doorknob. It turned and my heart went into full panic mode.

Sarah pushed in behind me, not wishing to be left behind. We entered the house through a long dark hallway and quietly tiptoed past a laundry room, bathroom and kitchen. We looked in all directions for Hans. Another distant howl gave me hope and fear at the same time.

We entered Curt's living room where a staircase curled up to the next story and another staircase headed straight down to a basement or cellar. The stairs going up were lit. Those going down were dark. I thought I heard a moan coming from downstairs. Sarah heard it too and squeezed my arm. I forced myself to look down, all the way to the big lump lying at the bottom. In the dim light, the lump could have been anything. But I suspected it was Hans. Fear hobbled my nerve and froze my body.

Solow whined, bringing me back to life and reminding me of what I needed to do. He sounded like he was downstairs somewhere, so I pulled myself together and took the first step down with Sarah still hanging onto my arm.

Suddenly I felt a presence in the room, someone breathing behind us. I started to turn but too late.

Someone bounded across the room and butted us over the edge.

I remember hitting walls on both sides as I bumped and bounced down the stairs, all tangled up with Sarah's arms and legs. I don't remember landing at the bottom or being dragged down the hall. When I awoke, all I knew was that my head hurt worse than all my other hurts put together. As I became more conscious and the fuzzies cleared out, I opened my eyes. But I couldn't tell if they were open or not since the room was black as Tavia's heart.

I tried to roll onto my side, but a body that felt like Sarah was in the way. On my other side, I felt a bigger body that I figured was Hans. They were not moving.

Suddenly I heard heavy breathing. I sat up, leaned forward and received a warm lick on my cheek from a friend. Solow was like a tonic to me. My heart pumped faster just knowing he was there with us. I wrapped my arms around his neck. He cried and whined and told me about everything he had been through.

I pulled myself up against a wall and staggered about ten feet until I finally found a light switch. Having light was almost worse than not having light. I saw, for the first time, Hans' bloody face as he lay quietly on his back. He looked like he had been shot with a bottle of catsup somewhere above his eye. I wondered if he was alive. Sarah was sprawled on her stomach, looking pale, but breathing.

Solow began licking Han's forehead. I didn't try to stop him. If Hans was dead he wouldn't care and if he was alive, at least his face would be clean. After a good licking, I noticed that the remaining bloody area was just an inch-long scratch very near his receding hairline. It looked like a bullet had taken out a small bit of flesh as it grazed his temple. Nothing too serious, compared to dying. Finally, I gathered enough courage to see if the man had a pulse. I removed my glove and placed a cold hand on Hans' neck. His body jerked, scaring me all the way back to the far corner of the room.

"Oh ... my head," he growled. Solow licked him on the lips. Hans opened his eyes and looked around. He watched Sarah sit up and scratch her head, and then he looked at me sitting in the corner waiting for everyone to acclimate.

Solow whined and wailed to Sarah, letting her know what a terrible time he had had with the witch. She hugged him and then tried to stand. On the second try she made it.

"Hans, are you all right?" she asked, as he sat up slowly.

"I think so. Actually, I think I may have been shot ... at least, someone was." He looked down at his old down jacket and then felt his forehead. "Oh my! My head hurts. Where's my gun?" A drop of blood ran down the side of his face.

"Careful, Hans," I said. "It appears you've been shot, but I think the bullet only grazed your head." I touched a throbbing goose egg on the back of my own head.

With saucer eyes, Sarah held a hand to her mouth and gazed at the wound on Hans' forehead. She spun around, checking out the windowless room full of workout equipment, and then saw herself in the wall of mirrors.

"Where are we?" Sarah croaked, running a hand over the top of her head. "Ouch! Omigosh, I have a huge lump on my head."

"Join the club." I watched poor Sarah lean against the mirrors. She was trembling and her teeth chattered uncontrollably. No wonder. The room was as cold as a freezer full of popsicles.

I focused on getting us out of the icy room, but even before I tried the door, I figured it was locked. Tavia wasn't going to let us run to the law. When Sarah saw me try the door knob and it didn't turn, she sucked in some air and let out a sob.

"What are we going to do now?" she wailed.

"Anyone see my gun?" Hans asked, not realizing yet that Tavia or Mark probably had it and had already used it on him.

"What I'd like to know is, are we alone in this house or are the Thorntons still here. Any ideas on how to get out of here, Hans?" I didn't poke fun at him about being shot with his own gun.

He tried to stand and finally gave up. He sat with his eyes closed, shoulders sagging, rocking back and forth. "We are obviously below ground level since there aren't any windows," he growled.

I checked my pockets for keys, hairpins, screwdrivers or any other object we could use to unlock the door. No luck, just a very old mint candy in a clear wrapper that might turn out to be my breakfast.

I sank down the wall to the floor, and Solow curled up next to me. I tried to stay alert, tried to think of a way out. After all my years of painting murals at new construction sites, I should know about doors. Eventually, I was able to bring up a memory of carpenters installing doors at the Willow Mansion. I did a freeze-frame in my mind, watching two young, shirtless men setting the door in place. I remembered that hot day. The more I pictured the action the warmer I felt. And then I concentrated on the hardware and how the two pieces of hinge fit together like fingers intertwined.

"That's it!" I blurted. "We need to pull the pins."

Sarah cocked her head to one side and Hans gave me a dull stare. Solow seemed optimistic as his tail thumped the floor.

"Solow's collar! Why didn't I think of that before?" I pulled my gloves off and unbuckled his collar with my cold, stiff fingers and waved the metal buckle for everyone to see. No one looked or listened. Still sitting, I turned and scooted a few inches toward the door, pushed the metal edge of the buckle between the top of the bottom hinge and the pin, and pushed up.

Since the doors were obviously as old as the house, the pin didn't move on the first try or the second. I broke a nail, growled at the hinge and then gave my best effort. After several minutes of hard work, the pin moved up one-tenth of a quarter of an inch, far enough for me to grab it with my fingernails and pull up. I jerked and twisted the pin side to side, freeing it from its rusty bondage.

"One pin up and two more to go," I said as I rubbed sore fingers with my left hand. The pin in the middle hinge was just as stuck, but it was easier to reach. I worked on it until finally it let go and moved upward.

Once I had both pins out, I needed Hans to reach the third one.

"Hans, do you feel up to helping me?"

"I'll help you," Sarah said, even though she was shorter than me by at least five inches.

Hans hoisted himself up on his feet, his weight wobbling from side to side like a walrus. He shuffled over to the wall, leaned against it for support and pulled off his gloves.

"Just push this buckle between the top of the hinge and the pin." I handed him the collar and he went to work. On the second try the pin popped loose and he pulled it free.

"OK, Sarah, you can help now. Grab the bottom hinge."

"Hans, take the top one and I'll work the middle. On the count of three, pull the door. OK … one, two, three … pull!" Hans pulled the door away from the jam and Sarah and I helped as much as we could. Solow joined in with a long howl.

"Let's do this quietly since we don't know if Tavia is still here," Hans said, as we pulled the free side of the door toward us. Wood splintered, cracked and gave way. Hans ripped the door the rest of the way, allowing us our escape into the hallway. We huddled together, listening. There was nothing but quiet. We crept past a couple of closed doors and stopped in front of the staircase leading up to the main rooms of the house.

"Should we turn on a light?" Sarah whispered. The light from the exercise room was getting further away and there were no lights ahead of us.

"Absolutely not," Hans whispered. "I'll go first and

look around." He stumbled on the first step but was able to right himself without help. He moved slowly, one step at a time. When he reached the top, he walked across the wood floor and knocked over something big, a floor lamp maybe. At that point, he flipped a switch and there was light. Sarah, Solow and I stormed up the stairs and looked around.

"Nice place," Sarah whispered. From the living room, I tried to see to the top of the next set of stairs, but it made a turn and it was dark up there. I hoped Hans would volunteer to go up first, but he was busy picking up a bronze statue he had knocked off a three-legged table.

"I'll take a peek up here," I whispered as I slowly crept up the first couple of stairs. No one followed except Solow, who seemed to be fearless. He sniffed around and trotted on ahead, his short legs struggling to reach each step. We finally made it to the second floor where all was quiet, dark, and definitely warmer than the workout room. I decided to sit on the top step to catch my breath and let Sarah and Hans catch up.

Hans huffed and puffed his way to the top and plopped down beside me. He held on to one of the oak spindles of the railing with one hand and his head with the other. He looked miserable.

Sarah was right behind him. "Do you think we should be snooping around?"

"I'm sure Mr. Anderson wouldn't mind. Besides, Solow will bark if anyone's around." Her worry lines relaxed a bit and she followed us down the hall. We searched each of the four bedrooms, three bathrooms and office. The only reminder of the witch and her offspring was a mug with half a dozen cigarette butts swimming around in cold coffee.

"I wonder why they left," Sarah said.

"We don't even know why they came here in the first place," I said. "Now that we found Solow, we should get out of here and go home."

"I'm going to finish my business with Tavia first," Hans said.

"Hans, leave it to the law. You don't have your gun anymore. Tavia has it and she already shot you once. Let the police do their job ... please," I begged. "Let's drive down the street to the house with all the police out front. Hans, you should see a doctor."

Hans mumbled something under his breath as we descended the stairs and began inspecting the living room. I peeked into the kitchen and Sarah checked the bathroom and dining room. Hans flipped on the front porch light, walked out the front door and stood on the porch.

"Where's my car?" he roared. Sarah and I ran to the door and looked down the street. Not a car in sight for three blocks and, of course, the black SUV was gone too. He kicked the door and stomped into the house. "She took my car ... I can't believe she took my car," Hans groaned, shaking his head in disbelief. He hurried down the hall and flung open the door to the garage. We were right behind him, hoping to see a vehicle, any vehicle. A riding lawnmower would do.

"All I see are two motorcycles designed for the 'under-eight-crowd.'" My hopes were dashed. I felt like I just got the wind kicked out of me. Children's motorcycles in a blizzard—not much help.

"My purse was in the Lincoln," I stammered. "A woman should never be without her purse. Right, Sarah?" She nodded. Her purse was also in the car. "I'll call 911." Unfortunately, every phone in the house had had its connection cut. Not yanked, but cut with scissors or a knife.

"I think I'll just turn up the furnace," Sarah said.

I sat on the sofa staring at the knotty pine rafters, and Solow curled up at my feet for a long winter's nap.

I heard Hans putting about, making a thorough tour of the house, opening every closet and drawer. I figured he was looking for a weapon. He finished his search at 9 pm and came back empty handed. I thanked God for that, as we didn't need any more bullet holes in our escort.

"Hans, would you like me to clean the wound on your head?" Sarah asked.

"I'll take care of it, thank you," he growled, and walked off in search of bandages.

"Anybody hungry?" I called out.

Sarah perked up. "I'll check the fridge," she said, trotting down the hall to the kitchen. By the time I wandered down to the kitchen, Sarah had emptied the whole refrigerator and freezer onto the counter. Catsup, mayonnaise, mustard, two cans of V8 juice, a petrified onion, half a carton of thick milk and two little cans of frozen lemonade concentrate. Maybe I wasn't hungry after all.

"Let's check the pantry," I suggested. "Ooh, I see peanut butter."

"And saltine crackers … and instant coffee," Sarah beamed. She fired up the stove to heat water for coffee and I spread peanut butter on crackers for the entrée. "Josephine, do you think this is stealing?"

"No, I met Mr. Anderson and I think he's the kind of guy who would want to help stranded folks like us," I said. Sarah bought it and smiled. "Besides, he's crazy about Solow. That reminds me, he hasn't eaten either as far as I know. Solow," I called out. I stepped back and tripped over his paws. I should have known he wouldn't be late for dinner. I tossed him a peanut butter cracker and watched him smack his gums together about thirty times trying to swallow the thing.

"Maybe he would like some of this dog food," Sarah said, pointing to a sack of Dooley's Doggie Kibble in the far corner of the pantry.

"Good idea." I found a bowl and poured some kibble for Solow. "Where's Hans? He must be hungry too." Just then Hans turned the corner, red faced and cursing the snow outside. "Hungry?" I asked.

"Coffee! Wonderful! Where is the food for our dinner?"

"You're looking at it ... peanut butter on crackers," I said. He groaned. "It's better than what the Donner Party had." After a limited menu for dinner, we settled ourselves in the living room and watched the local news.

"Oh, my!" Sarah squeaked. "There's Steve and David ... and Alberto."

My heart leaped when I saw David out in the snowstorm talking to a reporter. He looked so handsome. Unfortunately, he was hatless in his lightweight jacket, and his voice was full of concern because the three of us never showed up at 440 Northwind. I wanted to let him know I was OK, look into his dark eyes and ....

"It looks like the whole police force is over there," Hans said.

"We need to get word to them. But how can we? The snow is getting worse," I said.

"We could bundle up again and run for it," Sarah offered, "It's only four or five blocks." I knew how much she wanted to see Steve. Hans sat shaking his head which was pasted up with several colorful "Sponge Bob" bandaids.

"We would never make it," he warned.

I thought to myself that he probably wouldn't, but Sarah and I were slightly younger and in better shape. Sarah looked at me and I looked at her, and we began stuffing ourselves into winter jackets and other warm clothing. I pulled my hat down and winced as it slid over the goose egg.

I found a flashlight and a pair of rubber boots in the coat closet.

"The boots fit like a dream," Sarah said. I checked to make sure the flashlight worked.

"Hans, we're going, but I'll leave Solow with you. If we find a house with someone home along the way, we'll stop and ask for help. Either way, we'll be back as soon as we can."

Hans was miffed, but he wished us luck. He held onto Solow's collar so he wouldn't follow and then turned back to the TV program in front of him.

I opened the front door and we stepped outside. Windblown snow collected on our eyelashes as we made our way down the wide stairs to the walkway leading to the street. I sunk into a foot of new snow and shuffled along on numb feet. Instantly, my Nikes and Levis were soaked. Sarah trudged forward with her head down, leaning into the wind, but at least her feet were dry.

I tried to think about where Tavia might be, but the cold must have numbed my brain. Living in a mild climate my whole life had left me inexperienced when it came to blizzards. Every cell in my body was fighting to keep warm and keep going forward.

Northwind Boulevard had no cross streets, but I estimated three blocks to the turn and then one or two blocks down the hill to 440. Many hours had passed since we drove by the place. I prayed for someone to still be there. As we passed by our fourth house, Sarah suddenly began waving her arms and shouting. I saw the lights from an oncoming car and tackled Sarah, pulling her away from the road and down to her knees.

"What are you doing?" she screamed. "We need help."

"Wait a second. Let's see where this car is going." A black 4-Runner passed by us.

"It's going ... oh, Josephine, it's going to our house ... I mean Mr. Anderson's ...." We watched the SUV turn into Curt's driveway and then the headlights went out. Because the snowfall was so heavy, I figured they probably hadn't seen us.

"Now what?" Sarah cried.

"I'm not letting her take Solow again." I began running toward the house with all the strength I could muster, which wasn't much. Sarah hurried along about twenty paces behind. Finally, I stumbled up Curt's front stairs and leaned on the front door, panting. Sarah held onto the railing, pulling herself up the stairs to the porch, breathing hard. She pointed at the window, her eyes wide and her mouth unable to utter a single word.

I stepped back from the front door, afraid to go in. Should we use the backdoor and take them by surprise? My heartbeat was so loud, I figured it would give us away no matter what door we chose. Considering what Tavia had already done to me and my friends, there was no telling what she might do next. I was afraid to go in, but just as afraid of freezing to death outside.

Sarah just stood staring through the front window. I moved a few steps back and to my right so that I could see what she was looking at. I saw people inside. The information hit me like a snow storm in July.

"It's them, it's them," Sarah whispered.

"I know." We fell into each others arms and bawled as the front door opened.

CHAPTER TWENTY-THREE

If ever there was a reunion that would stick in my memory, the one at Curt's cabin would be it. Hans opened the front door and Sarah and I stumbled into Curt Anderson's warm and lovely vacation abode. Solow bayed and his tail wagged like crazy. David threw his arms around me, sending warmth to every inch of my frozen body. Sarah was having a similar experience with Steve. Alberto took Sarah's wet jacket and hung it in the coat closet.

"We were just about to go outside looking for you girls," David said. "Guess you saw us first?"

"Something like that," I said, too astonished to go into detail. Sarah had already crashed on the couch. Steve pulled her rubber boots off and sat down beside her. David helped me out of my jacket and sat in the loveseat beside me.

"Josie, you're drenched." He pulled off my shoes and socks and wrapped a knitted lap blanket around my feet.

"Is anyone looking for Tavia?" I asked.

"Actually, the police are looking for the three of you," David said. "We reported you missing in the storm when you didn't show up at the four forty address. Finally, I called the Quintanas and asked Alicia if she had heard from you or knew where you might be. She remembered that Tavia and Curt Anderson had had a fling a few years ago and suggested his place, but she didn't have an exact address. It seems Trigger had been up here with Curt's soccer team last summer. Anyway, Alberto drove me to a phone booth and I found the address in the phone book. Someone had already put a pen mark next to it."

"That would be Hans," I smiled.

"What I don't understand is ... why didn't you stop at the Thornton house to at least let us know you were in town?" Steve asked.

Hans squirmed in his chair, jowls jiggling, as Sarah answered the question.

"I think we ... ah, expected to go back there as soon as ... ah, we found Tavia."

Steve nodded. David raised an eyebrow and tilted his head. Alberto used his cell phone to call the police, letting them know we had been found. As soon as he finished the call, Al began building a fire in the massive rock fireplace.

"Now, tell us what happened to you when you got here," David said.

Hans volunteered his version of what happened, but said nothing about how the gun was taken away from him. I was glad not to be talking and happy to be able to feel my feet again. I felt warm and safe sitting next to David. My eyes grew heavy as Hans' voice droned on, telling his manly story.

The sound of a doorbell woke me. I checked my watch. Half an hour had passed and the police were at the front door. The two officers certainly knew how to dress for a storm. Hans offered them a place to sit, but they preferred to stand just inside the door where they could drip snow water on the tile floor instead of the pale peach carpet.

"I hope you folks plan to spend some time in this neighborhood," Officer Walters said. "All the main roads are closed for the next twelve hours."

Steve nodded and said we would stay put.

Hans gave the officers a short version of our encounter with Tavia and her son.

Walters took a few notes.

"The Thorntons won't get far in this weather," the other officer said.

I rolled my eyes in disbelief.

Walters saw me do it. "We're still looking for the Thorntons," he said, staring directly at me. "You folks might want to tune into the weather station on your radio. These storms can be unpredictable. By the way, can someone show us where you folks were held captive by the woman and young man?"

Hans pulled himself up from his comfortable-looking chair and walked the two men downstairs. They finally surfaced some twenty minutes later.

"Nice job on those door hinges," Officer Walters said to Hans as he pulled the earflaps down on his sheriff's issue, fur-lined cap. The two officers left.

I glared at Hans and watched his face turn crimson.

"I think I'll try to get an update on poor Garth," Hans said. "Mind if I use your phone, Al?" Alberto handed over his cell phone and Hans walked down the hall and out of hearing distance. He was gone a long time. I didn't think anyone else noticed since we were all relaxing and enjoying Alberto's fire. The scent of burning pine wafted through the room, enhancing the residual joy of the reunion.

Sarah fell asleep with her head on Steve's shoulder and I nodded off for another half hour. When I awoke, Hans was just returning from the kitchen. He began explaining to the group how many calls he had had to make before he found Willy.

"The boy is doing fine and should be able to go home tomorrow," he announced, smiling for the first time in two days. Just as Hans handed the phone back to Alberto, it began to play an electronic version of the cancan. Hans took the phone from Al and walked back to the kitchen before answering it. When he came back to us a few minutes later, he explained that earlier he had made calls to some of the hotels in Crystal Bay. One of them had called back.

"Does that mean Tavia and Mark have been sighted?" I asked, feeling a burst of adrenalin rush through my body.

"It means they are registered at Cal-Neva under a fictitious name ... 'Anderson.' " Hans laughed. "Imagine that."

"So you asked for Thornton and then you asked for Anderson?" I said.

Hans nodded. "Along with a good description of the trollop and her offspring."

"Not much we can do about it," David said, "but I'll put in a call to the Sheriff's Office and let them know where to look. The weather won't stop those boys. That reminds me, we should find the weather station. Anyone see a radio?"

"I saw a radio in the kitchen," Hans said, and trudged through the house to retrieve it. Minutes later he lumbered back carrying a portable radio. He set it on the coffee table and turned it on. The radio was already tuned to the weather station.

Steve turned off the TV and we all stared at the radio as if it had a picture. The report could not have been worse. Heavy snowfall was predicted for the next twelve hours with gusty winds from the north, creating a chill factor of three below. But if the bulk of the storm hit north of Tahoe, all bets were off.

"I get cold just thinking about it," Sarah said, yawning and stretching. "I'm ready for bed."

"Me too." I turned and kissed David goodnight, ignoring the disappointment in his eyes. Solow and I followed Sarah up the stairs. She found a nice room with twin beds and an adjoining bathroom.

"I'm so tired I could fall asleep standing up," she moaned.

"Yeah, me too." But I had no intention of falling asleep because I was sure that Hans was planning to go to town in the only vehicle at our disposal. I saw the gleam in his eye when he found out where Tavia was staying. I was certain he would try to leave and if he found Tavia, she would probably shoot him again and we would never get the 4-Runner back.

I crawled under the covers, still wearing my pullover sweater and almost dry Levis. I fought to keep my mind active, to stay awake so I could catch Hans sneaking out later, but I was exhausted. Solow's snoring from across the room was a familiar lullaby to my ears. I smiled in the dark and closed my eyes.

Four hours of sleep wasn't much, but I awoke at three in the morning, eyes wide open, with one thought on my mind. Where was Hans? I quietly climbed out of bed, crept downstairs and hurried to the front windows for a look outside.

"I knew it!" I whispered to myself. "The stupid 4-Runner is gone." I ran back up the stairs, yelling all the way to the top about Hans taking the SUV to find Tavia.

Sarah stood at our bedroom door looking like she had just woken from a bad dream.

"If you're looking for Hans, he's right there." Sarah pointed down the hall.

"Were you calling me, Josephine?" he asked in a husky voice, and then yawned.

"Oh, Hans … what are you … ah, doing up?" I asked, feeling my cheeks redden.

"Have you been sleepwalking, Josephine?" Sarah asked. I almost said yes, but instead I exploded.

"Did you know the 4-Runner is missing?"

"Certainly, the men were hungry last night. Since there was no food to be had, they drove to town," Hans explained, checking his watch. "It is rather late, but I'm sure they'll be back soon."

Feeling like a fool, I said goodnight and went back to bed. Solow had slept through all the commotion. Actually, he was probably too embarrassed to show his face. I curled up under the down comforter, closed my eyes and listened to the absolute quiet—but not for long.

A door slammed. I heard heavy footsteps and people laughing. I sat up and listened, finally recognizing the voices downstairs. The guys were back, shushing each other and laughing. Three bulls in Curt's china shop. I watched Steve and Al from the landing as they carried bags of groceries to the kitchen. Finally, David came by, looked up and saw me.

"Josie, what are you doing up?"

"Just waiting to see what three guys might bring home from the grocery store."

He set his bag of food on the tile floor and met me halfway as I came down the stairs. His cheeks were cold, but his lips were warm and my heart was doing a fast cha cha cha.

"I'm wide awake. Let's put this food away," I said, as we stood in the dimly lit hallway listening to Steve and Alberto laughing in the kitchen. When we rounded the corner, I had to shield my eyes from the bright kitchen lights. Four full bags of groceries, not counting David's bag, sat on the counter while Steve and Alberto swigged beers at the bar and bragged about their winnings at Cal-Neva.

"Did you win anything, David?" I asked as I helped him put away the groceries which mainly consisted of spam, bacon, chorizo, and multiple cartons of eggs, not to mention three 6-packs of beer.

"I didn't spend much time at the casino. Actually, I did some snooping at the hotel."

"Did you ask about the Andersons?"

"Yeah, it seems there were three Andersons staying there ... in a three-room suite, but they checked out before the police got there."

"Darn!" She had slipped through our radar, but then I thought of the possibilities. Either an entirely different Anderson family had checked in, or a third person was traveling with Tavia and Mark. Could be the pilot, but that would mean she was in on the shooting and everything.

"Did you find out anything else? Do you know where they went?"

"They had a good description of the woman, but no forwarding address."

"I'm not surprised," I said, as my pent-up anger for Tavia reignited.

"Come on, I want to show you something," David said, taking my hand and leading me to the front porch.

"David ... how ... wow! Hans will be so happy."

"Yeah, it was parked right there in the hotel parking lot. The only one of it's kind. Steve's pretty good when it comes to breaking-into cars. Luckily, the key was still in the ignition."

"That old Lincoln is wonderful to ride in. They don't make 'em like that anymore." I climbed into the back seat and hugged my long lost purse. I reached over the front seat and grabbed Sarah's quilted hippy bag. As I backed out of the Lincoln, I noticed the 4-Runner from the night before. David explained that Alberto had borrowed the SUV from his friend, Sergio, a pilot friend who was living in Tahoe.

"We didn't want to take any chances," he said, "so we parked them close to the house. Now I'm going to make sure they're locked." He squeezed my hand and then proceeded to check all the doors.

"Retrieving the car was brilliant, David." I wished I had been at the hotel and snooped around with him. I was dying to know who the third "Anderson" was. Could it be Curt Anderson?

"So how are we going to find Tavia?" I asked.

"The police will find her, don't worry."

"I'm getting a little tired of watching my back, if you know what I mean."

"I'm here. You're safe." He wrapped an arm around my shoulder. "Tomorrow we'll call the airport and a few hotels to see if anyone has seen them."

We took our time going back to the kitchen. I asked David how the drive in the snow went. He laughed, "You really don't want to know." And then he explained that they never were in mortal danger—just a lot of slipping and sliding.

The smell of bacon frying stirred the hunger in me. We rounded the corner and watched Steve straighten and re-straighten the strips of bacon as they bubbled up and curled in the frying pan. Alberto stood at the counter breaking a dozen eggs into a bowl.

"Need any help?" David asked.

"Sure. Make some coffee," Steve said. We went right to it, hot water and instant coffee. Steve looked up from his bacon project and frowned at the instant coffee granules.

We ate heartily that morning before dawn. I laughed and talked and let go of the tension from the last few days. The sun was coming up when I finally crawled into bed.

CHAPTER TWENTY-FOUR

It was Monday afternoon and I hadn't even opened my eyes yet. Might as well take my time, I thought, and enjoy the warmth of my bed. But when I opened one eye, I remembered where I was. I thought about getting up, but it was too late to rush. I blinked as sunshine streamed into the room, illuminating tiny dust particles dancing above the wood floor. Sarah's bed was empty and Solow was gone. I wondered what I might be missing and finally crawled out of my cozy cocoon.

After a quick shower, I towel dried my hair, pulled on my same old sweater and Levis and headed downstairs barefoot. The whole gang, including Solow, sat in the kitchen eating another round of scrambled eggs, bacon and chorizo. Acid indigestion reminded me of the caloric feast I had enjoyed a few hours earlier.

"Josephine, try some eggs. Steve made them." Sarah turned her smile from me to him.

"Maybe later, I don't seem to have an appetite yet." I leaned over and kissed David's cheek while he chewed on a bite of fried spam. And then I remembered I hadn't brushed. Oh, my fortune for a toothbrush.

"This spam meat-thing is rather good," Hans said. "And you should try some of Al's chorizo."

I yawned and sat down at the bar with a cup of instant coffee, not wishing to eat until after the next ice age. Solow wagged his tail each time a scrap of food was tossed his way. It looked like each contributor was trying for the "most-generous human" title at the expense of Solow's manly physique.

"I can't believe how much work I have to do in the next couple days," Steve whined. "And here I am, stuck in Tahoe."

"Hey pal," Al said, "the sun is out and it looks like the storm has moved on. Maybe we can go home today. Those meteorologists have a fifty percent chance of being right, and it looks like they were at least thirty percent wrong."

"Actually, I'd like to go back to Cal-Neva and get my money back," Steve said.

"Or make another donation," David chided.

"I thought you said you won ...." Sarah cocked her head to one side.

"Well, I did ... sometimes, but not everytime," he muttered. She smiled knowingly.

Alberto swiveled off his stool and stretched. "Who wants to fly home with me?"

Steve said he wanted to and Sarah jumped up ready to follow Steve anywhere. She collected the dirty plates and went to work washing the counter tops with a soapy sponge. I washed dishes while David and Steve shoveled snow off the sidewalk and driveway. I wrapped the leftover meats in foil and Sarah put them in Curt's freezer. It was the least we could do after holding a slumber party in his house.

"I guess you two will be riding with me," Hans said,

as David flopped down at the kitchen table for a breather. I felt like staying in Curt's house all day with David and Solow. But I pulled on my dry shoes and the borrowed foul-weather gear, grabbed my purse and joined David and the gang as they migrated to the front yard.

Al, Steve and Sarah said their goodbyes and left for the airport in Sergio's Toyota 4-Runner. Minutes later, Solow and I followed Hans and David to the Lincoln. We all piled in and Hans cautiously drove the car around the slushy circular drive.

Fortunately, Northwind had already been visited by the snowplows. Snow covered everything in sight except the road where the plow had carved a nice clear path. The sky was blue, the air crisp and I felt thankful and content. My hound dog sat on my left and my sweetheart sat on my right, all the way to North Shore. Tavia could go fly a kite for all I cared.

We had only been on the road for a few minutes when, suddenly, Hans jerked the car into a left turn down an alley and parked behind Cal-Neva. He made a hasty explanation about having to use the restroom. David turned in his seat to look at me just as I was rolling my eyes in disbelief.

David laughed. "Shall we walk the dog?"

"Sure. Solow would love to take a walk," I tugged on Solow's leash to get him started. He looked up with disinterested bloodshot eyes. After some gentle coaxing, he finally climbed out of the car. We walked up an alley and over to the sunny open area near the front entrance to the casino. An ocean of gamblers were crowding into the building. Another ocean pushed its way out the automatic exit doors. David stood behind me as we watched for Hans. I noticed a tall, well-dressed gentleman in his early fifties elbow his way through the masses. He seemed to be in a great hurry to leave the casino.

"Charlie!"

The attorney turned his head to look at me, one hand shielding his eyes from the sun. He put on a handsome smile full of straight white teeth and a dimple in each cheek.

"Well, well, Josephine ... and ... Danny." Charlie cleared his throat.

"It's David," I said as we all backed away from the crowd and found a place to stand near the street. Solow stood behind my legs.

"Sorry, old man." Charlie looked over his shoulder at the front doors as if he were expecting someone. He leaned down to pet Solow, but my dog walked to the end of his leash and Charlie gave up.

"What brings you to Tahoe?" I asked.

"Oh ... ah, meeting a client. Work never stops." He shrugged his shoulders as if to say he was the attorney most in demand and he had no idea why he was so popular. "This is a real coincidence isn't it? I mean, after seeing you only two days ago." He wiped a bead of perspiration from his brow and then looked back at the door. "Enjoy your vacation, folks."

We watched Charlie hurry down the sidewalk, hang a left and disappear into the alley leading to a parking lot behind the hotel. I looked at David and he looked at me. We were probably wondering the same thing since neither of us believed in coincidences.

Just then, Hans stormed out of the casino and joined us.

"I'm not sure, but I think I just saw ...." Hans looked right and left, sucking up high altitude air. His face was red as he narrowed his eyes. "I think I saw the Thornton's attorney, Charlie Wellborn." He gulped some more thin air. "But I lost him in the crowd."

"It was Charlie," I said. "We just had a little chat with him."

"You don't say. I wonder if Tavia knows he's here. She's going to need a lawyer and a lot of luck from now on." We agreed with Hans on the "luck" thing, and headed for the parking lot. Just as we turned the corner of the Cal-Neva Club, a classic white Jaguar whooshed up the alley, turned left onto the main drag and sped away.

"That was Mr. Wellborn," Hans muttered. "Quite a coincidence."

Even Solow rolled his eyes.

The parking lot was cold and shaded by rows of pine trees. We carefully made our way around patches of slippery ice, climbed into the Lincoln and headed west. The highway was lined on both sides with high banks of freshly plowed snow. By the time we powered up the mountain and parked in front of the Dinky Diner, most of the new snow had melted. It was four o'clock and I was starving. I had talked myself into having a burger since that was what Mr. Dinky knew how to make. We ordered three hamburgers with fries and hot coffee.

The burgers arrived promptly along with plenty of conversation from the perky old waitress. I tried the coffee and decided I would rather drink hot tar.

"You folks win anything at the lake?" the waitress asked, batting her faded blue eyes at Hans. He shook his head as he sat staring out the window, quiet as a chair full of marshmallows. The woman finally took the hint and trudged back to the kitchen.

David and I reflected on all the coincidental encounters and what they might mean. Like, why would Charlie drive up to Tahoe just before or during a big snowstorm? Was he looking for Tavia? Was Tavia looking for Wellborn?

"If Mr. Wellborn is representing Justin and Tavia … doesn't that constitute a conflict of interest?" I asked David.

"In my book it does," he said, "but Justin might not be a suspect much longer. Tavia seems to be a little crazy and her guilt is becoming more obvious." He sipped his coffee and nibbled a fry. His burger was long gone and I was halfway through mine.

"I wonder why Charlie looked so nervous at the casino," I said, almost to myself.

"Because he saw me, and he knew I saw him," Hans muttered. "The man is up to no good. I trusted him a few years ago when Mr. Thornton first hired him. Let me see, that was right after Willy married Tavia. But Charlie has changed and so has Tavia."

"What exactly is he up to, Hans?" I asked.

"Mr. Wellborn was hired to represent the family. Sometimes I think he has more impact on Thornton affairs than Willy," Hans frowned and stared into his empty mug. "Tavia had nothing when she met Willy, just a scrawny eight-year-old boy and a lot of debt. Like

Mr. Thornton, I was completely taken in, swallowed her sad stories and even felt sorry for her. We were all duped."

"Don't worry, the law will get her," David said. Hans stared at something only he could see until he decided to continue his rant.

"Six years ago she was beautiful and Willy was alone. You see, Mr. Thornton's wife died. I introduced Tavia to my friend because I understood how lonely he was. Willy came from money, had good looks and a son. She went to him like a bear to honey. She took over most of the decision making on the west coast while Willy spent more and more time on the east coast. I wonder if he knows about her plans for a mall."

"You're Mr. Thornton's friend. Maybe you'll have to fill him in," I said "especially the part about hitting Jim on the head so he wouldn't be able to show an incriminating email to his boss—her husband."

"I dread telling Mr. Thornton the facts, but it must be done," Hans whispered.

"Hey, it's already getting dark outside. Maybe we should get back on the road," David suggested. We stood up and walked to the car with serious gloom hanging over our heads. We climbed in, Hans fired up the engine, circled the parking lot and pulled onto the highway. The last thing I remembered was Solow's snoring.

When I awoke it was dark outside and David was gently shaking my shoulder. I felt like I was five years old again, like the old days when Mom and Dad would talk and drive while I slept in the backseat. I hated to leave my warm nest, but David helped me out of the car and gathered my things.

Solow circled the Chevy loaner, tail wagging, ready to go home.

"Just a minute, Solow," I said as I searched my purse for the car key.

"Hans looks tired," David said. I agreed that we should leave for home right away and let Hans rest. I checked my watch. It was only nine-thirty, but it seemed later. I handed the cold weather gear to Hans, but he pushed it back into my arms.

"Keep them. You might need these things someday and Heaven knows I don't need them. Good night." He pushed the garage door button, leaving David and me standing outside in the dark.

"Guess he was in a hurry to relax," I said, climbing into the passenger seat. David lifted Solow into the backseat. I smiled in the dark. I had my dog again.

David jumped into the driver's seat, drove us up Highway One to the Watsonville airport and parked next to his Jeep. By that time I was ninety percent awake and ready to take over the wheel. David kissed me and we drove our separate vehicles toward Aromas. I lost sight of David's Jeep somewhere along the way. Either he was in a hurry to get home or he had stopped off somewhere.

As I drove up Otis Road, I decided not to go straight home. I wanted a little more time with David. I zipped up his driveway only to discover he was not home yet. I sat for awhile counting the stars that looked so close and bright. Finally I gave up, turned the key and drove the short distance home. I laughed as I pulled in next to David's Jeep.

"Well, Solow, I guess David came for a visit." I noticed the porch light was on and as we approached the front door I heard the TV. Solow sniffed around, marked a bush and then ran into the house behind me. David sat glued to the TV watching the 10:00 news.

"Hi, Josie." He patted the couch cushion where he wanted me to sit but kept his eyes on the TV screen. My mouth dropped open when I saw the familiar female news reporter standing in front of the Physical Therapy Center talking about the Thornton Corporation being in legal trouble over the promised Solar Research Center. The reporter went on to say that a spokesperson had reported that they knew of no plans to build in Pajaro.

"Poor Willy," I whispered. David nodded. The woman went on to say that the police were investigating for fraud and wanted to talk to a "person of interest." A picture of Tavia's son, Mark, flashed on the screen.

"What? Mark's just a kid, the unlucky son of a crazy woman. He didn't do anything. He's only fourteen," I growled.

"We know that, Josie. Don't worry, the truth will come out." David put an arm around my shoulder, touching one of many sore spots on my bruised body, while Solow laid his head across David's feet.

The camera zoomed in on the chesty news reporter wearing a tight pink suit. She explained that another "person of interest," Tavia Thornton, had not, as yet, been located. She said the police wanted to question her about the death of an employee.

"That's more like it!" I stood up, arms raised, as if I

were rooting for the 49ers. Solow jumped up, ran down the hall and didn't come back.

"I think Solow just put himself to bed," I laughed, feeling a little guilty for accidentally scaring him away. Just then, there was a knock at the front door. Sarah burst through the doorway before I could get up from the couch. Her cheeks were rosy and her eyes sparkled. Steve was just a step behind her.

"Hi, guys. When did you get home?" Steve asked.

"Five minutes ago. Have a seat. You won't believe who's in the news." I pointed to the TV. Sarah and Steve sat down as David and I made room for them.

"Look, it's the Therapy Center and that woman from KPUT. I remember her," Sarah said. We all focused on the screen while the woman with the microphone explained that the new Therapy Center might not be able to open its doors until the Thornton family's various legal problems could be resolved.

"There goes the deadline Hans was so concerned about," I said. The news switched to a local car lot commercial where a man dressed like a cowboy pretended to be an honest car salesman.

David put his arm around my shoulder. Steve followed David's example and put his arm around Sarah's shoulder. If she were a cat, she would have been purring. Steve looked calm and happy, for an excitable rooster.

"Josephine," Steve began, "I owe you an apology. I realize now that Tavia Thornton really did steal your truck ... and, you know ...." Poor man could not say the words. He obviously missed his VW bus. His face had changed, and I thought he was going to cry just thinking about that old tin box on wheels.

"That's OK, Steve. I know it was a wild story. I could hardly believe it myself." It felt good to be back on good terms with the rooster.

It was not Sarah's habit to sit still very long. She bustled around making popcorn and tea for everyone and then the four of us sat back and watched an old movie. She refilled the bowl of popcorn and freshened our tea. At midnight, when the movie ended and just before I turned into a pumpkin, the guys left. Sarah trudged up the narrow steps to her tortuous bed while I joined Solow in my room. My bed never felt better. Our breathing fell into sync as Solow and I drifted into dreamland.

Not for the first time, my happy dreams twisted into a nasty nightmare. I witnessed dozens of little mutant Tavia dolls on roller skates armed with chunks of petrified spam. They pelted me with the salty meat as they chased me up a snowy hillside. I happened to be wearing lead boots and sank deeper and deeper into the snow. Just as my head was going under, David rang a bell and the chase ended. I woke up sweaty, exhausted and wishing I had never heard of the woman named Tavia.

I opened my eyes and looked around in the dark. The bedroom was unnaturally quiet. No doggie snores. I panicked for a moment, jumped out of bed and stumbled into the kitchen. Maybe he was just hungry and looking for food. After all, nothing else was likely to get him out of his bed. I searched every room except Sarah's. As I stood looking up the dark staircase wondering if Solow could have climbed up to the top, I heard his long toenails clicking across the wood floor behind me.

"Solow, why are you up?" I scratched behind his ears and turned to go back to my room. A little blinking red light caught my eye. I must have slept through the phone ringing. There was a message on my answering machine. I pushed the button.

"Watch your back woman," a female voice warned.

"Same to you," I told the machine. Solow and I went back to bed for an uneasy sleep.

CHAPTER TWENTY-FIVE

The kitchen phone woke me up from a restless sleep. I staggered out of bed in a somnambulistic state, trudged down the dark hallway and entered the kitchen where Sarah stood in her pajamas holding the phone to her ear. Her eyes were as big as Aunt Clara's biscuits. Her bare feet seemed to be frozen on one square of linoleum.

"Is it for me?" Sarah nodded and handed the receiver to me.

"Hello?"

"Josephine, did you get my message?" Tavia cooed.

"Just wait ..." I sputtered. My cheeks were hot and I heard my heart pounding in my ears. There were so many things I wanted to say to Tavia. They all tried to come out of my mouth at once, creating an unintelligible garble.

"Listen, deary, I know where little Trigger is and where he goes to school. If you want to keep the boy safe, don't pull any more of your silly tricks ... just accept the council's decision."

"Who's being silly? You're completely bananas." Too bad she had already hung up. Sarah and I stared at the phone as if it were a poisonous spider. How in the world did she think she could get away with causing more trouble now that the police and news reporters were hot on her trail?

"Now she's threatening to hurt Trigger." I was so angry I was shaking. "I'll call Alicia. What time is it?"

"It's only a little after five." Sarah wrapped her arms around herself and shivered.

"I'll call anyway. We wouldn't want her to send Trigger to school today." I dialed. Alicia sounded like she was coming out of a deep sleep.

"Hi, Alicia, sorry to call so early, but I just had a call from Tavia. She's threatening to harm Trigger. She said she knows where he goes to school."

"Do you think she would …?"

"Allie, I know she would do something crazy because she's off-the-meds crazy."

"OK, I'll take him to work with me today. He'll like that. Will Solow be with you?"

"Naturally. I have to keep an eye on him so he doesn't get dognapped again." What a crazy world we were living in, and all because one woman didn't have the courage or good sense to give herself up to the authorities.

Sarah kept shivering, but she was more than cold. She was scared.

"Sarah, would you like to spend today with Alicia, Kyle and me?"

"Um … that sounds nice. Thank you, Josephine." She smiled and trotted back to bed.

I was wide awake and angrier than a rattlesnake in a gunny sack. I pulled a phone book out of the kitchen drawer, put on my reading glasses and looked for Thornton. The name wasn't listed, and I wasn't surprised.

Hans would know their address. I looked up his number and dialed. Talk about your early morning grouch.

"Take it easy, Hans. I know what time it is, but we have a situation here."

"Josephine, I'll see you at work three hours from now ...."

"Can't wait. I've got to go on the offense with Tavia. It's the only way to get the upper hand, don't you see? I can't keep wondering where and when she'll strike."

"Mr. Thornton would not want me to give out his address to just any ... I mean to you."

"Look, Hans, she threatened me last night and this morning she threatened Trigger, Alicia's little boy. The woman has gone completely bonkers and there's no telling what she'll do next. You ought to know—after all she shot you in the head." There was a long silence on the other end. I could almost hear Hans' brain beginning to wake up.

"All right, but don't say I didn't warn you. It's 3250 Sandy Lane in La Selva Beach and you didn't hear it from me. Goodbye." He hung up.

I had been so engrossed in the conversation with Hans that I didn't even notice Sarah standing in the dining room.

"I decided sleep would never work," she said. "We're going somewhere, aren't we?" Before I had time to answer, she turned and walked to her room to get dressed. I fed Solow, pulled on my old Levis and a colorful paint shirt, and stuffed a street map into my purse. I grabbed a jacket on the way out. Sarah climbed into the Chevy and I helped Solow into the backseat.

As I backed the car down the driveway in the

pre-dawn light, I suddenly remembered Oliver.

"We have to make a quick stop at Rosa's," I said. As we motored up Rosa's driveway, it was plain to see we would not be alone. A familiar looking black BMW sat next to Rosa's dusty Firebird. Wood smoke curled up from the brick fireplace and Oliver was not around to greet us.

Sarah looked at me. "Guess we don't need to feed Oliver."

"Right, but I do want to make sure ...." Before I could say another word, the front door opened. Andy stepped outside in his pajama bottoms and t-shirt and did a hundred and eighty degree scan of the property.

We scrambled out of the car.

"Josephine, what are you doing here?"

"I came to feed Ollie. You know Sarah, right? Oh, there's Ollie." I bent down and scratched his head as he purred a greeting. "So, is Rosa home?"

Andy's Scandinavian cheeks turned red. "She's sleeping. I heard you drive up and thought I'd try to keep everything quiet for her." He stepped back and leaned against the front door. "She's had a rough time."

"Will you be at work today?" I asked.

"No. Mr. Thornton and I had a talk. I'm staying here until they catch his crazy wife."

"How's your dad?"

"Haven't seen him." Andy shrugged his shoulders, turned and opened the door. Before I could ask another question, he was inside. Sarah had already ducked back into the car. I climbed in and we thundered down Otis, then San Juan Road toward Watsonville. I handed the map to Sarah.

"See if you can find Sandy Lane in La Selva Beach." Not an easy task as we flew down the road. She was a good sport, but her hands were shaking like a bobble-head-doll on the dash. Before long, the map was a crinkled mess. I pulled into the Therapy Center parking lot next to a couple of pickup trucks. It was amazing to me that the carpenters started work everyday at seven, a whole hour before I usually woke up

"Here, give me the map." I held the mangled paper at arms length and located Sandy Lane, just one dust particle from the Pacific Ocean. I fired up the Chevy and we headed north, exiting the freeway one ramp before Aptos. I already knew what downtown La Selva Beach looked like. It was about the size of Aromas minus one feed store and one little grocery store. The main street was three blocks long and surrounded by beautiful neighborhoods full of average older homes with high price tags. Location, location, location.

At seven-thirty sharp, we rolled through the quiet little town of La Selva (Spanish for forest) Beach which seemed like a contradiction since there was no forest near the beach. I turned left onto Sandy Lane and followed it several blocks to a house numbered 3250, located at the end of the cul-de-sac. The choice piece of property was the size of four regular lots.

The Thornton's unusually large two-story house was perched on a cliff overlooking the ocean. The first story was concealed from the street by weathered redwood fencing and an automatic wooden gate that swung open as we watched. A late model black 'Vette rumbled out of the compound and passed by us going in the only direction available to it.

"Wasn't that Garth?" Sarah stammered. Neither of us had expected to see anyone up and around so early in the morning, least of all, Garth.

"Josephine, what are you doing?" Sarah shouted, as I leaped out of the car and ran toward the gate. I had no time to explain, but Sarah would figure it out. I barely had time to squeeze through the narrow opening before the gate completed its journey and automatically locked itself in the closed position.

Cold salty air blew strands of hair across my face. I pushed the hair back, looked around and decided the front door might be too obvious a place to start. Instead, I opted for a back entrance located under a deck. The door was weathered and stubborn, but finally opened as I pulled hard on the doorknob with both hands.

I stood in the dim light of a four-car garage wondering what to do next. I looked around. No lawnmower, motorcycle, shovel or even a can of motor oil anywhere, just one shiny black Porsche. In my neighborhood, most of the garages were so full of storage items there was no room for cars. I promised myself if I had a garage built someday, I would keep it clean and always park my truck inside.

As I stood alone in the middle of the car barn, I heard footsteps behind a door to my left. Before I could take one step, the door swung open. Willy stood like a statue, his mouth open and his hand frozen on the doorknob. Finally he came to his senses.

"Josephine?" He scratched his head in disbelief. His sweat suit looked wet under the arms and the thinning hair above his forehead was dark with moisture.

"Sorry, Sir. I … ah, wanted to find … I mean …." My

cheeks felt so hot I thought my hair would ignite.

"I know. You're looking for Tavia. Half the state is looking for my wife." He folded down into a sitting position on the doorstep and hung his head. I had to hold back tears as I watched him and imagined what he must have been going through.

"I just came home from a run." He wiped his brow. "Trying to clear my head, you know. I'm very concerned about Mark. He's only fourteen. Tall for his age. What's going to happen to him?" he mumbled.

"I understand your concern," I said softly. Does Mark have a real father, I mean, besides you?"

"No. I'm the only father he's ever known. According to Tavia, the father died in a plane crash when Mark was only two."

"That's very sad. How is Garth?"

"Doing well. He just left. It's his first drive alone since he … ah, became ill. He and Carlos have something planned for today."

"The reason I'm here is because Tavia called this morning and threatened Alicia's son, Trigger."

"Oh, my God," he whispered, wrapping his hands around his shoulders. He looked up into my face with sad eyes. "What can I do to help?"

"I wish I knew. Maybe you know some places where we can look for her."

"I'm afraid not," he said. "She's always been a very independent woman."

I turned my head and rolled my eyes. Poor man knew nothing about his wife.

"When was the last time you saw her?"

He was quiet for a moment. "Valentines day. I gave

her a diamond brooch. She threw it at ... I just don't understand. I'm sorry, Josephine. I'll open the gate for you." I thanked him and walked out the gate. Solow howled when I ducked back into the Chevy and Sarah looked relieved.

"Did you find anything?" she asked.

"Just, Willy." I drove us back to Highway One at twice the speed limit, then south about twelve miles, hung a right at Pelican Lane, a left at Long Drive and stopped at the gate in front of "Fore at the Water." But this time I took a different tact. My rental idled in plain sight while an elderly woman made her way to the window. Without one question, she pushed a button to open the gate. Sarah and I looked at each other and laughed. The straight-forward approach was definitely the best. A couple of minutes later, I parked near the third building.

"Are you going to talk to Curt?" Sarah asked. She leaned over the back of her seat and petted Solow's chest and ears. He sat on the edge of the seat, slack-jawed and drooling with his eyes at half-mast.

Rather than answer a really dumb question, I suggested Sarah attach the leash to Solow's collar and we would all take a walk up the maze of stairs and ramps to apartment number 303.

A reluctant sun glinted off the east-facing windows but did nothing to abate the morning chill. However, by the time we reached the third floor, my heart was beating with purpose and I was warm as a teapot. Solow pointed his nose at the door with the numbers 303 screwed onto it and howled clear down to his toenails. Some people would have thought he was dying, but I recognized it as a happy howl.

"I'm pushing the doorbell but nothing's happening," Sarah said. "Maybe he's not …." I saw someone peek through the blinds and a second later three front door latches clicked and the door opened a crack.

"I remember that howl," Curt laughed as he pushed the door wide open. "Come in." He quickly herded us inside, and then stepped outside for a look at the parking lot. "Just needed to make sure we don't have any uninvited guests." He stepped back inside, closed the door and bolted it. "Now, ladies, what can I do for you?"

"Have you met Sarah?" I asked, lowering myself down onto a fat floor pillow. I crossed my legs like a yogi master.

Sarah walked up to Curt and they shook hands. "Lovely place you have here," she said. "And isn't the ocean beautiful today."

Curt smiled. He obviously hadn't shaved in several days and there were food stains on the front of his t-shirt. I wondered if he had experienced cabin fever.

As if reading my mind, he said, "It's good to have company. I usually act like I'm not home. I even keep my car parked down at building four, but I couldn't resist your dog. He's quite special."

Sarah and I nodded our heads, and I reminded Curt of Solow's name.

"Yes, Solow, old boy, come here." Obediently Solow walked over to Curt and placed his chin across the man's Mickey Mouse slippers, a very high compliment. "Nice foot warmer," Curt said. We all laughed.

"You're probably wondering why we're here,"

I began.

Curt tilted his head as he glanced at my colorful paint shirt.

"Things have gone from bad to worse …."

"I know about Garth," he mumbled. "What will she do next?"

"Tavia dognapped Solow," Sarah said.

"I didn't know about that, but you obviously got him back."

I unfolded my legs, wrapped my arms around my knees and began telling Curt all the latest Tavia dirt. He clenched his jaw when he heard about the threat to Trigger.

"We're here, asking for help because we don't know where else to go. The police can't find Tavia. But she's out there, free to call and make threats … or worse. Does Andy know anything new?"

"I just talked to him last night. He moved into Rosa's house. Seems her brother had to take a business trip to Atlanta. Anyway, Andy feels better now that he's in charge of watching over her. He asked me to join them, and I'm probably going to do it. Anything to keep Rosa safe."

"Including a 'yes' vote?"

"If I have to."

"What difference will it make at this point?" I asked. "Everyone knows about Tavia's plan to build a mall instead of a Research Center. The jig's up."

"She has done some terrible things. I think she's crazy and I don't think she'll stop just because we know what she's done," Curt said. "She thinks the supervisors will vote yes next Thursday and everything will go the way she planned it. Believe me, she's completely delusional. Andy told me she was crazy a month ago. Now I believe him. If I vote 'no' Thursday, someone will get hurt. I know it. She's that crazy!"

The poor man stared out the window at silvery seagulls swooping and soaring freely. I felt sorry for the big, powerful councilman who was afraid to poke his head outside, let alone do his civic duty and vote.

"If it was just Tavia, that would be one thing, but she has a partner," Curt said. "I don't know his name and I don't want to know." Charlie flashed across my mind.

"Look at the time," I said, "eight-thirty. We're meeting Alicia at nine." Sarah nodded, Solow stretched his chubby legs and we all made our way to the front door.

"Josephine, maybe you would like to come by and see us tonight when I get settled in with Andy and Rosa."

"Sure, and Solow can warm your feet."

CHAPTER TWENTY-SIX

I should have figured the Therapy Center would be closed because of the murder investigation that was heating up, but it took my friend, Sarah, and me by surprise. The back entrance was blocked by a couple of Sheriff's cars, lots of yellow tape and a sign posted on the door stating that an investigation was in progress.

"We'll try the front door," I said, optimistically. I whipped the car around to the front of the building.

"Look, Josephine, there's Alicia's station wagon."

I parked in front of the main entrance next to a green Volvo and a yellow motorcycle. I helped Solow down from his seat and we walked up to the massive glass doors. Alicia had arrived early, as usual. We found her, black boot and all, near the top of my eight-foot ladder painting imitation cracks on the plaster.

Monday, she and Kyle had created a nice three-dimensional architectural effect that framed the entire park scene on both sides and across the top. The walls looked at least a foot thick. The Trompe L'oeil gave the picture a finished look.

"Alicia, I can't believe how much you accomplished while I was gone."

"Kyle helped," she said. "We decided to work late since you were out of town. Kyle volunteered to work today even though he has classes on Tuesdays."

"Kyle, thank you. But from now on, you go to all your classes."

Alicia backed down the ladder and dropped her brush into a pail of water. "I see you have your handsome hound with you. I guess you'll be watching him closely. Sarah, I'm glad you're here. I didn't see you come in."

"I'm Josephine's guest today. Anything I can do to help?" Sarah had already begun restacking the paint cans and sorting various supplies.

"Sarah, you can wash brushes and ...." Hans and Trigger arrived. "Oh, hi Hans and Trigger, where did you guys come from?"

"I was listening to the deputies talking to Hans," Trigger said.

"How are you feeling, Hans?"

"Nice of you to ask. Let's just say that I look better than I feel. I have an appointment to see my doctor this afternoon."

"You don't look too awful," Sarah said.

"Thank you, I guess. How are you ladies doing? Oh my, the painting is really amazing." Hans stepped back and gazed at our work with wide eyes.

"Do you think it looks like the sketch?" I asked, fishing for more compliments.

"Better ... and so big ... and look, swings, a slide and a dock ... and the two geese are magnificent. Nice touch." Hans was practically giddy. The once "crotchety old man" had turned a corner in art appreciation.

"So, Hans, how did you get into the building?" I asked.

"The police escorted me in through the backdoor because they wanted to question me. There must have been half a dozen of them buzzing around here earlier. Seems our friend, Tavia, called the police early this morning. She said there was a bomb in Willy's desk. The police turned the whole place upside down and didn't find a thing."

"Oh, my God!" I whispered. Alicia crossed herself and Kyle paled.

"Probably did it for attention," he growled and stalked off in the direction of the elevators. Trigger watched him go.

"Can I go with Hans ... please ... please?"

"Not this time, honey. I want to know exactly where you are," Alicia said.

"I'll be right here in the building ...."

"Not good enough. I want you to be close to me. Why don't you teach Solow some new tricks?"

"But ...." he whined.

Alicia cut him off with her "tough-love mom" look.

Trigger's shoulders drooped as he shuffled over to Solow who was stretched out on a tarp near one of the therapy pools. In no time, Trigger had found a piece of paper and a popsicle stick. I watched him make a small boat, which he dropped into the pool. Just before the little sail boat capsized, I noticed there was a curious red design on the paper. I dropped my brush in water and dashed over to Trigger.

"Hey, Trigger, what was on that piece of paper?"

"Oh, someone scribbled with lipstick ... that's all." By that time I had already flattened myself out on the concrete floor with my head and shoulders over the water. I reached out and grabbed the boat before it could sink, unfolded the paper and held up the dripping note. "Watch your back woman," it said in bright red lipstick.

"What's the matter, Auntie Jo?"

"Nothing, honey, just a note from someone I know."

Chester sauntered up the hall and stopped at the edge of the pool next to Trigger.

I looked up to his smiling face.

"We're playing 'boats,' OK?" I gathered myself up and showed him the note.

"The red lipstick looks familiar," he said as he swayed his hips like Tavia.

"Trigger, show me exactly where you found this piece of paper. It's very important."

Trigger stuttered, "I found it here." He pointed to my red folder. "It was right there, Auntie Jo, on top of the folder."

"Thank you, honey. Here, you can have some of my scratch paper." I handed him several pieces of plain white paper from the folder. "Maybe you would like to draw pictures with this pencil," I suggested. He seemed happy to have something to do.

"Or, you could practice your multiplication tables," Alicia added from across the hall on her eight-foot perch. Chester proceeded up the hall. I took the note over to Alicia who was descending her ladder one kah-thunk at a time. She looked down at the scribble and shook her head.

"I know, I feel the same way," I said. "Like, when will she give up this useless campaign." I crumpled the paper in my fist.

"Jo, how do you like the bird nest? Kyle painted it."
Alicia pointed to a robin's nest painted to look like a
bird had built it high up in a crevice in the wall.

"Nice work, Kyle," I said. His ears turned red.

Alicia grabbed a brush and started back up the ladder. She stopped and looked at me from the third rung.
"What are you thinking, Jo? You look like you just hit
the mother lode."

"Better. I think I know how we can find Tavia."

"OK, what's the big pla ...?" Before she could finish, I started moving up the hall, yelling over my shoulder that I would be back. Yellow tape cordoned off the
staircase so I rode the elevator. I turned left on the second floor and found Hans in his office. He sat at his
computer watching an old movie. When he heard me
walk in, he turned it off.

"Well, what brings you to my office, Josephine?" he
asked in a pleasant voice.

"Hans, you know how some men keep a picture of
their wife on their desk? ... ah, do you know if Willy
has a picture of Tavia on his desk?"

"He did last time I looked. He's in there now." Before Hans could finish his sentence, I was out the door
and halfway to Mr. Thornton's office. I knocked and
Willy opened the door. He wore a dark gray suit, a
black tie, a slouch in his shoulders and downcast eyes.
My heart broke every time I looked at him.

"Hi, Mr. Thornton. I, ah, just had an idea and I was,
ah, wondering if you might have a picture of your wife
... somewhere around here." I squeezed past him and
circled around the large office.

"Yes, a photograph. How can I help you ...?"

he asked.

"Actually, I have an idea. What if we made a hundred or so copies of a picture of Tavia and handed them out to some of the picketers, you know, people who love to get involved in a cause. They marched in the rain to save Mr. Mendoza's farm. Maybe they would be willing to scour the countryside to find your, ah, wife and step-son."

"I'll have to think ...." he mumbled.

"Does Tavia have a set of keys to this building?"

"Well, yes, of course. But you don't think she's still in California?"

"Oh, I'm sure she's around. She had a busy night calling me and the police, but she was right here in this building last night or early this morning. We just found another threatening note near one of the therapy pools."

"Oh, I'm sorry, Josephine." He looked up at the ceiling for a moment. "Would you like to finish the mural some other time? We no longer have a deadline or a grand opening to worry about." He cleared his throat and melted down into his black leather chair. "Take it. It's over there." He pointed to the trash can beside his desk.

"The picture?" I was already moving in the right direction.

"Yes. If there's a chance you can find her, who am I to stop you. But more than that, we need to find Mark and make sure he's safe."

"You don't think she would harm her own son?"

"I'm not sure of anything at this point." His voice faded as I left the room holding a framed color photograph of Tavia behind broken glass. In a matter of seconds I was around the corner, standing in front of Hans explaining my idea. When I told him I had permission from the boss, he agreed to help.

"The copy machine is in Andy's office. He's not here today, but you can use the equipment," Hans said with a sigh. "The phone is there if you need it."

"Thanks," I chirped as I headed out the door. I entered Andy's cluttered office, home to several computers, printers and a large copier. I noticed one blackened and slightly melted printer still in place. The small metal trash can on the floor smelled of wet ashes. I decided housekeeping was not Andy's forte, but I had to give him some slack since he was probably going out of his mind with worry over Rosa.

I dug Tavia's picture out of its frame, laid it upside down where the arrow pointed, set the dial for one hundred 8x10 color prints and let the copy machine do the rest. While it pounded away, I snooped in Andy's desk for clues to help us find Tavia and whoever H.C. was. Like Willy, I was also anxious to locate Mark.

Far back in the top desk drawer, behind the paper clips, post-its, pens and last years Easter candy, I found a manila folder of interest. The only reason it interested me was because it had been shoved so far back in the drawer. Jackpot! The folder contained two emails from H.C. about the impending mall project. The first one was a copy of "Megan," the email I had rescued from Justin's house and stupidly handed over to Charlie Wellborn. The second email was even more enlightening than Megan.

As the last prints slid into the trough, I called Steve

on Andy's phone. Steve's enthusiasm was through the roof as I explained what I wanted him to do. For a minute I thought he might cock-a-doodle-doo over the phone. Instead, he said he would get right on it and hung up.

I gathered up my one hundred pictures and the manila folder and took the elevator to the main floor. As I walked past the staircase, Deputy Sayer stood up from his crouched position where he had been dusting for fingerprints.

"Ms. Stuart." He looked at my stack of paper and smiled. "Need some help?"

"Deputy Sayer, actually, no … thank you," I said as I hurried past him and headed down the hall to my friends. I wasn't about to donate evidence to the Sayer-Lund investigation team that moved at the speed of a banana slug.

"What have we now?" Alicia asked, standing in the hallway with hands on hips.

"A project to keep us busy this afternoon."

"Like, we aren't going to, ah, paint this afternoon?" Kyle said, as he walked closer to me for a look at my stack of prints. "Are all those pictures of Mrs. Thornton?" He looked more than mystified.

"Yes, and we're all having lunch at El Milagro in two hours," I announced. "Steve will meet us there." Sarah smiled ear to ear. I picked up a brush, filled my palette and began painting. Alicia and Kyle followed suit. Sarah organized our paints and Trigger worked on his homework. Solow, as usual, slept—paws twitching, probably dreaming of a Fluffy chase.

The time dragged for me, but finally it was time to

go. We all piled into Alicia's station wagon, including Solow.

As we approached El Milagro, Alicia asked, "What's going on? The restaurant is packed. We might as well have walked down here since there aren't any parking spaces." She whipped the car around, doubled back and parked a block away. After a brisk walk, we inched our way inside the building and finally made it to a table Steve had saved for us. The room was crowded with ex-picketers, many of whom I recognized from the City Hall experience.

Steve stood up. "How's this, Josephine?"

"Steve, you're amazing," I saw two large maps spread out on his table, one of Santa Cruz County and one of Monterey County. Just then my phone began playing Beethoven's Fifth.

"Hello. Oh, Mr. Thornton … I'm having trouble hearing you."

"Mark is with me. He's OK. Just wanted you to know."

"Thank you. I'm so happy for you." I hung up feeling like barbells had been lifted from my shoulders. I told my friends the good news and they clapped. A handsome guy wearing a baseball cap, a long-sleeve plaid shirt and boot-cut Levis over actual boots, stood up and wrapped an arm around my shoulders.

"David, I didn't recognize you in that hat. Are you one of the volunteers?"

"Doing my civic duty," he replied with a smile. "I ordered some tacos and burritos. Hope you're hungry."

"Thank you, David. That was sweet of you." It took me a second to regain my composure. Finally, I spoke to the friends around me.

"Steve is going to circle areas on the two maps which are likely places for Tavia to be hiding out or causing trouble. The airports and bus stations are already covered by the police. We will distribute pictures of Tavia and assign search areas to groups of four, that way we can have searches going in about 25 different areas at once. Give Steve your suggestions of where to look for her," I said, pointing to the maps and trying to make my voice heard over the noisy populace.

"How about my school?" Trigger suggested. Steve circled a four-block area around the school with a red marker.

"Good thinking, Trigger," Sarah said. "What about Mr. Mendoza's farm and the Therapy Center? And Fore at the Water," she offered. He circled them.

"How about Otis Drive?" David shouted out. Steve ringed the neighborhood.

"Sandy Lane in La Selva Beach?" Another red ring, and so it went. Other people came by with suggestions. Trigger turned out to be a big help because he wasn't shy about approaching people and encouraging them to report ideas to Steve. Alicia suggested her neighborhood, including Justin's house. The maps became redder as more and more participants hovered around the table.

Our food was served to us by the little ten-year-old girl, youngest of the Milagro family. We gave our ideas to Steve, munched on nachos, burritos and tacos and drank our soft drinks. We had 22 red circles when we finally ran out of ideas.

Everyone seemed to know Steve and they all took

on his enthusiasm. They were eager to know their as-
signments. Trigger passed out pictures of Tavia with
Steve's cell phone number written on the back. Steve
sent people off in groups of three or four, making sure
that at least one person had transportation for his or her
group. By the end of the hour, the restaurant and parking lot were almost empty.

Steve assigned Otis Road to David, Alicia, Trigger
and me, while he, Sarah and Alberto took Fore at the
Water. We walked outside together and then separated.
Steve's group clamored into Alberto's SUV. David took
off in his Jeep; and Alicia, Trigger and I walked up the
block to the station wagon.

As I approached the Volvo, I suddenly had the feeling that icicles were piercing my heart and all the blood
drained out of my head. Hot tears ran down my cheeks.
Alicia caught my arm as I tilted toward terra firma.

I saw a smashed window, the car door ajar and an
empty backseat. I dropped my head back and screamed
at the winter sun until tears choked off the sound of my
rage.

CHAPTER TWENTY-SEVEN

Alicia drove, Trigger read a book and I stewed in surreal silence. I should have taken Solow with me into the restaurant. I should never have left him in Alicia's car where Tavia could find him. I should have, should have, should have. I was driving myself crazy with guilt, even though I knew Tavia was the guilty party. On top of that, I felt bad for Alicia who was stuck with a damaged station wagon.

"Allie, I've been thinking. I know how Solow feels when Fluffy runs circles around him. Tavia's doing the same thing to me."

She nodded. "Hang in there, Jo. A lot of people are out looking for Tavia. When they find her, they'll find Solow. Kleenexes are in the glove compartment."

"Thanks Allie. Sorry about your car," I whispered as I popped opened the glove box. "Guess I'll call 911, but I don't know what good it'll do."

"Mom, it's cold back here," Trigger complained as his hair blew to one side.

"Honey, we're already at the Center. Say goodbye to Josephine." Her car idled while I transferred myself to the Chevy. I waved a sad goodbye, and followed the Volvo all the way home, driving like a zombie with nothing but Solow on my mind. I pulled up behind

Alicia in David's driveway. I climbed out of the car and stood with Alicia by the Volvo.

"Looks like David's already home and searching his property," Alicia said. "Maybe we should look around your place before we do anything."

"No, I need to tell him about Solow first. Tavia can burn down my house for all I care … (sniff). I just want my dog back."

"Ok, Jo, I understand."

We watched David walk the perimeter of his house holding a phone to his ear. He saw us and headed down to the station wagon. He dropped his phone into a pocket and gave me a hug.

"You guys look like your lunch didn't agree with you. Where's So …?" His eyes stopped at the smashed-out window. "Don't tell me she …."

"Yeah, she punched out my window and took Solow," Trigger growled, looking thoroughly disgusted. I had nothing to add. Besides, it felt like I had a basketball caught in my throat. David put an arm around my shoulders. We stood like that for a long time, long enough for my anger to subside a wee bit.

"David," I hiccupped, "maybe we should tell Steve about the dognapping so he can pass the word, you know, so everyone will look for Tavia and Solow."

"I just talked to Steve. He said someone spotted an empty red Jag parked down at the Watsonville Market. The group assigned to that area checked out the store, but when they came back outside the Jag was gone."

"It's Fluffy all over again," I said.

David wrinkled his brow.

"It's like Fluffy taunting Solow by running circles

around him, only it's Tavia that's circling us. I still love
Fluffy, but I could easily shoot Tavia."

"Don't worry, Josie, we'll get her. Hans called and
left a message. He said that Charlie Wellborn has
washed his hands of Tavia. In fact, Wellborn is the one
who dropped Mark off at the Therapy Center. Apparently Charlie told Mr. Thornton he couldn't work for
him anymore. Has a job offer in Chicago."

"Isn't that where O.J. went? Is he driving a white
Bronco?"

"Good point," Alicia snickered. Things were starting to make sense to me.

"Actually, Charlie's business card says H.C. Wellborn and I've been thinking, what if he's the 'H.C.' person who sent the 'Megan' email about building a mall?
Maybe that's why he was so anxious to get Megan back.
Maybe he thought it could end up as incriminating evidence.

"How did Charlie catch up with Mark?" Alicia
asked David.

"Mark managed to get away from his mother and
hitchhiked to Mr. Wellborn's house. According to Mr.
Thornton, the boy tried to find Willy first, but his step-
father wasn't home so he thumbed a ride ten more
miles to Charlie's place. Charlie was leaving town but
agreed to drop Mark off at the Center."

"Hope it didn't inconvenience him," I snarked.

David's phone rang. "Yeah, Steve … where did you
say they saw her?" David's eyes narrowed.

"OK, Steve. Thanks for the heads up."

"Well? What did he say?" I pressed.

"Steve said Kyle's group saw Tavia driving south

on Highway One and followed her car out to 'Fore at the Water' in Moss Landing. They're about to meet up with the volunteers stationed out there which happens to be Steve's group. Steve called the sheriff's deputies to let them know where to pick her up."

"Did they see a dog in her car?"

"Steve didn't mention it. Sorry, honey, he was in a hurry."

"Tavia doesn't stand a chance with all those people out there," Alicia smiled.

I almost smiled, but not quite. I couldn't smile until I had Solow home again and Tavia behind bars. I suggested we all go to my house for hot chocolate and wait to hear what happened. Besides, a good dose of chocolate might help my disposition. An hour later, David answered another phone call from Steve. The news was not good.

"Well, what happened?" I asked, breathlessly.

David wasn't smiling. "The Jag is still parked in front of building three, but Curt's white Mustang is missing. The Deputies put out an 'all-points' on the Mustang."

I punched the sofa with my fist and kicked the rocking chair. Tears ran down my cheeks. David held me close until I was able to get a grip.

"It's getting dark," Alicia said. "How late do you think people will keep looking?"

"Guess we can start all over again tomorrow," I said, reluctantly. "I'm sorry everyone, but I'm going to lie down." I had been up since five in the morning. My energy was gone and my heart ached for Solow. I wasn't good company and I knew it.

Alicia and Trigger said goodbye.

David walked them to the Volvo and didn't come back.

I shuffled down the hall and crawled into bed at five o'clock in the afternoon so that I could punch my pillow and wallow in misery. At least, that was my intention. After an hour of feeling sorry for myself, I began to feel pent up anger pushing me to do something. I had to at least try to find Solow.

I bagged up a few items for dinner, grabbed my jacket and a thermos of hot tea, and hurried out to the rental car. The evening was cold and about to get colder, so I went back inside for the snow jacket Hans had given me. I grabbed the teal hat and gloves, a little pillow from the couch and a lap blanket Myrtle had crocheted for my fortieth birthday. I envisioned myself doing a stakeout somewhere.

As I cruised down Otis onto San Juan, I imagined Solow sitting next to me—his head out the window, ears flying like kites. I laughed to myself at the thought, turned up the radio and swallowed a bite of tuna sandwich to the beat of YMCA. I was determined to find my dog and nothing could stop me. I felt invincible. If someone had given me a pair of tights and a cape, I would have leaped tall buildings in a single bound.

A golden three-quarter moon reflected in my rearview mirror as I drove past El Milagro. Many of the picketer volunteers were gathered in the parking lot. I guessed they were celebrating the fact that someone actually saw Tavia, even thought no one caught her. The crowd spilled out into the road. A teenage girl, talking to a group of her peers, took a step back into the road.

She turned, saw me coming and froze in the headlights.

I slammed on the brakes and swerved. The other half of my sandwich and a slice of Sarah's homemade cherry pie wrapped in foil landed on the floor under the dash. If Solow had been with me, the floor would have been clean in no time. Brakes squealed behind me.

After that close call, I decided to drive slowly over to the market in Watsonville where I would pick up the food mess and ask Robert some questions. I noticed bluish headlights in my rearview mirror, but when I pulled into the grocery store parking lot, the lights disappeared down the block. My state of alertness was over the top.

I parked under a streetlight and watched Robert push several shopping carts into the cart corral in front of the store. I leaned over to the mess on the floor and shoveled the spilled food into a bag with one hand as best I could. I promised myself I would clean the red cherry stains off the light gray carpet at the first opportunity.

I took a deep breath, climbed out of the car and walked into the store. I eventually found Robert in the produce aisle unloading a box of cantaloupes.

"Hi, Robert. See any outlaws tonight?" He laughed. "Seriously, did you see a woman about my height but skinny and busty wearing four-inch heels?"

"Actually, I saw one like that a couple of hours ago with black hair that looked like a bad wig." He pushed the melons into a perfect row. "She bought a sandwich from the deli, a can of Red Bull and a roll of duct tape. She was in a real hurry to pay."

"She ought to be," I mumbled to myself. "Thanks,

Robert. You've been a big help." I was tempted to buy a sandwich but decided I didn't have time. Instead, I headed over to Justin's house. Again, I was slightly aware of bluish headlights following me.

I parked in front of Justin's two houses. He answered my knock on the cottage door and seemed glad to have company. I sat down on the sofa and stared out the window at the moon reflecting on the lake. Looking south, I saw lights from the second story of Alicia's house.

"So, what are you doing out on a cold night like this?" he asked, rubbing the top of his shaved head.

"Lost my dog and I'm trying to figure out where Tavia Thornton is so I can get him back. Since you know her, I thought you might have some ideas where she could be staying, who her friends are, that sort of thing."

"Does she have something to do with your dog being lost?" He tilted his head to one side. I nodded. "Just because I know her doesn't mean I would know …." There was a knock on the door. "Excuse me, Josephine." Justin opened the front door.

I heard a familiar howl and then that female voice I detested. My heart stopped, restarted and then began to thump loudly in my ears.

"Y'all hush up, dog," Tavia bellowed. "Justin, honey, just put your hands up and I won't shoot you," she purred as she dropped her purse on a kitchen chair.

Justin walked across the room with his hands high, a gun at his back.

"Well, look who's here, my favorite freaky painter," Tavia chirped as she marched Justin to the couch where

I was sitting. I saw a little ol' Chevy parked outside.
Yours?"

I ignored her. Instead, I turned my head to face the
window and carefully watched her reflection in the
glass. Solow rested his chin on my knee. I held his
wrinkly muzzle in my shaky hands. Justin made a sudden move and she pointed the gun at me. He froze.

"My plan was to take care of you, Josephine. But if
I get rid of you both, how's anyone going to pin Jim's
accident on little ol' me?" She smiled wickedly, and
threw a roll of duct tape at me. I quickly swiveled my
body and raised my hands to protect my head.

Solow whimpered. He leaned against my knee,
shivering.

"Ok, now the fun begins. Justin, down on the floor
… sit. Woman, wrap his wrists and tape them to his ankles … atta girl." She laughed as I did her bidding.

I searched my mind for a way to stop what I knew
would happen next.

Tavia waved the gun. She told me to sit on the floor
beside Justin and tape my own ankles together. She had
a wild look in her eyes as she grabbed the tape from
me, ripped off a piece with her teeth and wrapped it
around my wrists, never letting go of the gun.

"Now, Joan, touch your ankles." I reluctantly
obeyed. She promptly taped my hands to my ankles
and then stood up to admire her work.

"I have one question, Tavia. Why did you take
Solow?"

Tavia tilted her head back and cackled. "I just
wanted you to suffer like I suffered when you were
snooping around, marching and messing with my

plans for a 'yes' vote from the supervisors. Guess you won't be getting in the way of my mall again," she smirked, as she centered her wig.

"Nice disguise for a witch," I said, just before she smacked my face with the palm of her hand. My cheek stung, but it was worth it.

She turned and wiggled her way on spiky heels to the kitchen where she snatched up her purse, found a book of matches and lit a cigarette. She held it up for us to see as she sashayed her way back through the cottage and into the bedroom.

I was starting to sweat and beads of perspiration began to show on Justin's head.

When Tavia finally came out of the bedroom, I asked her a couple of questions.

"Were you behind the killing of Mr. Mendoza's dogs and his lettuce? Who helped you?"

Tavia smiled.

"You won't get away with this. Everyone's looking for you … and …."

"I'll be going now. Sweet dreams, y'all," she said, as she ripped the phone cord out of the wall, and slipped out the front door.

"Justin, do you smell smoke?" Suddenly a flash of hot fear raced through my body.

"Yeah, stay calm," he said as he flexed his arms trying to rip the tape apart. As big and strong as he was, he could not pull his hands apart or even free them from his ankles.

"I'm sorry I did such a good job taping you. Oh no, I see smoke coming from the bedroom!" I screamed. Solow must have sensed the level of my panic when he howled long and low, bringing tears to my eyes. Would he have to die too? I was scared speechless, almost.

"Justin, quick, do you have any scissors?" I choked. Smoke snaked its way into the room.

"Yeah, in the kitchen … in a drawer," he said as we both began scooting across the floor on our butts. It seemed like a long way, and I was breathing hard when I finally made it to the kitchen counter. The drawers were about three feet above the floor and might as well have been located on Mars.

"Justin, do you have a cell phone?"

"No. Do you?"

"It's in the car," I groaned as the reality of possible death penetrated my consciousness. "Justin, I'm going to try something." I squirmed a few feet over to the front door, lay on my back and extended my arms and legs as far up as I could—all the way to the doorknob, kind of a goofy-looking yoga pose. My feet kept slipping away from the metal knob. It seemed like forever before I was able to turn it and pull the door open with my feet.

"Nice work, Josephine. Ladies first."

"Solow, here Solow. Come on boy … now, outside, go on." I coaxed him, threatened him, promised him the moon and finally he sauntered out the door. I scooted outside next and Justin brought up the rear. We inched across the little moon-lit porch and bumped down one cement step onto a cold concrete patio.

"I'll go down to the lake. You go up to the road. We'll yell like crazy, OK?" I said.

"Sure. Good luck." Justin immediately began scooting his way up the moderate incline to Jim's house and beyond, one cheek at a time. I rotated my body 180 degrees and began the slow tedious journey over uneven brickwork, down to the beach. Solow ran ahead and barked at the ducks. Deep-throated geese honked at him, scaring him back to me. I heard Justin about forty yards away, bellowing out his plea for help. I rounded the back corner of the cottage screaming and yelling for help.

The dog next door barked and growled. On the other side of Justin's cottage, a porch light flickered on. I saw a woman step out of the blue house and look around. Before she could step back inside, I screamed with everything I had. She stopped and stared into the dark.

"Help, fire!" I yelled, over and over.

She cautiously stepped down the wooden steps to her cluttered back lawn and circled the palm tree.

"Who's there?"

"It's Josephine. Please call 911." By then the woman was at the fence looking over at Justin's bedroom window that glowed red.

"I'll call, don't worry," she shouted as she ran back across her lawn, up the stairs and into the house. A couple of minutes later she was back at the fence with a phone at her ear. "Are you all right?"

"I'm OK, but get some scissors. I can't move."

The woman ran back into the house. While she was gone, I had crazy thoughts like, would she return? After what seemed like an eternity, she reappeared, rounded the fence and stumbled across the beach following my pleading voice. Ordinarily I would have thought twice about sitting in the dark on a beach full of duck poop.

But that night, even the two cranky geese couldn't get my attention. I watched Justin's window with trepidation as the glow became redder and brighter.

The neighbor woman shined a flashlight in my face and then down my folded body to my feet.

"Oh, my!" She pulled a pair of scissors out of her coat pocket and nervously began clipping tape.

"Don't worry. You won't cut me ... ouch. That's OK—don't mind me. Do you hear sirens? I hear sirens. Thank God ... and thank you so much ...." I said as I ripped the rest of the tape off my shoes.

"I'm Greta. I didn't catch your name."

"Josephine Stuart. And this is Solow." I tried to stand up as soon as the tape came off, but it took a couple of tries before blood circulated down to my jellied legs and feet. "We need to find Justin and cut him free," I told Greta.

The sirens stopped. Greta and I rushed over to the path and watched three firemen race down the hill, past Jim's house and enter the cottage. In a matter of minutes the glow in the bedroom window turned into white smoke, which was just about the time Deputies Sayer and Lund arrived.

"Thanks, Greta. Excuse me. I need to talk to the deputies." I ran up the path with Solow at my heels, all the way to the street. A fireman was crouched, cutting tape off Justin's hands and feet. Solow licked Justin's cheek.

"Are you all right, Justin?" I asked, as he tried to stand up. "Take your time. It was like that for me too." Moments later he was able to stand.

"You really kept your head back there ... maybe not

at first ...." he chuckled.

"And you were awesome, Justin, scooting all the way up here on your rump." Solow and I circled him casually and noticed goose bumps in the moonlight where the seat of his pants was partly gone. I ran a hand across my backside and was relieved to find that I only had a couple of small spots where the fabric had worn through.

Half an hour later, the firemen were loading up their equipment and getting ready to leave. I heard one of them telling Deputy Sayer that the fire had started in a mattress and if newspapers hadn't been involved, it could have smoldered for hours. According to the young fireman, someone had added paper to the fire, making an easy case for arson. He said there would be a preliminary investigation in a matter of an hour or so, and he would stay at the property until the fire investigator arrived. After an hour of questioning by the deputies and later by the investigator, Justin and I were allowed to go.

"Josephine, I hope you're not going after Tavia again." Justin said.

"I have to. She tried to murder us tonight with a slow, painful death by fire. It doesn't get any worse than that." Even though I had Solow again, my rage was at an all-time high and my blood sugar was zilch.

"Tell you what, we'll go together. I'll drive," he said, firmly.

My stomach growled. "I'll go with you if we stop and get something to eat."

"No problem. I'm hungry too." He helped me into his SUV, hefted Solow into the backseat and left his smoky cottage behind.

CHAPTER TWENTY-EIGHT

The night was unusually cold; and when I squinted at the moon just right, it seemed to have a sad face. I felt a little better after a burger and fries. Solow gulped his very own burger and settled down for a nap in the backseat. Justin finished off two burgers and then drove us down to the Watsonville Market, the elementary school, the park and all the usual spots in between. It was getting late and the roads were almost empty. Not a white Mustang anywhere.

"I'll try Beach Street to Pajaro Dunes, but I don't think we're going to find her tonight, Josephine."

"We can never find her, but boy can she find us." I looked at the side mirror and watched a pair of bluish headlights following us down Beach Street. "Stop!" I shouted.

Justin stomped on the brakes. We jerked forward against our seat belts and Solow landed on the floor with a thud. At the same time, tires squealed and screeched behind us, followed by a loud metal on asphalt sliding, grinding, a thud and then silence.

"What was ... why did you ... oh my God!" Justin looked past me and out the window. I followed his stare to a spot of moonlight on chrome, and a tire rotating in the air as if it were still going somewhere.

"Something's in the ditch. Looks like a white car on its side," I said as feelings of guilt and fear engulfed me. I climbed down from my seat and stood on the side of the two-lane country road. Justin paced back and forth looking for a way down to the vehicle wedged on its side in an irrigation ditch.

It was hard to tell how deep the water was, but it looked to be four to six feet deep. The whole passenger side of the car was down in the murky water and the driver's side faced the stars.

"Justin, back your car up and shine some light on this thing." He raced around to the driver's seat, backed up and angled his SUV to point toward the accident.

"Help me, y'all!" a muffled voice floated up from the ditch.

"That looks like a Mustang," Justin said as he stood on the slippery bank holding onto a skinny willow tree for balance. I hung onto the same tree trunk, completely panicked and wondering what to do next.

"God, please help us," I muttered. My heart was pounding in my throat and time seemed to move slowly as crazy thoughts raced through my head. I remembered that my phone was in the Chevy rental back at Justin's house. How could we save the victim of this rollover? Did I cause it to happen? Was I an irresponsible person? I just wanted to save this trapped person, even if it turned out to be the woman who tried to murder us.

"Can you see anyone in there?" I asked, through chattering teeth.

"Just one lady friend."

"Is it really her?"

Moonlight reflected off the Marine's nodding head.

"Help ... please help me," came another cry from the car. I let go of the tree and leaned out over the Mustang with my hands on the door. I was bent at the waist as I stretched my head out to the driver's window.

"Roll it down!" I yelled.

"I can't. I'm hurt. Help me."

"Roll it down. Now!" I shouted. "You can do it, just push the stupid button ... there, that's better."

"I'm so scared. Help me!" the woman screamed. Hollow-looking eyes, blackened from smudged mascara, looked up at me. Her black wig was askew as she reached out the window and grabbed my hand. "You have to help me," she wailed. "Please, Josephine."

I noticed Tavia had inadvertently pushed all the buttons and rolled down windows on both sides of the car. Water rushed in. Half the steering wheel was submerged and Tavia's teeth were chattering worse than mine.

Tavia finally let go of me as Justin stepped up onto the car door. I moved back. He flattened himself across the cold metal, reached down into the window with one long arm and released the seatbelt. She grabbed his jacket sleeve and held on.

"Mrs. Thornton, we're going to pull you out of there. Do you feel any pain in your neck or back? Can you feel your feet?" he asked.

"My feet are cold. Get me out of here. Josephine, please don't let me drown. I didn't really mean to hurt you ... I was just jealous. Please forgive me," she moaned.

I didn't pay much attention to what Tavia said. I only knew that we had to get her out of Curt's Mustang before she became hypothermic.

"You're not going to drown. The water isn't very deep." I said.

"Water's coming in … help me, I'm drowning," she howled.

Justin rolled his eyes.

"Josephine, step back. I'm going to pull her out."

Tavia already had one of his arms so he grabbed her other arm and pulled her through the window like a skinny rag doll.

"Ouch, you're hurting me," she complained, as I helped her down to the ground. I held her in a sitting position while Justin spread his jacket over the dirt and weeds. We eased her down onto the big down jacket. Justin and I collapsed nearby on the bank, trying to catch our breath.

"Thank you," Tavia sobbed. "I was afraid y'all might not help me. I wouldn't blame you if you didn't." She curled up on her side, knees to chest and closed her eyes. I wondered when was the last time she slept, or ate, or had her wits about her. When was the last time her harried mind had been at peace?

Approaching headlights caught my attention. I jumped up, ran into the road and waved my arms. A pickup truck pulled over and stopped on the other side of the road. A portly gentleman hurried across the street to see what had happened. I asked if he had a phone. He nodded and immediately dug into his coat pocket, pulled out a cell phone and dialed 911.

My breathing slowed, my mind cleared and my

rage slipped away. The nightmare was over at last. Help was on the way and I couldn't wait to see David. I would let him hold me for a very long time and tell him the rest of the story.

ACKNOWLEDGMENTS

Read My Lipstick *was created with the help of my generous and talented family and friends. Thank you, Avery and Jennifer, for the cover. Thank you, Wendy, Marlene and Tomi, for your sharp eyes and red pencils. Thank you, Michael, for solving so many late-night computer problems. Thank you, dear husband Art, for your patience through it all.*

Made in the USA
Las Vegas, NV
24 January 2024

84826461R00225